Jessica Ruston was born in Wa
in the worlds of theatre, film a
written screenplays and two no
novel *Luxury* was highly acclaim ondon
with her husband. For everything y u need to know about
Jessica, visit her website www.jessicaruston.com.

Praise for *Luxury*:

'A wonderful debut: Ruston is staggeringly assured' *Sunday Express*

'What better way to banish in-flight boredom than with a mixture of sex, scandal, bitching and bling?' *Glamour*

'There's nothing guilty about this pleasure' *Elle*

'Pure escapism for a rainy October weekend – a real page-turner!' *Woman*

'Twists and turns and everything you need to keep you glued ... Smashing fun all round' Adèle Geras

'Compulsive' *Sun*

'A scandalous look at life lived at the top; a good old-fashioned blockbuster' *Bookseller*

By Jessica Ruston

Luxury
To Touch the Stars

Non-fiction

Heroines: The Bold, the Bad and the Beautiful

To Touch the Stars

JESSICA RUSTON

headline review

First published in 2010 by HEADLINE REVIEW
An imprint of HEADLINE PUBLISHING GROUP

First published in paperback in 2011 by HEADLINE REVIEW
An imprint of HEADLINE PUBLISHING GROUP

1

Cataloguing in Publication Data is available from the British Library

ISBN 978 0 7553 7032 0

Typeset in Sabon by Ellipsis Books Limited, Glasgow

Printed and bound in Great Britain by
Clays Ltd, St Ives plc

HEADLINE PUBLISHING GROUP
An Hachette UK Company
338 Euston Road
London NW1 3BH

www.headline.co.uk
www.hachette.co.uk

For Clemency

Acknowledgements

Thanks to my agent, Simon Trewin, for his unwavering support, advice and cheerleading, and his assistant Ariella Feiner.

A huge thank you must go to my editor, Sherise Hobbs, for her astute and helpful comments at every stage of the process and for helping me make this book the best it could be. Also to George Moore, Rosie Gailer and everyone at Headline, who make the journey to publication such a pleasurable one.

For generously giving their time to help me when I was researching the book, sincere thanks to Maggie Cochrane, Sheila Finlayson and Eugenie Teasley.

To Jack, as ever, love and thanks.

Prologue

He was watching from his position inside a taxi, just up the road from the villa, as they arrived. This golden, glittering family, their skin touched by the gloss of wealth and privilege. Their luggage unloaded for them, their feet hardly touching the dusty ground of the streets of Anacapri before they were stepping inside the property's gates where the tiles would have been swept clean in preparation for their arrival, and where they would be able to slip their sandals off and feel the cool stone beneath them.

There was the old caretaker, welcoming them as they emerged from the fleet of vehicles, one by one. A passer-by paused to watch their arrival, struck by the family's beauty and shimmer, as people always were, before carrying on his way. First came Fran, young and beautiful, despite the scar that ran down her face. Then Blue and Adam, his boyfriend, Blue jumpy as ever, his legs twitching as he swung them out of the car and blinked in the sunlight. No Flip, yet. He would be in the office still. Catching a later flight, probably. Always working. And then there was Violet. Stepping out of the car, her arms full of bracelets, her hair twisted up into a knot on top of her head, wearing a loose silk sundress. Her silver flashed in the sunlight and reminded him of a splash of seaspray.

'I drop you here?' his driver asked, turning to face him. 'You go inside Cavalley family villa? Very rich family. Big party soon, for Signora Cavalley's birthday. Been coming to Capri a long time. You are going to the party? You friend of Signora Cavalley?'

The watcher shook his head. 'No, I'm not going to the party. I don't know the family. Take me back to Capri town, *per favore.*'

The driver shrugged, and drove off down the hill.

Part One

Chapter One

Violet Cavalley had come from nothing. From nowhere, she liked to joke, when interviewers asked her about her background. She gave different stories, depending on her mood. 'I'm the daughter of a Ukrainian builder,' she would say, a wink telling them it was not true. Or was it? 'A French marquis, disgraced and exiled.' 'A shepherd, who lived in the hills of Scotland and raised me alone.' A thousand exotic tales, none of them true. Like a diamond she had been born out of almost nothing, and she had polished herself until she sparkled as brightly as light.

Like the diamonds she was wearing as she walked through the gardens of the villa in Capri. The large courtyard at its heart had been transformed into an outdoor dining room full of scented candles. The air was heavy with their fragrance – gardenia, peony, freesia, rose. Tables were arranged in the centre of the space, each topped with mirrored glass. Lanterns cast flickering shadows over the feet of the guests as they walked down the avenue in the dusky light. Sixty guests, one for each year of Violet Cavalley's life, were gathering. Family, friends, colleagues. Violet watched from the edges of the garden. The life she had built so carefully was displayed before her.

Dark-red candles rose up from the centre of the tables in pillars of wrought iron, surrounded with blood-red flowers. The chairs were covered in the palest duck-egg-blue chiffon which dropped to the ground in puddles, and on the back of each chair was a single red flower – a rose, or carnation, or gerbera.

She did a quick head-count now. Twenty, thirty, one, two . . . Forty-three guests were milling around the courtyard, gradually gravitating towards their seats, as directed by the seating-plan which had been engraved on a huge ornately framed mirror propped up on a stand in the corner. She could see her friends' faces reflected in it as they looked for their places. Kalisto Kauffman, her oldest and closest friend, was already seated and holding court. He saw her watching him and winked at her from across the courtyard. There was her daughter, Fran, straight-backed and smiling, chatting politely, her eyes flicking around nervously. What was wrong with her? She had been jittery all afternoon since coming back from visiting the castello again. No time to worry about it now.

Blue and Adam were making their way through the arched stone entrance which was covered with billowing dark-red chiffon (a small air-pipe had been run from outside to keep the fabric dramatically puffed out). Their arrival brought the head-count up to fifty. Blue wore a perfectly cut three-piece suit in the palest baby-blue velvet, with a candy-striped blue and white silk shirt. He was smoking a pale-blue Sobranie cigarette. Ever the showman. His partner, Adam, walked, as usual, half a step behind him, letting Blue go first, soak up the compliments, dazzle and flutter. Adam was good for him, Violet knew. Steady, constant. 'People like us need people like him,' as Blue had put it.

In the distance she thought she heard a rumble of thunder, and looked up at the sky. But it was clear.

As they sat, their starters in front of them, Violet remained standing. Before each guest was a bowl of champagne risotto,

on. 'I said to him, "Signora Cavalley has no brother, no sister. You must leave," I told him. But he said . . .'

And before he spoke, Violet knew the words that were going to come from his mouth. The words that she had dreaded hearing for so long.

'He says Signora Cavalley does not have a brother. But he says Signora Cavalley is not . . . *is not Signora Cavalley*.'

Violet stared. The courtyard had fallen silent. Everything had slowed down. She felt as though she were floating; her arms and legs were numb.

'Hello, Violet,' a voice said, from over Pietro's shoulder. 'That's what you're calling yourself now, isn't it?'

And as she collapsed, she looked beyond Pietro, into the shadows of the courtyard, and into the eyes of her brother.

Earlier that day

Violet Cavalley had spent her life in the single-minded pursuit of her goals. She was decisive, clear, resolute. But now, for the first time in as long as she was able to remember, she found herself utterly unable to make a decision. She sat on the striped window seat that faced directly out to sea, in the bedroom of her villa in Capri, and wondered how she should divide up her empire amongst her three children. How she would choose.

To bestow Cavalley's on one of them would be to burden them with a responsibility so heavy that there had been times in her life when she herself had not believed she would be able to go on carrying it; and she was the one who had created it. How would they – the heir, the chosen one – cope with the burden of being the person with whom the buck stopped? The person upon whom the livelihoods of thousands depended? Who could not easily take a day off, who could not just wake up one morning and decide to turn over and drift back into an unfinished dream.

She loved Cavalley's, the company that she had built from nothing into one of the world's most valuable brand names in fashion, loved it as strongly and as fiercely as her children. She and it were bound tightly together like tendrils of honeysuckle around a rose. And like two plants they had grown together, from the weedy and undeveloped shoots of an idea in the mind of a green girl, into a woman and a business with strong, deep roots that clung tenaciously to the earth beneath her feet. Cavalley's was as much a part of her as her own skin, and just as impossible to shed or to think of giving to someone else.

It wasn't just about the responsibility, of course. It was the bad luck that haunted her. It was why she had not let Cavalley's be split up and sold off or become public. Maybe if she had done it earlier, it would be easier, she thought now.

She ran her finger along the windowsill. Violet had owned the villa for more than twenty years. It was the place where she had spent countless summers with her family, hundreds of evenings dining on the terrace that she could see from her room now, lingering over dinner and wine in the candlelight. Hundreds of afternoons working in her study upstairs while the children and guests napped under parasols by the pool or splashed in it. Had she sacrificed too many hours like that? Working, always working? Once, when Fran was small, six or seven, she had been sulking about having to wait to go on some outing on the island she had set her heart on, and had accused Violet of liking work more than her, in that melodramatic way small children have. Violet had turned and stared at her, and Fran's eyes had become wide, afraid that she was going to be in trouble, standing in the doorway of Violet's room, half inside it and half out of it, ready to scamper away in her white cotton skirt and sandals.

Violet had stood up, and said, 'Right, that's it,' in a stern voice. 'We're going to take the afternoon off. Girls only.' And she had taken her daughter for her first manicure in Capri Town, and bought her a new dress, and they had drunk virgin Bellinis on the terrace bar of the Quisisana.

Fran. It hadn't been easy for her, growing up so much younger than the others. And then after the accident . . . Frangipani was as beautiful as the flower she was named for, was clever and ambitious, more ambitious than most girls of her age and class, many of whom were busy tripping around Town getting paid to attend nightclub openings, if they were doing anything at all. Fran was halfway through a law degree at King's College, and worked in the Mount Street salon in Mayfair at weekends. She worked hard – too hard, her mother sometimes feared – but she was still young. Inexperienced. And there was no way Violet could entrust sole care of Cavalley's to her. Not now – it would be too much, too soon. One day, she could well prove a worthy figurehead, but not yet. And Violet needed someone *now*.

The problem was that she didn't feel that any of her children were in a position to be handed the reins of Cavalley's. They were all of them missing some essential part that would be needed by whoever stepped into her shoes. And she wanted that person to be family – of her blood. She could not risk passing all that went with Cavalley's to an outsider, however close. Kalisto, her oldest friend, would not do it, and she regarded him as family – as good as. He had kept his own label smaller than it could have been, purely because he didn't want all the worry and stress that went with running a company of this size, and in her heart of hearts she didn't blame him. He now had the luxury of designing for a successful line run by someone else – having sold out to Violet a few years ago – and now, it seemed, he had the best of both worlds: the protection and clout of Cavalley's behind him, along with the freedom to be creative and not have to worry about the balance-sheet or property fees or employment law.

Fran was too young; it wouldn't be fair to steal her youth by giving her such a job, but also, Violet worried that she lacked the ruthless edge required by whoever took over from her. Fran, despite her crisp, cool shell, had the tenderest of hearts. She had always been the child who Violet would discover weeping over a ladybird with a broken wing that she had found in the corner of her bathroom, who would insist on funeral services for dead pets, and who would, when taken to the toy shop and asked to select a new teddy bear for a treat, inevitably find the one with a wonky arm or an eye sewn on not quite straight and choose him. Violet knew it was because she was worried that no other child would choose the imperfect stuffed toy, and he would be left at the bottom of the pile.

Once, a long time ago, Violet had wondered whether Blue might be the one to end up leading Cavalley's. But that was before. Before everything with Scarlet, before his demons got worse and his condition became unmanageable. Before. There was no question of him running the company now. He was a talented designer, however, one of the best. His dresses had made Cavalley's into a name to contend with for red-carpet events, joining labels such as Armani and Marchesa on the list for Oscar nominees and starlets en route to Cannes; in fact, it was seeing Blue's designs that had inspired Violet to build up the business around his clothes, and it had paid off, tripling the company's value in the first year, and exponentially ever since. Her son drew like other people breathed or walked, his black Fineliner an extension of his long, thin fingers, flying over the pages of his sketchbook as easily and lightly as a dragonfly hovering over a lake, pulling out of his imagination more beautiful, shimmering creations. Yet he was fragile, so fragile. He had to be constantly protected from stress, could not cope when plans changed and his carefully ordered world shifted even slightly. No, there was no way he could run Cavalley's, not now and not ever – though Violet hoped his designs would always be at the heart of it.

The obvious choice, then, was Flip. Violet knew this. She also knew it was what everyone was expecting her to do, eventually. Announce that she would take a smaller role, or that she was signing over some more control to him. No one was expecting her to step down right away, of course not – why would she? But he had been working with her closely for years, had plenty of responsibility already. He was the logical choice. She trusted him. Didn't she? Of course she did. She trusted Flip like she trusted herself. Out of all of her children who were still here, he was the one who knew her best, he was the one she worked with the most, who had sacrificed the most for her and for the company. He deserved it. And yet.

There was something that stopped her wanting to bequeath Cavalley's to him in its entirety. She wasn't sure what it was. He didn't have great flair, but did he need that to run the company? Blue would be around to provide all the style, after all, and Tillie, Flip's girlfriend, worked for Violet and was a talented junior milliner whom she had been nurturing. Tillie would support him, and it would be good to have a woman's touch still steering the ship, even at one remove. Maybe, maybe . . .

Flip

Flip Cavalley waited for his assistant to put his coffee and the morning's papers and cuttings down on his desk, then waved his thanks to her as she shut the door of his office behind her. The voice at the other end of the phone belonged to the Head of Sales in Cavalley's office in Shanghai – a market into which the company was expanding with a speed that had surprised even Flip and his mother, and which showed no signs of slowing. It seemed there was an insatiable demand among Shanghai's high society for the quirky couture hats that his mother was so famous for, and an almost limitless pot of money with which to purchase them. There might have been a global recession, but it didn't seem to have reached China.

'I also recommend that we think of a limited edition collection, for China only, in the mass-market side,' the voice continued. 'There's a high demand for what customers perceive as unique, even in the mass market, which might seem to be something of a contradiction in terms. It would also provide us with an opportunity to include some traditional Chinese design, possibly. I wonder if you might suggest this to Mrs Cavalley?'

Flip made a noncommittal sound, and began to glance through his correspondence. He had been on the call since 5.30 a.m., in his office at home in Berkeley Square, and then taking the call with him as he walked, as he did every morning, to Cavalley's headquarters above the original salon on Mount Street. He looked out of the window. The street woke up slowly and late. This was no 7 a.m. in the City, where the streets would already be packed and the day well underway with people treading on one another's toes to get to meetings, coffee cups in one hand, laptop case in the other, *Financial Times* tucked under an arm, the pavements already littered with free newspapers. Here papers were still being delivered, trolleys full of dark-red sides of beef trundled into Allens of Mayfair, the famous butcher's, and a man in a deerstalker tweed hat strolled slowly along the street, smoking a pipe in the pearly-grey morning sunshine. It was a tiny pocket of London where everything felt calm, refined; where it still seemed reasonable to linger for three hours over lunch of a plate of oysters and a bottle of white wine at Scott's, where within a radius of just a few yards you could buy a rifle, a Porsche, a couture Violet Cavalley hat, a set of leather luggage, a French-trimmed rack of lamb, a diamond ring, an Old Master, a Monte Cristo cigar, perfume in a cut-glass bottle and a tailormade suit. Flip sometimes found it difficult to imagine much that he would want to buy that was *not* for sale on this one street; Mount Street had been his second home since before he could remember. His first memory, indeed, was of cutting his head open in the storeroom underneath the salon. The street and the shop were part of the fabric of his life.

The thought of the *FT* reminded him, there was an interview with him scheduled to run today. Ending the call, he opened the cuttings file and turned over the pages of articles about Cavalley's, his mother, a rare photo of Blue in public at a gallery opening. He paused over that for a moment, touched, as he always was, by Blue's face staring into the camera, his eyes shocked, as usual, that anyone wanted to take his photo. The photographer must have been quick, since he had caught him before his hands had started to flutter in front of him, his long fingers moving quickly, as though drawing images that only he could see in the air; they were still holding the gallery programme and a glass of white wine, a straw Trilby on his head, circled with a pink-striped trim. Also as usual, Flip was surprised to see the faint crow's-feet around his brother's pale eyes, and the lines in his forehead, the changed boundary of his hairline. In Flip's mind, Blue would always be sixteen, and it never ceased to come as something of a shock to see that he was not. Or not on the outside, at least.

Flip sighed and turned the page over. Here it was. *Heir to the Cavalley Throne* the headline read, above a large photograph of Flip sitting – looking somewhat regal, he thought to himself – on an antique chair that had been stripped down and painted with a punky, gold-leafed skull-and-crossbones design. His eyes moved quickly over the image. His dark suit was classic, well-cut – cut by Blue – with a deep-purple silk lining. The photo had been taken in the workshop in Battersea, the chair positioned on top of one of the worktables, activity going on all around him. At his left foot, a woman was hand-sewing silver sequins on to peach chiffon; at his right, someone shifted images around on a mood board, moving photographs of crocodiles and crumbling houses and beehives on the page in the swirling, mysterious process involved in creating a collection. On the walls, Polaroids of celebrities wearing Cavalley hats were visible – here was a top model blowing a kiss to the camera in a red bowler hat, there was a minor royal in a vivid cobalt-coloured and heavily feathered headpiece.

In the corner of the room, half of a tailor's model was visible, draped in a tightly corseted ball gown, and Violet herself was standing in front of it, pointing to the area above the model's neck, sketching a design in the air with her hands, watched by Kalisto Kauffman, her best and oldest friend and creator of the dress. The two worked closely together, and had done for years; Violet designed all of the hats for Kalisto's catwalk shows, and was co-owner of his shops on Bond Street and Savile Row. She had been the one to encourage him to create a diffusion line that could be sold in boutiques and department stores, and had invested in it. This had made him his first million (and many more since).

The image was impressive, Flip thought, gazing at the photograph. He looked young but not immature, handsome but with enough rough edges that he could not be accused of being a pretty boy, a pampered Little Lord Fauntleroy. The sub-heading was less pleasing. *But with Violet Cavalley showing no signs of slowing down as she approaches her sixtieth birthday, will eldest son Flip always be The Man Who Would Be King?*

'Fuckers!' exclaimed Flip. 'Fuck'. Examining the photo again, more closely this time, he noticed that the lighting had been digitally altered so he appeared in shadow, as though lurking backstage. There was only a sliver of his mother in the image, but somehow your eye was still drawn to her. She appeared lit from above: Golden Girl Violet.

Flip skimmed the article. Nothing was misquoted, he had said everything that was printed, but everything read badly. He sounded spoiled, expectant. *'Of course I'd like to be in sole charge of Cavalley's one day. Who wouldn't? It's a multi-million-pound company.'* And: *'Every child of successful parents feels that they have something to live up to – it's our blessing and our curse.'*

Idiot. Idiot! Why had he said that? He sounded petulant, and 'poor me' – all the things he despised in others. 'Poor me, with my famous mother and immense fortune at my fingertips; poor me, with a job I walked into and a successful company that will one day be mine.' He knew that was how he sounded. He could kick himself. He knew better than to talk honestly to journalists, to open up to them, however many times they'd chatted in the pub, or however many so-called friends they had in common. He knew better. So why had he?

Flip knew. It was a weight in his chest, a stone that was growing inside him. He bit his lip, and carried on skimming the article, trying to take in what he needed to know without dwelling on his self-pitying, inane remarks. There was a lot of stuff about the business, about how Violet had come from nowhere, the mysterious young woman who appeared in London's swinging sixties like *a snowdrop, overnight, or so it seems, arriving fully formed, fully fledged, amidst a harsh winter, heralding Spring*. For crying out loud, talk about hyperbole, Flip thought. All of her major triumphs were mentioned – the Oscar, the ballets, the catwalk shows, the eventual recognition by the establishment, the honours, the weddings, both her clients' and her own. And of course, here it was, of course it would be here. The Cavalley Curse.

> *The Cavalley Curse, as it has become known in recent years, seems to have blighted the otherwise charmed life of Violet Cavalley. Violet herself laughs it off, in public at least, as rumour, gossip, coincidence. But sources close to her allege that, despite her claims to the contrary, she is deeply troubled by the thread of bad luck and misfortune that appears to dog her personal life at every turn. Is such tragedy the price demanded by the Fates for success? The Cavalleys might be the latest great family to suffer the slings and arrows of outrageous fortune, but they are far from the first – think of the Kennedys, the Onassis family, the Redgraves. Or is it simply the decadence of privileged lifestyles that brings with it a moral decay that infects and insidiously . . .*

Flip could not read on. He closed the file of papers and rubbed the back of his neck with his hand. The rumours of the curse had been following the Cavalleys for years. They would not go away now, he knew. Once something was named – labelled, like that – it became eternally linked with its subject, casting a shadow over its gilded surface. And, God knew, there was enough evidence for it. Flip blinked. *He would not think of that.* But it wasn't the mention of the curse or of the tragedies that hung in its wake like ghosts at the feast that bothered him. It was the way he felt inside.

He burned with – yes, with jealousy. He could admit it here, in his own head, in the privacy of his office, even though the admission made him clench his teeth. *He was jealous of his own mother.* It burned inside him like a forest fire. The article was meant to be about *him*, the interview had been with *him*, the photoshoot was of *him*. And yet, as ever – it was all about Violet.

'I can't believe you let them run it like that,' he raged. 'I can't believe you approved it.'

'Flip, I didn't. It was your interview, I was just in the background.'

'But you weren't just in the background, were you, Mama? You're never in the bloody background.'

Violet sighed, and Flip glowered as his driver wove in and out of the heavy M25 traffic towards Heathrow, gliding smoothly between lorries and holidaymakers, finding spaces where there were none.

'Flip, listen to yourself. I'm sorry if you feel pushed to one side,' Violet said, 'it's not my intention.'

'I don't . . .' He found it hard to speak. 'I don't feel like that. I'm not that childish.'

'Forgive me, darling boy, but then maybe you should try and stop acting so childishl—'

Flip cut her off and threw the phone down on to the seat next to him. On his other side, Tillie squeezed his hand.

'She won't listen to me. Cavalley's can be bigger – it can be better. But she has to let me start making some decisions. We should be exploiting the Chinese market more. Jason's right – we should be getting in there before our competitors do. We should attract local investment and build quickly. Spend less time on couture and more on what makes the money.'

Tillie stroked his hand with her thumb. 'She won't ever let go of couture. And I think she's right.'

Flip snorted in exasperation.

'She is,' continued Tillie. 'It's what gives Cavalley's value. You can buy a cheap hat anywhere, pick it up, throw it away. People don't do that with Cavalley's; even the mass-market ranges last. You lose couture and you lose what makes it special.'

'You stop losing millions of pounds a year,' he snorted.

'Not overall.'

'It's not just the couture. She's stuck in her old ways, to the point where she can't see the future.' Flip swivelled round in his seat to face his fiancée. 'I can make it better, Till. *We* can make it better.'

'Are you sure it's not just that you want to do it your way?'

Flip shook his head. 'No. But, even if it was, what would be so wrong with that? What's wrong with wanting a chance to show that I can do it – to be in charge?'

Tillie shrugged. 'It's not your company, darling. It's hers. It's always been hers.'

'And don't I know it.' Flip's voice was bitter.

'Sorry. I don't want to fight with you about it. I just want the chance, that's all.'

'I know.' Tillie pulled his hand to her lips and kissed it. 'And I love you for it. As long as it's not at the expense of what really matters. Which is family.' She prodded him in the chest. 'Go on, send her a text. Make it up before we get to Capri.'

'All right,' he grumbled. Then he groaned. 'Oh God.'

'What?'

'Just the thought of it all. Family dinner. Boodle. Mungo.'

'Oh Flip.' Tillie frowned, and Flip felt awful. 'You mustn't say that. He's your son. He adores you – worships you. Make an effort. Please.'

'I know, I know. I just find him impossible. He's so – so needy. Like . . .' Flip stopped himself. It wasn't fair to complain about the boy or his mother to Tillie. To anyone. They had done nothing wrong. He resolved to make an effort tonight, a proper effort to talk to his teenage son. Take him down to the terrace after dinner and give him his first cognac, maybe. Do some of that father and son bonding he was always hearing about. He cheered up, leaned over and kissed Tillie full on the lips.

'I'll spend some proper time with him this weekend, I promise. You've worn me down. How can you be such a nag when we're not even married?' he teased.

Tillie waved the ring on her finger at him. 'Nearly,' she joked. 'I'm practising.'

'Hmm. I can still change my mind, you know,' he said, mock stern, stroking the side of her face.

'Just you try it. Anyhow, your mother wouldn't let you. She's planning the wedding of the century.'

'Tell me if she gets too much.'

'I like it. It's nice to have someone who cares.'

Flip looked at her tenderly. Tillie was an orphan, just like his mother. It was one of the things that had brought them together, Tillie told him, that had made them closer than boss and employee, or friends, or future mother-in-law and daughter-in-law – all roles that they had played during the years that they had known one another. When Tillie had started working at Cavalley's she had been untrained but obviously talented. Violet had seen her potential straight away. Seen something of herself in her. There was a fire in the girl's eyes that Violet recognised; a determination to make something better of her life. So Violet had spent time with her, given her responsibility, promoted her. Tillie had a flair for marketing, a knack for knowing what people wanted and how to give it to them. She had progressed quickly up the ranks. And then, when she had reached a level where no one could accuse her of sleeping her way to the top, she finally allowed Flip to take her out on the date he had been badgering for since her first day.

He kissed her nose. 'Good. Anyhow, I think she prefers you to me at the moment.'

Tillie shrugged. 'I don't really blame her.'

'Neither do I.' He smiled.

'Now send that text.'

'Yes, Miss.'

'Mrs, soon.'

'I can't wait.' Flip picked up his phone and opened a new message. As he did so, his phone rang. 'Damn. It's Boodle.' He sighed. What did his ex-wife want? She was going to see him in a few hours. His hand hovered above the phone. Tillie reached over and flipped it open. He glared at her, and she pointed at the phone. 'Go on,' she mouthed. Flip rolled his eyes.

'Hello, Boodle. What can I do for you?'

He listened as she wittered on about a delayed taxi and a birthday present for his mother, and he closed his eyes and let her words wash over him – and he never sent the text.

There was a knock at Violet's bedroom door. She sighed and stood up; she would carry on thinking about the problem later. Nothing was going to happen today, after all. As she stood, she felt a sudden twinge, and winced. '*Momento*,' she called out, knowing that Pietro would wait until she told him to enter. She stood still, waiting for the pain in her back to subside, breathing slowly through pursed lips.

When she opened the door, a few seconds later, a bouquet of pink roses and peonies took up the whole space.

'Signora Violetta, beautiful flowers for you – from a secret admirer, I think?'

Pietro came inside and carefully placed the arrangement on the low table in front of the sofa. Violet reached down and opened the little white envelope that was tucked into the side of the blue glass vase holding the flowers. Their scent hit her, sweet and rich, and her hand shook a little. Pietro's eyes gave away his concern with a slight wrinkle at their corners. She must reassure him.

'*Ecco*,' she said, holding her hand out, spreading her fingers wide. 'I'm like a schoolgirl getting her first Valentine. So silly, at my age.'

He smiled, relieved. '*L'amore domina senza regole*,' he said proudly. Love rules without rules.

Marry me, the card said. Violet smiled. Every day since Patrick Byrne had walked into her life, long after she had given up on finding someone with whom she could share it, he had asked her to marry him. They had met three years ago, at a dinner party that Violet hadn't wanted to go to, and he had charmed her immediately. He was funny, affectionate and, most appealingly of all perhaps, he didn't take either himself or Violet too seriously. Their relationship was quite unlike any that Violet had experienced before – which was, she supposed, why it was so special.

'I'll never marry again,' she had told him, the first time, and the time after, and the time after that. 'I'm too old.' And, 'What would my children say? It would look ridiculous. And anyhow, I don't believe in marrying twice. I made those promises once.'

Patrick just shrugged, and carried on asking. 'I'll wear you down one day,' he joked. 'You'll run out of excuses eventually.' Violet couldn't help but admire his tenacity and find it attractive. But she couldn't marry him.

She smiled as she read the second line of the card. *A thousand-and-thirty-second time lucky? Yours, in hope eternal, Patrick*. One thousand and thirty-two days, she had known him. And she had been happy in his company for every single one of them. People had married on far, far less. They lived separately but closely, both agreeing that they were too old to merge their households and start playing house. Both happy with the arrangement that had evolved, where they met once a week for a date that felt like the definition of romance, and the keys they held to each other's homes that felt like the comfort and companionship and security they both valued. People wondered why they didn't marry, she knew that. Violet shrugged to herself. It didn't matter what other people thought. It never had.

'*Grazie*, Pietro,' she began to say. But as she opened her mouth, the pain in her back returned, and she gasped.

'Signora? Signora Cavalley!'

Violetta, she thought. *Call me Signora Violetta*, as normal. But everything was not normal, and she could not speak, and her eyes were shut tightly, as if by shutting they could ward off the wave of pain that had spread from her back around her body and all through it, and then there was nothing.

His hand was the first thing she was aware of when she woke up. The cool skin of his fingers, lightly stroking her temple. She did not move.

'I'm still alive, then,' she said quietly, without opening her eyes.

'Unless you've taken me with you, and heaven is a villa in Capri, in which case I've got away with a surprising level of bad behaviour for a Catholic boy,' Patrick said. She opened her eyes and smiled at him. He wore jeans and a navy linen shirt that was as crinkled as his eyes at their edges. 'How are you feeling?'

Violet mentally worked her way down her body, as you might do after a fall or an accident. 'All right, actually. No more pain.'

'Ah. That'll be Doctor del Conte's magic working.'

'Has he gone? How long have I been sleeping for?' Violet pushed herself up on her elbows and reached for the glass of water that had been placed on the table within easy reach. She thought, not for the first time, how lucky she was to have so many people around her to attend to her every need. Being ill was more bearable when you were rich.

'A couple of hours. I think—'

'I don't want to cancel the dinner tonight,' she interrupted, before he could speak. His forehead wrinkled. 'I'm not arguing about it.'

There was a pause. 'I wouldn't dream of it.' Patrick stood. 'Are you going to tell them this weekend?'

Violet pursed her lips. 'I'll tell them when I'm good and ready.'

'That's not an answer.'

'I argued with Flip earlier.'

'Neither is that.'

'Oh, stop it.'

'You have to tell them, Lettie.'

'I don't *have* to do anything,' she snapped suddenly. 'It's my business, and I'll deal with it how I see fit.'

Patrick nodded. When he spoke, his voice was calm but firm. 'Well, that's fine when it comes to everything else. But this isn't everything else, is it? It affects them as well. It's not just about you any more, my lovely girl.' Patrick's face was sad. He looked out of the window. Violet was filled with an urge to hold him, and she got up from the sofa and went over to his side, wrapping her arms around his body and leaning her head on his shoulder. As she held him, she could feel his chest moving, his breath coming unevenly, as he tried not to cry. She watched the froth of the sea rise up in white foam in the wake of a speedboat whizzing towards the harbour, and laced her fingers with his.

Illness might be made more comfortable, the rough edges softened with cashmere blankets and private hospitals and doctors who came to your bedside where you lay in linen sheets. It could be made more convenient, with people to shop and fetch and carry and care for you, chauffeurs to drive you to appointments and the knowledge that you would not be made to wait.

But there were some things no amount of money could protect her from. The look of worry in Patrick's eyes was one. The main reason that she was putting off telling her children was not because she wanted to shield them from pain – pain was coming, whatever she did – but because she could not bear the thought of looking into their eyes and seeing *that look*, the one that said she was an invalid now, a patient, not their indomitable mother. Not Violet Cavalley.

Fran

Fran trudged up the dusty road towards the centre of Anacapri, pressing herself against the wall as a scooter, followed swiftly by a truck carrying crates of fruit, whizzed past. A driver whistled at her as he sped down the hill, and she spun around and glared angrily at the departing vehicle, catching the man's eye in his wing mirror as he disappeared. The make-up that she wore evened out her skin and concealed the redness of her scar, but it couldn't hide the ridge that ran down her left cheek, nor the fact that her jaw sagged slightly on that side. She carried on up the hill, wondering why the pavements seemed to run out just on the bits where the road bent and you couldn't see what was coming. It was like a real-life version of a computer game: you had to peer out from around the wall and scamper to the next bit for safety. But she had escaped the villa and her family and the rest of the party, at least, and now she had a couple of hours to herself before she had to go back and be Violet Cavalley's daughter.

Her mother had gone into her spotlight mode, as Fran thought of it – holding court like the jewelled spider at the centre of her web, surrounded by acolytes. She had turned into the brittle version of herself that was nothing like Fran's real mother, all surface and sparkle and sharp edges. It would be the same until they got home now, Fran knew. She would flit about from friend to ex-lover, flirting and charming and dazzling them all. Everyone would say how wonderful she was, and how talented and clever, and wasn't Fran proud of her, wasn't she lucky, and Fran would stay in the background and think that she much preferred her mother when she was at home in the big kitchen of their house off the King's Road, wearing an old cashmere jumper and jeans, drinking pots of tea as she doodled new designs and absentmindedly worked her way through whole packs of digestive biscuits, before complaining that Fran should have stopped her.

Fran had reached the centre square of Anacapri now, and it was full of tourists eating *gelati* while they waited for buses, and huddles of taxi drivers trying to entice them into their funny topless cars. A tanned street-sweeper in orange overalls winked at her from behind his mirrored sunglasses and she turned away and went into the side alley that her map showed her would take her up to the ruined castle, where she was heading. Strange how even the street-sweepers here looked like movie stars, all stubble and shades and suntan. The side street was quiet, apart from a dribble of German tourists just in front of her, and she dawdled back by a little fruit stall set into the stone wall to let them go first. An old lady, the skin of her face scrumpled up like a raisin and the colour of almonds, held a huge grapefruit out to Fran as she walked past, waving at her almost threateningly and saying something in Italian she didn't understand. Fran scuttled on up the alley, past shops selling limoncello in lemon-shaped bottles and citrusy perfumes, floaty cotton skirts and big straw hats. She paused by the hat shop, amusing herself by wondering for a moment how her mother would react if she arrived back at the villa wearing one of the wide-brimmed raffia ones. Not well. That was an understatement. A girl with yellow-blond hair caught her unawares and squirted her with one of the bottles of scent she was wielding. It smelled of a garden by the sea.

'The castello was built in the late nineteenth century by . . .'

She ducked around the woman standing with a red umbrella held aloft in front of her tour group, and made her way inside the castello. She had been here every day since they arrived on the island a week ago. The first time she had come just for something to do, telling her mother she was interested in the history of the building, but it was the gardens that had transfixed her, the gardens that she kept coming back to.

Today it was different though. She couldn't relax. What was changed? The gardens were no busier than usual, no less beautiful and well-tended than the day before, or the day before that – but something was different. She walked along the path towards the back wall, towards the sea. Then she realised. It wasn't anything about the garden itself that was different, it was someone *in* the garden. Someone was watching her. Fran knew the feeling all too well. She had grown used to it. People looked at her a lot – doing double-takes. Staring. Not seeing *her*, but only her scar. It was all they could see.

This wasn't someone looking at her face, however. He or she was behind her, over her shoulder. It was the sort of sensation you got when you were walking down a street in London and turned suddenly to see an old friend 100 yards behind you, trying to catch up, or when you were walking home at night and something made you turn into a busy street and take the long way round to avoid remaining in the shadows any longer. Fran had been taught to listen to her sixth sense by the man Violet had paid to come and train all of her children about how to avoid being kidnapped. 'You're being hysterical, Mum,' Fran had protested. 'We live in London, not Baghdad or somewhere. People don't just go around kidnapping teenagers.' But Violet had insisted, so she had jumped, kicked and blocked her way through two days of intensive personal safety training with a big bearded man called Clive. Fran had grown more and more used to these impulsive fears of Violet's. It was all to do with the family curse that her mother believed in – more and more these days, it seemed. Fran herself didn't believe in curses, or magic, or anything other than logic and science. She was a rationalist. But Violet did, and Violet was the one who made the decisions.

'Listen to your gut, Miss Fran,' Clive had said, over and over again. 'It's the most important lesson I can teach you. If you take only one thing away from this, it should be that.'

Fran had thought that for the amount of money her mother was undoubtedly paying for the training, she would be expecting her to take away a lot more than that . . . but now his words rang in her ears and she slowed her walk very slightly.

Be logical, she told herself. You aren't going to be kidnapped. You aren't going to be attacked. Not here, in a public, walled garden on an island. And yet . . . there was *something*. She touched the petals of a flower curling round a pillar, then leaned in to smell it, glancing behind her as she did so. She couldn't see anyone other than the group of tourists, who were making their way back inside the house. There was no one there. But still the feeling lingered.

She had a sudden urge to run after the other visitors so that she wasn't left alone in the garden, which had seemed so lovely just a few moments ago but which now felt sinister and unwelcoming. Oh, for goodness' sake, she told herself. It's the middle of the day, in a tourist attraction, and you've spooked yourself for no good reason. You're behaving like your mother. *But are you going to take the risk*? the little voice in her head asked. *Is it worth it? Think of your mother. What if it is someone out to do you harm? It's not as if you're from just any old family, is it?* She tried to silence the voice. This must be what it's like to be Blue, she thought. A constant battle inside your own head.

Fran took her mobile phone out of her slouchy shoulder bag. You're being pathetic, she admonished herself as she dialled. There is no bogeyman, no one waiting in the shadows. Just like there is no Cavalley Curse. It's an invention, a myth, a paranoia.

But as she rifled in her bag, she felt someone's eyes watching her again. She jerked her head up quickly, before they had a chance to move. There was a man on the other side of the square, watching her. He was wearing a T-shirt and dark trousers, had short black hair shot through with grey, and dark, tanned skin. She couldn't tell how old he was from this distance, but he wasn't young. Probably just a local man, she told herself. You're seeing faces in the shadows. But still, she called up Tony, the family's driver.

She told him that she was tired and didn't want to walk back. He would pick her up from the square *subito*, he said. 'I have already left.' She caught up with the group as they were leaving and began to walk back down the sloping stone alley to the square. As she put her phone away, she looked back at where the man had been standing. Just for a second. There was no one there.

Tony pulled up beside her almost by the time she had wandered down and sat on the wall to wait for him. 'Did you have a nice time, Miss Frangipani?' he asked as she slid into the cool of the air-conditioned car. She secretly loved that Tony insisted on using her full name. To everyone else she was Fran. Sensible, bright Fran. Fran, the youngest. Fran, who was adored and spoiled by them all. Fran, who was different.

But to Tony, who had been driving the family since she was small, she would always be Miss Frangipani. Sweet Frangipani, she had been called when she was little, and she had hated it then, not wanting to be sweet. Wanting to be tough, like her brothers. 'Fran,' she insisted on being called, 'my name is Fran. A grown-up name.' They had humoured her at first, but Fran was easier to say than Frangipani, and so it had stuck. Then the accident happened and no one seemed to think of her as girly and sweet any more, and they avoided talking about make-up and things when she was in the room. Now part of her wished she could go back to being Frangipani, and cast off the slightly severe role she had created for herself.

'Yes, thank you. What's been happening at the villa?'

He caught her eye in the rearview mirror. 'Miss Boodle should be arriving soon. I'm going to collect them shortly. Your mother's in her room. Doesn't want to be disturbed, she said,' he replied evenly, and winked at her. She rolled her eyes and stared out of the window. They were stuck in the square, blocked in by one of the island's orange buses, which couldn't move down the narrow street because of a funeral. Women in black lace with heads lacquered stiff with spray poured out of the hearse and descended like crows upon the waiting crowd on the pavement. There was a lot of crossing themselves and gesticulation. Fran rather admired their capacity for full-blown grief. It was effusive, external. None of the thin-lipped British way of things here. Death in Capri was communal, public and wore patent-leather high heels. Fran brought her attention back to what Tony was saying.

'Been resting for a couple of hours this afternoon.'

Fran sighed. Her phone was still in her hand, and she began to text Tillie. *Coming back now*, she typed.

'Oh God, Tony. Probably some drama or other. I wonder what it is this time.' She carried on tapping into her phone.

'Don't be too hard on her,' Tony said. 'She's probably nervous, that's all.'

'Ha! Nervous about what? My mother's never been nervous in her life. I don't think she even knows what it means.'

Tony tutted. 'Now now. She's a very talented lady, your mother.'

'So everyone tells me.'

Tony smiled. 'Just be nice to her.'

Fran huffed loudly so that Tony could hear. It was part of their routine. They had been playing this double-act since she was a recalcitrant four year old, gazing up at his pale-blue eyes in the rearview mirror as he drove her to school. *Be nice to your mother*, he had said then. *She's a busy lady, so sometimes I have to step in for her. She'd bring you every day herself if she could*. And: *She doesn't mean to tell you off*, when Fran and Violet had argued. *Be nice to your mother*.

The funeral procession had moved off down a cobbled side street towards the church now, a trail of mourners following the coffin, men in short-sleeved shirts with their hands stuffed into their pockets bringing up the rear. Tony put the car into gear and began to move off.

Fran was sick of being different. Different at home. Different in public, because of her face. Different at school, even. Oh, plenty of her schoolmates' parents were famous, but there always seemed to be something that singled her out. When she was at prep school her mother would sometimes drop her off wearing some bizarre creation, a fuchsia-plumed fascinator or a top hat with full-length black veil like a Victorian widow, claiming that she needed to give her creations a trial run. Fran couldn't see why that trial run needed to be the school run, but there was no arguing with Violet when she was in full flow. Or she had been singled out because, once more, her family was in the papers, some new disaster, some new crisis having befallen them. Or her mother was whisking them all off on tour with the band whose costumes she was helping to design, or to collect an award or go on a research trip that she insisted was a better education than sitting in Double Geography looking at it on a map. 'I'll take you to the actual place.' Her teachers couldn't do much about it, but they didn't like it, and she could never get her mother to understand that the GCSE examination board wouldn't accept an illustrated photo-essay about Los Angeles or Sydney or Shanghai in place of the essay questions everyone else had prepared. And then, later, of course, there was the other reason that she stood out, when people looked at her twice, their eyes shifting quickly away when they began to see the extent of the damage.

Frangipani Cavalley. No one could quite work her out when they first met her. She had olive skin and green eyes, an exotic first name and a surname that, by the time she was a teenager, was already synonymous with mystery and tragedy.

'Cavalley,' people said, turning the name over on their tongue, trying to remember where they had heard it, and then, as it came to them, a look of curiosity spreading over their face, the outer reflection of a hundred questions they wanted to ask and a hundred rumours they had heard whispered. But whatever they asked, whatever they knew about her or did not know, they always, always, looked at one thing first. Her scar.

As they pulled into the driveway of the villa, Fran picked at the edge of her thumbnail, peeling off the navy-blue varnish in little flakes. The driveway was circular, a huge urn in the centre, and three cars were leaving as they arrived. Blue was in the back of one. Where was he going? The other two were empty, presumably going to pick up guests as they arrived at the marina. She hopped out of the car and went to find her mother. It was five o'clock. She wanted to try and talk to her before everyone got there and Violet was taken up with the role of hostess and being the star. Fran would never get her by herself once that had happened. And now that she had made her decision, she wanted to tell her mother about her plans before she lost her nerve again. Fran's exterior was tough, because she had made it so, but inside she was still the youngest child, trying to find her place within the maze of her family, and not get lost.

Blue

'Blue is free inside, Blue is no one's bride . . . no one's mind. Blue is his own man, his own mistress and his own master . . . master of fortune, fortune favours the brave. Blue is brave, brave and true, true to his own will . . . will . . . will . . . Will you, won't you, won't Blue, don't be blue, do be Blue . . .'

The words comforted and soothed Blue with their rhythm as he walked briskly through the boutique-lined streets of Capri Town looking for the bar where he had agreed to meet Adam. Bar Napoli, it was called. Blue had looked it up in one of his guidebooks and it had said it was a 'well-positioned people-watching spot serving well-made cocktails and some of the best antipasti in town'. It sounded nice. But people-watching? He was unsure about that. Did it mean people would be watching *him*? Like an animal at the zoo, a monkey scratching its balls while people laughed and pointed, a dancing bear someone poked a stick at – and that thought made him want to cry, though he didn't quite know why – something at the edges of his brain, some memory floating into view that he did not want to bring into focus – so he stopped it, blocked it off with a black wall. He was nervous. He hadn't wanted to go to the bar but Adam had insisted. Adam said it was right and so it was right and must be done. His hands bounced against the side of his legs.

This town was like a film-set of a town, he thought, all polish and gloss, as if it had been erected overnight. But what was behind the shopfronts? Maybe there was nothing there at all. Hollow. Hollowed out and crumbling on the inside like a scarab beetle or a tortoise shell, like a tomb or . . .

'. . . nonono, don't do that, you'll give yourself the shudders, the shivers. Find the bar, meet Adam, and it'll be Adam and Blue, A and B and no C to play the third wheel, Alpha Beta no Omega. In the beginning there was Adam and in the end there had better be Adam or there would be no Blue . . .'

Adam had promised him a Bellini, a drink that always made Blue feel happy, so he had said he would come even though really he had wanted to stay at the villa in his room with his sketchpad and his cigarettes, but Adam had told him he could bring his cigarettes and must leave the villa where he felt safe. Blue stopped short in the middle of the street and the woman who had been walking behind him tripped into him and muttered something angrily in a language he didn't recognise. He didn't look at her. He had felt safe at the villa and here he did not. And Adam had known he would not, he must have known. He knew everything about Blue. He was trying to undermine him, pull the rug from under him, make him walk on shaky ground where there were no foundations, no net to catch him and he could fall at any time . . .

Blue looked around him and everywhere he saw danger. Mannequins in shop windows had pointy black shiny limbs with huge bags hanging from them and clothes that he knew weren't as good as his clothes, weren't as carefully designed or well-made, but he wouldn't go in and start looking at them, he remembered, he remembered, he had done that once before and it had not ended well. He clutched on to the memory without making himself remember it. He was walking a tightrope again. Balance, balance, and weave, weave between the – no, that was an obstacle course, with things to weave between; he was mixing his metaphors again. Like a cake. 'Make a cake, bake a cake, pat-a-cake, pat-a-cake baker's man, bake me a cake as fast as you can.' He was a baker's man. Adam was a good baker, he made delicious scones that Blue liked to eat piled high with strawberry jam and clotted cream until he felt sick. Adam never stopped him though. Wanted him to get fat? Fat and lazy like a slug so Adam could keep him inside in a glass box and no one else would want to look at him and none of the nice things would happen . . . Blue pulled himself back. No. Adam wouldn't do that. 'You're not being very fair,' he told himself. 'You must be fair, fair play, playground, fairground . . .'

A waiter waved to him from a restaurant with tables outside. 'Lunch, signor? Special of the day, veal parmigiana.' How did he know he was English? The place had pink napkins weighted down with heavy-looking cutlery that Blue didn't like the look of at all; it glistened at him threateningly. 'Turn away, turn away from that, turn, turn, turn . . .' He knew he must, so he turned and started to walk back in the direction he had come from. No, that wasn't right, he was walking away from Adam, and Adam would be angry. He must go on. Must plough on, battle on like a brave little soldier, head down, no surrender. 'Onward Christian soldiers, marching as to . . .'

On he marched, his arms swinging and his hands tapping his thighs when they passed them, like a touchstone, reminding himself he was still here, still Blue. People stared at the thin, fragile-looking man striding down the street, his arms almost windmilling and his lips moving in a silent recitation. His progress was stuttering, he took a few steps quickly and then paused, gathering his nerves, his hands working in that familiar rhythm. He was typically well-dressed in the slightly costumed way of one whose image is part of their brand, for whom design is everything, in a pale pink patterned shirt and white trousers and waistcoat, a white straw Trilby on his head, but there was something slightly off about the picture, something too symmetrical, almost, and as he neared him it took Adam a few minutes to realise that it was because Blue held a slim, white cigarette in each of his whirling hands.

A blonde woman was coming towards Blue on the arm of a tall, pompous-looking man in a suit, and as she neared him she giggled and whispered something to her companion, who steered her towards the other side of the street and away from the muttering Blue. The sight tugged at Adam's heart and made him want to weep and shake the couple all at once. 'Can't you see?' he wished he could say to them. 'Can't you see he's not just some mad person? He's Blue – he's beautiful and talented and, well, yes, a little mad too maybe, just now.' But not frighteningly so or in a way that made him someone you had to cross the street to avoid mocking him as you did so. He wouldn't hurt a fly. Adam rushed to catch up with him.

At least he had realised where Blue would have been heading and had managed to get down here before – well, before any number of things happened. You could never quite predict the outcome where Blue was concerned. He could get himself into difficult situations sometimes. He got so caught up in his litany of words and ideas, in the conversations that he had with himself because his brain got too full and scattered and he couldn't focus, just leaped from one thing to the next. That was when he was at risk, when he didn't see the cars coming towards him on the road on to which he had wandered because he wasn't paying attention to where he was going, or when he started to take his clothes off because it was getting dark and just somehow carried on until he was naked in the middle of Hyde Park at four in the morning in January, or when he had become fixated on examining the structure of a jacket in a department store and so had begun to unpick it in order to see how it had been constructed and ended up getting arrested for criminal damage. All things that had happened in the last year or so.

'Hey,' Adam called out now. 'Blue!'

There was no response. Adam wasn't surprised – Blue would be oblivious to all but the refrain in his head and the movement of his body until Adam was close by him. He called again anyway.

'Blue, wait up.'

Something in him needed to call out, to voice his alliance with this dashing, dapper man who was attracting so many glances and raised eyebrows. *He's not just some nutter,* calling out his name seemed to tell the world. *He's a person, he has a friend – more than a friend, a partner, one who won't allow you to smirk and mutter about him as if he's deaf and blind.* Blue might be deaf and blind to it now, but in his quieter moments he was all too aware that he made an unusual sight.

'Am I terribly shaming?' he would ask sometimes, at night, as they lay side by side watching boxed sets of the comedies Blue liked to play over and over again, because he knew the jokes and when they were coming. Unexpected humour unsettled him. 'I don't want to be an embarrassment to you. I don't want people to think badly of you because you're with me when I'm on the ups.'

That's what he called his swings of emotion. There was 'on the ups' and there was 'in the pits' – the cycles and rhythms that formed the pattern of Blue's life, and now of Adam's as well. Adam would pull Blue closer and ruffle his hair when he asked that, and Blue would smooth it back down again into its neat side parting, precisely, almost preciously.

'Anyone who thinks badly of me because I'm with you is stupid, aren't they?' Adam told him. 'What, they see an average-looking bloke with splinters in his hands walking along the street with you, Blue Cavalley, famous designer and best-dressed man in town, *Tatler*'s fifty-third most invited party guest of 2009, no less.'

Blue smacked his arm for that, but looked pleased. 'Don't mock me.'

'I'm not mocking you, I'm mocking the people who make up lists of how many parties people get invited to and think it's something to be proud about. But what, they see us together, you and me, and they're going to feel sorry for me? You've got it the wrong way round, mate.'

'Don't call me "mate". It's what you call fat men sitting at the bar in the pub.'

'You are my mate, though. My soulmate.'

Blue smiled and blushed. 'Well.'

He was. And he was proud to be so. Adam was a practical man, and he had lost enough to know that he had to hold on to what was good in his life. And Blue was good. He caught up with him and touched Blue's shoulder gently, careful not to jar or shock him.

'Blue,' he said softly. 'You raced off. I've only just caught up.'

Blue stopped but didn't turn around, just took a puff from the cigarette in his left hand and then from the one in his right. Adam could see him thinking. Blue's face broadcast his every thought like a rolling screen.

He knew what had happened. Earlier, Adam had suggested taking him for one of his favourite cocktails in the bar in order to get him out of the villa, stop him sinking into the whirlpool of drawing and smoking and drinking that he would get caught in if he just remained in his room there. He wanted to remind him that there was a world out here, away from his mother and the other Cavalleys and the strange little bubble they seemed to inhabit sometimes. But the suggestion had obviously flicked a switch in Blue's mind, as sometimes happened, and he had just set off, like a wind-up toy across the floor of a child's nursery, only stopping when it was picked up, or hit the wall.

'Hey. Shall we get that Bellini?'

He had to be careful with him. Didn't want to suggest that Blue had done something wrong, which could send him spiralling off in one direction; nor did he want to crowd him and make him feel like he was being controlled or manipulated, which could set him veering off in another.

'Adam,' Blue said softly, thoughtfully. Still not turning, not looking at him. But he dropped the cigarette in his left hand to the ground and then raised the hand to waist height. Adam waited while Blue thought. He could see his brain working to catch up, process the situation he found himself in. For a second he looked like Adam thought he must have done when he was a small boy, fearful of the world around him, a little lost, a little at sea. And then his face changed and he turned to Adam with a smile on his face and said, 'A Bellini, you say? What a lovely idea, good man, my good man, my man.'

He held out his hand, and Adam took it, and they walked towards the bar together. Adam allowed himself to relax a little and listen to Blue chatter about what they should both wear for dinner as they went. The crisis had been averted. For now.

Boodle

Boodle Lockington-Barr hung up the phone call to her ex-husband, Flip Cavalley, and wriggled uncomfortably into her seat on board the aircraft, wedged in by her not inconsiderable girth. Her husband, Willy, called the tyre of fat around her hips her 'steering wheel', and sometimes took hold of it and pretended to manoeuvre her around by it, making childish brrm brrm noises. When they had first been married she had found this quite amusing – endearing, even – but after ten years of marriage to Willy, the joke had started to wear a little thin. Well, after about two years, if she was honest.

She was further jammed into the seat by the thick cardigan that she had had to take off already. 'Honestly, Mum, it's not even cold,' they had all said in the car, but she had muttered something about air conditioning on planes and needing to wear layers, while they had rolled their eyes. Layers were the way to dress when one was travelling; she was sure she had read it in Nicola Formby's column in *Tatler*. They had all been right, of course. Her children were far more confident travellers than she was. Caitlin, who was eight, and even Ellie, her youngest, had trotted happily on to the plane and found their seats, settling down straight away, and were now bickering over who got to play with the Nintendo DS first.

Boodle hated flying; it made her nervous and uncomfortable and infinitely aware of all of her shortcomings. How plump her hips were, how uncoordinated her wardrobe, how meagre her budget. How, when Nicola Formby wrote about the importance of layers when flying, she was referring to gossamer-thin wisps of satin and cashmere and silky jersey, in inky navy and co-ordinating neutrals and bright white camisoles and ballet-wraps and flowing scarves, not Marks & Spencer T-shirts in an array of mismatched colours and a Boden cardi that had lost one of its 'jazzy' flower-shaped buttons.

Boodle's lack of style didn't bother her much, these days. It was one of the pleasures of living where they did, in the draughty old rectory in Northumberland, that she didn't have to worry about what she looked like – indeed, she frequently went for days without looking in a mirror – although when she finally caught sight of herself in a shop window or in the mirror above the basin while she was helping Ellie to brush her teeth or wash her hands, she got a shock when she saw a frizzy-haired, pink-faced woman with fine red lines around her nose, and rough skin that still blushed like a teenager all too easily. Still, most of the other local mums were the same, being farmers' wives or countrywomen born and bred who had no time for the glossy magazines that Boodle still subscribed to and pored over in the bath with a big bar of Green & Blacks. It was only occasionally that she was made painfully aware of how awful she looked – when she drove down to Mungo's school to watch him play rugger or pick him up at the end of term, filling her estate car with trunks and tuckboxes and muddy boots and the smell of fourteen-year-old boy, which she complained about but secretly relished, and had to say hello to all the glossy blondes who had four children and hips narrower than their sons'; or when she took the girls to London for a half-term treat day, buying them pancakes in the tea room in Harrods and stealing glances at the glamorous Arab women all around her.

Or when she went to see her former mother-in-law. Violet Cavalley had never been anything other than kind to Boodle, and Boodle had never felt anything other than deeply inadequate in her presence. Actually, in her absence as well, come to think of it. Violet was everything Boodle was not. She had a brilliant career which she had built from nothing. She was a darling of the fashion world, hailed as the first real genius in the world of millinery in decades. And of course everyone loved the mystery of her background – the rise from nowhere and nothing, the glamour of a true rags-to-riches tale. It wasn't just the career, either, it was her children – the deeply glamorous and bohemian offspring that she had raised, practically single-handedly, all of them different in looks but joined by the strand of DNA that they had in common – Violet's. Flip, the eldest, and physically the most like his mother – dark and strong, with a look in his eyes that warned anyone from standing in his way. Blue, delicate Blue, whose long limbs looked as if they were jointed by hinges, like a puppet, and whose pale face and haunted eyes told of a reality inside his mind that was quite other from the rest of the world's. Then there were the missing ones – the lost children – the ones whose presence was felt still, even in their long absence. Scarlet, whose golden curls had caught the light in a way that might almost, one day, have competed with Violet's own magnetic splendour; and Sebastian, whose wild nature was matched only by his wildly good looks. There was, from the very beginning of his life, something a little out of control, a little too rampant, about him, Boodle knew from photographs and family stories. The Cavalley family was one with plenty of stories, told and untold. They had entranced Boodle from the beginning.

Boodle was nervous about going back into that family, taking her own with her, she admitted silently to herself now, as she sweated in her sticky aeroplane seat. She had always felt like an outsider with her first family of in-laws. Not elegant enough, not funny or clever or in with their in-jokes enough, however hard she tried. Actually, the harder she tried, the worse it had been, she remembered. She could see them pitying her, sharing quick glances, cringing. Trying to hide from her the fact that they were doing so – well, most of them. Flip never bothered, that was the worst of it. He would roll his eyes and openly laugh at her when she tried to make a clever remark, or to tell a joke. 'Oh Boodle, you never remember the punchline properly, do you? Poor thing.' He would kiss her on the head and pat her shoulder as if the dig was affectionate, as if he found it endearing, but she knew better. She wasn't good enough. She had never been good enough. Not for Flip, and not for his family.

Violet had welcomed Boodle into her family and home as best she could, she had taken her shopping and given her hats that Boodle still wore occasionally to weddings and christenings to this day – without telling Willy where they had come from, as he would have sulked until she took off the only beautiful links to her former life that remained, and put on some drab bit of felt from the old-fashioned boutique in the nearest town with anything more than a post office and pub.

It was ironic, she was well aware, that Willy was always trying to live up to the shadow of Flip. Boodle and Willy had never acknowledged this essential truth between them; how could they? She couldn't tell this good man, who had taken her and Mungo on and given her two lovely daughters, that she still woke up some nights hot with the memory of Flip's touch and the intense excitement it raised in her that she had never again experienced, and knew she never would; or that when she saw him, as she did occasionally at Mungo's school events, when Flip managed to fit them in – he was busy, she reminded herself, very busy – she imagined how her life would be, had they stayed married, how they would look together now – not very good, given the state of her appearance, maybe, but if she was still Mrs Cavalley she would have more time, she would make more effort . . . And that when her ex-husband kissed her cheek, she always, without fail, had a deep and dark urge to hold on to him, to make his touch last longer, to bury her face in the thick, soft cashmere of his overcoat and breathe him in . . .

Oh dear. Boodle took a deep breath and accepted a gin and tonic from the flight attendant, ignoring Willy's querying gaze. She rarely drank in the daytime, and he didn't really approve of women doing so. Sod it. She was going to need it on this trip, so she may as well start as she meant to go on. It wasn't just seeing Flip, and Violet, and all the rest of them, feeling inadequate and shabby and unsophisticated, that she was afraid of. It was putting her children into that world, and making them feel the same. Making them feel not good enough, as she had always felt. She couldn't bear the thought of that, that her lovely girls and her beloved boy were going to be held up for comparison to the Cavalleys, and found wanting. They didn't deserve that. Was she doing the wrong thing, taking them at all? They had all been so excited to be invited, but they didn't know what she knew. Didn't know what the Cavalley family could do . . . *Oh, stop it, Boodle!* She tried to pull herself together, but had a sudden sense of history repeating itself, and shivered.

Violet. Boodle hadn't seen her for years. What would she be like now? The same, probably, just as beautiful and captivating. Just as flawed. And she *was* flawed, Boodle had no illusions about that. However in awe of her former mother-in-law she might still be, however much she adored her, despite everything, for her kindness and warmth to Boodle when she was a young, inexperienced bride, Violet Cavalley was no saint, and she was not perfect. But oh, how she glittered with charisma still. That was obvious from the photos Boodle had seen of her since they had last met. She was slim, and beautiful – not just pretty, or attractive, or well-groomed – but properly beautiful in the way that made women unable to keep their eyes off her, and men unable to keep their hands off her. Her movements had the natural, easy sensuality of someone who was fully confident in their skin. Boodle had never had that – she had always erred on the clumsy, overexcited puppy side of things. Violet lit up the room, she glowed, she sparkled. Boodle had never sparkled. Not even on her wedding day – despite what people had told her to the contrary. 'The bride is always the most beautiful woman in any room,' they had said. But she had known, even then, that Violet was the one people were looking at, and Cressida Cavalley, Flip's first wife, the bride they were all remembering, even while Boodle was walking down the aisle.

By the time they landed at PRJ airport on Capri Island, Boodle had drunk two double gin and slimlines, and was feeling a little light-headed. When she got up to reach for her hand luggage from the overhead locker, she stumbled to one side, and had to right herself by putting her hand on the seat in front of her.

'All right, Boo?' Willy asked.

'Yes. Stood up too quickly, went a bit woozy.'

He patted her rump absentmindedly and herded Caitlin and Ellie towards the exit. Willy had the same attitude to his wife and children as he did to his gun dogs – give them plenty of exercise, fresh air and food, and treat them with kindness but a firm hand, and one would be rewarded by obedience and affection. With Boodle, his approach was mainly successful. Much as Willy might resent Flip, he had paved the way for the easy life that Willy enjoyed now, since Boodle didn't expect much in the way of attention from a husband. When it came to his children, however, things weren't quite as straightforward. Caitlin was a Daddy's girl, and Ellie adored both of her parents equally, to the point where she had to buy both a present on one of their birthdays, lest the other feel left out – she had a sense of fairness and a horror of injustice that led her father to joke that they were raising a trial lawyer. And then there was Mungo, who was always somewhere in between.

Boodle watched him now, as he loped down the aisle of the plane, all elbows and undone work boots that were all the fashion, and a thick wodge of wavy hair that fell down over his forehead, apart from when he pushed it back in a hairband. Willy had been horrified by that, the first time he saw it. 'What the bloody hell are you wearing a girl's hairband for?' he had said. 'Take it off at once.' Mungo had responded with a dark, baleful glare, and by sloping off to paint his nails black with a marker pen and Boodle's clear varnish.

Mungo didn't quite fit in anywhere. Boodle knew it, Willy knew it, and she was pretty sure Mungo himself knew it. He wasn't Willy's son, and they had little in common, despite many long hours spent trying to get them to bond. Day trips, courses, activities that they might both enjoy – they tried it all and it all fell flat, for both of them. The boy was too rebellious and strong-willed for Willy, who found his girls much easier to get along with. Mungo also reminded Willy too much of the boys who had bullied him at school, all dark eyes and grunting, and he looked too like his father for Willy to ever really be able to feel like his parent. Maybe it would have been different if Mungo had been younger when Willy came along, but he was seven by the time he and Boodle married, old enough to resent this pink-faced, bespectacled man with a weak chin who was the very antithesis of the masculine strength that his real father embodied. But Mungo didn't fit in with his real father either.

He was too soft and reminiscent of Boodle for Flip's taste, too hard and reminiscent of Flip for his stepfather, too ungainly and parochial for Violet, too awkward and unsophisticated for all of them. Too into Emo for Northumberland, too used to country ways for London. Too rich for the local comp, where he had been for a year and been bullied, too poor for his boarding school, where he was still bullied, but just by a better class of thug – and this time he had not made the mistake of telling his parents.

Boodle was nervous, partly due to all the usual reasons, but also because she intended to confront Flip about his relationship with Mungo. Enough was enough, she had decided. Flip had to get to know his son – his only son – better, and Boodle thought she had found just the way to make it happen. She was determined to stand up for herself for once, but more importantly, to stand up for Mungo. Flip would be pleased she had done it when he got to know the boy, she knew he would. Maybe he would be grateful enough to her that . . . 'Stop it, Boodle, stop it now,' she admonished herself. 'You have a husband, a good husband. Flip doesn't want you, he never did, and he never will. Just be thankful for what you've got.' She hefted her bag and woolly cardi towards the little bus that would carry them all to the terminal, the girls skipping along, the only members of the family who seemed entirely unworried about the prospect of the weekend ahead. They were just excited about the party. Boodle didn't blame them. Despite her nerves, she too was looking forward to the prospect of a weekend surrounded by the trappings of the Cavalley family's glamorous life.

'Wow!' The girls launched themselves into their room like little rockets, dropping their rucksacks on the floor and racing to the balcony, their eyes wide as plates, trying to take everything in all at once. They had twin princess beds, pink silk draped in swathes over the white-painted metal of the four-posters, they each had their own little dressing-table, and they had their own bathroom.

'This room is the best room in the world ever, like a princess's castle before the giant comes to get her,' Ellie said breathlessly. Boodle didn't bother to ask what giant she was talking about. There was no understanding what went on in their heads, half the time.

'You're next door, Mungo,' she said, squinting at the letter that had been waiting for them at reception, a thick pack of instructions and directions and information all printed on dove-grey laid paper that was soft as cottonwool in Boodle's slightly damp hand. 'Through that door, I think. Don't bash the frame with your bag . . .'

'All right, all right, calmez-vous, clipboard,' he grunted at her as he went through, determined not to be impressed, as always. But then she heard his fingers click against each other and a long, drawn-out, 'Coo-ool,' and she knew that the magic that Violet managed to spin around herself and those with her, everywhere she went, had reached out and touched him as well.

Boodle poked her head around the door, keen to get a glimpse before he locked her out, as he no doubt would as soon as possible. The room was the perfect lair for a teenage boy; it had dark-blue walls, in sharp contrast to the girls' pastel-coloured confection of a room next door, and a low futon piled high with cushions and pillows. There was a pinball machine in one corner, and an iPod dock in the other.

'Boodle . . . I'm so glad to see you.'

Boodle turned to see Violet in the doorway, her cobalt-blue silk tunic melting into the walls, making her jewellery and eyes stand out against her pale skin.

'Violet.'

The two women kissed. 'And Mungo. Goodness me.' She looked up and down the long limbs of her grandson, who was easily taller than her. 'Don't worry, I won't say it. It's good to see you, as well.'

Mungo nodded. 'Hi, Grandma. The room's cool.'

Boodle raised an eyebrow. 'Gosh, an unprompted compliment. You are honoured. Deservedly, of course,' she added in a rush. She didn't want Violet to think she took any of it for granted.

Violet smiled. 'Shall we have a drink downstairs? It's been such a long time.'

Boodle nodded and trotted along after her ex-mother-in-law, who walked with quick, neat steps down the marble corridor towards the lift. Though Boodle was the taller of the two women, she seemed to need to rush to catch up. 'Don't make a mess,' she called after herself, as she shut the door to the children's rooms, knowing as she said it that they would already be pulling all of their possessions out of their cases and scattering them everywhere. She promised herself that she wouldn't nag them, or Willy, this weekend though.

'Have you and Willy found your suite yet?' Violet asked, as the lift slid to a halt in front of them.

'Willy's gone along there now. I wanted to get the kids settled. I'm sure it's as perfect as theirs are. Honestly, Violet, how do you do it? It's almost as if you had the rooms decorated just for them.'

God, she was gushing. How embarrassing.

Violet stepped into the lift and waited for Boodle to follow her.

'I did,' she replied.

Boodle's mouth opened but no sound came out. She had forgotten what life with the Cavalleys was really like.

Chapter Two

The party started at six. Guests had been arriving in Capri all day, dispersing from the marina to their various hotels, dresses in dry-cleaning bags, suits in their carriers. It was the talk of the island. They arrived, now, in their ones and twos, dressed like beautiful butterflies, tripping in high heels down the villa's driveway, hands heavy with jewelled rings, embellished little bags on the women's wrists.

The villa could have been made for parties, its sweeping gardens looking out to the backdrop of the sea, providing the setting and decoration all in one. It had a feeling of luxurious splendour, but an informal one. Of possibility, especially at this time of the evening. You felt that anything could happen, as night fell, and it was intoxicating.

Fran stood under one of the arches, watching. The guests came together and swirled around each other, like a froth of bubbles flying in concentric circles around a whirlpool. And at its centre, as always, was Violet. She wore a purple silk dress, one-sleeved, one-shouldered, gently ruffled at the bottom, and a pair of purple satin mules with a Perspex wedge sole. Inside the translucent sole of each shoe was a glittering little disco ball that caught the light as she tripped around the courtyard. They had been made specially for her, of course. The picture shifted, as she moved on, from group to group, glowing, glittering, gleaming. Fran might sometimes disapprove of her mother to her face, but secretly, she never tired of watching her when she was like this, knowing that she was related to her. It still made her feel special, even now, even having lived with it for her whole twenty-something years. It was like watching an actress step out of the cinema screen and take your hand, it was like seeing a portrait in a gallery come to life. Violet might dress the heads of the stars, but there was no doubting the fact that she was a star herself; the brightest one in the room tonight.

'You look like her, you know,' a voice said at her shoulder.

Fran turned. Boodle was wearing a strapless satin dress in a raspberry colour that did not flatter her ruddy cheeks, and that cut into her belly at the waist, but Fran was glad to see her.

'No, I don't. I don't look like anyone. Why would I?'

She smiled at her former sister-in-law, to soften her words. The rest of her siblings laughed at Boodle, but Fran remembered how kind she had been to her when she had been married to Flip, how much effort she had made to spend time with her. Boodle must have forgotten she was adopted. It wasn't really surprising, Fran supposed. No one ever really talked about it, so it just sort of faded into the background.

Boodle sat down on one of the seats, fiddling with the strap of her shoe. It was cutting into her foot already. She never had been able to wear high heels. Serve her right for trying to look sophisticated.

'You look like you. I mean, I know you're not blood-related. Of course,' Boodle said in a hurry, looking embarrassed. 'I just meant . . .' She was flustered. 'Well, it's like dogs, isn't it?'

'Dogs?' Fran was confused.

'You know. Dogs and their owners get more like one another.'

'Right,' Fran said.

'Oh God. Fran, I don't mean you're like a dog. Obviously.'

Boodle panicked, as something else occurred to her. 'Or that Violet's your owner, or anything. I mean, just because you're adopted, doesn't mean she loves you any less . . .'

Fran put a hand on her arm. 'It's all right, Boodle. I know what you meant.'

Boodle sighed with relief. 'Thank goodness. Silly old cow, always putting my foot in it, Willy says.'

'You're not old.'

'Hmm. But the rest is spot on, right?' Boodle laughed. 'Is Flip here yet?'

Boodle's voice was casual but her fingers were rearranging the perfectly laid out cutlery in front of her as she spoke. Fran noticed, but simply replied, 'Upstairs, getting ready. They'll be down soon.'

Boodle winced at the 'they'. Stupid of her. Flip was engaged; she was married. Of course he was a 'they'. *Let it go*, she told herself. *How many years has it been? Too many to be clinging on to romantic notions, that's for sure.*

'Hard, sometimes, isn't it? Trying to find your place amongst them?' Boodle's eyes were misty as she spoke. Fran looked at her in surprise.

'Sorry,' she said, smiling at Fran. 'It's just . . . I know it can't always be easy for you. Being a Cavalley is a full-time job, isn't it? And if you feel on the edge of things a bit . . . well, I just wanted to say that I understand. It wasn't that easy for me, either. In a different way, of course. But I just wanted you to know you can always talk to me. I know I'm not your sister-in-law any more. Not anything, really.'

'Don't say that.'

'It's true. I'm just a mum. But I'm part of your family still, sort of. I hope. And I know what it's like when, whatever you do, it never feels like it's quite enough.'

Boodle's eyes were sad, and Fran nodded.

'Thank you,' she said quietly. Didn't trust herself to say any more.

'I'm going to sit back down. Don't want to miss any of the food. Are you coming?' Boodle saw Mungo and started to head towards the top table, where the family were all sitting, then remembered she was seated with Willy, on the adjacent table. Mungo was with the family proper. Of course. He was the grandson. It was as it should be.

'In a bit. I'm going to wait here till she's done her speech.'

Boodle nodded. Fran made sure she was never centre of attention. Sitting by her mother while the whole courtyard gazed at them would be her idea of hell.

'All right. I'll see you later.'

Fran watched as the guests were all seated and the first course served, and her mother called for silence. She leaned against the cool of the stone pillar, and wondered what it must be like to be able to just stand up in front of people and talk like that. Confident, self-assured, no nerves. Never feeling you had to dip your head to stop people staring, or turn your face away.

'To lost loves.' The courtyard rose in their toast, and then Fran saw Pietro come into the courtyard, walking quickly over to the top table. Her mother's head tilted, listening to him, her expression unreadable at first, then frowning, clearly confused. Fran moved closer. Pietro was talking to Flip now, her brother's dark hair combed neatly into a side parting, his thick shoulder leaning forward as he stood at Violet's side. Tillie sat next to him, her tiny body close to his, their outfits perfectly co-ordinating, like the perfect couple they were. It seemed that with each day they got more alike, more neatly and comfortably joined. Fran thought she would never have a relationship like that; she settled for being part of their lives, basking in the glow of warmth she felt when she was with them, staying the night at their flat or being taken out for dinner by them, knowing that they were hers, her family.

She moved closer still. She could hear what Flip was saying now. Other people in the courtyard were starting to notice the conversation, so awkward and uncomfortable did the normally charming and grandfatherly Pietro look.

'He says he is Signora Cavalley's brother. I'm sorry, signor . . .'

Fran's eyes were on her mother's face as Pietro carried on speaking. It was quite, quite white, and her eyes were staring straight ahead, over Pietro's shoulder, to a tall figure standing in the loggia beyond. Fran observed her mother as Violet took her hand off Flip's arm then raised both hands to her mouth, touching her slim fingers to her lips as though shushing herself. And then, as Pietro spoke – quietly, so that only those closest to him could hear – she saw her mother's body crumple in on itself like a helium balloon that had been punctured, falling towards the ground. Patrick, on her other side, grabbed her and supported her, and then the courtyard was full of noise and movement, people standing to see what had happened, women crying out 'Oh!', Patrick calling for someone to 'ring the doctor, ring Doctor del Conte' as he lifted Violet gently in his arms and carried her towards the house, her sequinned and beaded train trailing behind him as he went. And all the time Fran stood completely still, Pietro's words ringing in her ears.

'He says Signora Cavalley is not . . . is not Signora Cavalley.'

As Violet lay in Patrick's arms, and was lowered on to the sofa in the villa's drawing room, her eyes flickered open for a moment. In front of her was motion, people coming towards her. Noise. 'Doctor, call Doctor del Conte,' she heard someone saying. An Irish accent. She wanted to shrivel from it, and couldn't work out why. It was Patrick. Patrick whom she loved, who was so kind. And then she remembered. As he stroked the back of her right hand, she could feel his thumb running over the scar there. And she heard another voice. One she had not heard for years, so many years.

'I'm not lying. She's my sister. That bitch is my sister, and I know she's dying. It's time she told the truth about where she came from. About who she is. I can prove it,' she heard him tell the others. 'She wears a crucifix on a chain around her neck. It has her real initials on the back of it. Go on – look at it. On the back. M . . . V . . . G. I'm no liar. Not like *her*.'

She could hear him being ushered away, hear Flip shoving and pushing him and shouting at him to leave. 'Can't you see she's ill?' he was saying.

I'm ill, she thought then. I'm really ill. She hadn't believed it until that point. The doctors had told her she was dying, had little time left, should 'make the most of it', whatever that meant. Go swimming with dolphins, or some other supposedly life-affirming rubbish. But it had felt as though it were happening to someone else – until now. Why was *he* here? Why had he come back? Money, she thought to herself. They all want money. And she drifted off again, unable to keep herself from bobbing under into unconsciousness. Patrick was stroking her hand still, and she wanted to tell him to stop. 'Don't listen to him,' she wanted to say. '*I* want to tell you. I want to tell you all the truth.'

But she couldn't speak. And then the darkness engulfed her.

Belton-by-Sea, 1956

Accidents happen. They happen in the distracted turn of a mother's back and the tug of a kettle cord or the slam of a car door. They happen in a sudden gust of wind and an unlatched gate, in the twist of a head to the back of the car and a ticking-off, in the drunken fumble of a finger holding a cigarette.

Accidents happen – that's what people say, isn't it? No one's to blame, there's no use crying over spilled milk.

May Gribbens's accident happened in the trip of a foot up the icy steps of the caravan and a smashed pint of milk that she would cry over, just not until later, not until she was safely hidden under the pile of quilts at the back of the caravan, cradling her hand and watching the blood soak through the makeshift bandage that she had wrapped around it. May's accident happened in the slip of time between her trip and the caravan door opening, before she had time to pick up the broken glass and wipe away the milk, or to work out how she could replace the precious contents of the bottle that were now dripping down the steps. May's accident happened in the tail end of a wail of rage, in the stamp of a booted foot on a bare hand, in the crunching and slicing of glass sinking into flesh as it was pressed down into it. May's accident wasn't an accident at all.

It was cold. Bone-crunchingly cold. Every morning when she woke May lay motionless, not wanting to stretch her legs out because that would mean them edging their way into the parts of the sheet that hadn't been warmed by her body, and that were icy damp still. Her breath frosted in the air and she began to wiggle her fingers and toes to bring them back to life, steeling herself to make the journey from bed to floor, which, when she eventually worked up the courage to make she did in a leap, hurrying to put her clothes on before her lips began to turn blue, and then to light the wood-burning stove. She loved their caravan. It was small and smelled of sawn wood and the oil that had been used to wax it. It was one of the old wooden ones – they couldn't afford a new motorised one, and Jimmy claimed not to want one anyway. 'Newfangled rubbish,' he said. 'There's nothing wrong with the old ways.'

'If there was nothing wrong with the old ways, why'd they invent something better?' her mother retorted, and May thought she had a point. The new ones were cosy and snug inside and had tables that screwed to the floor. But she did love their old wooden one, with the little cupboard set into the wall where she kept her things, and the piles of quilts and blankets that she and her brother Mattie slept on, that covered the ledge bed underneath her parents' bed at the back.

She pulled her jumper on and shoved her feet into shoes and opened the door, breathing in sharply as the cold air hit her face and burned her cheeks. The hedgerows sparkled with a thick frost that the morning sun would not thaw for hours. Cold. She hopped down the steps of the caravan. She had the milk money in her pocket, and she would be back by the time everyone else was up and wanting their tea. If she hurried she could fill the kettle and get it on as well. It was little things like that, that weren't really little things at all, that made her days go better. If her mother woke up well, she didn't go downhill till later in the day. Sometimes not at all, but those days were rare. If she woke up wrong, things often didn't pick up again all day. Those days were bad. May had learned to do what she could to avoid those days.

Her father was different. Jimmy was all right until he drank. Then everyone knew to stay out of his way. Even aged six May knew that it was not normal that she only felt close to her mother, safe with her, only when they were staying out of the way of her father.

They had been moved on from the last site. They were always being moved on, bundled off in the middle of the night, half-asleep, dimly aware of the wheels turning and voices speaking in whispers, waking up somewhere new, knowing when you woke up in the morning and the air smelled different, and the shadows made by branches that trembled outside the windows made a different shape on the floor, that you were going to step outside to a new view.

The Gribbenses' life was an unsettled one. Jimmy sharpened knives and mended pots and pans for the pubs and houses nearby, and he satisfied his urge to keep moving by taking their second smaller caravan up and down the country doing the same when he had exhausted the local work, leaving Moira and the children on the site with the handfuls of fellow travellers who had become their extended family. There was always a child or a dog for May and her older brother Mattie to play with; they were dirty and unwashed most of the time, but they didn't know any different so they didn't care, and on the bad nights when Moira and Jimmy's voices became ugly and twisted, and the caravan was filled with rage and bitterness and regret that welled up inside them and made their fists tighten and fly, there was usually a spare bed or bit of floor in a nearby van for May and Mattie to decamp to and take refuge in.

But now the Apple Field was gone, torn up in a trundle of developers' machinery and soon-to-be-buried for ever beneath a housing estate, and the families they had grown up with had scattered, and the Gribbenses had taken to the road, heading for no one knew where, and May had a bad feeling about how and where they were going to end up. There were jobs going at a building site, Jimmy had heard, but when he got there they were all taken already, by a tight-knit group of local men that he was not part of.

Everywhere Jim went looking for work he was turned away. A door shut that had been open moments before, a sign suddenly flipped over to read *All Positions Filled*, a nod that turned into a shake of the head. No one wanted them around. Jimmy Gribbens had arrived in England with nothing but hope and the energy of a young man eager to work, sure that he was going towards a better life. He had heard tales back in Cork of men making millions, normal Irishmen like him going across the water and making their fortunes, and he dreamed of success and riches like every other young man who had grown up cutting peat and patching his clothes with blanket squares. Now he realised he had been wrong. Wrong to fall for the myth that England was going to welcome him with open arms like the villagers at home would, with their familiar refrain. 'You are always welcome here,' they said, back in his home town, repeated so often it was like a song. Not in England, he wasn't. *Blacks and Irish need not apply*. They were on the outside, looking through the smeared windows at other families gathered around warm hearths. Lower than dogs.

He was an outsider here – everywhere, it seemed. No one wanted a gyppo to work for them, especially not one like Jimmy, with his rough voice and his hands that shook a little as he lit his fag, and the booze on his breath. His eyes flicked from side to side and he looked 'shifty', people said to each other in low voices. 'Can't be trusted. Quick with his temper and light-fingered to boot,' they said. May knew it was her mother who was more likely to steal than Jimmy, but she kept her mouth shut. She had long learned about keeping her trap shut. She could spot the signs early – the uneven lurch that Jimmy's legs took on when he'd been drinking, her mother's mouth set into a crooked line when she was in the dark place – and to keep quiet, in the shadows. To keep small.

She was a very lucky little girl, the doctor had said the next day, when May's mother had finally realised she would have to take her to the hospital. Her face was white with pain and she held her hand up in front of her chest like a puppy with a wounded paw, hanging limp and lifeless. The woman needed her daughter to be able to use her hands.

'I can't support a cripple, on top of everything else,' she said, glaring at May as if she had done it on purpose. May kept quiet.

She had broken three bones in her hand and had to have a

thick line of stitches that ran from her wrist up her hand and snaked around her finger, where the glass had sliced through the flesh and into the tendons. But the bones should knit together and come right in time, and with luck the tendons would not turn out to be permanently damaged. The scarring would fade, in time.

It was lucky that she was left-handed, wasn't it? So lucky.

'How did you do it again?' the doctor asked, as she finished dressing the wound and securing the splint that would protect the little girl's hand as it healed. May stared at it and knew that it would take more than a wooden cradle to protect her in the way she really needed. She looked up at the doctor, who was concentrating on tying up the final stitch, and kept her mouth shut.

'It was an accident,' Moira said, her voice unfamiliar to May – soft and gentle, full of regret and sorrow. Like a real mother. 'Gets overexcited, don't you, May?' She patted her daughter's shoulder. 'Running too fast to get to the pictures in town, tripped over and went flying, and there was a broken beer bottle in the gutter.'

The doctor tutted. 'People just don't think, do they? Still, accidents happen.' She looked up from her notes and said, almost as an afterthought, 'Pretty name, May. Reminds me of the rhyme "Here we go gathering nuts in May . . ."'

'It's just when she was born,' Moira said.

The doctor nodded. 'I see. Well, it's a fine tradition to continue, naming your children after the month of their birth. May Violet. After her eyes, I assume?'

Moira shrugged. The doctor gazed at her. The woman obviously didn't care what the child was called. Poor little thing.

'Yes, a very pretty name.'

At sixteen, May was still just over five foot, but all of a sudden she wasn't so skinny any more. She was still slim, but the curves and smooth lines of adulthood had rubbed out those of her childhood body. She looked like a woman, not a girl. She attracted lingering looks from the fishermen that she walked past every day on her way to Mrs McLeod's who just a few months ago had not noticed the child walking in front of them, and wolf whistles from the boys selling fruit in the market in the square.

The Gribbens family had settled in Belton-by-Sea, in a flat that Moira despised and that Jimmy refused to call home. 'Home is the road and always will be,' he said. Moira ignored him. She had finally got her way – a flat, a street, a life away from the road. And still, she was mired in misery.

'You need to eat more. I've no time for my girls fading away. What good are you to me then?' Mrs McLeod would call over her shoulder, her hands busy as she steamed hats on their blocks, her fingers red and rough from years of hard work. May smiled. She had been with Mrs McLeod since she was fourteen. The woman was more of a mother to her than Moira had ever been, and would often shove a sandwich at her, pushing the plate full of thick slices of bread and ham under her nose as she worked, accepting no thanks, but just gruffly muttering about the inconvenience if one of 'her girls' were to faint at their station. But, it was motivated by a genuine concern for her apprentices and workers; a world away from May's mother Moira, who only worried about her eldest child's capacity to take care of things at home and help her with the sewing Moira took in to try and make ends meet. In the years since the Gribbens family had settled in Belton-by-Sea, Moira's bitter despair at the path her life had taken had solidified into a thick lump of resentment that weighed her down and stuck in her throat. She made dresses for the well-to-do ladies in the town, and took in mending too, but it didn't bring in enough, especially not after the cash for a bottle of gin and a few pints in the pub had come out of the pot; and however much May tried to make sure the money they did have didn't all get spent on booze, there was still never enough to pay for food, and so May went without, more often than not, because Mattie was growing so fast you could almost see it, and now there was Maggie, May's little sister, to worry about as well.

It was Miss Hankins, one of the women Moira sewed for, who alerted Mrs McLeod to the skinny, dark-haired girl with violet eyes who sometimes came to fittings with her mother and who always gazed at Miss Hankins's hats with an intensity that made the woman sure she was memorising every detail of the mohair cloches and tweed Trilbies, not just idly watching as her mother worked.

'I shall go to Madame Fournier's next month,' Miss Hankins said one day, as she stood waiting while Moira pinned up her hem. 'I was thinking something in peach.'

Moira nodded, her lips tight around the pins she held between them, an unhappy display of concentration mingled with dissatisfaction.

'Right you are, Miss Hankins,' she said. 'A nice peach. Or maybe a pale pink to match?'

'Madame Fournier is ordinarily of the opinion that matching one's hat to one's suit in summer is somewhat vulgar.'

'Oh. Right you are,' Moira repeated. She didn't care what colour Miss Hankins bought her overpriced hat in, but she was one of her best clients, one of her only regulars, so she had to keep her sweet, whatever the cost.

May handed her mother the tape measure as she reached out for it, and wondered who this woman was that held such sway over the wardrobe of Miss Hankins, herself a woman of strongly held opinions.

'Madame Fournier is my milliner, May. Do you know what that word means?'

May shook her head.

'She makes my hats. You like my hats, don't you? I've seen you notice them.'

May nodded. Her mother shot her a warning glance.

'I never touched nothing I wasn't meant to,' she blurted out.

'It's all right, May. Fetch my maroon felt hat from that box and bring it to me.'

May hopped up and went to the leather hatbox that Miss Hankins was pointing to, and undid the straps. Inside was a maroon pillbox, with a stiff black veil and a patent-leather bow on the side. It was beautiful. Elegant and grown-up. She lifted it carefully out of the box and carried it over to Miss Hankins as one would a crown on a velvet cushion, her arms held out stiffly in front of her. The older woman took it in her thin hands and turned it over. Sewn inside was a silk label, with the words *Madame Fournier, Mayfair, London* embroidered on it in elaborate italics.

Miss Hankins ran her finger over the letters and gave May one of her rare smiles.

'There,' she said. 'Madame Fournier. The best milliner in the country.' Her eyes flicked down to the scar on May's hand, and as May pulled it away and slipped it into her pocket, their glances met. Miss Hankins wondered what the story was behind that. But not for long. It wasn't hard to guess what the girl's life was like. Moira was an average seamstress, but May's eyes burned with a fire that told Miss Hankins the girl would not be long for Belton-by-Sea.

She was right. May was getting out of here as soon as possible – and never coming back, not if she had anything to do with it. The thick rope of a scar on her hand which had never healed as well as the doctor said it would, because the splint hadn't been replaced and the cut had got infected and no one had taken her to another doctor, was the most visible reminder of the accidents that seemed to befall May regularly, but it was far from the only place on her body that had been burned or cut or somehow damaged by those who were meant to care for her. There was the bit of gravel in her elbow from the time she had tripped over her father's boot and gone flying. There was the corner of her mouth where she had split her lip on the edge of a doorframe. There was the thumbnail with a ridge down the middle that had been trapped in a cupboard hinge.

So Mrs McLeod and her workshop became May's refuge, after Miss Hankins took it upon herself to give the girl an opportunity, after realising that no one else was paying any attention to what happened to her. She went to see the woman who mended Madame Fournier's creations when Miss Hankins couldn't get up to London for the great woman to take care of them herself. When May was there, she felt as if she could breathe again. There was no looking over her shoulder at the sound of a door opening in case it was her father home for the night, stinking of whisky and stumbling into walls, no heart-sinking as she listened her mother's sighs and her story of woe, that she repeated to herself again and again, a miserable mantra, her voice becoming thicker and thicker with gin as the hours passed. She loved everything about her job there, from sorting the rolls of felt and keeping the floor swept, to carefully packing hats in pillows of tissue paper inside their smartly striped boxes. She wasn't afraid of hard work, as Mrs McLeod often noted approvingly, and she didn't mind being given the dirty jobs, like scrubbing out the buckets of size or cleaning the inside of the steamer.

Anything was better than home.

The only good thing about home was Maggie. May's little sister was as fair-haired as May and Mattie were dark, with their mother's pale English skin and blue eyes. But Moira's skin had lost its rosy freshness and was now greyed out, and her eyes were dull, her hair lank and lifeless. Maggie's eyes were clear and bright, and her hair fell in soft curls down her neck. It had never been cut. Like most things to do with her children, especially Maggie, Moira could never be bothered, and May was the one who ended up making the decisions about whether to cut her hair or what to dress her in, in the mornings, so she kept it long, and tied it in plaits with bows made from the tail-end of reels of ribbon that Mrs McLeod let her take from the workshop. Yes, Maggie was the one good thing about the Gribbens family, as May saw it; the one thing that was not yet spoiled by it.

Mattie was a thug already, May knew it. He was a street-fighter and a tough talker who had learned from their dad to communicate with his fists and his feet; and May was shorter than she should have been because she had never had enough to eat. The family was blighted with a canker that had warped both her and Mattie already. They were not like other children. They could both read and write, and Mrs McLeod was teaching May to get her numbers better by making May help her with the books, but their education had been patchy, and May knew that you could see simply by looking at them that they were not the sort of clean, well-cared-for children she saw on holiday with their parents, walking along the pier hand-in-hand with them, on their way to buy ice creams. Those children had no bruises between their ribs. If they had scabs on their knees it was from falling over while learning to ride a bike, their dad pushing them along and running beside them, not pushing them aside and into a table corner or doorframe; if they had shadows under their eyes, it was from staying up late reading comics under the bedclothes with a torch, not listening to their parents batter each other and hoping that they didn't turn on them.

But Maggie was unblemished. She was possibility.

May had grown up with her mother's tale of woe embedded into her consciousness.

'I was young and foolish, and I thought he loved me. He was so different to any of the other lads around our way – Irish, exotic. I thought it sounded romantic, travelling up and down the country, free as a bird. Ha! What's romance when you've got a baby hanging off your tit in a cold caravan and no money to heat it? I should have left when I had the chance, before I had you brats tying me down, while someone else might still have wanted me. But no, oh no, I stayed because I loved him. I thought he would settle. I thought the drinking would get better. Stupid cow. It never gets better, nothing ever gets better – and how can you make it better when you're working all hours just to feed your children, who're never grateful anyway . . .'

On and on it went, round and round, like a spiralling whirlpool of gin-drenched misery, dragging Moira down until she fell asleep over her sewing. Then May would get up and move the needles and scissors out of the way so her mother didn't hurt herself if she rolled over on to them. Then she would go to bed, curling up next to Maggie's warm little body, and listen to the radio, beneath the covers, the volume on low as she drifted off to sleep.

May loved to imagine the disc jockeys on their boat off the coast, not far away, but part of another world. Bobbing around, their voices soothing and magical, talking of London, and pop stars, and beauty products and clothes. Sometimes they had special guests and May would imagine the singers traipsing on to the boats in their glamorous outfits, and dream of being on the boat with them, being interviewed herself. 'So, May,' they would say, 'tell us how you became who you are today – designer of some of the most glamorous hats and outfits that the country has ever seen. Where does your inspiration come from?' And

May would flick her hair mysteriously and look at the interviewer through dark glasses and talk about the secret pain behind her genius.

'This is Radio Caroline, on one nine nine metres, your all-day music station, Britain's first commercial music station. My name's Tony Blackburn, your disc jockey for the next hour . . . a quick pause while I change the discs . . . it's blowing a gale out here this evening . . . the water's splashing up over the sides of *Radio Caroline* . . . Four kinds of Sunsilk shampoo . . . Lots of girls have dry hair – do you? You need gentle Sunsilk with Lanolin cream . . . Four kinds of Sunsilk shampoooo . . .'

One day, as she was walking home, making her journey last as long as possible, she noticed a boy noticing her – a boy whom she had not seen before. Belton-by-Sea was a small town, and she knew almost everyone there, but this boy was new. He was looking at her with interest, but without intent. His face was heavily freckled, and his hair a ruddy reddish colour, and he had a snub nose that almost made him look stuck-up, but his expression was so open and his smile so easy that there was no chance of this. He grinned at her as he noticed her noticing him noticing her, and winked. Winked! She blushed and hurried home, her cheeks hot with excited embarrassment.

The tall boy with a freckled face wasn't like the other boys she knew. None of them gave her this feeling of her mouth being full of dust and her tongue being too big for it, of a tight knot in her lower belly that trembled and flickered when their eyes met. But he did. Something about the way he moved. The way his eyes turned towards her. Something gentle, something full of innocence and hope.

That night, as the rest of the house slept, she didn't turn the radio on, as usual. She just lay there, running the wink over again and again in her imagination, the image replacing her usual fantasies of London and escape and adventure, turning it around and around in her mind like a delicious bit of toffee that she was trying to save by sucking rather than chewing. She had only seen him for a few seconds, had looked away quickly when he winked at her, and then had been too embarrassed to look back, but now she wished that she had done. He was tall, she could tell that much by the length of his legs sticking out from under the table at the café. What had he been eating? She hadn't seen. Something exotic and unusual, she would have liked to think, but that was unlikely given that egg and chips was about as unusual as the café got. His hair fell over one side of his face and he was wearing a simple shirt and trousers that were not especially fashionable, but that May could already tell, even in the brief glance that she got, were perfectly cut. May knew clothes. His teeth were extremely even and white. Very, very white. They glinted enticingly at her in the summer sun. She tingled at the memory. That wink. That cheeky, friendly wink, which spoke of a conspiracy between the two of them that, though they had never spoken, she wanted to be a part of; that told of shared adventures to come and shared secrets to be created in the space between them.

The next day he was there again, his legs stretched out in the same way as before, too long for the space under the table, too big for his body almost, and yet perfectly in proportion when he stood up, which he did as soon as he saw her. They carried him swiftly towards her, clad in light-grey trousers that were, again, perfectly cut and tailored, and which crossed the square before she had time to decide whether to slow her pace or to quicken it. It wouldn't have mattered, he would have caught up with her in a second anyway; she wasn't tall and her shoes were too small for her.

'Well, hello there,' he said, and she stopped in her tracks.

'You're American!' The words came out of her mouth more accusingly than she had intended, and he grinned.

'Guilty as charged, ma'am,' and then he held out his right hand and bobbed his head. 'Bryce Hawthorn, delighted to make your acquaintance.'

'But where are you from?' she asked. The only American accents she had heard were actors and singers on the radio, but this was different, silkier and longer; he made all of his vowels last for what felt like an age, and she thought she could listen to him talk all day.

'Goose Creek, South Carolina.'

'Oh.'

'It's in what we call the Deep South. Right next to Georgia?'

She had no idea where that was, so smiled politely and he laughed. 'Well, it's very beautiful and very warm, if that helps any.'

'Sorry. I don't know much about America. Or much about anywhere, really, 'cept here. My name is May – May Gribbens. I'm pleased to meet you.' Why did she sound so prim all of a sudden? Something about this tall, slightly stooped young man made her want to appear like a lady.

'Well, Miss May, I wonder if you might be so kind as to allow me to buy you a drink?'

May hesitated. It was nearly six, she should be getting home – Maggie would need feeding and putting to bed soon. But why should she not have some fun? It wasn't as if she ever went out with the other girls who were doing apprenticeships in the area, and who tended to hang around together: Lorrie, Peggy and Sheila. They went out dancing at the weekends, and to the music hall, walked along the seafront holding hands with boys. May was younger than most of them, and never got asked out by boys – because she was always at home minding Maggie or cooking the dinner, not hanging around by the arcades and the café, batting her eyelashes. Waste of time, boys were, she had always thought. But this boy was different. He wasn't some local lad, after a quick squeeze under the pier that he could brag about. She could tell. He was sophisticated, different – foreign. Didn't she deserve something good to happen to her?

'All right. The tea room on the other side of the square does a lovely hot chocolate.' May's sweet tooth was almost insatiable – she could never get enough sugar.

'With cream?' he asked. 'Hot chocolate has to have cream on top. It's the law.'

She smiled. 'They even put a flake in it if you pay extra,' she said.

'I think we can probably stretch to that.' And he held out his arm for her to take, and they crossed the square together.

Later, as she was walking home, May couldn't even really remember what they had talked about, or anything that he had said, she had been so transfixed just by the tones of his voice, moving up and down. She gazed at him as he was saying something about a farm and no geese in the town really and biscuits which weren't like the biscuits they had here, and architecture and how beautiful England was – and none of it really went in. She just stared at his lips and imagined the sounds coming out of them curving through the air towards her. Soothing her, swaddling her in a gentle cocoon that she wanted to remain in for ever. She had never met anyone like him before, never knew that such a person could exist, so big and yet so gentle, so polite, so worried about pleasing her. Everyone in the café had stared when they came in, little May Gribbens with the tall American boy, and she felt an emotion that she didn't recognise at first as pride. She felt proud to be with him. It wasn't something she was used to feeling. He pulled the chair out for her and waited until she had sat down and was settled until he did so himself;

he helped her on with her coat when she realised what the time was and jumped up out of her chair in a panic to leave, half an hour later than she should have been, because she was having a nicer time than she could ever remember having before in her life.

'Woah – cat on a hot tin roof! What's the hurry?' he said, when she did that. 'I'm sorry, am I boring you? I've been going on about America, I know. I just . . .'

His 'I's sounded like 'Ah's, like delicious little sighs that made her want to weep with pleasure.

'No, no, it's not that, I promise. It's lovely, I had a lovely time, I just have to go . . .'

She was out of the door and in the street, her heart racing, while he was still scrabbling in his pocket for the unfamiliar coins to leave on the saucer on the table. She had to get home. Her father was around, back from weeks on the road, and it hadn't gone well; there had already been one big fight this week, and it was past six now. He'd be heading back from the pub expecting dinner, and she didn't know if her mother would have done it and there would be hell to pay if he wasn't fed.

'I'll walk you home . . .' Bryce had caught up with her already, and was alongside her when she was halfway down the promenade.

'No!' She trotted along, her shoes pinching. Should she take them off in order to get back quicker? But she wasn't wearing stockings and the gravel would hurt her feet, so it might not be any faster. No, she would keep them on. She glanced around her. The Black Horse, the Ram, the Crown, all were up ahead, and Jimmy could be in any of them, getting ready to leave. The last thing she wanted was to bump into him with his cronies leaving the pub. Or, worse, he could be behind them, catching up with them even now, coming from the Red Lion. She glanced back over her shoulder. No one was there.

Hurry, May, hurry, hurry home.

Bryce's face had fallen at her exclamation, she saw, but he was still loping alongside her, one of his strides matching two or three of hers. May paused, despite her hurry to get home. She didn't want him to go any further. Didn't want to risk him seeing Jimmy, or worse, Moira coming to fetch Jimmy from the pub as she sometimes did. This boy had just given her the most precious gift – an afternoon of happiness where she had felt special. Like a princess, and she hadn't had to worry about looking after anyone, or anyone getting drunk and what would happen if they did. She wanted to keep the afternoon perfect, unsullied by the muck of her family. And God forbid he saw where they lived, he'd never want to speak to her again. It was obvious he was used to better.

'Please.' She stopped and moved round in front of him, blocking his way. 'You can't walk me home, you just can't.' Her voice was full of panic, but he seemed to take it for something else.

He too stopped. 'Of course. I completely understand. Have a good evening, ma'am.'

He looked terribly disappointed, but didn't take another step. He was far too much of a gentleman to push it. Oh, the way he spoke. Those little sighing 'Ah's again, and he had called her 'ma'am'. Ma'am! Like the Queen of England. That nearly weakened her resolve, and made her let him walk her a little further down the promenade to stretch out the time. Nearly.

But not quite, because then, in the distance, behind Bryce, she saw the familiar figure of her father, head angled towards the ground, thank God, his walk an uneven stumble, and she yelped. And then quickly, before she lost her nerve, she stood on tiptoe, gave him a quick kiss, and then took off running in the direction of home, her lips burning with the memory of his slightly stubbly cheek all the way.

Bryce watched her take off, her slim calves kicking up behind her and her worn cotton coat gathered around her shoulders and flying out behind her, and had to stop himself from running after her and picking her up like a doll and kissing her, as she had just kissed him, but for longer, on the lips, holding her tight.

Instead, he turned and looked round to try and see what had sent her racing off.

The man walking towards him was swarthy, not tall but broad-shouldered, and his face was lined in the way that came not through age but through the sun, deep lines tracing across smooth skin. His black hair stuck up in a messy quiff and spread down his face into thick sideburns. He wore an open-necked shirt and dark trousers, and Bryce could tell two things about him straight away. Firstly, that he must surely be related to May, and secondly, that he was a man who would shout with his fists rather than his mouth. The idea that this man, who must be her father, might be someone May was scared of, made Bryce's own fists clench in his linen pockets.

Bryce may have had the manners of a prince, but he was no soft Southerner. He was a farmer's son. Wealthy his family might be, but pansies they were not, and Bryce had grown up with animals, farm labourers, and four older brothers, and had had to wrestle all three at times. It was one of the reasons he had been keen to leave – the casual everyday violence of life on the farm, the way you were so close to life and death. It unsettled Bryce, was too bloody and gutsy for him.

The man was getting closer, his eyes still cast towards the ground, his progress weaving. Bryce looked back over his shoulder to see where May had got to. Not far enough to be sure of safety – the promenade was long and wide and open, and nearly empty at this time of night. If the man looked up and managed to focus, he would surely see his daughter running, stopping every so often to hop, her shoes obviously pinching her feet. The sight of her hopping tugged at Bryce's heart, and he decided.

Turning back, he put his head down and walked quickly towards the man, hands tucked into his pockets, his body a solid barrel. In just half a dozen steps he had met him, head on, in a collision that sent the shorter man tumbling towards the ground. A noise emerged from him like a lamb being wrenched from its mother, and Bryce almost turned and ran himself, but he didn't. The image of May's legs kicking up behind her and the memory of her lips on his cheek held him firm.

'Whatthafuck . . .' The man shook his head, confused.

'I'm sorry. I didn't see you,' Bryce said, trying his best to disguise his thick Southern accent by mimicking the Dorset lilt that he had been surrounded by since he came to town. He was recognisable enough as it was; he hoped that if he didn't sound too foreign the man would forget him more easily. Because he intended to meet May's father again, under more amenable circumstances, and before too long. He was standing now, pushing himself up on his fingers. Jimmy Gribbens looked up at him, his eyes dark pools of tar.

'You takin' the fuckin' piss?'

Bryce shook his head. 'What? No, I'm not taking— Sorry, I just wasn't looking where I was—'

He was cut off by the thick thud of an uppercut to his jaw, and then a swift punch in the guts. He doubled over, winded.

'Ugh.'

'Yer mocking a man with an Irish accent? What, an honest workin' man isn't to be respected no more, just mocked by some Yankee?'

Oh. His plan hadn't worked then. That part of it, at least. But it didn't matter. From where he lay on the ground, he saw no slim unstockinged calves flicking up, just the dirty frayed hems of Jimmy's trousers as he shuffled down the promenade. May had got away. He had thrown his body in front of danger for her like an old-fashioned suitor laying his cloak over a puddle, and won. And maybe tomorrow he would win the girl.

The next day, she didn't appear in the square. He waited, drawing and doodling all afternoon, but by seven she hadn't appeared and he went back to his boarding house. The day after that he returned to his usual place, and that morning he did see her, scurrying across the square on her way to work, the collar of her coat turned up, a scarf round her neck. It was blustery and the wind was cool, but not cool enough for what she was wearing. Bryce waited until she had reached the far side of the square, passing the cries of, 'Apples, Lady May, lovely apples this mornin'?' and 'Come and see me later, my sweetheart, I'll give you a good price on crabs,' and then hurried up to her.

'May,' he said, and touched her hand, but she ignored him and carried on, walking down an alleyway that led off the square. 'May!'

She spun around and hissed at him, 'You can't talk to me. Don't talk to me!'

'I just wanted to see if you were all right after . . .'

He trailed off. She had tugged at her scarf so it came loose and showed a dark bruise stretching the length of her jaw, the skin swollen and purple under the skin.

'Oh, my.'

'Yes, oh my. What did you think you were doing, starting a fight with my dad? And why? And you didn't come out of it well, either, did you?' She glared at his chin, bruised in almost a mirror image of hers, but less vivid. Jimmy Gribbens obviously had a practised and familiar swing.

'I was just trying to make sure that he didn't see you.'

She gazed at him. Oh, that voice. 'Make sure that he what?'

He shrugged, in a motion that made him look about ten years old. He might as well have been scuffing his plimsoles on the ground in front of his mother for all the bravado he showed now.

'You were worried about getting home. I figured . . . I figured I'd buy you some time. It was stupid.'

She shook her head and her face softened. 'No. No, it wasn't stupid, it was sweet. Well, maybe starting a fight with him was a bit stupid.'

He nodded. 'Yip. That part was kinda stupid.'

'Look, I have to get to work. But . . .'

Bryce looked down at her, his eyes full of hope. Oh, he was like Maggie, trusting, desperate for her to say yes – yes to what? What did he want from her? She wasn't sure, but nor was she sure that it mattered any more. Her heart was leaping, and she knew that whatever it was he wanted from her, she would give, because of the way he looked at her, and the way he had touched her hand with his. It had been so gentle, as though she might shatter if he wasn't careful, that had melted her heart.

'I have to make up my work from yesterday. I can't lose my place with Mrs McLeod. It's the only . . . And . . .' Her eyes darted down the street, like a trapped bird.

'Go. Go to work,' he said. 'I understand,' even though he didn't, not really. He just knew he wanted to stop her looking so afraid, would do anything to make her feel better. 'I'll meet you tomorrow, it's Saturday. You can get away?'

She nodded quickly. 'He's gone again now, won't be back for a while. Time for this to fade before next time,' she said, pointing at her bruise and smiling wryly. Bryce's own heart went brittle and cracked at the thought of this girl's life being punctuated by beatings from her father, the man in her life who should protect her, not harm her. Well, Bryce would just have to protect her his own self.

'Meet me by the Crazy Golf hut at five,' she said. His face was blank, but he nodded eagerly, and she smiled and touched his hand. 'Next to the pier!'

And then she was gone, her collar back up and skitting down the alley and into a door in the wall. Bryce stood for a minute, smiling. He had gotten himself a date! A second date, even, with the prettiest girl he had ever seen. His face throbbed, and he touched it. He didn't care. It reminded him of her, not that he needed reminding. It also marked her upon him, not that she could be any more imprinted on to his skin than she already was, just by the touch she had given him before she left. He curled his hand up and shoved it into his pocket, as if by doing so he could carry her touch with him. Then he wandered dreamily down to the door that she had entered. A dark-green wooden stable door, both halves shut. *McLeod's Millinery* was stencilled on it in fading white paint. *Workshop only, all enquiries to Horsely Street.*

As he stood there, the top half flew open and would have hit him in the face, right on the spot where he was bruised from his altercation with Jimmy, if he had not leaped back with the quick reflexes of one used to being around skittish stallions. In front of him was a woman who was almost as wide as the door she stood in, her hair covered with a red and white kerchief and her face almost the same colour.

'I can tell what you're doing, you know,' she berated him, 'and I'll be having none of it, do you hear me?'

Bryce pressed himself back against the far wall and looked from side to side. Was she talking to him?

'Yes, I'm talking to you,' she continued. 'Mooning around my girls – I know your game. Well, shoo, go on, be off with you! Tomorrow's Saturday and you young things can do as you fancy, and none of my business, but until then, you keep your hands and eyes to yourself.'

Bryce gulped, and nodded. 'Yes, ma'am.' Behind the woman's immensely wide hips, he could just see May's big eyes, smiling for once, her hands shooing him away, and a gaggle of other girls all giggling. The woman turned to them. 'And you lot can skedaddle, an' all! What do I pay you for – not to stand around gawking while I get rid of your fancy men, that's for sure and no mistake.'

However, her Scottish accent, which was almost as broad as her girth, had softened in the face of Bryce's terrified expression and polite response, and before she closed the stable door again, she winked at him. 'Now, get on with you,' she admonished again. He smiled and bowed, doffing an imaginary cap with a flourish.

'I take your leave. Good day, Missus McLeod, and I trust it is a pleasant one for you,' he said in his broadest Southern accent, and then he turned and walked down the alley towards the seafront, Mrs McLeod's, 'Well, I've never seen the like of it – bowing, indeed, I ask you!' carrying down the street behind him, and images of May carrying him forward on a cloud of what he thought just might be love.

Two days and two dates later, and he knew it for sure. It was love, it was love, it was love. This was what he had been waiting for, for all of his twenty-two years. Because Bryce was a true romantic. He had grown up with parents who held hands over the breakfast table and who even after thirty-five years together and five children still wrote each other love letters. His mother kept them in shoe boxes beneath her side of the iron bed they shared, tied up in little packets of ten with string (she may have been a Southern woman and a romantic like Bryce, but she was also a farmer's wife, and deeply practical, and there was no way she was wasting her best ribbon on old love letters that were kept under her bed). So Bryce had always believed that one day he would find the girl with whom he would spend the rest of his life, the one for him. Someone he could build a family with, someone to come home to, someone to whom he could say 'Team Hawthorn!' and touch knuckles like his older brothers used to on the football pitch, but instead of it being a precursor to knocking the wind out of someone's sails in a tackle it would be the precursor to a tender kiss. Ah, he was soppy, he knew it, but he also knew there was a strength in allowing yourself to be gentle, a special form of power in restraint. Bryce had never pushed himself forward (apart from at mealtimes, when if you didn't you missed out, and Bryce loved his food more than almost anything), but had ambled along, quietly getting things done and waiting for his girl to show up.

And now he was sure she had done just that – in this funny little town by the sea in England, of all places. He had not expected that, when he arrived here at the beginning of the summer. His plan had been to spend his vacation from the Royal College of Art here, drawing and reading and walking along the cliffs. Because though he loved the buildings in London, and spent hours walking around looking steadfastly up so he did not miss anything, frequently walking into passers-by and lamp-posts and dogs as he did so, he did not like London as a city. It was too big, too noisy, too full of people and smog and smoke and horns. From the day he had arrived the previous September he had been dreaming of the countryside, had taken day trips out to Surrey and Kent at weekends when he could, but his time was so full of work and study that it was only a few snatched hours here and there, and he longed for fresh air and clear skies. So he had waited until the summer holidays came around and then booked a room in a boarding house in a town that looked about the right size to give him the fix of small-town country life he was craving, and packed his suitcase and his sketchbooks and got on the train.

When he had arrived he had spent an hour just breathing in the sea air. It smelled indefinably different from the sea air at the beach house where the Hawthorns spent August to get away from the oppressive heat inland, but it was still the ocean and it connected him to home, and for the first time since he had arrived, Bryce realised just how deeply he missed that home. But the small town was good for him; it let him recharge and take stock of all that he had seen since he arrived. He spent hours filling his sketchbooks with pencil drawings of the limestone buildings and coastline, of the fishermen going out to sea and returning with their nets full, of the pier and the promenade. Whereas in London his work was led by his tutors, who pushed him to draw clean straight lines and solid angles, here he was free to follow where his pencil and his fancy took him, and he let his imagination loop the loop on to the page.

Bryce had always assumed he would marry an American girl. A Southern girl from a local family probably, one who would be happy to live in the city, since despite his love of the countryside, Bryce had no desire to live on a farm or plantation for the rest of his life; he was interested in buildings and buildings were in cities, but spend plenty of time in the country. One who could bake a perfect peach cobbler and hold her own in the bustle of his family; a girl who went to church on Sundays, and who smelled of cornflowers. But apart from an abortive romance with a girl called Alice, whom he had attempted to court in his teens and who had chosen his older brother, with whom she now had three children, Bryce hadn't come across anyone there who might fit the bill. And now he had met May, who didn't fit the bill in any of those ways. She had a strange accent and a terrifying father, she was, he was almost certain, much too young for him, she clearly had a quick temper and she was an apprentice milliner with rough red skin on her hands. She smelled of glue and damp wool, and he doubted she had ever heard of a peach cobbler or even grits. And yet somehow this girl with wild hair and a flash in her eyes fit the bill in his heart absolutely.

They met at the hut by the Crazy Golf course. He was pretty much always there half an hour before they had agreed to meet, part sheepish at his keenness, part uncaring but just desperate to see her. The man who ran the course looked at him suspiciously as he sat on the bench, waiting, so he walked up and down in front of the course, his hands behind his back, conscious of the lump that the gift he had bought her was making in his jacket pocket. He didn't care what people thought. He just wanted to make sure he was there when she arrived, so that she would know he was waiting for her. He wanted her always to know he was here for her. That day, when she did arrive, she was out of breath and pink-cheeked and he stood to greet her with what he knew had to be a stupid grin.

'Come on,' she said, and took his hand. He allowed her to pull him along the beach, the salty wind beating his face, and felt pure happiness.

Inside the beach hut it was cool and slightly damp, and the wooden floor creaked ominously as they entered, but it was covered with blankets and there was a little wooden table in the corner that held an old biscuit tin and a lantern with a stub of candle inside. May lit it and then closed the door behind them.

'I never knew these huts were here,' Bryce said.

'They're tucked out of sight – it's why no one came and used them. The family who own the big house in Belton built them in the twenties, some landowner's idea of a great plan. Didn't think about the fact that people wanted to be near the shops and the prom, not tucked away behind a big cliff. And it's the cold side of the sea, so no good for swimming.'

'The cold side? Is there a warm side?'

'Ha ha. There is – well, a warm side for England – but this isn't it. Anyhow, that's why I like it. No one comes here apart from me, and sometimes the odd camper. But they're usually scared off by the black wolf.'

'The black wolf?'

May smiled. 'Don't tell me you've been here for – how long?'

'Six weeks and three days.'

'Six weeks and the all-important three days, and you haven't heard of the black wolf. Have you actually been into any of the pubs?'

'Twice. I don't really drink much.'

May cocked her head slightly. Another point in his favour. She filed it away.

'Ah, the black wolf. Want to hear about it?' He nodded. 'Sure it won't give you nightmares?'

He poked her knee. 'Hey! Nothing gives me nightmares.'

She shrugged. 'Don't say I didn't warn you, then.' She huddled down into the pile of blankets and drew her cardigan closer around her shoulders.

Bryce listened as she told him the local legend of the black wolf, drawing all the drama out of it that she could, as if she were telling it to a child around a campfire. Her face was animated, her expressions exaggerated. He didn't really pay attention to the story – it was some old tale about a wolf that had been killed by a local farmer, and whose malevolent spirit was said to stalk the cliffs, carrying off children and animals. He just gazed at her face, watching her come alive before his eyes. She was a different person here, away from the streets where she had been panicking about being spotted; she was relaxed and free and sparkling with energy.

'So?' She was staring at him, clearly waiting for an answer to something. 'Do you want to see where it's meant to appear? The black wolf?'

He watched her eyes, flicking between his, waiting for an answer. And then he leaned forward and kissed her. The kiss came out of nowhere and she jerked in surprise – and Bryce went bright red and leaped back.

'I'm sorry!' He was sitting back on his knees looking shocked. She couldn't help but giggle.

'Why are you sorry?'

'I shouldn't have done that. It was ungentlemanly.'

'Oh, Bryce. What do you think – that it's the first time I've been kissed? You just took me by surprise, that's all.' She scooted over towards him, and lifted her face to his. 'Now, I'm ready. Try again.'

He swallowed, and paused; he appeared to be steeling himself.

'Well, if you don't *want* to . . .'

'I just don't want to get it wrong.'

'Oh, for goodness' sake.' She leaned forward and, kneeling in front of him, kissed him. His eyes were still open when she started, but after a second he closed them and pulled her down on to his lap with one of his long arms.

It *was* the first time that May had been kissed, and from the way the whole thing had come about, and then from the way their teeth bumped together and they had to awkwardly rearrange their noses, she could tell that Bryce was not much more experienced than her. He was fumbling and awkward, she could feel his hands hovering over her body by their heat – first her waist, then her shoulders, then her chest – but he seemed unable to put them down anywhere, as if he was scared to touch her. She broke off the kiss, and looked into his eyes.

'Violet,' he said softly.

'What?' She tilted her head to one side.

'Violet eyes.' Bryce stroked the skin of her cheekbone. 'They're near the first thing I noticed about you. I saw you, walking all hurried, and I thought, There's a girl who's going places. And then you looked up and I saw your violet eyes and thought it was Elizabeth Taylor come to Belton-by-Sea.'

'Don't be daft.'

'As I live and breathe.'

May blushed. 'It's my middle name. Violet. I always liked it more than May.' May was the name her parents called her when they were shouting for booze or their dinner. May was pain and keeping your shoulders down and your head low in the hope that no one would notice you. May was the girl who never had money to go to the cinema, who had never been allowed to buy sweets or a comic with the other children, who had shoes that were too small and a skirt that had been patched so many times it was hard to tell what colour it had been to start with. Violet – Violet could be someone else. The girl on the radio, the girl in the magazine wearing a jaunty scarf and carrying a smart shiny handbag, the girl who had friends and a boy to hold her hand when she walked down the street. May only realised that she was crying when Bryce wiped away a tear.

'I like Violet better too. I think you're a Violet. I believe that you are Violet.' She bit her lip. He kissed it again, tenderly. Her hands found his and she held on to them.

'What about you? Have you got a middle name?'

'Cavalley,' Bryce said.

'What?' May roared with laughter, throwing her head back. 'That's not a name! That's – well, it's a surname.'

Bryce grinned. 'It is so a name. It's a family name. A name passed down for generations, a name given to all the Hawthorn boys. An honourable, venerable name, I'll have you know, Miss Violet.'

'Oh, really?'

'Yes, really. And when we're married and have scores of children, they'll all be given it as well.'

May hooted. 'Cheeky.' But her heart thumped with the thrill of it. 'All right then, Cavalley. Close your eyes,' she said.

He did as he was told and then waited, his eyes shut, his full lips trembling slightly. She pulled her V-necked jumper up over her head and then quickly unbuttoned her blouse. It was now or never. Her hands were shaking. Nice girls didn't do things like this. But for the first time in her life, she felt safe, as though she were with someone who would look after her whatever happened, and she just wanted to be close to him, wanted his arms around her as she leaned into his chest and inhaled the musky scent there. And so she took off her blouse, and then waited.

'Open your eyes,' she said, and he did as he was told, his pupils widening when he saw her kneeling topless in front of him, her breasts level with his face.

'Oh,' he said.

Suddenly she felt shy and exposed, and reached for her blouse again to cover herself with. He didn't want her, after all, of course he didn't – why would he? He took her hand to stop her, and kissed her fingers.

Bryce's shyness seemed to have fallen away, along with May's blouse. He lifted her up, those big hands scooping her bottom neatly on to his lap, and then he pulled her down towards him so she had to part her legs and hook them around him. He then took a handful of her hair and twisted it around his fingers, pulling it gently so that her head tipped back and her neck was exposed, and he was faced with an expanse of olive skin from her waist up to her jaw. She shivered.

'Are you cold?' he asked. She nodded. He placed his lips on her skin, transferring their heat to her, moving quickly over her body, then he lifted her again and laid her down on the blanket, took his shirt and trousers off and lay down on top of her.

'Skin to skin,' he whispered. 'Best way of keeping warm.'

He kissed her, his long body covering her from head to toe. She shifted underneath him slightly and he pressed back against her.

'I read that somewhere as well,' she said. 'But there's a problem.'

'Oh?'

He was working her skirt up, his fingers pushing it up around her waist. May wasn't sure whether the feeling in her stomach was nerves or excitement. She wanted to do it with this boy, she was sure of it. But what if she did it wrong? What if she disappointed him, or he laughed at her? But then she brushed against the bulge between his legs, and he groaned, and pulled her tight to him, nuzzling at her neck, and she realised that there was no right and wrong, there was just the two of them, their bodies and the space between them that grew smaller with each touch, each stroke. His hands went behind her and tugged at her skirt, and she reached around and undid the clip, and then shy, reticent Bryce had disappeared entirely as he pulled her skirt off and almost before it was off he was working himself between her legs, his hips heavy on hers and his breath hot against her face.

'Have you got a . . .'

'I don't have anything.' They both spoke at once, and he continued, 'I didn't think we would . . .'

'It's my first time,' she said, suddenly embarrassed. 'You can't . . .'

But then he moved up so that their hips were level and eased himself inside her, and it hurt less than she had thought it would, and Bryce was gentle and strong all at once, and as he moved inside her she began to cry. 'I'm sorry, am I hurting you?' he asked. She put a finger on his lips and smiled.

'I'm fine, don't worry,' she whispered, and he nodded and kept moving – he couldn't stop now. 'You're not hurting me.

You're making the hurt go away. I'm happy,' she said. 'Bryce Cavalley Hawthorn, I do believe you've made me happy.' And he smiled down at her with his big, kind brown eyes, and she felt safe and warm and she wasn't cold any more, and didn't think she ever would be again, as long as she stayed right here in his arms.

May found out that she was pregnant on the day England won the World Cup. She was just sixteen. She walked slowly through the streets of Belton towards Dr Loughlin's house. It was 9.30 and the town was full of people going about their usual Saturday-morning errands, baskets of shopping over their arms or on the front of their bicycles, dogs being walked, children being chivvied along and told not to dawdle. Normal lives going to and fro, and May walked among them knowing that her life was going to change for ever – had already changed for ever. She didn't need the doctor to confirm that she was pregnant, but she knew that she should be seen and examined, or whatever it was that they would do, exactly.

A baby. May had worked out that, if she was right and she had fallen pregnant that first time with Bryce, in the beach hut, she would be getting on for three months by now. There had only been a few occasions, so not many to choose from, and she had missed two periods, so it hadn't taken her that long to realise what was going on. But it hadn't been just that. She hadn't felt right for weeks. She had noticed that she felt tired, more tired than she had ever felt in her life. She had to drag herself out of bed in the morning and found her eyes drooping halfway through the day at work. And she was hungry. She found herself sneaking morsels from Maggie's plate as she sat next to her in the evening, shovelling food into her chuntering mouth, something she would never have done just a few weeks ago. She normally ended up giving Maggie some of her share so the little girl never went to bed hungry. And then her waist began to feel just an inch or so thicker, a tiny bit puffy, like it did before her period came – but it didn't go away, and her period didn't come. And then she knew for sure.

As she walked she remembered what she had read in the book that she had peeked into in the library. Ten weeks', she thought she was, and that meant that the foetus was probably just over an inch long, or the size of a small strawberry. What would it look like, she wondered, this little nugget of life inside her? Would it have her violet eyes, or Bryce's brown ones? Her nearly black curls or his reddish-coloured hair, her olive skin or his freckles? The child wouldn't be fair, she could be pretty sure of that. But then, how could she really know? Bryce's parents might look completely different from him, and she knew the grandparents played a part in how their grandchildren looked.

The grandparents. The thought made her shiver. What would her parents say? She could predict her father's reaction easily enough. He would call her a hussy, a whore. She expected him to throw her out. Her mother . . . May wasn't sure what Moira would say or do. It wouldn't be supportive or sympathetic, she knew that much. But May realised now that she hardly really knew her mother at all. What was going on behind those grey eyes? She had no real idea. One thing was certain though. Jimmy and Moira were hardly cut out for the role of loving grannie and grandpa, cooing over a newborn in a Moses basket, were they? They hadn't exactly taken to the role of parents brilliantly, so she had no illusions about the care and concern that they were likely to extend to the next generation.

And what about the other set of grandparents? What would they say when Bryce told them that he had got a girl into trouble – an English girl, no less? She had no idea. The thought that she didn't even know what his parents looked like made her suddenly feel ashamed. What sort of a girl had a baby with a boy whose family she hadn't even met, and whom she was not likely to meet before the baby was born? A hussy, a whore, that's what sort. More to the point, how would she tell Bryce? He was back in London, studying, working hard, writing her long love letters at night. She kept them in an old cigarette tin under her bed. That would have to be how she gave him the news that would change his life for ever – a letter. She didn't know what words she would use. But somehow, in her heart, she knew he would be glad.

But despite all the questions in May's mind, all the unknowns and what-ifs and what-will-bes and what-will-Bryce-says, there was one thing that she was absolutely sure of, and that was that she was going to have a baby, and she was going to keep it. There would be no backstreet abortion carried out by a dirty-fingered gypsy woman with a tin kettle of hot water and a coat-hanger, no hot baths and half-pints of gin to try and bring on miscarriage, no giving it away to a nice couple who couldn't have a baby. This was their baby, something precious and special that they had created between them, that had come into being out of nothing other than their love, and she was going to take care of it, come what may.

And because of that, because of how much she loved Bryce and their baby already, even though she had only known him for a few weeks and the baby wasn't even a baby yet, not really, she knew that now more than ever, for the sake of the small strawberry-sized baby she was carrying, whatever else happened, she had to get away.

'It's not the way we do things. Family should stay with family. Bastard or not, I don't want a grandchild of mine being shipped off to strangers.'

At the word 'bastard', May curled her arm protectively around her stomach.

'Not the way who do things? We're not travellers any more, Jimmy.'

'You don't stop being who you are just because you stay in one place for a few years, you stupid bitch. May was born on the road, she's a traveller in her soul, just like I am and just like you are, wherever you were born – and you know it.'

Silence.

Then: 'We turned our back on that life when we settled.'

'I've never settled.'

'And don't I know it.'

'I never promised to change.'

'But it changed them, it changed us all. They're not your kind any more.'

'They'll always be my kind. It's in our blood.'

Moira's sigh carried through the closed door, almost loud enough to rattle the windowpanes in their frames.

'She's good, Jimmy. A real talent. Missus McLeod says so. She's the one who can keep us afloat – I can't do it for ever. We need her here with us, not off having babies. Or here, with another mouth to feed, when the boy disappears back to his own. They won't stand for it, they won't like it. What, the ladies'll keep her around with a bastard? Ha. What then? You're going to support us all with scrap? Mattie will feed us with thieving, with selling stolen stockings?'

'Don't rile me! Don't.'

Jimmy made a strange noise, a cross between a grunt and a yell, and her mother cried out, and May buried her head under the pillow and held on to the scrap of hope that came with the words, 'She's good. A real talent. Missus McLeod says so.'

'We'll send her away to have it. She can stay here till she starts to show, and then she can go away to have the baby. It'll only be a few weeks, and they'll take care of everything.'

'Who's going to pay for it?'

Moira tutted. 'I'll find the money somehow. *We'll* find it. It'll be less dear than having a baby to support.'

Jimmy grunted. 'All right. All right.'

May lay awake and shivered. They wanted to send her to one of the homes for wayward women, for girls who had 'got into trouble'. She had heard tales about those places. Girls went there when the bulge under their coats could no longer be passed off as puppy fat, or concealed with a thick jumper, and they came back, six weeks or so later, pale-faced, thin, weepy. Some of them weren't allowed to see their babies before they were taken away, she had heard; they were just pulled from them and given to women who couldn't have children, newborn and squalling, and the girls lying bleeding and unable to do anything. The thought made tears spring to her eyes. She touched her stomach. 'I will not let them take you away,' she said. 'I will not let them. Because you're mine. *You are mine*.' And even she was surprised by the ferocity of her feelings.

She left the next night. She lay, waiting, until her parents had gone quiet. Then she waited for another hour. It was four in the morning by the time she crept out of the door – the witching hour, she always thought of it, far more than midnight. The hour that felt like the back of a cave where nothing echoed. She knew she didn't have much time, and she knew she mustn't dawdle, or she'd lose her nerve. May Violet Gribbens, or Lady Violet, as Bryce called her, was tough and she was determined to protect the child she was carrying, but she was still only sixteen, and she was scared.

Before she left, she put her head round the door of the cupboard where Maggie slept and listened for a second; her breaths were even and deep. May closed her eyes. Could she leave this little girl, so innocent, so helpless, to the childhood she had had? May leaned down and tucked the sheets around her chin. Maggie stirred.

'Bye bye, sweetie,' May whispered. 'I love you.' She kissed her forehead. And, before she straightened up, she took off the little crucifix that she wore around her neck, and put it around Maggie's. She would need it more than her, now. And then, she slipped silently out into the night, to find Bryce, and her future.

Chapter Three

Violet sat at the big table outside the villa, letting the sun warm her skin. It had been two days since the party. Two days spent with doctors, with her family, telling them all what she had been putting off for months. She was exhausted. She could hear Patrick directing the loading of their luggage into the cars that would go to the airport ahead of them. Back to London, to the house she loved and the business that she missed. London, where she had built her life for over forty years, in the city that had protected her and absorbed her as if she was its own child. She had never felt lost there, not in the dead of night in a Soho backstreet, nor when wandering aimlessly around a market in the East End looking for bits and bobs for inspiration. She didn't need a map to tell her she was home.

'Be careful with my lady's boxes, there. That's fragile, make sure it goes on top.'

Violet smiled. She loved listening to Patrick. Had never thought she would choose to listen to the smoke-edged brogue of an Irish accent again. But his was different from her father's. Very different.

Violet had not thought about her father for a long time. He and Moira, Mattie and Maggie, they had all remained bundled up in a corner of her brain, like an old trunk pushed to the back of the attic. But now – now the trunk was open, and memories were spilling out. Seeing Mattie's face again had been like looking into a strange mirror. She had seen parts of herself reflected in it, parts that she had tried so hard, for so long, to deny. The doctor said that was what had brought on the collapse. It wasn't really anything to do with her illness, except that her body was weakened by it, hence 'more susceptible to physical manifestations of emotional trauma', he had said. Violet had raised an eyebrow and stopped herself from saying that she felt as though her whole body was a physical manifestation of emotional trauma.

She was waking up in the night, at strange times and for no reason, overwhelmed by a single fragment of memory – of standing by the sea in Belton, stealing a moment to herself as she walked to Mrs McLeod's, or of lying next to Maggie in her narrow little bed and singing her to sleep, as she had done later, with her own children, the same old crooning songs that she had picked up from camps the family had stayed in. Of Bryce, his funny, stretched-out voice, holding her in his long, freckled arms and telling her of all the wonders they would see together. Drawing with his stubby pencil the bones of a building that she dreamed would one day be hers. Drawing her dreams. And the memories were so vivid, so acute. It was as though suppressing them for so many years had made them all the more potent. She would suddenly be overcome by them – the sound of the sea breaking against the pebbled beach as she walked past it, cool salt air on her face. The sensation of Maggie's skin next to hers, soft and powdery and damp. The smell of Bryce's Camp Coffee and bacon frying on a Sunday as she lay in bed with Flip on her stomach, still all drowsy and in a half-sleep. And the memories would bring tears to her eyes.

She did not want to remember. But the memories did not listen to what she wanted, and did not stop coming even now – until, blessedly, she was interrupted by Boodle, wanting to talk to her about her son before the rest of the children came down. Violet was grateful for the distraction.

'I'm worried about Mungo,' Boodle said, sitting next to Violet at the table on the terrace. She had packed Willy and the girls off on a boat trip around the island.

'He seems like a normal teenage boy to me,' Violet commented. 'I've lived with a few of them. They're all silent or grunting, it's quite normal.' She sipped her drink. Boodle looked out at the sea. Despite her worries, she felt herself relaxing.

'It's more than that. Oh, he's not into, you know, drugs or anything,' she said quickly, in case Violet thought badly of him. 'And he never gets into fights. It's just . . .' She paused.

'Go on.'

'It's a little . . . delicate.'

'Boodle. You should know me better than to think of me as shockable, after all these years, surely?'

She was right. Boodle carried on. 'He won't listen to Willy at all. Doesn't respect him. He thinks of him as – well, as lesser, I think.'

'Lesser than what? Or whom?' But Violet already knew what the answer would be.

'Than Flip. But Flip will hardly ever see him. I'm worried that Mungo's going to end up with no one he can really talk to. No father, I mean. He's got me, of course, but I'm his mother, and it's a father he needs.'

Violet nodded. 'Flip's never really made enough time for him, has he?'

Boodle shook her head. 'No. I know why – I know he didn't find it easy. I couldn't understand it back then, but now I do. But . . .'

'But Mungo is his son, and he needs him, however painful Flip finds it.'

'Yes.'

Violet thought for a long moment. 'Do you blame him, Boodle?' she asked. 'Do you really blame Flip for finding his relationship with Mungo difficult?'

Now it was Boodle's turn to remain quiet.

'Sins of the fathers, that's what they say, isn't it?' Violet went on. 'But what about the sins of the mothers?'

Boodle looked back at her, and blushed. Violet was right. Boodle could not claim to have played no part in the story that she and Mungo both now found themselves in.

Caroline Calthorpe, who had not been called Caroline by anyone other than an irate teacher since she was three years old and became Boodle for reasons that no one seemed able to remember now, gazed at the set of pale-blue boxes that contained her wedding stationery. Caroline and Philip. Who were those people? Mrs Philip Cavalley. Boodle Cavalley. She couldn't quite imagine it – she'd been practising her new signature since Flip proposed, and it still didn't look right. Half of her friends didn't even know that her real name was Caroline, so entrenched was her nickname. Her own father had once, when booking the family's flights to France for his brother's wedding, booked her ticket in the name of Boodle, meaning that her ticket didn't match her passport; she hadn't been allowed on the flight and had had to follow everyone on the next day, once it had all been sorted out.

Boodle and Flip had been together for just six months, after meeting at the Fire Ball, which took place in the Hippodrome in Leicester Square. Flip was older than most other men there, and by far the best-looking, Boodle and Sarah-Louise had decided right at the beginning of the evening. Boodle hadn't been able to believe it when he had asked her to dance, and shortly afterwards, manoeuvred her into a dark corner and groped her thigh through the thick fabric of her ball gown with its black velvet bodice with a sweetheart neckline and raspberry taffeta skirt. Boodle hated the dress. It was too long and she was wearing flat shoes – black-patent ballet pumps, which made her calves look thick. Thicker. She had wanted a strapless dress with a short puffball skirt, like Sarah-Louise's, but her mother had put her flat foot down. 'What on earth would your father say if I bought you a dress which exposed your chest to half of London?' So Boodle's dress had sensible elbow-length sleeves, which made her sweat.

She had finally persuaded her mother to let her have her hair permed, but the process had simply made it a bit frizzy, rather than giving her the mass of tumbling pre-Raphaelite ringlets that she had envisaged. Ringlets didn't seem to have arrived at 'Curl Up and Dye' in Oxted yet. So, Boodle's mousey frizz had been backcombed at the front and pinned into a quiff, and pulled back into a French plait fastened at the end with a black velvet scrunchie. Boodle had just turned eighteen, and this was the first ball she had been allowed to go to – and even then, only after a protracted vetting process involving long and torturous phone calls to Sarah-Louise's parents, the parents of other acquaintances of Boodle's who were attending and, most humiliatingly, the organisers of the ball who were clearly somewhat baffled as to why the mother of a legal adult was quizzing them about their plans to ensure that teenage drunkenness did not rage out of control.

The Hippodrome was bigger than she had realised and inside it was noisier and more crowded than she had hoped it would be. When she arrived, alone, because Sarah-Louise had to be there early as one of the ticket committee, she had stood outside and had a sudden moment of panic when she almost turned tail and fled after the disappearing red lights of her father's Volvo. Hordes of teenagers were cramming themselves into the doors of the Hippodrome, tickets in sweaty palms, a mass of spotty necks in their fathers' dinner jackets and tartan taffeta and black velvet headbands. 'Fiona – Fiona! Over here!' 'I've got a bottle of Mirage, it's all I could find. Katie's bringing some Bailey's, as long as her dad doesn't find out.'

Boodle waited in line, getting pushed to the back of the queue by the scrum again and again, until eventually she spotted Sarah-Louise inside the doors and managed to attract her attention by jumping up and down and waving her arms. Sarah-Louise looked embarrassed, but came out and rescued her, dragging her through the crowd by the arm.

Sarah-Louise pulled a silver hip-flask out of her handbag and gave it to Boodle. 'Here. Have some of that, and then let's go and dance.'

Inside, the music was even louder, and the air was sticky with Marlboro Light smoke and Malibu and Coke, and sweaty bodies. Boodle followed Sarah-Louise on to the dance floor and lost her again as she was grabbed by a tall blond boy who she immediately started snogging enthusiastically. Boodle stared helplessly, but strangely captivated as the boy pressed Sarah-Louise up against a pillar and began to grind his hips against her in a bizarre-looking dry-humping motion. Sarah-Louise responded by grabbing his bum and pulling it towards her, her stubby-fingered hands working his flesh. Boodle was shocked. The music changed to 'The Locomotion', and Sarah-Louise and her partner seemed to begin timing their thrusts in time with the music, and Boodle felt slightly despairing and too old and at the same time too young to be there.

'It's rude to stare, you know.'

Boodle jumped, and found a tall young man, in his early twenties, looking down at her with an amused expression on his face.

'They certainly seem to have got the knack, don't they? My goodness. Is she your friend?'

'Yes. She's a Brosette. I don't know why she suddenly seems to like Kylie so much. It's a mystery.'

He laughed. 'Can I buy you a drink? You don't look as if you're enjoying the dancing much. I never dance.'

'Oh, me neither. Yes, please, a drink would be lovely.'

'Come along then. My name's Flip Cavalley. Let's find the bar and somewhere we can talk.' He looked at her, a question in his face, and she realised he wanted to know her name.

'Boodle. Boodle Calthorpe.'

Things like this – men like Flip – didn't happen to girls like Boodle. He was everything she wasn't – suave, sophisticated and confident. He told risqué jokes and let his eyes, and later, his hands stray to her chest. No one had ever touched her there before. No one had even kissed her before, unless you counted a peck on the cheek from the boy who had been forced to be her dance partner in the school production of *The Pirates of Penzance*. And now, all of a sudden and all at once, in the space of – she glanced at her Swatch; she had met him at about 10 p.m., so just over thirteen hours – not only had she been kissed but all sorts of other things as well.

She lay staring up at the floral wallpaper that, inexplicably and claustrophobically, covered not only the walls but also the ceiling of the spare bedroom she was in, and took an inventory of her body. As well as the smell of cigarettes and aftershave and, undeniably, sex, there were other new and unfamiliar things about her body. Her lips felt bruised. The skin on her face was slightly swollen and tender to the touch, and when she looked in the mirror of her compact she could see that it was red and irritated. Stubble rash. She had heard about it from other girls, but had never had it herself. She sighed, proudly, and continued. There was a small oval bruise on the inside of her arm. Boodle stroked it. It was from Flip's thumb, she remembered, pressing into her flesh as he pushed her back against the red velvet banquette. She put her thumb on top of the mark and imagined his thumb still there, touching hers, and a thrill rushed through her at the memory.

Her cheeks flushed as she remembered how he had worked his hand up between her legs and begun to tug at the waistband of her knickers. She had pushed his hand away, but more because she had felt she should than because she had wanted to. She wasn't sure whether he had been frustrated or whether he had respected her for doing so, as her mother had always said men respected girls who didn't 'go too far'. Boodle was still a bit unclear about the actual mechanics of going too far, as she and her mother had never had the sort of close relationship that meant they could discuss such things openly, so what she knew about sex she had mostly picked up from floating around the sidelines of other girls' conversations at school. Laughing along with them, she had tried to look as if she knew what they were giggling about, while her mind whirred and churned with trying to remember words like 'shaft' and 'fingering' in order to look them up in the dictionary later, which was never much help.

'I should be honest with you,' Flip said, on their third date. 'I know it might seem – premature.'

Boodle's eyes were wide. Was he going to – no. Not even her romantic nature could convince her that he was about to propose after only a pizza, a dinner at Langan's and a picnic in Hyde Park. But something inside her skipped a beat, and she realised that it was what she was secretly hoping for, and had been since she first set eyes on him at the ball.

'Honest is good,' she said quietly, and smiled.

'I like you, Boodle. I like you a lot.' Boodle blushed. Oh God. Maybe he *was* going to.

'I like the fact that you don't pretend to be older than you are, like all the other girls. You're not like all the other girls at all, are you?' He reached forward and pushed her hair away from her face. Boodle bit her lip. She couldn't reply.

'You're kind. You're gentle. You've never been drunk, you're not interested in fashion.' Boodle looked down at her outfit with dismay. She knew it was too frumpy. But Flip still seemed to be paying her a compliment, not criticising, so she didn't say anything.

'You'd rather read a terrible romance novel or watch one of those godawful soaps than go to any of the places I could take you, most of the time.'

Oh dear. He had seen her copy of *A Florentine Fantasy* in her bag the other day, then. She had thought she'd managed to conceal it in her bag, under the copy of the *Independent* that she had hastily bought at Waterloo for that exact purpose, on their second date.

Flip continued, 'Basically, I like that you're an old-fashioned girl. Well brought-up. But . . .'

Of course there was a 'but'. How could she have thought there wouldn't be a 'but'? Was it going to be 'but I've already got a girlfriend'? Or 'but I'm moving abroad'? I'll go with you, she thought. I'll wait. I'll do whatever it takes. I'm not letting you go. But she couldn't have predicted the 'but' that was coming.

'But I've already been married once. I'm a widower. I . . .' Flip's eyes were full of pain, and Boodle wanted nothing more than to take him in her plump arms, but she recognised that she had to let him finish, should not touch him.

'I'm sorry, I don't find it easy to talk about. I don't *want* to talk about it,' he said, more firmly. 'But the fact is, I had a wife and son, once.' Boodle's heart turned over at the mention of a son. Oh, poor Flip. Poor, poor Flip.

'And they died. And I don't want to get married again, or have children. I can't get married again.'

And now Boodle's heart thudded. She sensed that she was about to be asked something bigger than whether she would agree to marry Flip, even. She was about to be asked whether she would agree to *not* marry him.

'I understand I'm not offering you a great package here, Boodle. If you decide to walk away, I'll understand. I won't hold it against you, or try to change your mind.'

She looked at him and her romantic nature swooned at the thought of being the one to save him. She would be patient, she would be gentle. He would change his mind. And she would be part of his golden, gilded world. She would be a Cavalley, and nothing would be able to touch her.

Boodle nodded. 'I understand. I want to be with you, Flip. I don't care about anything else. Just you and me, together. That's all that matters.'

And it was true. For now, that was all that mattered. Boodle and Flip. The rest could come later.

Boodle stood in her smart hotel suite, gazing at the beautiful dress hanging behind the door. In her heart of hearts, Boodle would have preferred to get married in the local village church, where she had been going since she was a child and where she had gone to see so many local brides arriving, standing at the gate and waiting for their car to roll up and catch that first, magical glimpse of their dress. She'd always imagined that one day she would be that bride, on her father's arm, and the local village children would be waiting to see her, their excited faces the first things she saw as she pulled up to the church. But Flip was a London boy – no, not a boy at all, a London *man*, she thought proudly – a London man, and so the wedding should be in London. Anyhow, the tiny Surrey church would not be big enough for all his friends, and his mother's glamorous fashion crowd, of whom, if she was honest, Boodle was scared.

The thought of walking up the aisle, watched by hundreds of pairs of critical eyes all appraising her dress, and appraising *her* – less than kindly, she was sure – terrified her.

Oh, pull yourself together, Boodle Calthorpe, you're a grown woman now, you're soon to be a wife. A mother. Or so they thought. It wasn't a lie, she told herself now, not really. She might be pregnant. She had been flushing her pills down the toilet since the first night. How long did it usually take, anyway? Her period was due soon. Maybe this time. She could fudge the dates. It wouldn't matter, when they were married, and the baby was born. Their baby. And she was doing it for the right reasons. Definitely for the right reasons. It was what Flip needed. A wife, a baby. Not to replace the ones he had lost, of course not. But to move on from them. Yes, she was doing the right thing. And holding that thought at the front of her mind, Boodle went to call Sarah-Louise to help her get dressed.

There was a rustle at the back of the chapel and Violet, along with the 250 other guests, craned their necks to see. First, Boodle's mother walked smartly down the aisle on the arm of an harassed-looking usher whom she had no doubt been haranguing outside about the correct walking speed for such occasions. He deposited her in the front row and gratefully took his own seat. Then the familiar whisper of anticipation that preceded the entrance of every bride started up, followed by a hush.

Boodle was almost invisible beneath acres of lace-edged veiling. A thickly flowered coronet of peach and cream blooms held the veil in place, and her hair fell in her long-desired ringlets to her shoulders. Her dress, an off-the-shoulder design, had puffed-up silk sleeves which ended at the elbow with a ruffle of lace, and were trimmed with peach flowers. The bodice was ruffled around the neckline, and the skirt fell in huge ruffled folds to the floor and out behind her, for half the length of the chapel, it seemed. A large bow was positioned just above Boodle's bottom – an unfortunate choice of detailing, Violet thought, as it really wasn't the feature she would have chosen to accentuate – and from beneath it rolled yet more bows and ruffles. An immense bouquet trailed down the front of her dress, ivy curling out of the flowers and almost to the ground. The matrons and wives on the bride's side of the church oohed and aahed. The fashion lot on the groom's raised perfectly combed eyebrows. Then came four small, podgy-faced girls looking both overwhelmed and overexcited. They were almost more beribboned and beruffled than Boodle herself, if that were possible, their silk dresses festooned with bows and tied up with full sashes of peach silk like little presents under a Christmas tree; even their peach ballet slippers boasted large bows on the toes. They carried shepherdess-style baskets overflowing with peach and cream flowers which they were to scatter before Boodle's lace-clad toes once the ceremony was over.

When they arrived at the Heminsley Club, in Mayfair, where the reception was taking place, Boodle went upstairs to her room straight away to redo her make-up. She reached up and began to unpin her veil from her head-dress. Where was Sarah-Louise? Shouldn't she be up here helping her? Boodle realised that she was about to cry, which would make her look even more pink-eyed and puffy, so she took a deep breath and concentrated on her under-eye concealer. Her hand wavered. Sod it. She needed a drink. She poured a glass of champagne from the now slightly flat bottle that she and Sarah-Louise had had a glass from earlier while getting ready, drank it quickly, then poured another.

The door opened and Flip slid inside the room.

'All OK up here?'

Her heart swelled with love. She was Mrs Flip Cavalley now,

and no one could take that away from her. Ever. She held out her hand to him and he took it.

'All OK, pookie.'

'Come along, then. They're waiting for us to make our entrance.'

As Flip led her into the ballroom, and Boodle heard her new name announced by the gilded Master of Ceremonies, as he asked the guests to 'please charge your glasses and stand, to welcome Mr and Mrs Cavalley,' she knew that her happiness was complete. She was touched that Flip had turned her advances down earlier – he obviously wanted to make sure the night was as special as she did. She must just keep an eye out to make sure he didn't drink too much: her mother had warned her about that.

As she took her seat though, Boodle felt a horribly familiar sensation in her pants. A damp stickiness that she knew she could not ignore. Today of all days, in this dress of all dresses . . . She leaped up from the table and, pulling her skirts around her, rushed to the ladies'.

'Darling? Shall I come with you?' her mother called after her. 'Are you going to be able to—'

'I can manage,' she called back. 'Morning sickness.' Her mother nodded indulgently. She couldn't wait to be a grandmother.

She was going to have to wait a bit longer than she thought, Boodle knew, as she lifted up her skirts and carefully removed her blood-stained pants from under her dress. Damn. She had hoped that this month would be *the* month. She was just going to have to carry on trying.

Twelve months later, Boodle stood in the changing room of Rigby & Peller, looking at her reflection in the mirror and wondering if the set of lilac silk teddy, French knickers and loosely draped dressing-gown really did as much to conceal her 'mummy tummy' as the friendly but brisk assistant, with her hair set in a tight head of curls that reminded Boodle of her matron at school, claimed. She turned to the side and tried to suck her tummy in, but the bulge was still evident.

Boodle was determined to pull her marriage back from the brink. Things were not good. She jiggled Mungo's buggy with her right foot, watching as the flesh on her thigh juggled along with the motion. It really was no wonder Flip didn't come near her any more, was it? She was hardly an appealing erotic prospect. And things hadn't been right for months. She had known that he suspected her of lying about the pregnancy, not long after they married. She had tried to claim a miscarriage, but he hadn't believed her. And eventually, after a long night of him shouting at her, and her weeping, she admitted it.

'Yes,' she had said, exhausted. 'Yes, I made it up. I'm sorry.'

It had been an awful night. She had trapped him, he had raged, when she had known he didn't want this, and why. How could she have done it to him? If she had loved him, at all, she would not have done it.

'It's because I love you so much,' she had sobbed. 'I wanted you so much.'

'Jesus, Boodle,' he had snapped. 'I'm not a fucking toy. You don't just decide you want a husband and lie to get one.'

He would have left her, she knew it. But, inadvertently this time, she had trapped him again. She really was pregnant.

And so, against his instincts, against his better judgement, but knowing what life had been like for Violet as a single mother for all those years, Flip did what he thought was the right thing. He stayed.

Boodle regretted the way she had gone about everything, now. But she couldn't regret the reason for the gulf that had grown up between herself and her husband. How could she, when the reason for it was the perfect little boy sitting gurgling happily in front of her? He didn't care how far her breasts had dropped towards the floor, or how much her belly sagged, or even the lies she had told to get him. He just cared about the food that they provided, and the comfortable pillow it made for him to lie on. Boodle sighed. If only everyone's needs were as straightforward as those of her son.

It felt to Boodle as though her life, the whole world, even, had been riven in two, split into 'before' and 'after' Mungo and motherhood by a great and uncrossable chasm. Before was frivolity, selfishness, stupid ambitions and worries that she could now hardly believe she had wasted precious energy and breath on feeling or discussing. She couldn't believe she had wasted time and money shopping for anything other than baby clothes, spent her evenings in cinemas and watching the soaps, frittering away her life on dinners out and reading *Harpers & Queen* and fretting over which pair of court shoes were best.

Later, of course, the feeling subsided somewhat, not disappearing but fading into a more muted version of itself, and the rest of the world began to seep back into her consciousness. Mungo was still the pivot around which her life revolved and without whom her life meant nothing, but she began to feel as though she were waking up from a long sleep, and became aware of other people and things once more. Flip, the rest of her family, friends, even, slowly came back into focus; she started to watch TV again in the evenings while she nursed Mungo, rather than just staring at his perfect face, the curls on his forehead and his perfect, thick eyelashes as he drowsily drank.

She hadn't noticed during the first weeks of Mungo's life, but Flip was more distant than ever with her. She woke up from her baby-induced haze, only to find that, as so frequently seemed to be the case in Boodle's life, she was just a little bit too late. While Boodle felt as though she had lost a layer of skin after

Mungo's birth, it seemed as though Flip had grown an extra one. There had been a period after their marriage where he had seemed, if not happy, then content. She had really thought that he was over Cressida and Jasper, and would be able to settle into their life together. Oh, she was not the love of his life, as he was hers – she knew that in her heart of hearts, despite her innocence. But she had hoped beyond hope that she could make him happy, that in time he would come to love her in a different way, and to value and appreciate her for who she was. And that would have been enough for her, as long as she had him, as long as she could tell herself that she came first, and that she was Mrs Cavalley.

'Everything all right in there, dear?' The plummy voice of the sales assistant came from behind the curtain. Boodle sighed.

'Yes. I'll take the lilac set.' Boodle piled her hair up on top of her head with one hand and looked at the array of underwear and nightwear hanging around the dressing room, suddenly feeling more confident.

'And . . . and the corset, with the stockings. And the garter belt!' she called out as the assistant retreated.

She bit her bottom lip. Nothing ventured, nothing gained, she thought to herself.

That evening, Boodle fed Mungo and put him to bed half an hour earlier than usual, so that she had time to set the scene for when Flip got back from work. She had been to Marks & Sparks and bought the ingredients for the best meal that she had learned at Leith's, where she had taken a four-week course. It had been a wedding present from her mother, and Boodle had entered into the spirit of it with gusto. This was all part of her new life, her new role as a wife, and she was determined to make a good go of it. She learned how to make a shortcrust pastry, prepare, poach in court bouillon and serve a whole salmon with a cucumber scale decoration, and make a cheese soufflé that never sank in the middle. In fact, she pondered now, by the end of the four weeks she had learned more than enough to carry her through married life; more than many professional caterers knew, but she hadn't learned what she really needed to know, and what, a couple of years later, standing in the kitchen of the little Chelsea mews house that she shared with her husband, stirring her Béarnaise sauce, she wished someone had told her. How to make her husband desire her, how to make him look at her in the way she saw other men looking at their wives. Maybe if her mother had been a different kind of woman, she would have taken Boodle to one side before her wedding and given her the advice she really needed, instead of the somewhat awkward and embarrassing moment they had shared in the hotel.

So, Boodle was taking matters into her own hands. So to speak. She chuckled at her little joke. Maybe she would say something along those lines to Flip, later, in bed. 'I don't want you to have to take matters into your own hands, darling,' she could say, with a saucy wink, as the strap of her teddy slid off her shoulder . . . But then she went to the fridge to get the steaks out so they came up to room temperature before she cooked them, and she caught sight of her reflection in the stainless-steel front, and remembered that she wasn't really a saucy-wink kind of a girl.

She wasn't a seducing-her-husband kind of a girl either, or so Boodle decided later, when she was taking off her carefully applied make-up in the bathroom, wiping the smeared mascara off her cheeks with cottonwool balls soaked in cleanser. However upset she might be at her failure to persuade her husband to make love to her, even when she had cast her dignity aside and told him straight out that she would do anything he wanted, even 'that thing' that she still could not bring herself to name, Boodle knew the importance of sticking diligently to one's skincare routine.

The evening had been a disaster from the moment Flip walked in the door.

'God. What's that smell?' she had heard him call from the hallway. He would be standing there, briefcase under one arm, going through his post, she knew. Boodle sniffed, trying to work out whether he was referring to the cooking smells or the fragrance of her physical preparations. She *had* used rather a lot of bath oil, far more than usual, as well as all her other lotions and potions. She was wearing the teddy and French knickers already, and had laid out a simple coral-coloured shift dress on the ottoman in their bedroom to wear for dinner, one she knew that he liked. She heard him coming towards the bathroom, and grabbed the dressing-gown to cover herself with before he entered. She planned to unveil her new purchases after dinner.

'Boodle, why are you in your underwear?'

Too late. Flip's head was round the bathroom door, his expression quizzical and a bit annoyed.

'Is Mungo ill?'

'Ill? No, why? Oh, I see. No, I put him down a bit earlier tonight.'

'Why?'

Boodle pulled the gown around her waist and slipped past Flip into their bedroom. She picked up the dress from its resting place on the floral ottoman with its Laura Ashley upholstery that she had saved up for and bought herself. She loved it. They had the matching duvet cover and scatter pillows on their bed, which Flip thought was 'twee and unadventurous', but had let her buy anyhow.

'I thought we could do with some . . . grown-up time.' She smiled nervously. Flip stared at her. She steeled herself – this wasn't going that well, he hardly seemed thrilled at the prospect, but she made herself carry on. He was probably just tired from work.

'Why don't you go and have a shower, make us a drink? I'll be through in a moment to finish dinner. I've made something special.'

She had spent hours planning the meal, getting all her recipe books and folders out, with their carefully clipped recipes from the *Mail* and the *Telegraph* neatly organised in sections according to course. Something rich and satisfying, indulgent, but nothing so heavy that they would feel weighed down after eating. Eventually she settled on a starter of moules marinière, followed by fillet steaks with Béarnaise sauce and green beans, and chocolate fondants (which she privately thought of as her signature dish). She had chosen some good red wine and decanted it, taking care not to spill a drop as she did so, and she had polished her silver candlesticks and cutlery that she had inherited from her grandmother. Everything was perfect.

Except it wasn't. 'Shower? Something special? Have I forgotten an anniversary or something?'

She could see him counting the possibilities off in his head – birthday, wedding anniversary, Valentine's Day . . .

'No. Like I said, I just thought we could spend some time together. Just the two of us. Go on. Give me a minute and I'll join you in the living room.'

Flip gave an almost imperceptible shrug, and went off downstairs. Boodle could hear the clinking of ice in a glass, and relaxed for a second. Good. He was having a drink, maybe he was going to go along with her plans. For a minute she had been worried that he would throw the whole thing into disarray by saying he was tired, just wanted a bowl of soup, or had to go back to work or something. She slid the dress over her head and reached around the back to do the zipper up. It was awkward to do it herself, but she wasn't going to ask him to do it. Maintain the mystique, the article in *Cosmo* that she had read at the hairdresser had advised (she would never have brought *Cosmo* into the house, it was far too racy; she liked Flip to think she only ever read *Harpers* and *Tatler*). Then she took a deep breath, practised the slow glance over her shoulder that she planned to use when she got up from the table and invited him to join her in the bedroom one last time, and crossed her fingers, praying that Mungo would not wake up and start crying for her.

He did wake up, of course he did, just as Boodle and Flip were digging into the mussels, their fingers covered with creamy, winey juices. Boodle had stuck one finger in her mouth and was sucking the sauce off it, and trying to work up the courage to do the same to Flip's finger when the monitor that they hardly needed because the house was so small but that Boodle felt nervous without, crackled into action. Boodle's hand shot towards it automatically, almost as if by holding the white plastic box in her hand she was already offering her son some kind of comfort. She started to stand.

'Wait and see if he settles himself,' Flip said.

Boodle froze, half-standing, her bottom hovering above the chair. She could feel her breasts beginning to leak already.

'He's hungry.'

'Didn't you feed him before he went down?'

'Of course. But . . .'

She was torn. But only for a second.

'I'll just quickly see to him, and then I'll be back.'

Flip sighed, and went back to his mussels, shrugging. Boodle could have cried. Damn it.

By the time she came back, Flip was on the phone, and her mussels had gone cold. She quickly cleared them away and turned the gas on to heat the pan for the steaks. She had taken her dress off after feeding Mungo – even hesitating for a few seconds had resulted in bigger marks on the thin silk than she could dry off quickly, and so she had taken it as a sign, and slipped the silk dressing-gown on over her underwear. It would be sexy, wouldn't it? Your wife cooking your dinner clad only in lilac silk – surely Flip would find that a turn-on?

'All right?' Flip was in the kitchen door, the cordless phone in his hand.

'Who was that?'

'Mama.'

Boodle nodded, and quickly tried to change the subject. She did not want to start discussing her mother-in-law.

'How do you want your steak?'

'Blue. Boodle . . .'

'There's some lovely red wine open, pour us some, can you . . . Yes?'

Now was a good moment to have a trial run of The Look – she turned her head towards Flip, her chin down, her lips slightly pouting and her eyelids lowered. 'What is it, darling?' she asked softly.

'What's all this really about? Is there something you want to talk about? Hang on, why are you making that face?' He was staring at her lips incredulously. She hastily pulled them back into their usual position. He could be extremely obtuse sometimes, her husband; he obviously hadn't got the message at all. Honestly, what more did she have to do to make it clear that she wanted him – swing naked from the chandelier? Not that she could do that, it was quite fragile and wouldn't support – oh, stop it, Boodle. She was just going to have to come out with it. She took a big swig of her drink, gathered all of her courage, gave the Béarnaise sauce one final stir, dropped the steaks on to the smoking griddle and then turned to him, jiggling one shoulder as she did so and tugging at the back of the gown with one hand so it sank down around her waist, leaving her shoulders and upper arms bare.

'It's about you, and me, and . . .' Boodle searched frantically for inspiration. She had started reading *The Joy of Sex* before Mungo was born, but had stopped before she got to the chapter on talking dirty, and it wasn't something that she had a natural talent for.

'And this,' she carried on, gesturing to her body with one hand. 'It's about the fact that I've been here all day, thinking about you. Waiting for you to come home . . .'

Her mouth was dry. Oh God, she couldn't do it. Flip was giving her a very strange look indeed. Come on, Boodle. Your marriage is at stake here, she told herself firmly, and so she continued, 'Feeling myself become wet at the thought of it . . .'

She felt a rush of exhilaration as she said the word 'wet', and almost laughed out loud at her brazenness. And saying it had another effect, she realised with surprise, a physical one. She felt herself becoming excited for the first time in months. Maybe there was something to this dirty-talking thing after all. She glanced towards him. His mouth was open.

'Take me, Flip,' she said breathily. 'Take me now.'

'Bloody hell,' he said. 'Boodle . . .'

'I know!' she squealed excitedly. 'It hardly sounds like me at all, does it? I can't believe—'

'No, not that – oh fuck, Boodle, get that off, you're on fucking fire!'

And as he rushed towards her, grabbing a tea towel and shoving her towards the wall, she realised by the sudden heat on her back and smell of acrid frazzling as the flame caught the end of her hair, that he did not mean in any erotic sense of the word.

After he had patted her down and she had changed her sooty,

damp clothes, Flip pulled his jacket on and opened the front door. 'I'm going to meet James for a catch-up. Don't wait up.' He stepped out into the street and breathed the fresh air in with relief as he did most times he left the mews house. The place was suffocating. It was stuffed full of flowery cushions and fussy food and the weight of his wife's expectations and the burden of her disappointment. James was Cavalley's Sales and Marketing Manager and Flip's best friend in the company. But he wasn't going to meet James – he just knew that his friend would cover for him without question, should the need arise. Cover for him – why beat around the bush, even to himself? Lie for him, was what he meant.

As Flip walked down the narrow cobbled street towards the King's Road, seeing the streetlights and headlights of passing black cabs get closer, he felt himself begin to relax in a way he could never even come close to when he was at home. It was all wrong. His house should be the one place he felt comfortable, where he could shrug off the working day and unwind; instead it was the place he felt the least at ease. It wasn't him; he didn't like the house and he didn't like his life there. Boodle was always at home, she never went out any more, always sitting there on the sofa, immobile, her big cow eyes staring up at him, wanting something from him that he had no idea how to give. Something that he didn't possess. Love for her – real, passionate love for her. He just felt suffocated by her, by Mungo. Trapped in a relationship that had gone far further than he had ever intended.

It was as if the more she yearned for him to love her, the more she mooned and waited and silently asked him to pay her attention, the more he felt something that approached revulsion, the more he pulled back and found her very presence an irritant rather than a blessing. She was heavily present, all the time. There was no respite from her loaded glances and martyrlike offers to do things for him, make him a cup of tea or open a window; it felt like every little favour, however small, that he accepted from her was something more that he owed her, tied him more irrevocably to her, like an anchor being driven deeper and deeper into a muddy seabed. He was trapped, and what made it worse was that it was a trap of his own making.

He had thought he was doing the right thing. Or the only thing he could do at the time. Acquiring a girlfriend, someone he didn't find that attractive, but who was nice and polite, dependable and responsible. A suitable companion whom he could take to dinners and who would do all of those things that he had thought he needed and wanted. Someone who would never, ever come close to filling the void that Cressida and Jasper had left, but since he didn't expect them to, he wouldn't be disappointed by them. Well, he had been wrong. Very badly wrong. He had made promises to Boodle that he had known he had no chance of keeping – promised to love her when his heart was still bound to his first wife, promised to cherish her when she was someone whom he simply did not hold in the precious esteem necessary to carry out such a vow. Promised to put her first. But he had already made those promises once. And *they* came first. Cressida, and Jasper. They would always come first.

And still they haunted him. Cressida's face, golden and smiling. The sound of Jasper's gurgling laugh. The feeling of his little body in Flip's arms, Cressida's head leaning happily against his shoulder. He had to make them go away. But all he really wanted in the world was for them to come back to him.

'Another, sir?' The barman held the bottle of bourbon up in front of him.

Flip took his head out of his hands. He nodded, and pushed his glass towards the bottle.

'Yes. Another.'

*

'Hi.' Violet and Boodle were interrupted by Fran, standing a few feet away. Violet looked up at her. She was such a beautiful girl, despite the scar, she thought, and then admonished herself, as always. You shouldn't even notice it, after all this time, she told herself. But she did. Violet noticed it the most of anyone. Every time she saw it, the guilt pierced her heart.

'Tillie said something about a family conference.' Fran walked over and sat at the table, opposite her mother. She was barefoot, as she always was here, despite years of Violet telling her to 'put some shoes on, you'll tread on something'. She never had.

'Yes. I thought it better to talk to everyone here. Before we all disperse back to London. There's a lot to—'

'Who is he, Mama?'

Boodle stood. 'I should leave you to it.'

'Oh Boodle,' Violet said. 'Sit down, for goodness' sake. When are you going to accept that you're family?'

Boodle did as she was told, and hugged Violet's words to her.

Violet turned her attention back to Fran, whose worried expression sent a pang through her mother. It was as though her youngest child were being made to re-evaluate everything she had known until this point. Violet knew how she felt. How many times in her life had she discovered something that had turned her world upside down? Too many. And oh, how she wished she could have protected Fran from the uncertainty and disappointment that went with those discoveries. But she could not. Violet had to learn how to let go.

'He's telling the truth,' Violet replied. 'He is my brother.'

Fran nodded. Violet could see her absorbing the knowledge, its implications. 'Have you seen him – recently, I mean?' she asked.

How deep was the deception, was what she was really asking.

How fresh the lies were. But they were old. Violet could reassure her of that, at least. The secrets she had kept were so well buried in Violet's mind they hardly even felt like secrets any longer. Just part of another lifetime, one that bore no relation to the life she lived now. And she wanted to keep it that way. She had worked hard to keep it that way. Mattie might have reappeared out of nowhere – why? how? – but the rest . . . the rest, Violet would keep out of sight. She had known for a while that she would be forced to cause ripples in the smooth surfaces of her children's lives because of her illness. That was bad enough, but she had not bargained for this. She looked at Fran. Took her hand across the table.

'I haven't seen him since . . .' she counted back the years in her head . . . 'since before you were born. There's a long story, there, my darling.'

'Yes. I realised last night,' Fran began, then paused, 'that I have never asked you about – well, about you,' she continued. 'You were just my mama. I never really thought about what happened before us, before you had us. Your childhood, where you came from. You never talked about it. I'm sorry I didn't ask.'

'Darling girl, it's your job not to ask. I'm your mother. You're not meant to see me as a real person. Not until you're much older, at least.'

Fran smiled. 'I am older, now. I'm going to have to be, aren't I?'

Violet took a deep breath. 'I will tell you about Mattie. About where I came from. But . . .'

'But first you need to rest,' Fran interrupted her. 'There'll be time, Mama. There will be time.'

She stroked Violet's wrist with her thumb. Here it begins, Violet thought. Here is the moment when she starts to take care of me, not me of her. I did not think it would come so soon.

'I talked to Patrick yesterday. With Flip.' She looked at her mother. 'You haven't been well for ages, have you?'

'It's been a few months. Not that long, I . . . sorry, darling. You should have heard about it from me. Before now.'

Fran shrugged. 'It's all right. I like Patrick.'

'Flip doesn't.'

'Oh, Flip.' Fran smiled. 'He just doesn't like the thought of anyone else being the important-est boy.'

'True.' Violet laughed. When Fran was little, she had asked her mother, 'Am I the important-est, Mummy? The important-est little girl in the whole world?' 'Yes,' Violet had always replied. 'Yes, you're the important-est little girl, and Flip is the important-est big boy, and Sebastian is the important-est medium-sized boy, and Blue is the important-est quite big boy.' 'And Mummy is the important-est of all,' Fran would say, almost reverently, still at the age when she thought her mother knew everything, ruled the world. No one could remember where it had come from, who had said it first; the word had just gradually, over the years, become woven into the language of their family.

Fran glanced at her watch, a silver face that was tied around her wrist with a striped ribbon. There were a few minutes before the others were due to come down. She glanced at Boodle, who smiled at her encouragingly, and then looked her mother in the eye and said, 'Mama, I want to come and work for you. I want to work at Cavalley's.'

Violet was momentarily taken aback. Fran was wearing a familiar, determined expression. The same one she had worn when she was a little girl and would hold her hand out for sweets or, later, when she was learning to play tennis, hitting ball after ball until her swing was just right. Fran's school CV was an embodiment of the maxim, so oft-repeated but so rarely true, that anything was achievable if one put one's mind to it.

'You do already.'

'No, I mean properly.'

'Oh Fran.'

'I mean it. I . . . Patrick told me there isn't much time.'

Violet frowned. 'He shouldn't have.'

'Of course he should have. We need to know, Mama. You can't keep doing it all. Not now.' Fran looked over to the pool. 'Months, he said, not years. And . . .' Her voice was choked suddenly. Violet reached over the table for her hand, but Fran did not take it, just spread her fingers wide and flat on the cool marble. Grounding herself. 'And if you're going to not be here, then we all need to help. I don't want to waste time at college, when I could be learning what I'm going to need to know.'

'You're doing so well though. I don't want you to cut your course off because of – because of me.'

'But it's not. It's because of me. I want it. I chose Law because I thought it would be useful, and I thought I had a lot of time to decide. You know, to think about things, have a gap year, do all of that stuff. Stuff that normal kids do.' She smiled a little, to show she wasn't cross. Their family had never been normal. 'But I don't have that time now. And that's OK, because it's made me decide. I'm doing well at college but I can do better at Cavalley's, I know I can. I'm my mother's daughter. There's nothing else I want to do, Mama. There isn't anything. Anyhow, you can't leave it all to the boys, can you? Girls have to stick together.' Her eyes filled with tears. Suddenly the reality of her mother not being there seemed much closer.

Violet nodded. 'True we do. But—'

'No, I've decided,' Fran interrupted. 'And you always said you'd support me whatever I wanted to do. Didn't you?'

Violet had to concede that she had.

'Well, this is what I want to do.' Now Fran lifted her hand

and took Violet's. Her tears had subsided again. 'This is what I have to do. You understand that, don't you?'

Violet nodded. She, of all people, did understand Fran's need to follow her heart. To prove that she could do something, to show her mother, during the last few months of her life, how strong she could be, how far she had come. She could not deny Fran that. And she knew the girl was right: she would do well. Violet could see it in her. She had the hunger, the desire to show the world and everyone in it what she could do. And she had the love of beautiful things that you could not teach, the innate sense of style that Blue had, but tempered with a clear-sighted head for numbers and business that Violet thought was unique among her children; not even Flip had quite the same natural knack for it. And, maybe most importantly, Fran knew what would suit someone, had the sixth sense that Madame Fournier had impressed on Violet as being the most important part of running a successful salon, all those years ago.

'Am I too early? I can come back.'

Violet, Fran and Boodle lifted their heads. Tillie stood, a few feet away, as if waiting for permission to join them. Her legs were brown in her little pink and white sundress, and a pair of white Jackie O-style sunglasses pushed her blond curls back off her face. For a moment, and not for the first time, Violet was reminded acutely of Scarlet. The way she stood with her weight on one hip, the hair, the easy smile. Memories.

'No, sweetheart. Don't be silly.' Violet gestured for Tillie to join them and she did so, sliding on to the bench next to her. 'I want all of the family here – it's important.' She turned her head to Fran again. 'Think it through some more, darling girl. It's a lot of change all at once. You can always do a bit of both.'

Fran shook her head. 'Too late. I've already spoken to King's College.'

At that moment, Flip strolled over to the table, shirtsleeves rolled up around his elbows, a cigarette in his hand. Mungo was a little way behind him, slouching along. 'Blue's not coming down.'

Violet raised her head, concerned. 'Is he all right?'

Flip reached down to pour himself a coffee from the pot in the centre of the table. 'I haven't seen him. Adam rang our room, said he wasn't up to it.'

'Blue? I heard him walking around a lot in the night,' said Boodle.

'How did you know it was him?' Flip said, irritation seeping out of the sides of his voice. 'It could have been anyone.'

Boodle looked hurt. 'He was pacing up and down the corridor outside my room. I could hear him talking. To himself,' she added quietly.

'I'm sorry, Boodle,' Violet said. 'You should have rung me.'

Boodle flushed. 'Oh no, it's not a problem. I don't sleep much, anyhow. Was very hot as well.'

'Can we get on?' Flip said firmly.

'All right,' said Violet. 'I'll talk to Blue later. Maybe it's better that way.' She always watched what she said around Blue. His imagination was so reckless, so unpredictable, she had to think about every metaphor she used, every detail of anything that might be disturbing. She would not have been able to be as open as she needed to be if he was there.

She looked around at the faces of her family. Flip, smoking angrily. His sorrow always emerged as rage. And Boodle's presence always made him prickly. Poor Boodle. She couldn't cope with the heat at all. Everyone else looked sun-kissed, sun-softened. She just looked plump and uncomfortable, her T-shirt sticking to her and her toes squeezed into flip-flops that would give her blisters. Mungo was embarrassed by her, and she knew it. He sat, a little away from her, his chair pointedly tilted towards his father, leaving Boodle looking at the side of his head. Fran was opposite her, her face worried still, her scar already covered with the make-up she wore every day. Even when she was alone she covered it.

Around the table then, her family were gathered, but with gaps. There was no Blue. There was no Scarlet. And there was no Sebastian. Violet's stomach lurched and she told herself to focus on the now, on the ones who were there. This was too important. She must not let the memories rise up and overtake her.

'All right,' she began. 'You all know that I'm ill. Very ill. I feel well enough, most of the time. I don't want you to worry or fret over me too much – if you can help it. I really don't feel as bad as you might think. But the thing with the type of cancer I've got . . .' She took a breath. Saying it made it real. *She had cancer*. She carried on: 'Is that by the time they know you've got it, it's too late to do anything very useful about it.'

'How long?' Flip asked. Violet looked up at him. Always direct, always to the point. There had never been any messing around with Flip. He was the only one not sitting; his foot was on the chair and his arm rested on his knee. Smoking, smoking. Normally, she would tell him to get his bottom on the chair, or was he not planning on staying? Today, she must allow him – all of them – to do whatever they felt. Say whatever they needed, ask the questions they must know the answers to. And after today? They would have to find a new way.

'A few months. Maybe less.'

Boodle raised a hand to her mouth. 'Oh,' she said, and then apologised straight away. Flip just nodded, his mouth a straight line.

'How many? Three? Four?'

'I don't know,' Violet said. 'It's not an exact science.'

'It's just I need to know what preparations to make at work. Obviously things are going to change.'

'Well,' Violet said quietly, 'I'm sorry, darling. I can't give you a number of days before I'll be out of there.'

Boodle couldn't contain her sob any longer. 'Oh Flip, how could you? Your mother's dying, and all you can think about is work. Still. It was always . . .' She stopped herself, and buried her face in a tissue. Mungo sat awkwardly next to her and poured her a glass of water.

'I'm sorry, but someone has to think of these things,' Flip snapped. 'We can't all have the luxury of sitting around weeping and wailing. Some of us have to work.'

'Please be quiet,' Violet said. 'It's all right, Boodle. Everyone's upset. Everyone's worried. And Flip's right – there are going to have to be changes. Obviously. We all need to think about it.'

'Well, there isn't much to think about, surely?' Flip asked, lighting a new cigarette. 'The company's more successful than ever. It'll be a matter of transferring your shares, signing over power of attorney at some stage.' Fran frowned, and he held up a hand. 'I'm sorry, Fran, but it has to be faced. And we may as well pull the plaster off while we're all together, so we all know what's happening from the start.'

'Flip,' Violet said. 'Slow down. I haven't decided how things are going to progress yet. I'm meeting Gerald when we're back in London. I'll keep you in the loop, of course.'

'But—'

'But you thought I would just hand everything over to you?' Violet's voice was kind but firm. 'I'm afraid it isn't quite that simple, darling.'

Flip put his coffee cup down on the table with a clank. 'I'm sorry we fought, Mama. I was going to text you on the way here, but I got distracted. But is that really—'

Violet interrupted him. 'Darling. It's forgotten. And it has nothing to do with this. Whatever decision I make has to be for the good of the company – for the good of the family. You know me better than to think I'd change my mind because of a silly row, don't you?'

Flip shrugged, and took his cigarette to the railing overlooking the sea, running his fingers through his hair, trying to calm himself. Violet carried on. He could hear perfectly well from over there.

'Fran wants to be more involved in the business, and that's fine. Tillie's role has got bigger in the last year. Blue's designs have taken Cavalley's dresses into the top tier. There are lots of people involved. And it's important that I think about what's best for all of them.'

'And Mungo,' Boodle blurted out. 'Mungo wants to do work experience with Flip.' Everyone turned to look at her in surprise, including Mungo himself. She blushed again, but carried on. 'He must be allowed to be involved as well,' she said, and there was a thread of steel in her voice that no one had heard before. 'I won't let you shut him out.'

'Darling Boodle, no one wants to shut Mungo out, certainly not me,' Violet said.

Boodle nodded. 'Good. Because . . .' She stopped. Violet was staring at her, and her eyes reassured her, but also reminded her that Mungo was sitting next to her, and he was only a boy still, despite his height and emerging stubble. There were conversations that his teenage ego was still too fragile for.

'Because I just want to make sure he gets a chance to find out what his family do. And make his own decisions.'

Violet nodded. 'Of course. Mungo, you're welcome at Cavalley's whenever you like. I hope you know that. I'd love to show you around.'

Mungo looked embarrassed. 'Thanks, Grandma.'

'So, I must move on.' Violet paused. 'Flip.' He waited a moment, raising his hand to his face and rubbing it, then turned to her. His eyes were red.

'Yes, Mama?' he said.

'Might I have a cigarette?'

He smiled, took one out of the packet and came over and handed it to her, then lit it for her with a silver lighter. 'It's been a long time since I lit your cigarettes.'

'I know. I just felt like one, suddenly.' She looked at Mungo again. 'Mungo, you're never to smoke. If I find out you have been, I'll cancel the car I've got on order for your seventeenth. And when I'm gone I'll come back and haunt you.'

Mungo's lower lip dropped and his face was a combination of pleasure and pain. He couldn't help himself, 'A car? Cool.'

Violet laughed, and so did Boodle. Even Flip smiled. 'Yes, cool. Right.' She paused, and inhaled on her cigarette. 'God, why on earth did I stop smoking? *When* did I stop smoking? I don't even remember, it was so long ago.'

'The doctor said it would be the death of you,' Boodle said. 'It was just after we got married. Remember? I was pregnant with Mungo. You said you had better make sure you were around for your next . . . for your grandchild.'

Boodle bit her lip. Violet glanced at her, quickly, then looked away. 'Yes, that's right, of course. Well. I don't think we need to worry about *that* any more. So, let's move on to the elephant in the room: the man who turned up at my party.'

Everyone was quiet. Violet took a deep breath. 'He told you he was my brother. And he told you that my real name is not Violet Cavalley.'

They all stared at her, remembering. Mattie Gribbens, as they had learned his name was, was staying in the Capri Palace Hotel, just around the corner, where Patrick had installed him the night of the party, after making sure Violet's health was not in immediate danger. He had been there since, ringing the villa every day, saying he wanted to talk to his sister. No one had known what to do about him. They had all been waiting for

Violet to emerge, and tell them. They might yearn for independence, her flock, but they still turned to her for guidance, to be led. She was going to have to be honest with them now, because one day soon, she would not be here.

'He was telling the truth. Or a truth, of sorts. He is my brother. And though my name is Violet Cavalley now, it wasn't always. Once upon a time I was called May Gribbens. May Violet Gribbens.'

No one said anything. A thousand questions floated in the air around the table, and all of them remained unasked. For now. She carried on.

'I did not have a happy childhood. That much will have been obvious to you all long before now.'

'You've never talked about it,' Tillie said softly. 'We – I always assumed there weren't happy memories. We can all understand that. Some things you want to leave in the past.'

Violet looked over at her and nodded. 'Yes, that's right. But some things won't be left in the past. Some things can't be buried for ever. Remember that, all of you.'

Tillie looked away and lowered her sunglasses.

'What does he want?' Fran asked. Violet turned to her.

'Money, I expect. He found out I'm dying, and he wants what he thinks is his piece of the pie. Don't worry – he's not going to get it. He's got nothing to bargain with. Because I have nothing left to lose.'

Violet shut her eyes for a second, them carried on, 'It's time to tell the truth. I don't want to run from my past any longer. My childhood isn't why I did what I did. Lots of people have miserable times when they're little. They get over it, they move on. Oh, I was never going to go back home and visit my parents every weekend. But it was what happened later that made me run.'

Flip was sitting at the table now and he looked up at her. 'After I was born?'

Her gaze was tender. 'Yes.'

'To do with my father?'

She nodded. 'Yes.'

Flip knew his father had died when he was just a baby. Violet had told him that Bryce was killed in an accident, on a visit back to see his family in America. That he was buried there.

'Bryce – your father – didn't die as I told you.'

Chapter Four

They had been happy. That was what she remembered afterwards. How happy she had been with Bryce. How she had felt as though she had walked into someone else's life, a life where good things happened, not bad, a life where no one hurt her or ignored her, a life where she was loved and cherished and did not wake up every morning full of dread, her heart pounding in her chest, but full of hope, her heart soaring. A life where she was Violet, not May, and soon to be Violet Hawthorn.

They would lie in bed in their little rented house at the very bottom of the King's Road, catching minutes in their hands before Bryce had to go to college, his arm curled protectively around her belly, making plans. 'Our wedding will be full of sunshine and flowers,' he would tell her. 'Our wedding will be special, just the two of us . . .' And then she would interrupt him. 'The three of us,' she would say, and he would grin his wide, white grin and lean down and kiss the top of her belly. 'Oh, yes, Ah forgot for a moment,' he would say, and she would glare at him, pretending to be angry, until he tickled her stomach and she collapsed into giggles, batting him away.

He would draw for her. Propped up on pillows, his sketchbook resting on his knees, his pencil would fly across the page as she talked, describing to him what the milliner's salon that she dreamed of owning one day would look like.

'It'll have a window there – no, there – bigger . . . yes! And a thick carpet. So thick you can take your shoes off and feel as if you're floating. Pale grey – like the underneath of a shell. And there should be mirrors, a big one on the wall – yes, that one – and smaller ones, so you can see from different angles. There, yes, and there.'

As she watched, her words became pictures in front of her eyes, as he somehow drew exactly what she was seeing. He was drawing her dreams.

And then the day came where everything changed.

'Things are bad at home, May. Worse than you can imagine. Mattie's in trouble. Bad trouble. He keeps getting into scraps. The police'll be on to him soon, May.'

Violet's breath was coming in thin, ragged gasps. Her father was standing on the doorstep. His thick, donkey-jacketed torso, with its familiar smell of oil and tobacco, almost filled the frame. She stood firm. She mustn't take a step backwards. Then he would be in the house and she didn't want him in the house, where Flip was asleep upstairs, untouched by the taint of her family. She had to keep him out.

'How did you find me? I didn't tell anyone where we were living.' She wanted to say to him, 'I'm not May any longer, don't call me that. I'm Violet. I am who I wanted to be.' But the words would not come out.

'Friends. Tracked you down.' He leaned against the door-frame, his shoulder slumping against it, and lit one of the dark-papered hand-rolled cigarettes he carried around with him everywhere he went. The smoke puffed out of the end of it and reminded Violet of despair. She knew who Jimmy's 'friends' would be. The network of travellers spread its tentacles far and wide. Violet had not been let go of yet.

'Your brother's really gone off the rails since you're gone,' Jimmy said, rubbing his scratty beard.

'He's always got into scraps. He'll come good.' She didn't believe it.

'He misses you.'

'Mattie don't miss no one.' Then she corrected herself. She had changed the way she spoke. She didn't want to slip back into her old ways. Into anything from back then. 'Mattie doesn't miss anyone. He can stand on his own two feet.'

Mattie had never needed her around. Not since he was a small boy. He walked alone, always had done. Violet knew that. She held her shoulders square.

'Dad, I don't understand. Why do you want me back? You never cared when I was there.'

'We're your family. We need you.'

'You're not my family. Not any more.'

Despite everything, despite the hurt and the anger, despite how desperately she had wanted to get away, saying that still hurt her more than almost anything. How could she turn her back on her family like that – how could she say the words, even? What kind of a person must she be, how cold-hearted, to be able to do that?

Just then, Flip woke up and began to grizzle. And for once, his crying soothed her. That was how she could do this. That was what would give her the strength to stand firm. Even so, she was distracted by it. And as she turned towards her son, she took a step back. And her father took one forward.

'Maggie's sick – real sick,' he said, as they stood in the narrow hallway.

'What do you mean?' Violet could hear Flip's cries getting louder; they were high-pitched and filled with real rage now.

'She's . . .'

Violet looked up the stairs towards Flip's bedroom.

'Go and get 'im, then. My grandson. I'd like to see 'im.'

She was torn. She didn't want to leave her father standing

in the hallway by himself, wanted to keep an eye on him. But she couldn't let Flip keep crying like that; he was hardly taking breath between each scream now. He would make himself sick soon.

She went to her son. Flip was standing in his cot, his fists curled tight around the bars, and his puce face stained with tears. She lifted him out and laid him against her shoulder, where he sobbed great wracking sobs that expanded his chest and broke her heart. She rocked him from side to side. 'Shh . . . Mama's here, my man, my little man, Mama's here. Too ra loo ra loo ra lay . . .' The rhyme soothed him and he quieted.

'That's what we always used to sing to you. Do you remember?'

Violet spun around. Her father was standing in the doorway. 'Get out! Get out of here!'

He stepped back. 'May. I'm your daddy. I'm not going to hurt him.'

His face was sad. She took a breath. Maybe she was being too harsh.

'Come on. Come downstairs.'

In the kitchen, she put the kettle on and prepared a bottle for Flip, who was still giving lurching sobs every so often, as if to remind her of his upset. Her father lit a cigarette.

'She got the flu. It was bad – real bad.'

She nodded. 'But she's better now?'

'No. It got worse, it turned into . . .' He paused. 'Into – ach, you know I'm no good with words.'

'What, pneumonia?'

He inhaled, and turned to look out of the window. 'That's the one.'

Violet shifted Flip to her other hip. 'Well, what does the doctor say?'

'He says . . .' Jimmy paused.

'Well?'

'He . . .'

'Violet? Hey, guess what happened today? I was offered—'

Violet and Jimmy both turned towards the door. Bryce entered, putting his battered brown leather satchel on the floor as he did so and at the same time taking in the scene before him.

'Oh.'

Violet watched as the two men stared at each other. Jimmy slowly exhaled a thin stream of cigarette smoke. Bryce's eyes crinkled at the edges. Finally, she broke the silence.

'Maggie's sick. Dad was just telling me.'

Bryce moved slowly towards her, his hands in his pockets, studiously calm.

'I sure am sorry to hear that, Mr Gribbens. I trust she's making a good recovery.'

Jimmy shook his head. His mouth had twisted into an uneven line. He had never liked the way Bryce spoke. Too fancy for his own good.

'Well, no, she isn't.'

Bryce was by Violet now, and he reached forward and took Flip from her.

'I was telling May, she's ever so bad. Can't breathe at night. You can hear her wheezing from the other room. Have you a drop of whisky, May? I get upset talking about it.'

'We don't keep liquor in the house, Mr Gribbens.'

'I wasn't asking you,' Jimmy spat back. 'May?'

She sighed. 'I don't have any. There's some sherry in the cupboard over there. I – Bryce calls me Violet now. I prefer to be called Violet.'

She was expecting an argument, but Jimmy just shrugged and poured the sherry. Saw Bryce watching him. Topped the cup up, and raised it to him. 'Cheers. You should join me.'

'I don't drink.'

'No. Course you don't.'

Jimmy's face was mocking as he stared at the young man holding his son. The meaning under the words was clear. Real men drank. Violet interjected again, pulling a chair out and sitting at the table, placing herself in between the two men.

'Look, tell me about Maggie. Do you need money for the doctor? Because I'm sure we can help.'

'It's not the money I've come for, May. It's you. You're my daughter. We need you to come home. We need your help. Maggie needs your help.'

'Absolutely not,' Bryce said firmly. 'Violet has responsibilities here. She left home – we left – for a reason.'

Jimmy's fist hit the table and he stood up. 'She left because you'd knocked her up. She left in bloody disgrace, tail between her legs, pregnant at sixteen. Shameful.'

'So why would you want her back home?' Bryce's voice was cold. Hearing Violet, whom he loved so, talked about like that, by her own father, made him furious. Violet was his family now, his wife, though they were not yet married, and he would stand by her.

'I'm not bloody well talking to you, boy,' Jimmy snarled. 'Look after yer baby, like a good lad. Leave me to talk to me daughter.'

Bryce drew himself up tall, and handed Flip back to Violet, who sat him on her lap. The baby was happily sucking his fingers now, oblivious to the tension in the room that had risen like a thick winter mist between the warring members of his family. His father, his mother, his grandfather, all facing each other down around the small plastic table, all afraid and angry and defensive all at once.

'I want her home because we need her there. Ach, come on, what do you care? You should be glad to get rid of her. No more responsibility for you. Knock her up, send her back home, go off back to America and forget about it all. It's not as though you're married.'

'We will be.' Bryce rested his hand on Violet's shoulder. 'We're to be married in a fortnight.' And he could not keep the pride and excitement from his voice. Violet patted his hand.

Jimmy laughed. 'Well, well. Dragging the whole thing out, aren't we?' Mocking. Cruel. 'Ah well. Maybe Maggie'll be all right. She probably doesn't need everything the doctor said, anyway.'

Violet pressed her fingers over her eyes and pushed down on them until she saw pink and orange circles but still the tears seeped out. She couldn't do this. How could she ignore the plight of Maggie, her little sister?

'I'll come.'

She felt Bryce's big hand on her shoulder.

'No, Violet,' he said softly. He knew how hard she had fought to escape. He was the one who comforted her in the night, when she woke and sat bolt upright, still inside a dream, sweat running down her back and her eyes alert, looking like an animal ready to run. He was the one who held her when she cried. He knew that the dreams had faded in the last few weeks and she was finally beginning to feel free, and he knew how easily she could be pulled back into the darkness.

'Will you stop interfering in things you don't understand?'

Jimmy was round the other side of the table, in front of Bryce. They faced each other down, a few feet between them.

'Bryce . . .'

'She knows her duty, always has done.'

Bryce looked at Violet, her face crumpled, her loyalties being torn in two. 'Violet, you're not going.'

She looked up him, unsure whether to feel grateful or worried by this sudden show of strength.

'If you can't protect yourself then I'm going to have to do it for you. It's *my* duty.'

He pulled himself up tall, and suddenly Violet saw how young, how terribly young he was, they both were, and felt an awful pang of guilt. He was a boy, and he was having to pretend he was a man, and it was her fault. She had brought him here.

Jimmy rounded on him.

'What business is it of yours?' He whistled through gritted teeth. 'What right have you got to fiddle around in my family's business? Yer may've got my slut of a daughter knocked up, but that doesn't mean anything in my book. Get back to your desk, boy, and leave us alone.'

His face was red and vicious, the blood pumping beneath it, angrily pulsating. Suddenly Violet understood what it meant when people said their blood was up.

'Maggie's sick, May, she's so sick. We need you. Maggie needs you,' Jimmy continued, taking another swig of his drink. He ground his cigarette out in a saucer on the table and lit another one.

'Please don't . . .'

'What?' He rounded on Bryce, arm outstretched, and as he spun around, the cigarette caught one of Flip's curls. There was a brief sizzle and the acrid smell of frazzled hair filled the room. Violet cried out and scooped Flip up, and backed away with him into the corner of the kitchen.

'Oh! You could have burned him!'

She checked the baby's face, which was unharmed.

Jimmy covered his shame with defiance. 'Well, I didn't fuckin' burn 'im, did I?'

Violet stared at him. 'Get out. Get out of here!'

'I'll get out, but I'm taking you with me.'

He made a move towards Violet, who cowered into the

corner, shielding her son with her arms and shoulder. Jimmy stretched his arm out to her but Bryce moved in between them.

'Don't you dare touch her.' His grey eyes were flinty and he broadened his shoulders.

'You can't stop me, you Yankee queer. I'm taking my daughter and my grandson, and you can—'

Jimmy was stopped by the thud of Bryce's fist connecting with his jaw. His head spun back and he staggered, lurching away. For a moment everyone in the room was still, stunned by the action; awaiting the reaction. Bryce held his hand up near his chest, as if it was unattached to the rest of his body. Violet covered Flip's head with her hand. She would have run out of the room with him, but she was trapped in the corner behind Bryce. She wasn't going to push past him and Jimmy to get out. She had seen her father's temper before. Flip breathed quietly against her. It felt like waiting for a volcano to erupt.

And then it did.

With a great roar, Jimmy rushed forward at Bryce, knocking him off his feet and down on to the floor. They fell in a pile with a great thump, and Violet gasped. They tussled, a knot of arms and fists as they struggled to gain dominance, and Violet was scared, scared for Flip and scared for herself. She screamed and turned in towards the chimney-breast and tried to hide herself and her son in the safety of the nook of the wall.

She heard the grunts of the two men, her father and her fiancé as they fought, and then a yelp, a groan, and she kept her eyes tight closed and whispered a lullaby to Flip.

'Too ra loo ra loo ral, too ra loo ra li, too ra loo ra loo ral, hush now, don't you cry . . .'

But Flip wasn't the one who was crying. It was Violet, and someone else as well, now. A wailing, keening sound came from her right, and she forced herself to open her eyes and turn around to the middle of the room.

'Oh God.'

It was Jimmy who was crying. He was sitting, slumped against the wall, his knees drawn up and between them, in his hands, a short knife. Bryce lay on his back on the floor, one hand up by his face. Blood ran from his stomach, down the side of his body, the pool of it beside his body growing. Jimmy looked up at Violet with the face of a child who has been caught misbehaving and is regretting it, too late. His eyes were pools of red in the red of his face. Everything was red, she thought. Red blood, red face, red eyes.

'I'm sorry, May. Oh Jesus. I'm sorry.'

Dying was noisier than she had known. It had been a few minutes before Bryce had actually died. For a second, when she opened her eyes and saw the horror in front of her she had stood, frozen, staring at her sobbing father and her bleeding fiancé. And then she had reacted. Taken Flip up to his bedroom and put him in his cot with some toys, kissing him on the forehead and whispering, 'I'll be back soon, be good,' and running back downstairs again. When she got to the kitchen, her father had gone.

Bryce's motionless body had lain on the floor and she knelt beside him and tried to press the wound in his chest together with tea towels, her cardigan, anything she could find. It didn't work. The blood flowed relentlessly through everything and in the end she gave up. He was dying, she could see that. There was too much blood outside of his body for him to survive this. And so she sat on the floor next to him and held his hand, the big, strong hand of the boy who had bought her hot chocolate and taken her dancing, who had kissed her so sweetly and had made her believe in a life outside Belton, who had, inadvertently, got her pregnant but who had stood by her, who had never thought of doing anything other than standing by her, and who had now got himself killed doing so. Violet watched as he drew his last breaths, which rasped fearfully in his chest. It was a dreadful, violent noise. She had thought dying would be quiet – people talked about loved ones 'slipping away' – but Bryce didn't slip into death, he gurgled and spat into it.

Part of her wished she had never met him. Or at least, she wished that when she had met him she had turned away, had followed her instincts. Because she had known, hadn't she, somewhere deep inside, that he was too good for her. She should have stopped him, like she stopped him following her that day on the promenade, should have held her hands against his chest until he turned away and not been swayed by his big eyes and his sweet, freckled face, and his gentleness. It was her fault. But he was the one who had paid the price.

She waited. Bryce didn't speak before he died. She had half been expecting him to open his eyes, or to whisper something. But he didn't. He just took one final, slow, laboured breath – and then, didn't.

Violet had no idea what to do next. She didn't cry. Just sat next to him, paralysed by the enormity of what had already happened and what she knew would happen next. There would be police, statements, forms. Would she be arrested? Would they think she had killed him? They would have to take him away. Would there be doctors? Who was in charge of removing bodies? How did people know things like this? How did other people know what to do?

She couldn't go out into the street like this. Her clothes were covered in Bryce's sticky blood. It was in the lines in the palm of her hand, it was under her nails, it stained her shirt. Everyone would know. They were going to know before long, weren't they? She couldn't sit here for ever. She had to do something.

In the end, she washed her hands and face in the kitchen

sink and put her coat on over her blood-stained clothes. She thought it would look suspicious when the police came if she had changed completely. She wondered, for a moment, how she could even be thinking like that. Was it strange that she was worrying about being accused of killing her fiancé? Should she be weeping and wailing and rushing out into the street to call for help? Strange or not, she buttoned up her coat then picked up Flip and walked quickly with him on her hip to the phone box by World's End, keeping her head down and hoping she didn't see anyone she knew.

When she got there, she hesitated for a moment. The Gribbenses didn't call the police. Travellers stuck together, sorted out their own problems. Cleaned up their own mess. In the cold damp of the phone box, her baby on her hip, Violet thought of the mess that she had been left with, the mess of Bryce's body and the blood everywhere, and began to cry. She could not clean up this mess by herself. She picked up the handset, and dialled.

Violet was drowning. She could feel it – a creeping certainty that life was rising up to swallow her once more. It was like being back in her childhood; once more she would wake at night unable to breathe, her hands scrabbling in front of her, her skin cold with sweat. She would blink in the darkness, wondering what had woken her for a second – but only a second, because then she would remember. The images would rise up in front of her, nightmarish, muddled in her still half-sleep. Her father staring at his hands like something out of a play, melodramatic, frozen, stuck. Bryce crumpled on the floor, blood everywhere, his pale-blue shirt, normally so perfectly pressed, covered in grime and blood and torn by the knife that had ripped through it.

And all the time, she was haunted. Haunted by the death of

Bryce, and the memory of her father sliding the knife in between his ribs. Haunted by what she had seen, and what she had lost.

It was as though he was in the very walls of the house where she had once felt so safe. It struck her as strange that someone whose voice was so quiet in life could be so very loud in death. She heard him as she lay in bed at night, the gentle murmur of his lips as he read over his notes from the day as he did every night before going to sleep, in an attempt to 'make them stick' overnight. She heard him in Flip's bedroom, telling his son stories about his childhood on the farm, and all the things they would see and do together when Flip was older. She heard him when she came in the front door, calling out to her, pleased that she was home. And most of all, worst of all, she heard him in the kitchen. Whistling to himself as he made tea or boiled water for eggs. Sighing happily and smacking his lips when she put a plate of food down in front of him. Standing up to her father, protecting his family. 'Don't you dare touch her.'

Dying.

Death was messy. It wasn't just the blood, it was everything else. It was the specks of dirt on the floor that Violet should have swept up earlier that Bryce was suddenly lying in when he fell. It was the black, greasy smears that always covered her father's sleeves and hands that were transferred to Bryce's skin and clothes in an exchange that seemed strangely intimate to Violet, and desperately unfair. Why should her father get to mark Bryce in this way, as he had done to her and her siblings? Taint him, even in his death. Bryce's goodness, the clean smell of his skin and hair didn't get left on her father. There was no fair exchange in this transaction.

And then, almost as if he knew she was awake and thinking of his dead father, as if the images were seeping from her head into his, Flip would start crying in his Moses basket, and she would get up and hold him close, taking him into her bed with her and whispering to him while they waited for the morning light to break over London.

The city, once again, was the only thing that kept her sane. She spent her days walking around London as she had when she and Bryce had first arrived in the city, as she made it her home by pacing its streets and letting their life seep into her and bearing her back to herself. Pregnant, she had slowly made her way through them as she grew bigger and heavier and had to go slower and slower. She had become rooted there, as she walked, she and Flip, tied to the streets of London: they had become part of their history. She had named Flip walking down these streets – he had been facing the wrong way in her womb and the midwife had told her they'd have to 'pull him out of the sunroof if he didn't flip himself round'. She spent hours pacing, willing the baby to 'flip, come on, Baby, flip', so when she went into labour and they found that he had indeed flipped himself the right way up, she had known right away that that was what she would call him. Philip, shortened to Flip.

Then, after Flip was born, she had pushed him through Chelsea and Kensington and the parks, talking quietly to him as they went, pointing out trees and buses and lamp-posts, palaces and gates and lakes. All the things that made London, London. And now, she walked again. Her progress was slower these days as Flip tended to insist on walking rather than being pushed, so they went on their meandering way together, her son stopping every few steps to pick up and examine a small stone, or to try and eat a worm; through the corridors of the V&A, Violet feeding her imagination and soothing her soul with the acres of beauty contained within the old building; down the wide avenue of the Mall to watch the Changing of the Guard and so Flip could laugh at the men in their bearskin hats. All the time, thinking, thinking, thinking. Gathering ideas, making plans.

And all the time, she had Bryce's drawing of her salon in her pocket, sitting close to her, giving her comfort. Giving her something to walk towards. The piece of paper, folded small, contained her dreams, her heart, her future. She would make it happen. She had to make it happen.

As she walked, she gathered strength once more. She began to feel as though she could cope: that, one day, she would make it out of the darkness. Her father was gone, who knew where, sucked down into the network of travellers and friends and acquaintances who had found her, who lived in the shadows, unregistered, unnoticed by most people, invisible. But they were there; Violet could see them. She had lived amongst them. She would see them as she walked, lurking in alleyways, drinking in the corners of pubs. She turned her head away, and walked. Walked, walked, walked on. She was not of that life any longer.

As she walked, she planned. She would get a job. And she knew where she wanted to work. Madame Fournier's salon in Mount Street.

She would walk past it, trundling Flip along the well-kept pavement, hoping to see a sign in the window, a handwritten note in elegant script maybe, saying *Help Wanted*. There never was. And she didn't quite have the courage to go in and ask. Not with her worn coat and her baby in a buggy. Why would they employ her? Madame Fournier could have her pick of young, elegant girls to work in her salon, girls whose hair was glossy and who wouldn't have to worry about getting home to pick up the baby from the minder. But still, she walked past the shop every day, and hoped and dreamed. She had enough money for a few more months, from Bryce's savings. By then, she would have put her plans into action, would be back on her feet, would have Flip weaned and settled with Ginny down the road who looked after other mums' children, along with her own, and who had Flip sometimes now. She had been the one who had looked after Flip the day after the murder, when Violet had been at the police station.

She shuddered to remember that day. She'd been there for hours, in a tiny room with two hard chairs either side of a table, sitting and telling them everything. All about her father. Her childhood, her background, when she had come to London and why, when she had got pregnant, when and where she had had the baby. Everything. Right up to when she had opened the door and seen him standing on the step in front of her, right up to the terrible sound that had made her open her eyes and turn around, and what she saw and how she had felt when she came back downstairs after it happened and saw that her father had disappeared. And that was the hardest bit somehow, the fact that he had made this enormous mess and had just gone, abandoned her to clean it up. Of course he had, of course he wouldn't have stayed – what did she expect, that he would stay while Bryce died and hold her hand and turn himself in? But still, the betrayal sliced into her. It was not just Bryce who had been cut deep by Jimmy's knife.

Violet was scared to tell them that it was Jimmy who had done it. Not just because he was her father but because of who he was, the sort of man he was. Whatever he had done, no matter the fact that he was guilty as sin and had brought it on his own head, he would blame her for telling, she knew that. You didn't grass, especially not on your family. On your blood.

But Violet had meant it when she had told him he was not her family any more, and so she told.

And then the letters started.

The first letter had arrived the day that Violet and Flip were due to move out of their little house, and into their new home, a small flat in Edith Street, almost a month after Bryce's death. Her present landlord had turned up on the doorstep as Violet was getting ready to leave. He had made his feelings very clear about the inconvenience of the situation.

'Middle of the month and a murder in the place. 'Ow am I supposed to let the place to anyone now, eh?'

Violet had just stared at him. He had had the sense to shut up then, at least, though his doleful eyes had continued to convey his discomfort. She had spent all day cleaning the place, including the floor where Bryce's blood had stained the cork tiles.

However hard she had scrubbed at the stain, it had not been enough.

'They'll 'ave to be replaced, all of 'em,' the landlord had reminded her. 'It'll take up all yer deposit money.'

She had sighed, and picked up Flip. There was no point arguing with the man. She would just have to start again. Before he left, he handed her a pile of post in a rubber band.

'I shan't be forwarding any more,' he said. 'Yer'll have to come and pick it up if anything else comes.'

Violet flicked through the envelopes. Bills, mostly. Something addressed to Bryce, a letter from his college, that made her catch her breath when she saw his name printed on the outside. And then there were two other letters, her name and address written in a familiar, round hand. The letter to Bryce had come as a shock, but these took the wind out of her.

Dear May,

Your brother has disappeared, run off with your father. Me and Maggie are here at home. I do not know where your father and brother have gone. Jimmy came back late one night in a terrible state. He wouldn't tell me anything about what had happened. In the morning he and Mattie were both gone. Then the police came and told me what had happened with Bryce. They are looking for your father but they won't find him easy. If you know where he is you should keep quiet. I don't know what will happen to me and Maggie now. Maggie is still very sick. I'm not well and can't work easy. And when I can get to work there is no one to look after her now. If your father goes down there will be no one.

Violet sat on the bottom stair, the memories flooding back of that day. Her father had been standing just in front of the spot she sat in now. She could almost smell his tobacco-y, tarry smell still. And then Bryce had come in, with his easy smile and his long arms that he would wrap around her. Her eyes filled up and she blinked, and then she opened the next letter.

Violet, the police came again today. They say they have found your father and taken him to the jail. He is going to stand trial for the murder of Bryce, which I know he did not do. He may not be a good man, but he is no murderer. You know that and I know it as well.

Violet threw that letter down, without finishing reading it. The writing was scrawled across the page, uneven. Violet could see her mother writing it now, drunk, self-pitying. 'He is, Mum,' she whispered to herself. 'I'm sorry. But he is.'

'Do you, May Violet Gribbens, swear to tell the truth, the whole truth and nothing but the truth, so help you God?'

'I do.'

The days that Violet spent in court, giving evidence against her father, passed in a haze. She was taken through her statement, through everything that had happened on the day of Bryce's murder and afterwards, and all the time she was aware of her father's dark eyes on her, hating her, willing her to stop. She didn't stop. She carried on. Told the court about the notes, which had continued to come through her letterbox, never with a clue as to where they came from or who had delivered them. About how they got angrier and the threats inside got worse and worse. About how she feared for her life, in the end, and that of her son. She told them how relieved she had been when the police had come to her door and told her they had tracked her father down and arrested him, and how guilty it had made her feel to think that.

She told them how the notes carried on coming, even then, with him insisting that he hadn't meant to kill her fiancé, that it had been an accident, that she was to tell the police that, and that if she did so, everything would be all right. And she told them how she knew it hadn't been an accident, how the knife, which had long disappeared and was no doubt deep at the bottom of the Thames by now, was a folding one that had to be flicked open. Jimmy would never have it loose in his pocket. She described the sound that she had heard as the knife went into her husband, the twisting sound of it, and what she had seen when she opened her eyes – how her father had stared up at her with blood on his hands and guilt in his eyes and how, just a couple of minutes later, he had been gone.

'Could it not be that he ran for exactly these reasons?' the defence lawyer had asked. 'Because he knew that, as a member of the travelling community who are, let us not forget, regularly discriminated against, the finger of suspicion would be pointed at him? Because he is not an educated man, and was afraid that that would be used against him? Can we not believe that he apologised to his daughter not because he was guilty but, on the contrary, precisely because he was *innocent*? Is it so hard to believe that a man who has accidentally killed his future son-in-law would be sorry for that?'

The jury members had scribbled notes on their pads of paper and Violet had shaken her head.

'I know my father,' she had whispered.

She had had to describe other occasions when he had been violent, go over rows she had seen him have with her mother where they had come to blows. Moira was not in court. She would not give evidence against her husband. There had been one final letter, just before the trial.

I am asking you, May, as your mother, who still loves you despite everything and wants the best for her family, do not stand up in court and tell everyone that your father is a murderer and your brother his accomplice. Do not do it if you have any love left for me or for any of us, including Maggie. If you do then I can no longer call you my daughter.

Violet felt the fingers of her family reaching out to her, calling her. But she knew that if she let them, they would pull her down again, and that this time, with no Bryce by her side, she would not escape. So she stood firm. She looked at Flip, his big eyes and his dark curls, and the freckles that were appearing across his nose, and she kissed him, and went off to court, Bryce's drawing still safely in her pocket. It felt like her talisman. Every day, she kissed her son goodbye, then got the bus to the court, and she stood up in front of her father and all of the people in the courtroom, and she told them everything that had happened, and then she went home and cried herself to sleep. She knew that every day she did this, she was breaking any and all remaining ties to her family, snapping them like brittle twigs, and as she did so she felt nothing but overwhelming relief and overwhelming sadness.

And then suddenly, one day, it was all over.

'Guilty,' said the foreman of the jury, and Jimmy Gribbens

let out a great roar of rage and despair that brought tears to Violet's eyes despite herself.

The court adjourned for the judge to deliberate. Violet sat in the small room where she had been taken to wait, sipping tea that she didn't want to drink, while he did so.

When they went back in, the room was quiet apart from the sound of reporters' pens moving across their notepads.

'James Gribbens, on the count of the charge of the murder of Bryce Hawthorn for which you have been found guilty, I will pronounce sentence in a few moments.' A scuffling and a murmur rippled through the room as people reacted. 'But first, I wish to explain the sentence that I am about to hand down and the reasons for the decision that I have come to. Mr Gribbens, the severity of your initial crime was great, let there be no doubt. You killed a man, and that is crime enough itself for the most stringent punishment. But the fact that the victim was your future son-in-law, and that your own daughter, your own flesh and blood, was sure enough of your guilt and afraid enough of your future actions to testify against you as she has done, with great bravery and strength of character, I might add' – here he turned his watery, metal-rimmed eyes to Violet and smiled at her benignly – 'increases the severity of the crime to one that must not be underestimated. Added to this,' he continued, 'once the act had been committed you did not hand yourself in to the police, nor even remain to face the consequences of your actions and help your daughter cope with the aftermath of what you had done.'

The judge's voice displayed genuine anger and outrage now.

'You left your daughter alone in the house with her dying fiancé and infant son. And then you ran . . .'

He paused and shook his head.

'And so, Mr Gribbens, for the reasons outlined previously and because it is my belief that your family, as well as the public at large, will be safer with you behind bars, I hereby sentence you to the mandatory life sentence for murder – without the possibility of parole at a future date.'

Jimmy's head was in his hands. His back shook. The court was agog. The judge banged his gavel. 'Quiet. Mr Gribbens, is there anything you wish to say?'

Jimmy lifted his head and then shook it. He raised himself to his feet wearily, as if his limbs were filled with concrete, not blood. The wardens began to lead him out towards the doors, his hands cuffed in front of him. And then he paused for a moment and looked towards the judge.

'Your Honour. Can I ask one thing?'

The judge raised his eyebrows, then motioned to the ushers. 'Go on.'

'I know it's not usual, but can I say one thing to my daughter, before I go down? I know she won't come and visit me. I don't expect her to. I don't expect to ever see her again. I'd like to say sorry.'

'And so you have.'

'I'd like to say goodbye, Your Honour?' Jimmy motioned to where Violet sat.

The judge shook his head. 'I don't think it's appropriate.'

Violet spoke. 'I'd like to hear what my father has to say, sir. If you'll allow it.'

The judge pursed his lips 'Very well.'

The officers walked either side of Jimmy, and he stood in front of Violet where she sat, hands in her lap.

'May.'

'Violet.'

'You'll always be May to me. To us.'

She didn't speak. He leaned forward, and his voice dropped to a whisper. 'You betrayed me, and you'll pay for it, I swear to you. You'll never escape. You've done a deal with the devil,

May Violet Gribbens – blood betraying blood begets blood. You're cursed. You remember that.'

She recoiled in her seat, and the judge snapped, 'That's enough. Take him away. Miss Gribbens, are you all right?'

She nodded. But her father's words rang in her ears. '*Blood betraying blood begets blood.*'

After the trial, Violet tried to carry on as normal. Or whatever normal was now, for a young woman who was still a teenager, who was already a single mother, a widow, and now, the daughter of a murderer. She got up every morning, cared for Flip, went to work at the part-time job she had got in the shop around the corner, selling newspapers and fags and chocolate bars, made ends meet in the way she had always done, the way she had learned back in Belton. By stretching, scrimping, saving. Cutting and pasting. Back in Belton.

She tried to put all memories of her family out of her mind. There was no point in dwelling on the past, she told herself. She had a new family now, albeit a tiny one, and she had to make a new life for herself and Flip. It was what she had wanted. An escape. And she had got it. But something kept pulling her mind back. *Maggie.*

Her mother's words about Maggie had touched her conscience, echoing through her mind as she changed Flip's nappies, and fed him, and pulled his little trousers up around his fat, dimpled knees. All things she had once done for Maggie. *She's sick . . . I can't look after her easy.* She could not abandon her to the fate that Violet knew awaited her with Moira. A childhood spent listening to her mother crying into her drink, of poverty, of grimy, grinding misery. Violet might not have much, but what she had was hers; earned not stolen, clean not smeared with grease. She could give her sister a better life. She had to go back to Belton, to the place that she had escaped from and to which she had vowed never to return, for Maggie. To get Maggie.

Violet shut the front door of her parents' flat behind her, and stood in the hall for a moment. It stank, a thin, watery smell of cabbage, maybe. Of neglect. The air in the hallway was cold and damp.

She jogged Flip on her hip, shh-ing him, and went through to the kitchen. The tiny room was also cold, empty of food or people or warmth. The sink was full of dirty plates, with a couple of inches of brown water at the bottom.

'Jesus.'

She looked around. Black grease was caked on to the hob, and the surfaces were sticky with grime. The remnants of a sandwich lay on the table. She prodded the bread. It was crumbly and stale, with mould around the edges. But someone had taken a bite out of it, even so. Someone with a small mouth.

It was worse than she could have imagined. Violet left the kitchen and walked back through the lounge towards the hall. Dirty washing lay in a pile on the floor. Moira's sewing machine stood on a table in the corner, a pile of unfinished work next to it.

Violet trod carefully, quietly.

'Mum?' she called out. She didn't think anyone was there. Had watched for a while before letting herself in with the key that she had taken with her. There had been no signs of life from the place. She would have been too scared to just walk in like that if her father had still been there. But he was in jail. Safely behind bars, she told herself. But still, she woke in the night, sometimes, imagining she heard the tread of his footsteps on the stairs. Still, when someone knocked at the door, she hesitated before opening it, checking the spyhole that she had had installed, making sure the thick chain was on tight if it was dark and she was unable to see out. Violet still looked over her shoulder as she went about her business. She was used to it.

Mattie wasn't here either. She had lurked in the alley before braving her old family home, had heard someone talking about him over the fence to a neighbour.

'Hasn't been seen for weeks,' they said.

'Gone the way of 'is father, and no surprise. Mending on the road? Thieving, more like. Dirty money, the only pennies they see now.'

'Shame. Moira used to be a good dressmaker once.'

'Before the drink.'

'Ay. Before that.'

So Mattie was still thieving. And her mother was still drinking. It came as no surprise, but it killed the tiny shard of hope that Violet still held in her heart. She steeled herself. All the more reason to get Maggie out of there.

In the bedroom, Moira's solid form was discernible beneath dirty sheets. She lay still. Violet stood in the doorway, her nostrils full of unwashed linen and something worse. She took a step closer.

Just then, her mother groaned and turned over, her body rolling across the bed like an enormous, seamy wave.

Violet took a step back. 'Mum,' she whispered, hardly able to bring herself to call the woman in front of her by that name.

Moira's voice was croaky as she pushed herself up on her arms and tried to focus on Violet. She was a mess. Her hair fell in thin stands by her pale, puffy cheeks, and her breath stank of gin.

'Get me a glass of water.'

Violet looked at her in shock. Moira's eyes hardly registered her at all. Didn't show any surprise at Violet's presence, or Flip's. Violet pulled her baby closer to her.

'Where's Maggie?'

'I got the flu. I need some water,' she said again.

'I'll get you some when you tell me. Where's Maggie?'

Moira closed her eyes, leaned her head back against the wall and shrugged.'Don't know.'

Violet leaned forward and slapped her on the cheek, hard. Her mother's head lolled to one side.

'You're not flipping sick, you're drunk.'

'I'm sick. Ask the doctor. He came – gave me some pills.'

Violet looked on the bedside table. There was a small brown pill bottle next to the bed. She picked it up and checked the label. 'It's empty.'

Moira shook her head. 'No . . . he only came yesterday. I've not had many. Due for another now, I reckon.' She held her hand out. Violet knocked it away, and left the room.

'Maggie? Maggie, sweetie, it's OK. It's only May. Where are you, darling?'

Violet shifted Flip to her other hip. He was heavy, wriggling, but she refused to put him down in this filth.

'Maggie? Come on, sweetpea.' Violet pushed open the door to Maggie's little box room, and what she saw made her gasp.

'Oh no. Oh no, Maggie.'

She knew straight away. Just as she had known with Bryce. The girl lay, tucked up in her little bed, under a quilt, her hair in dirty ringlets around her face. Violet knelt, balancing Flip on her knee, and gently pulled the covering back.

'Oh my baby girl.' She was dressed in a ragged cotton dress, one that Violet remembered making for her. It had a little bow that tied at the back, that Maggie always liked Violet to tie for her so it was stiff and stuck out. Around her neck was the crucifix Violet had put on her, only a few months ago, and which she now reached down and removed, holding the thin bit of metal in her hand as she wept. And next to

Maggie, on the grubby pillowcase, were the remains of Moira's valium.

Hearing how his father had died, in such pain, had shaken Flip to the core. Violet watched him as he let the story sink in, absorbing the horror of it. Wishing she did not have to tell it to him. Knowing that she did. Reliving it had exhausted Violet. She had gone through it all again as she told her family where they really came from, feeling once again the fear, the guilt, the grief. Remembering the smell of the flat where she had found Maggie . . . She shivered, and touched the crucifix bearing the three initials M. V. G. She needed to sleep. But first, she must face the last surviving member of her family. Her children had quietly melted away, shocked by what they had heard, kissing her and disappearing in different directions, all lost in their own thoughts. She sat, looking out to sea, and waited for her brother to arrive.

Brother and sister faced one another now, for the first time in decades. Violet looked at Mattie closely, her eyes scouring his face. It was rugged, hard, scarred. His eyes flickered around him quickly, taking everything in. His body was solid, taut: he looked ready to spring.

'Why are you here?' she asked him.

He shrugged.

'Why now?' Violet persisted. His eyes were so shifty, she thought. The boy she had once known was long gone.

'Someone told me . . .'

'Told you what?'

'That you were dying.'

Violet gave a little gasp that she quickly covered. *You're dying*. The words never lost their power. But she did not want Mattie to see the effect they had on her. She stared at him. Would she have recognised him, if she had passed him in the street? There was something in the eyes . . . but maybe that was just the resentment that was directed at her now, the old, familiar fury that she remembered so well.

'*Who* told you? Who *found* you? Hardly anyone knows that I'm . . . ill. Only two people know, or knew before today. They wouldn't have told you. They didn't even know you existed.'

'A friend. It doesn't matter, does it?'

'Yes, of course it matters. It matters a lot. I need to know who betrayed me. I need to know who I can't trust. I run a big business and—'

He sneered. 'Oh yes, we all know how important you are. What a big deal Violet Cavalley is. I've been watching you, you know.'

'So why didn't you come before now? Why wait? You could have got money from me, if you knew who I really was. You wouldn't have been the first.'

Mattie stared at her. 'You're not the only one who wanted to escape the past.' His voice was cold. 'Do you think it was easy for me, growing up, either? He expected you to go. Could always see you would, one day. You were always different. But me? He expected me to follow in his footsteps. Become like him.' Her brother's mouth was twisted.

'It wasn't my fault, you know. None of it.' As she said it, Violet knew it was true. Her childhood had not been her fault. Mattie's childhood, Maggie's – the pain they had all suffered and endured – it had not been her fault. As a child she had thought it must be – all children do, don't they? And as the eldest, she had felt it even more keenly. Her mother had ground it into her enough times, after all, with words and with actions. 'If only I'd never had you, I could still have got away, I could have been someone, been happy . . .' The words still hurt her, even now, at the age of sixty. She, May Gribbens, as she was then, had been the tether that had kept her mother trapped with her father, that had meant she stayed, and wept, and raged, and had Mattie, and Maggie, and all that had ensued . . . But no. She was not May Gribbens. Not any longer. And none of it had been that child's fault.

'Mattie . . .' Violet began.

'Matt. It's Matt. Like I said, you weren't the only one who wanted to leave the past in the past.'

For a moment, Violet thought that she had been wrong. Maybe Mattie – Matt – had changed. Had managed to slip through the clutches of their family, slip through their father's fingers. After all, she had done so – why not him as well?

'But now you're here, so presumably you changed your mind – about leaving the past in the past, I mean.'

He smiled, and the old Mattie returned. 'Well, I decided if you weren't going to be around for much longer, that I should make sure I got what I'm entitled to.'

'Entitled to? You're not "entitled" to anything. No one is. Cavalley's is mine. I'll leave it to whomsoever I choose. And I can tell you now that it won't be you. I have no ties to you, Matt. I owe you nothing.' Violet's hands shook.

'I don't want your fucking business. Don't be stupid. Think I'm interested in peddling hats – in peddling anything?' He laughed. 'I've done enough of that to last me a lifetime. No, I just want an easy life. I deserve it. And we're family. You owe me, whether you like it or not.'

Violet shook her head. *No.*

'I'll tell,' Mattie said. 'I'll tell everyone what I know about you. Who you really are. If I don't get what's right, I'll make sure everyone knows you come from muck.'

Violet looked up at him. 'It's sad,' she said softly.

'What is?' he spat.

'That he's won.'

'What are you talking about?'

'Dad. You said he expected you to follow in his footsteps, and you have. You've become everything he was. A violent, lying, lazy bastard, running from responsibility, wanting the world to hand him a living on a plate. You're no good, Mattie. You're just no good.'

Her voice had become harsh and ugly, and she made herself stop. She did not sound like herself. She sounded bitter, and full of bile, and she realised to her horror that she sounded like her mother. She closed her eyes for a second. She would not do this. She would not let them win.

Violet slowly raised herself from the table and turned to leave. Before she went, she paused. Looked back at her brother.

'Tell who you like,' she said. 'I've got nothing to hide any more.'

Chapter Five

Fran sat in her seat by the window of the private jet that was taking the whole extended Cavalley family back to London, her knees curled up underneath her and a pale pink Moleskine notebook on her lap. Her hair was pushed back with a pair of vintage leopardskin-framed glasses, and she held a pencil in her hand. Her iPod played the sound of a husky-voiced woman reworking two songs into one new one, a jazzy, swinging mash-up of old and new. The familiar rhythm of Gershwin forced up alongside a 1990s grunge track until they became friends, joined together at the edges by the licks and nuzzles of the singer's voice. It was just what Fran liked; old and new, traditional and modern, everything contradictory and even jarring, and yet somehow not. If she had been the sort of girl to go to a therapist, they would have said that it reflected how she saw herself – a contradiction, a jumble of opposites that somehow sat together and made her *her*. But she knew that already; she had no need of a therapist to tell her the things she already knew.

Fran was nothing if not practical, even in her most whimsical moments. She was the girl who would be dancing at a music festival, dressed in a floppy black velvet hat from the 1970s that she had dragged out of the back of her mother's wardrobe, and one of Kalisto's trailing velvet coats that she had snaffled from his wardrobe (Kalisto, as ever, unable to refuse her anything), flowers in her hair and each toenail painted a different colour, but who would have a special pocket sewn into her underwear so she didn't lose her money and train ticket home, and who would hide a secret stash of water and baby wipes and loo roll under a bush for her and her friends to use.

'A Boy Scout Butterfly' Violet had called her once. Fran smiled at the memory. Her mother had always given her nicknames. Boy Scout Butterfly, Frantastic Frangipani, Flower of My Heart, Almond Blossom, Frangimina . . . the list went on. Fran had always rolled her eyes at her mother and told her it was 'Fran, Mama, or Frangipani if you really must,' but nothing had stopped the never-ending stream of variations on her name tripping off Violet's tongue with almost every breath, and secretly Fran had been glad.

Had she done the same with Fran's siblings – with Flip, and Blue? And with her other siblings, the ones who were like shadows in the story of her past – Scarlet and Sebastian? The Lost Ones. What had Violet called her brothers and sister, when they were little, when they were playing, or hiding from her, or sitting down to eat their dinner? Fran didn't know. Their childhoods were separate to hers, not a shared past but a previous one. She was so much younger than them. Flip and Blue had joint memories, jokes from when they were younger that meant nothing to her, looks that would pass between them, or between them and Violet, from which she was excluded. Not in a malicious way, she knew, but still . . . Somehow she was always slightly on the outside, even when she was in the midst of those closest to her.

She was realising, more and more, that there was a lot about her family that she didn't know, had never bothered to ask. She had taken a lot for granted, always assuming that Violet would be there, that Flip and Blue would be there, that things would remain the same. How stupid. But there was still time, as she had told Violet. She was just going to have to make sure that she asked the questions. Before it was too late.

It was one of the reasons why she was so pleased that Flip had got together with Tillie. Fran had always got on with her, ever since Tillie started working at Cavalley's and Violet had seemed to take her under her wing, bringing her home for supper with the rest of them sometimes, making her part of things. Tillie had shown an interest in Fran, and it had been nice to have another girl around. She would be her sister-in-law soon, Fran thought now, and was pleased at the prospect. She would be a good ally, an important one, when – when Violet wasn't around. And maybe she could help Fran with some of the things she wanted to do, some of the questions she wanted to ask. Tillie was good at knowing what to say, at manoeuvring her way through tricky situations.

She had already helped her with one. Fran had confided in her, before they left Capri, and was pleased she had done so. Tillie had been the right person to go to. Following the family meeting, she had knocked at Tillie and Flip's bedroom door, to have a private talk with her future sister-in-law. Violet was resting, and Fran couldn't have gone to her with this, anyway – not now, she told herself. She was too weak. She needed to get her strength back first.

Mattie had been despatched to the hotel where he was staying, Patrick's sharp blue eyes and anger enough to keep him at arm's length. For now, at least. Her uncle, Fran thought. But – not. She sighed. It had been bothering her for a while, the question of where she came from. Not seriously enough to do anything about it, though. Why would she rock the luxurious, cocooned boat in which she floated through life? She had everything that she could ever need; she wanted for nothing, in either material terms, or in terms of love and affection. Her family had never treated her as anything other than just that – family.

There was no question in her mind that she was a Cavalley, just as Flip and Blue were. And yet.

As she got older, Fran wondered, more and more, *Where do I come from?* Just as Violet had never talked about her own childhood, neither had she talked about Fran's birth parents. Fran had asked, once or twice, when she was younger, when watching a film with an adopted child in it, or reading a fairy story, 'Where did you get me from, Mama?' And Violet would stroke her cheek, and tell her, 'I chose you from the Beautiful Baby shop. And you were the most beautiful one there. Still are.' But she would not be drawn, and over the years, Fran had stopped asking. She hadn't needed to know. Violet was mother and father and sister and friend, her brothers were protectors and champions and playmates despite the large age gap, she was smothered with love and affection, and mostly, she forgot she was adopted unless she saw a newspaper article that referred to *Violet Cavalley, couture milliner, with her two sons and adopted daughter, Frangipani.* Violet tended to try and stop Fran from seeing those, aware that they served as a reminder of something she might not want to be reminded of, but Fran still saw them sometimes, at school in friends' magazines, or on the bus. It was one of the occupational hazards of being Violet's daughter. The family was everywhere.

But now, Violet was dying and, much as Fran wanted to deny it, her mother was not going to be around for much longer to tell her that she was the most beautiful, the chosen child, most beloved. How would she go on, Fran thought now with a terrible pang, without her mother to tell her those things? Without her there at the kitchen table, drawing, her hair wild, tied up with a ribbon or a tea towel, both as likely and both looking as glamorously, peculiarly *her*. How would she manage without Violet there to swoop down on her, some new creation in hand, demanding that Fran model it for her so she could tweak it, at midnight. Without her to suddenly announce that she was taking everyone out for lunch, the whole office, to Flip's infuriation and the secretaries' delight, and whisking them all out to take over her favourite Italian restaurant for the afternoon. How would any of them manage?

So that was why, back in Capri, she had knocked on Tillie's door and sat on the edge of their unmade bed, while Flip was pounding up and down the balcony on the phone, and told her that she needed her help. 'I need to know where I come from, because . . .'

Tillie had taken her hand. 'Because she's not going to be around for ever, and you don't want to feel alone in the world before she goes?'

Fran had nodded. That was it, that was exactly it. She felt as though there had to be an overlap, that she had to locate this other, unknown part of her family before Violet was gone, or else she would be untethered, belonging to no one. And then she might slip through the cracks. It was silly, she knew that.

'And you can't just ask her,' Tillie continued. Fran shook her head.

'I don't want to argue with her, upset her. I don't want her to feel as though she's not enough, that all of you aren't enough.'

Tillie smiled. 'Honestly, Fran. I understand. I really do.'

And Fran knew that she did. They had agreed then, that Tillie would help her, as soon as they got back to London, find out who to contact and which forms she needed to ask for. It wasn't as though Fran couldn't have done it by herself, practically speaking. Boy Scout Butterfly . . . But it wasn't something she felt she could do alone. She needed a hand to hold, and Tillie's was the right one.

Fran looked over at her now, asleep in Flip's lap, a cashmere blanket over her shoulders, while Flip read some document or other on his iPad, resting it gently on the top of her head, and she grinned. They fitted together so neatly, the two of them. Fran couldn't imagine ever fitting together with someone like that. Her contradictions meant that she was self-reliant, difficult to get to know. She had had a couple of boyfriends, but they had always complained that she 'didn't let them in', and had melted away after a while. She didn't understand what they meant. And, if she was honest with herself, she suspected that the relationships had failed, not because of anything she had done or not done, but because of her scar. They had been put off by her scar.

She sighed. It still hadn't really sunk in, the severity of her mother's illness. It was still an abstract, something that she knew and yet did not quite know in her heart. She was pushing it away, dreading the moment when reality hit. She did so again now. Pushed it away, and forced herself to focus instead on the page in front of her. It was part of her big plan, and now she was going to have to speed it up considerably. She could do it though. She knew she could. She would have to – it was crucial that her mother got to see, and enjoy, what she had created.

Fran had designed a perfume. A perfume that smelled of vanilla and roses and had a hint of frangipani, but whose strongest scent was that of violets. She had been collaborating with an old French perfume house, spending money from her trust fund on the development of it, making secret trips to Paris whenever she could. The rest of her family were so busy with all of their various projects that no one questioned what she was up to during the hours she spent with her head in a notebook or tapping away on her laptop. Fran had always been secretive, private. They just assumed that she was writing some essay for college, or studying, or that she was weekending with a boyfriend who she didn't want to talk to them about, and she had let them think it, while she carried on putting her business plan together, refining the perfume until it was absolutely perfect, and working with a glass factory to manufacture a prototype of the bottle that she had designed herself.

She stole a glimpse of the drawing inside her notebook now. It was a thick piece of smoky, deep purple glass that would sit satisfyingly in the palm of one's hand, a stopper shaped like the flower it was named after in amethyst at its head. A beautiful bottle, more jewel than vessel. Fran was proud of it. Proud of how far she had got with it all by herself, of what she had already achieved. But a pretty bottle and a lovely scent were only the start, she knew. She needed serious investment now, more than her trust fund could cover. She needed proper market research, and distribution, retail expertise and marketing experience that stretched far beyond her own instinctive ideas. She needed the network that Cavalley's offered.

And she knew it could be a success – more than a success, a sensation. The market for fragrance and cosmetics was huge, it was where many of the big fashion houses made a large chunk of their profits, which could then be ploughed back into the business, underwriting the couture side, providing capital and growth and a brand awareness far beyond anything that they could achieve even with the most successful of fashion ranges.

She just had to find the right way to approach her mother.

'I want Tillie to be involved in the business, as she is now,' Violet told Kalisto and Gerald, who sat before her in the small, jewel-coloured drawing room of her house in Slaidburn Street off the King's Road. She had bought the house when her business had first started to do well, keen to own bricks and mortar, put down roots. The Cavalley home had expanded, over the years, to fit Violet's growing family, and was now spread over two buildings that she had knocked together to make one large house. She could have moved, bought one of the smart townhouses nearer the top of the King's Road, or overlooking a private garden. But she was happy here in the scruffier end of things, in the house that had grown with and around her, and that was knitted into the very fabric of her family's life.

'Whatever happens – independently of Flip, I mean. She and Fran are close. She's a good influence on all of them. Good for the family.'

Gerald nodded and made a note. He never came out with any criticism of Violet's plans and ideas directly, never had done, during all the years that he had been advising her. But he would work his way around to raising concerns or worries in his own, deeply tactful way. He raised a finger now, as he looked through the paperwork in front of him, his pen hovering over the page.

'Very good, Violet. Of course you must divvy up, so to speak, Cavalley's and its subsidiaries as you see fit. Tell me, do you envisage that Flip and Tillie will marry imminently?'

'I hope so.'

He nodded again.

'And would you expect this to happen . . .' he paused, and his frown deepened. Poor Gerald. Violet could see he was torn between the two absolutes in his personal code of conduct – the importance of impeccable manners, and that of scrupulous diligence to his work. She decided to rescue him.

'Are you asking whether they'll marry before or after I die, Gerald?'

He made a little 'ahem' noise in his throat. 'Yes, yes indeed, the exact timing of things could have certain implications with regard to the best way to structure the document.'

'I'll talk to Flip,' Violet promised.

'Are you sure about her?' Kalisto asked, from his position leaning against the wall by the shuttered windows. He suited the room perfectly and knew it, had placed himself to maximum effect: an immensely tall figure in a broad-striped three-piece suit complete with top hat and jewel-topped cane, and polka-dotted cravat, the fabric of his necktie co-ordinating with the room's wallpaper. Dear Kalisto. A truly dedicated creator, not follower, of fashion.

'Why?' Violet asked, a little sharply.

Kalisto walked towards the fireplace and gazed at his reflection in the circular mirror above it.

'She's not family,' he said eventually.

'Neither are you, if we're talking blood,' Violet replied evenly. 'But you're more family than . . .' She trailed off. The impact of Mattie's reappearance could still be felt; his nearness was somehow palpable. She didn't have to finish the sentence. Kalisto and Gerald had known her for long enough to be able to do so in their heads.

Kalisto pointed his cane at her. 'Correct, *petite fleur de mon coeur*, but the difference is, I don't want anything of Cavalley's. Gawd only knows I have enough terrible trials with my own little endeavour.'

Violet laughed. Kalisto's 'little endeavour' was one of the most sought-after couture tailors in London. But he was right in one respect – he had never wanted the responsibility and stress of the business side of it all. Violet had bought out Kalisto's company some years ago, leaving him in place to get on with the business of making beautiful clothes.

She stood and walked over to him, taking his big face between her small hands. 'It'll be all right, Kal. I promise.'

His eyes filled with tears. His worries weren't about Tillie, or who was going to lead the business after she was gone. They were just about what he would do. After she was gone.

She kissed the end of his nose, and he laughed. 'Oh, Lady Vi. Always taking little birds under your wing, aren't you?'

Violet shrugged. 'Elizabeth Fournier did the same for me. I'll never forget that.'

*

Violet had managed to get an interview at Madame Fournier's through one of those combinations of luck and tenacity that occur every so often, when the stars are aligned, as some say, or when the time is right, or just when someone sticks at something for long enough and refuses to let go, maybe.

One day after the trial, as she was slowly passing at early evening, she overheard one of the girls talking as she came out of the shop and locked the door. Violet had walked past the shop so many times now that she had almost stopped seeing it, almost stopped looking out for a card in the window.

'Leanne's leaving?' she heard.

'Getting married, ain't she, her hubby won't let her work. Right bossy one, he is. Still, guess he can afford to be . . .'

The voices floated off down the street.

People say it was 'meant to be' or that 'everything turns out for a reason,' but Violet didn't believe any of that. Things became 'meant to be' only if you made them so.

As she stood in the street outside Madame Fournier's salon in Mayfair, she felt a little thrill run through her.

'The best milliner in the country,' Violet whispered to herself now, remembering Miss Hankins's words as she prepared to ring the goldplated bell by the glass door. She looked at her reflection. She was wearing her old coat and worn, unpolished shoes. Her hair was dull and ratty, and her skin pale. She hadn't worn rouge or mascara for weeks. 'Violet,' she whispered to herself. 'You've let yourself go.' She could not go in like this. She looked down at Flip, gurgling in his pram.

'Right, Flip Cavalley Hawthorn. Come along. We've got work to do. We'd better hurry if we're going to get to the market on time.'

The next morning, Violet stood outside the door once more, this time feeling as though she deserved to be there. She gazed at herself in the mirror and saw a very different person staring back at her. Gone were the worn clothes and neglected hair. The little, dark-haired figure staring back at her wore a russet-coloured coat that she had made herself, on an old sewing machine borrowed from a neighbour. It was simple, but the darting and pleats at the back provided a swing that she knew anyone with a good eye would notice. Her dressmaking skills were better than average, and she had pressed them into service last night, sitting up until the birds began to sing, sewing the outfit that she had made with the fabric she had bought yesterday evening. She had had to take her final savings, and then had still been forced to plead with the stallholder to give her a discount, eventually promising to help him set up the next weekend. But it had been worth it.

It was the hat that she was concerned about, that she knew Madame Fournier would be looking at. It was the last thing she had made with Mrs McLeod, and was inspired by a Balmain hat that Violet had seen in a magazine – a dark red the colour of dried blood, constructed out of four large, stiff bows that formed a soft square, and worn on an angle, almost like a naval tricorn. It had the clean lines that she knew Madame Fournier would appreciate, a simplicity that was striking, and workmanship as good as anything she had ever done. Mrs McLeod had given it to her once it was finished, claiming the client had changed their mind. Violet hadn't believed her at the time, nor now she realised. Mrs McLeod had known she was pregnant, would have been able to see it, despite Violet's efforts to hide her pale face and changing shape. The hat was Mrs McLeod's leaving gift to her.

But would it be enough? She was about to find out. 'You can do it, Violet. Go in there and show her.'

Violet had to stop herself from gasping when she entered the salon, and keep the long-practised expression of professional composure. Stepping into the salon was like stepping into another world, a soft, rarefied world where the air was scented with a rich floral perfume and the carpet sank in soft dips beneath her feet as she walked. The whole room was manicured, as though it had been taken straight from the pages of a thick, glossy magazine and brought to life.

And, of course, it was full of the most beautiful hats Violet had ever seen. Neat little pillboxes for day, huge brimmed hats for weddings, jewelled and sequinned and beaded chapeaux for parties more glamorous than Violet could ever imagine going to. As she raised her hand to touch the plume on the side of one, she heard a voice over her shoulder, and quickly lowered it again.

'You like the feathers?'

She turned. Standing before her was a tiny, ancient woman with skin like dried rose petals, crinkled and papery-translucent, dressed in a bouclé Chanel suit in shades of the sea, all blending together into an emerald mix, and a purple silk cap covered with green beads that glistened in the light. The back of the hat flipped out like a little duck's tail, and Violet couldn't help but gaze at it. She had never seen anything like it.

'I love them. Are they white peacock?' The voice that came out of Violet's mouth wasn't quite her own. Something about the salon, the presence of this extraordinary woman in front of her, made her want to stand up straighter, speak better. Be better.

Madame Fournier smiled. 'That's right. My favourite. Like something from another world, I always think.'

Her accent was three-quarters clipped British softened with a quarter of chocolatey French. She gave Violet an appraising look.

'So, you are here for the job, I assume.'

Violet nodded. Madame Fournier's eyes burned into her,

taking in her coat, her shoes, her hat, running over her face. 'Hmm.'

Both the sound and her face were inscrutable. The amethyst necklace that encircled her little neck seemed to glow against her pale skin. Madame Fournier's eyes were dark and beady, like a magpie's. Violet was at once terrified of her and enthralled.

'Yes, madame. Shall I show you my—'

'No.'

The shake of her head was one small, neat movement. Violet felt huge, and deeply inelegant next to her.

'Tell me something. If you were alone in the store and a wealthy customer came in – a very rich lady, who you knew was a regular, and who spent a lot of money here . . .'

Violet nodded – a brief, sharp nod – emulating the precise movements of Madame Fournier almost unconsciously. Everything within Violet wanted to impress this woman.

'She has set her heart on a hat that is not flattering to her, that makes her look jowly and old – *pas jolie* – what would you do? She will not be steered towards anything else; every suggestion you make to try and get her to look at a more flattering option is rejected.'

Violet paused while she thought. She knew that the answer to this question might be the most important one she ever gave.

Eventually she said, 'I would make up some reason why I couldn't sell her the hat. That I had become confused and had already sold it to another customer – whatever I thought would put her off until such time as you were in the shop and could deal with the situation.'

Violet tried not to bite her lip with nerves as she waited for Madame Fournier to respond. Was passing the buck the wrong thing to say? Maybe she was looking for confidence, someone who would tell the woman herself? Or maybe she wanted Violet to say she would sell the hat to her regardless, because of her status and potential value? No, she knew absolutely that that was not the right solution to the problem. Retaining the integrity of Madame Fournier's name was paramount, and that would be damaged if customers were sold hats that were not completely right for them. The matching of the hat to the individual was one of the things Madame Fournier's name had been built upon, her instinct famously accurate as to what would suit.

The woman pursed her lips, her eyes appraising Violet.

'And risk looking stupid, or incompetent, in the woman's eyes? A silly girl who has got herself in a muddle?'

'It doesn't matter. She won't remember me once she has the right hat, the one that makes her crow's-feet disappear and her neck look long and elegant, and inspires everyone to compliment her.'

Madame Fournier nodded and the shadow of a smile appeared, and then was gone again. 'Good. Good girl. Hats have power. If you recognise that, then I can teach you the rest. They have the power to transform, don't you think?' She looked at Violet, a hint of amusement in her eyes.

Violet nodded. 'Yes, I do.' The truth of the statement was staring her in the face. Over the woman's shoulder, Violet could see herself in the mirror. Transformed indeed, from the girl who had stood outside the shop only yesterday. Mrs McLeod had done her proud.

Violet hesitated, and then reached for her portfolio, but was waved away.

'No. I don't want to see your drawings.'

'Oh.'

'I'm sure they're charming. But if you are going to work here you will learn from me. My way.' Then: 'Oh, one thing I forget to ask,' the woman said. 'What is your name?'

Violet paused for a second. Inside her jacket, she could feel Bryce's drawing, stiff, reassuring. Cavalley, she had called him.

She slipped her hand into the pocket, and felt the edge of the paper. This was her dream. This was her chance. And she took it. Hats have the power to transform, she thought.

'It's Violet,' she said softly. 'Violet Cavalley.'

After Violet's interview with Madame Fournier, she had collected Flip and gone straight to the Register Office on the King's Road. It was hot, and she had to queue to speak to a registrar. While she waited, she jiggled Flip from side to side, singing to him, 'Mama's going to buy you a mockingbird . . .'

Eventually, they reached the front of the queue and Violet faced the woman who was staring at her with owl-like glasses. 'Yes?' she said tonelessly.

'I have to cancel an intention to marry,' Violet said.

The woman sneered. 'What a shame,' she said, looking at Flip. 'Changed his mind, did he?'

'He died,' Violet said. The woman just stared. And shrugged. Why should she care? It was only Violet to whom the words signalled the end of her life. The end of one life, she told herself, pulling herself together. The end of one life, and the beginning of a new one.

'And I need the forms necessary to change my name. By deed poll. I want to change my name.'

Mary Wallop was the first friend Violet made at Madame Fournier's salon. It was her first day and she had arrived early – so early that she had to wait outside for someone else to get there and let her in. It would be a while before she might expect to be trusted with a key, if ever – Madame Fournier had made clear.

As she walked through Hyde Park towards the salon, Violet pulled her coat tight around her and turned the collar up. One day, she told herself as she walked, she wouldn't be cold all the time. She would have a fur-lined collar, to keep the back of her neck warm. She would have a coat with a lining that wasn't patched inside, and that was made of soft wool – cashmere, even – that would hug her like a cloud. One day she would have the heating on all the time, all day and all night if necessary, feeding coins into it as if they were nothing, letting the radiator blast out so much heat she wouldn't even have to sit close to it to get the benefit.

One day. It became her litany, as she walked to work every day, and back again. Her novena, her mantra. *One day, one day.* One day she would have toasted crumpets for breakfast every day, smothered with so much butter that it would drip through the holes on to her fingers. She would have a front door that didn't stick and that was painted bright red. She would have a carpet on the stairs that was thick and soft and that your toes sank into. One day she would have a bath deep enough to sink her whole self in over her head, full of bubbles and hot enough to make her skin turn pink and smelling of roses. One day. A long way off maybe, but one day.

She carried on walking, feeling the wind scald her cheeks and make her eyes water, and she put a finger up under her lashes so that her mascara didn't run down her cheeks and make her look a mess on her very first day. It was important that she look smart, Madame Fournier had impressed that upon her. 'You are the face of the salon, all of you girls. You must put your best face forward, at all times.'

Violet pulled her shoulders back and licked a finger and rubbed it under her lash line to make doubly sure, checking her reflection in the window as she waited outside the shop. The hats on display were winter ones still; the spring collection wouldn't come in until May. Madame Fournier didn't believe in displaying collections months ahead of time, like some of the designers did. 'Why show winter hats in summer and spring hats when we are still clearing up after Christmas?' she said.

'It makes no sense. If I am cold, I want to buy a warm hat. If I am going to be visiting Ascot, I do not wish to be faced with a tide of dark wool. It is common sense, no?'

Yes, Violet had nodded. She was in complete agreement (though she would have been pressed to think of anything she would not have agreed with Madame Fournier on). The display wasn't all greys and heathers though. Madame Fournier was cleverer than that. 'Now, I might want to buy a winter hat, but that doesn't mean I want to blend into the pavement, *n'est-ce pas*?' she had said to Violet, as she was showing her around the salon after offering her the job. Violet hadn't replied, assuming the question was rhetorical, until she became aware that the older woman was waiting for her answer with a slightly tilted head.

'No,' she had said quickly. 'Not at all, madame.'

Madame had given a small nod, and she had continued, 'I want to turn heads with what I am wearing on my head. I want to be the splash of colour in an overcast sky, like a child's balloon floating up through the rainclouds. I want to be a little pocket of glorious splendour in the midst of a dull world.'

The window certainly was that, so beautiful was the collection displayed within it. There was lots of red this season, so the window looked as if a field of poppies had descended on the salon. You could see it from the far end of the street, glowing, almost, with light and life and colour from behind the plate-glass. In the centre, an enormous, wide-brimmed hat had a crown covered entirely with scarlet silk tulips, their petals made stiff with wire and lacquered to protect them from the elements. 'A flash of summer in the depths of winter,' Madame Fournier had said softly as she pointed it out to Violet. 'Like a bowl of pot pourri to remind us that even in the darkest days, sunshine is only just around the corner.'

Either side of this magnificent centrepiece was a pair of red and white striped hats, smaller, almost pillbox in shape, with red veiling that covered the top part of the face, and a jaunty grosgrain bow at the back. 'Smart, prim almost – but never prissy,' was how Madame Fournier had described these two. 'I think they would be called something like . . . hmm, what, if they were girls? Priscilla, maybe? Yes. Clever, sensible, but with a good bit of pep.' Violet had smiled with delight at that. Of course the hats could have names – why wouldn't they? They had personalities, just as people did; any fool could see that just by looking at them. The hat at the front of the window, for example, was certainly no Priscilla. It was Violet's favourite, and it was a blowsy, forward puff of a hat. It was made from bright red velvet covered in very fine tulle of the same colour, and was the shape of an overblown rose, at the point where it was just on the verge of collapse. It was a hat that would look you straight in the eye and dare you to challenge it, Violet imagined, as she stared at it; a hat that would brook no arguments; a hat that would transform the wearer into someone stronger, someone racier, someone . . .

'The small ones have always been my favourites,' a voice said from behind her shoulder. 'Neat, inconspicuous, but when you look closer, there's always something you're not expecting.'

Violet turned in surprise and found herself looking into the perfectly powdered face of a woman twenty or so years older than herself, who was looking back at her with amusement. She had pale, smooth skin and her hair was set in big rolls that bounced gently as she walked. Violet could see that she was not beautiful – she had ordinary features, and her eyes were a bit too close together – but she was one of those women who did what the magazines called 'making the best of oneself'. Immaculate make-up, shiny hair that was fashionable but not too young for her, and a scent that was intoxicating. Indefinably but unmistakably adult, it was musky and slightly sweet and made Violet think of shadowy woods full of ferns. She wore a cream coat and low heels, and carried her matching bag in the crook of her arm. She was everything chic and grown-up and stylish, everything Violet was not – at least not yet. Violet found her voice, at last.

'I like the big ones. They're so – so exciting.'

The woman looked at her appraisingly. 'Do you now?' There was a flicker of amusement in her eyes, for a second, that Violet felt wasn't entirely friendly, but then it was gone, and the woman laughed. 'Come on. You'll need to get your head out of the clouds and into the heads of our ladies, if you want to learn how to sell hats to them.'

'I'm V-Violet,' she stuttered as she followed the woman through the door of the salon, watching as she removed her coat and brushed it off before sliding it on to a hanger and putting it away in the cupboard behind the desk, and gesturing for Violet to do the same.

'I imagined you were. Or do you think I just go around dragging passers-by in off the street and forcing them to work here?'

'No, I—'

'Oh, don't look so terrified, I'm only playing with you. I'm Mary. Mary Wallop.'

Mary had been with Madame Fournier for almost fifteen years, Violet discovered over the course of the next few days. 'Fourteen years, six months and three weeks,' she told her proudly, as they were tidying the dressing room at the end of Violet's third day. 'Madame took me on after things had gone . . . awry in my life,' she said, plumping the silk cushions and arranging them neatly on the chaise longue, 'and she never judged, nor asked questions that I wasn't willing to answer. Just gave me a job, and her trust, and I'll never forget that gift.'

Her husband had left her, Violet learned, and run away with a neighbour. Mary had been a customer of Madame Fournier's at one time, 'Not a regular, we weren't that well off, but I had three hats that Peter gave me as gifts, and when I needed a job – well, it was the first place I thought of. It felt like coming home.'

Violet understood that feeling. The salon was the first place where she had ever felt as though she truly belonged. It was her world, she had known it from the day she came here. It was as if she was meant to be here. She said as much to Mary one day.

'It's as if I was dropped in here, like a piece in a jigsaw, and the space was made just for me, you know?' she said one morning while they were sharing a cigarette before opening the shop.

'As if the shop was made for you?' Mary said, and there was a look in her eye that mocked Violet, repeating her words back to her and making her hear how arrogant they sounded.

'Oh no, that's not what I meant. Just that I've found where I'm meant to be,' Violet said quickly. 'You know how I feel; it's the same for you, isn't it?'

Mary took a long drag of her cigarette and looked out at the roofs of Chelsea, her mouth twisted in the corner.

'Yes. Yes, it's the same for me.' She exhaled. Then she turned to Violet and smiled. 'It's nice to have someone here who understands.'

On a Monday, Violet had a half-day off, and would usually spend it at the studio. It was her chance to watch the women work, these experienced women who had been making the finest hats in London for decades before going home to husbands who worked on the buses and mucky-kneed children. And she would sweep up after them and listen to their gossip and chatter over the noise of the machinery, and run errands, and generally make herself useful.

'You may look through my sketchbooks, Mam'selle Violette,' Madame Fournier said one afternoon, as Violet swept up bits of piping from underneath one of the trestle tables. 'See what you think of this one.'

She got down one of the large, black-covered sketchbooks that were stacked along a shelf in date order, their month and year painted on the spine in white. Violet took it and opened it reverently.

'This was ten years ago. A good year for my industry. A good year for me.'

Madame Fournier smiled as she watched Violet turn the pages, her eyes wide and her fingers careful. Inside the book was a world of glamour, of colour and shapes that Violet had seen in papers and magazines.

'Whenever you are here, you may read them. It is how you will learn. Really learn, not just the blocking and the sewing, but learn how to see. You must open up those pretty eyes of yours, Violet, if you are to be a designer yourself one day.'

Violet looked up at her, surprised.

'What are you staring like that for? I know that is what you dream of. Of course it is. Why else would you sacrifice what you do, this time with your son, if you did not have ambitions far greater than being a shop girl – even if in a shop such as mine?'

Violet had never mentioned Flip at work, had been determined that she would not use her motherhood as an excuse to go home early, that she would somehow make both roles fit in alongside each other. And there had been another reason, as well, why she had kept her beloved son a secret – she had been afraid she would be judged.

The women's eyes met, and for the first time that Violet could recall, Madame Fournier smiled. 'Come here,' she said, and reached into a drawer in her desk. 'I want to show you something.'

She handed Violet an envelope that was worn and fuzzy with age. 'Open it.'

Violet did as she was told. Inside there was a single, rectangular, sepia-tinted photograph. The image was of a woman with pin-curls, standing outside a large building. There was a sign to her right: Blakeham Hospital. She wore a simple drop-waisted dress, and a shy smile, her eyes not quite meeting the camera. In her arms was a baby.

Madame Fournier sighed. 'I've never shown that to anyone before, you know.'

Violet turned around, surprised 'It's you?'

'Yes.' The older woman smiled sadly. 'Nineteen years old, I was. She was called – well . . . I called her Martha. She won't be called that any more, I'm certain.' Madame Fournier's voice was soft and her eyes crinkled at the edges.

'Did you have to give her away?' Violet whispered.

'Yes. There was no choice, not then. Not for me, or girls like me. Oh, I know it's still not easy, even now. But it was a different time then. Babies were taken away.'

'Some of them still are.' Violet's heart clenched. Flip had almost been taken away from her. The thought of not having him now, was utterly unimaginable.

'What do you mean, "girls like you"?' she continued.

'I was in service. Brought up, if you can call it that, in a children's home. Then I got a job in one of the big houses nearby, as a scullerymaid. Oh, I was one of the lucky ones. I got out.'

Madame Fournier looked over as Violet's eyebrows shot up. 'I know. Not what you expected, is it?'

'None of this is.'

'No, I know. But Violet, I'm showing you this, because I understand. I know how hard it is for you, and how you have had to fight to keep your son. And I respect that. I admire the fact that you are trying to make a good life for him, and

I see talent in you that you may not even realise is there.'

Violet looked at the floor. She felt strangely ashamed.

'I don't want you to feel you have to lie about your child any longer – to hide him away, to pretend he doesn't exist. I lost mine. I have spent years pretending she never existed – to the world, and even to myself. It was the only way I could survive. But it killed something in me. I don't want you to have to deny your child the way that I did.'

Violet wiped a tear away from her cheek. 'How did you know?'

'It doesn't matter. What matters is that you can be honest with me.'

'Thank you. He's called Flip.'

'What a lovely name. Short for Philip?'

'Sort of. I call him Flip.'

Violet looked at the photograph again. She knew just how the girl in the picture felt, and her heart went out to her. She was alone. Afraid. Uncertain of the future and what it would hold for her. Abandoned by the man she had trusted, probably. But most of all, consumed with fierce love for the fragile little bundle in her arms, the daughter who would shortly be taken from her and whom she would never see again. The thought of it broke Violet's heart, and she could not bear to look into the young woman's face any longer. She turned the picture over and carefully put it back in the envelope.

Madame Fournier took the envelope from her and replaced it in the drawer.

'I thought you were. . . ' Violet didn't know how to phrase what she wanted to ask. 'I thought that you came from . . .'

Madame Fournier rescued her. 'You thought I was well-bred, upper-class? French aristocracy, maybe?'

'Yes.'

'Ah. Well, Violet, what can I tell you? People see what they want to see. I spent a lot of time in France during the war. But that was much later. I was just a Lancashire girl in service who got in trouble.'

'Oh.'

Madame Fournier touched Violet's face, and looked at it as she had done the first time they met, as if appraising a painting or sculpture.

'I told you, didn't I? Hats have the power to transform.'

And they did. Violet could feel herself changing. With every day that passed, she was leaving her old self behind. Her childhood was fading away from her. Her scars, too, were fading, although the scar on her hand would always be there. But the memories were falling away. Her mind was too full – of ideas, of excitement, of sheer exhaustion – to hold them in its forefront, and so they retreated, to a place where she could almost forget about them completely. Almost.

She started to get her own ideas. Reading the sketchbooks was like peering into a diary, but one with pictures and results and form. She could see into the imagination of a truly original mind; see how the spark of an idea developed into a scribbled phrase, then a pencil sketch, then a fuller drawing, turning, butterfly-like, into a creation atop a duchess at the races or a widow at a wedding. And as she watched the transformation of ideas, and of the clients who came into the salon, she herself began to transform, to shed her former self like a snake shedding its skin and take on a new confidence and poise.

She wasn't the only one who was changing and growing, day by day. On Sundays she took Flip to the park, watching with a bittersweet combination of sadness and pride as she noted the changes in his face from week to week. If she were taking care of him every day she probably would not even see them; they would just merge into a continuous cable of growth and development. But as it was she would see something different in his face every week: a new, wider smile, the fact that he could now focus on her when she was further away, slimming down of chubby wrists, an extra tuft of hair. He grew quickly and surely, and in no time at all he was able to stand by himself, with only a bit of wobbling. He grew stronger. And so did Violet. She wobbled less, as well.

One day, she was in the corner of Madame Fournier's studio, poring over a design for a hat made entirely of sequins, trying to learn the construction of it, when Madame looked up at her and asked, 'What happened to him, *chérie*?'

Violet's head jerked up. 'Who?'

'Your man. Flip's father.'

Violet stammered. She trusted Madame Fournier with all her soul, but she did not know if she could tell her this. 'Why d-do you ask? I m-mean . . .'

'I don't want to intrude. I apologise.' Madame smiled. 'I will not ask you again. I thought only that you might wish to talk about it.'

She lowered her head to her work again, and Violet realised that she did, in fact, want to talk about it desperately – about him, about Bryce, whom she had loved, who had saved her, and who she had killed. Because every day, still, she felt as though she had killed him. It was the canker and cancer inside her family that had led to his death, that she had led to him. He had walked into darkness to protect her, and he had not come back. And with a rush of tears that came from she knew not where, Violet told Madame Fournier everything.

One morning, Violet went into work as usual and, instead of being the first one in, found that Madame Fournier was already there. 'Leave the Closed sign on the door for a moment, Violet,' she called out from the little office at the back of the salon, 'and come in here, will you? Bring some tea for us.

'I'm going on holiday,' she said, not looking up from the letter she was writing, when Violet carried the tea tray into the small, floral-wallpapered room. Framed drawings of some of Madame Fournier's most famous designs were mounted on the wall.

'But you never go on holiday,' Violet had said in surprise.

'No.' Madame Fournier took a breath. 'I thought it was about time.'

Violet was confused. 'Is everything all right?' she asked.

'Of course. Why would it not be?' Madame Fournier folded the piece of paper she was writing and ran her finger and thumb along the fold to sharpen the crease.

'So. You will be in charge of the shop.'

Her friend and mentor was not herself – she was brisk, cool. Had Violet done something wrong? She couldn't have made her too angry if she was leaving her in charge.

'Won't Mary be upset? She's been here the longest.'

'I will deal with Mary Wallop.' Madame Fournier's voice was firm.

Violet nodded. 'How . . . how long do you plan to be gone for, madame?'

Madame Fournier gave a short, sharp sigh. Oh dear. Violet wished she hadn't questioned her; she had clearly made her cross.

'I'm sorry.'

'No.' She looked at Violet and her face softened. 'You have nothing to be sorry for, dear girl. The truth is . . .' She paused. 'The truth is, I can't say. I'm visiting an old friend who's unwell, and I shall stay with them until they recover.'

'I'm sorry,' Violet said again.

'Thank you. So am I.' She stood. 'So, I will be in touch. Until then, you are more than capable of managing the shop, and the other girls.'

Madame Fournier reached out and took Violet's hand. Her skin was cool and talcum-powder soft.

'If you are unsure about anything, just ask yourself what I would advise you to do. Look into your heart and ask yourself the question. You'll have the answer.'

Violet frowned. She didn't understand. 'All right.'

'Good girl.'

And Violet did manage. She found that she did have the answers. She rose to the challenge of running the shop, dealing with even the most difficult customers.

She was beginning to feel as if there was hope again. As though she might, one day, come out of the dark tunnel that she was trudging through, only managing to make any progress at all by simply putting one foot in front of the other and not looking at the road ahead. She had a routine, she had her son, her flat and her job. And the realisation that she had, finally, got what she had been seeking – freedom from her family. Although the reality of that was very different from what she had imagined it would be. It did not leave her feeling light and free as she had been when she had first come to London with Bryce. She had felt old for a long time now. Ground down and world-weary.

But somehow, the responsibility of being in charge of Madame Fournier's salon did not weigh her down further; it gave her a new energy. She was awake at dawn every day, before Flip, dressed and buzzing, ready to get in and get started. She was happy, for the first time in a long time.

One morning, Violet went into the salon as usual. Picked up the pile of post that lay on the mat and took it to the little kitchenette where she put the kettle on for coffee. She needed it more than usual this morning. Flip had been up half the night with a fever, and she had spent hours pacing the floor with his hot little body in her arms, laying cool towels on his forehead and trying to soothe his cries. These were the times she felt the weight of her solitude – not because of the work but because of the sheer loneliness of it. There was no one to hand him to for a moment while she went to the toilet, no one to reassure her and say, 'I'm sure it's just a bug, he'll be fine in the morning.'

She didn't know what to do about the workshop, either. It was coming up to the time that the girls would need to start on the new collection if it was to be ready, and Madame Fournier had left no indication as to what she expected Violet to do. There was no collection designed, Violet had looked through her sketchbooks and desk and found nothing. It was all very well telling her to 'ask herself what Madame Fournier would do', Violet thought crossly now as she waited for the kettle to boil, but she could hardly imagine a whole collection out of nowhere like that, could she? It was like asking her to be psychic; it wasn't reasonable. She had had no word from the woman for weeks, and time was running out. If she didn't hear soon she would have to – well, she didn't know what she would do.

The kettle whistled and Violet poured the hot water on the coffee and began to open the post as she waited for it to percolate. Just the smell of it began to perk her up. An electricity bill, a letter from the council about the leasehold, bills for fabric and special trimmings from suppliers . . . then Violet came to a small white envelope with Madame Fournier's elegant copperplate handwriting on the front.

Thank goodness for that. Hopefully the letter would give Violet some clue as to when her employer would return, or at least what she wanted her to do about the new collection in the meantime, if that was not to be soon. She opened the envelope and unfolded the letter inside as she walked into the main room of the salon towards the office, carrying the other post tucked into the crook of her elbow and the pot of coffee in her other hand.

When she was just a few steps into the main room of the salon, she read the first words of Madame Fournier's letter and dropped the pot of coffee, which spread in a thick, dark stain over the cream carpet. It read: *Dear Violet, If you are reading this letter then I am sorry to say it is because I have passed away.*

The paper shook in Violet's hand as she read on.

I should begin by coming clean and saying that I am sorry, for you deserve both an explanation and an apology. I misled you, dear girl. There was no sick friend – or rather, the sick friend was myself. I first discovered that I was dying some months ago. For a while I could continue as before, which gave me time to put the affairs of the shop in order and to make plans. But it quite soon became apparent that I would not be able to do so for much longer. So, I decided to go away. Dying is a messy, tedious business for all concerned, as you know all too well, dear child, better than you should, and I had no intention of subjecting you or anyone else to witnessing my demise.

Violet took a deep breath. She wished she could take back the angry thoughts that had been in her head only a few moments before.

I won't bore you with the details. Suffice to say, I have, for the last few weeks, had the best possible care in a small private hospital in the Alps. I always wanted to return to France, and now I have done so. Do not worry, as I know you will, that I have been in pain or alone, for I have been neither.

Violet smiled despite the tears that were streaming down her face. The woman had always been able to know what Violet was thinking.

So. On to business. I told you before I went away that I wanted you to trust your own judgement with regard to the running of the shop. I know you will have made the right decisions and that you will continue to do so. For the shop is yours. You will run it with all of the efficiency, flair and determination that I saw in you that first day when you walked in the door, and you will do both of us proud. You will have had enough practice by now. It will be hard at times, I am sure, but I am equally sure that you will rise to meet every new challenge. Violet, simply trust in yourself, and everything will be fine. And trust in the power of hats to transform.

I hope this all means that you can make a comfortable life for yourself and for Flip, dear Violet.

Yours, Elizabeth Fournier

Trust in the power of hats to transform. Madame Fournier had planned the whole thing. She had left Violet in charge of the shop to prepare her for this moment, to give her a trial run, almost. Violet walked to the front of the salon and looked out at the street in front of her. Mount Street. One of the best streets in London.

And then she turned back to look at the salon with new eyes. It was hers. She couldn't quite believe it. She was the one Madame Fournier had chosen. She wasn't quite sure why. Why she had picked her, not Mary Wallop, as one might have expected, or any of the other girls who had been there for longer than her, or one of Elizabeth Fournier's rivals, even? But she knew, in her heart, that her mentor had made the right decision. She would live up to the honour that she had been given – would spend her life making sure that she lived up to it. She laughed. She, little May Gribbens, owned a hat shop in Mount Street! It was as though all her childhood dreams had come true. But in order to obtain it, she had to lose the best friend she had ever had.

The first big decision that Violet had to make, once her inheritance of the salon had been confirmed in a meeting with Madame Fournier's solicitor and executor of her Will, was what she would do about the forthcoming collection.

'Can I offer you a sherry, Miss Cavalley?' Gerald Petherbridge, the lawyer asked her on her arrival in his wood-panelled office. 'I like to partake of one before lunch, I must confess.' Violet declined, then took the chair opposite his desk that he pulled out for her. 'I'd really like to get straight down to business, if that's all right.' She folded her gloves neatly in her lap. She was keen to make a good impression.

'Very well, in that case I had better begin. There is not much money in the estate in addition to the business, and what there is, as well as Madame Fournier's residence, has been placed in trust for her daughter – should I be able to track her down, that is.' Violet nodded her understanding.

'You have the leasehold to the salon in Mount Street, and the rights to continue trading there. But I would be remiss in my duties were I not to warn you that the business runs on a tight budget, and the leasehold is shortly due for renewal. There is no margin for error. In fact . . . well, Madame Fournier was a long-established client. We knew one another for many years.

I would not wish to malign her in any way, especially now that she is no longer with us. But it would be fair to say that her talents lay in the arena of design, not accountancy.'

'Are you saying there's no money to carry on running the business with?'

'Yes, I'm afraid that's exactly what I'm telling you. Well, day-to-day, you will be able to continue, as long as takings do not dip. But with the leasehold due for renewal, and some other overheads that need attention . . .' Gerald Petherbridge pushed a piece of paper towards Violet, and her eyes widened at the size of the numbers on it.

'I'm afraid you find yourself in a rather urgent situation, Miss Cavalley.'

'I see. Well, you'd better tell me exactly how much I need to raise, and how quickly.'

He made some more calculations, then jotted a figure down, and showed it to her. She took a deep breath.

'I think I'd like that sherry now,' she told him, 'if it's still on offer.'

After the meeting, Violet went straight to the workshop to talk to Madame Fournier's employees – *her* employees, she realised now.

'As you know by now, Madame Fournier left me her salon and the business when she died. I intend to honour her memory and her name with a collection that reflects the best of her work.'

Violet had had an idea, on her walk from Gerald Petherbridge's office to the studio. She would do a sort of 'greatest hits' collection, remaking a number of the most successful of Madame Fournier's hats and bringing them together for the first time. Her early work, the hats that had made her famous. Designs from the thirties, elegant little caps that were both simple in appearance and complex in their construction.

Wartime hats, austere and respectful, yet with a valiant spirit that was typical of Elizabeth Fournier's designs. Hats from all the eras Violet's mentor had worked in, hats from a career spanning more than fifty years.

The girls who worked behind the scenes, the ones who worked in the salon, Mary, and Billy – who was now driving deliveries for the business – they all listened as she spoke, promising them that she would not fail them, asking them to trust her. And they did – one by one, they all agreed. They would work together to ensure that the salon remained great.

So she pulled it together. Spent hours trawling through the archives, collating her favourite hats, planning how they would be displayed. She had named the collection 'Pinnacle', and had a catalogue printed up by the smart stationer down the street, listing all the hats. She would make them in a limited edition run, ten of each, and keep one for the salon's archive. And she did her sums carefully, with the help of Gerald Petherbridge, who sat with her as she worked her way through the books, helping her to understand them, tactfully waiting when she got confused. Violet's maths lessons had been patchy, as had the rest of her education. But the numbers added up now; with the money she would make from the new collection, she could pay the leasehold off and keep things running for a bit longer, they deduced.

The old customers had begun to fade away in the weeks before the re-opening, but Violet had been too busy planning to pay much attention to it, or to ask why. They would return when there was something to come and see, she trusted. When she re-opened, they would be back, bringing new clients in their wake, drawn by all the hard work she was doing. She trusted in herself, as Madame Fournier had told her to do.

She got to the shop early, on the morning the new collection was to be released, anticipating queues waiting to buy one of

Madame Fournier's designs. She had advertised the collection and opening day around town, sending Billy out to put up posters that she had specially designed. She'd had invitations sent out to all of the regular clients, expensive, gilt-edged invitations in tissue-lined envelopes.

And no one came.

Violet couldn't understand it. The salon was popular, people had always loved the designs. She knew she had chosen the best of the best, she had planned carefully and for weeks. But it was a flop. She stood in the window of the shop for hours, all day, the girls hovering behind her, not knowing what to do or say. One person came in, around lunchtime, and Violet leaped forward to greet them. This was it, it was beginning. Maybe there had been something else happening in Town that people had been to in the morning, some show or event or other, and people would begin to make their way here now. But the woman looked surprised, and then backed out. 'Sorry, looking for the perfume shop.'

Violet sat next to the tub in the small attic bathroom of her flat, bathing Flip. He batted her hand with his, waving at the sponge she held in it. 'Squeezy shower, Mama, squeezy shower.' She dipped the sponge in the water before squeezing it out over his head. He squealed with delight, and she smiled. The sharpness of her failure seemed less potent when she was with him.

But later, once she had put him to bed, she sat at the little desk in the corner of the room, with Bryce's drawing of the salon she had dreamed of above it, and wept. To have failed so completely at something so important, to have so badly let down the first person to ever really place any trust in her, was almost more than she could bear. 'I'm so sorry, Elizabeth,' she cried. Then she read the letter Madame Fournier had sent her once again.

Trust yourself, it said. The words comforted her. *Trust your instincts.*

Something was niggling at the back of her mind. Violet sat for a moment, thinking, her tears dried. Then she picked up her bag from its place on the floor beside her, and dug around in it for the address book that contained the salon's client list. She opened it at random. Ran her finger down the page till she came to a suitable name. Yes, Miss Fisk. She had been a client of Elizabeth Fournier's since 1955, it said here; she bought two hats from each collection, without fail. Violet had spoken to her shortly after Madame Fournier's death, and the woman had promised to support her in continuing the salon. 'Elizabeth was a good friend to me,' Miss Fisk said. 'I'd hate to see her work disappear now she's gone. I'll do anything I can to help you out.'

There were plenty of women like Miss Fisk, Violet recalled now, who had come forward after Elizabeth died with stories of the loans she had given them here and there, credit extended beyond what anyone would consider reasonable, kindnesses both small and large during times of need of one kind or another. These women had written to Violet, assuring her of their continued patronage, of their faith in her. Letters, postcards, phone calls.

Violet pulled the drawer of her desk open, and took out a pile of them that she had brought home from the salon to read. '*Anyone Elizabeth Fournier trusted is someone to be reckoned with,*' one said. '*Madame Elizabeth was so kind to me after the death of our daughter, Katie,*' read another, '*and I never had the chance to thank her properly. I hope that, one day, I will be able to repay the kindness she showed me, through my loyalty to you, in her name.*' '*Madame Fournier gave me my first job. I could not stay with her for long, as my husband was posted abroad, but without her faith in me I would never have become who I am today. I am so sad that she has gone, but so pleased to see that she has continued to put trust in young talent until the end.'*

So many letters. So much love and respect and gratitude for Madame Fournier. So many promises of support. *So why had none of them come?*

The next morning, Violet called Mary Wallop into her office. She had spent hours on the phone the previous evening, and by now had pieced together what Mary had been up to over the last couple of weeks.

'I put the posters up like you told me, Miss Violet,' Billy had told her on the phone. 'Of course I did.' His voice was hurt.

'I know, Billy. I believe you. But tell me – which is the one nearest to my house? Do you remember? I just want to see one.'

'Erm, there's one by the pub – the King George. On the left-hand wall. Violet, was it not the right place—'

She cut him off. 'It was the perfect place, Billy. Please don't worry.'

She put the phone down and raced around the corner to the pub; Flip was asleep upstairs, she couldn't leave him for long. She got to the pub and searched the side of the wall. No poster was visible. She looked harder: she had to be sure. Then she saw it – or what was left of it. Just the CLE of the word Pinnacle was visible. The rest had been torn off. She ran back home again.

The remainder of her phone calls confirmed her suspicions. None of the dozen women Violet rang had received their invitations to the relaunch. None of them knew anything about it. 'I assumed you just weren't ready yet,' said one. One or two had seen a poster before it had been taken down, but hadn't received invitations, and so 'had thought you were only inviting favoured clientèle,' sounding a little sniffy. Voilet had reassured and explained, as much as she could, told them she had no idea what had happened, apologised. Promised to let them know as soon as it was rearranged.

But Violet had a very good idea of what had happened. *Trust your instincts,* Madame Fournier had told her. So she did.

'You took the posters down, didn't you? It must have taken you hours. That day you took off, the same day as Billy was out putting them up. That was no coincidence, was it?'

Mary Wallop said nothing. Just stood defiantly in front of Violet, in her pale yellow dress and red lipstick, her face blank.

'I found the invitations,' Violet continued. 'Or some of them, anyhow. Addressed, sealed, stamped. Shoved in the bottom of the rubbish. What did you do with the rest? Burn them? Throw them away?'

'You can't prove it was me.'

'I don't need to. I know it was you. *You* know it was you. You were in charge of taking the invitations to the post office. They never arrived. Some of them were in the rubbish. I don't need much more proof than that. But I would like to know why.'

'Why what?' Mary's face was a sneer.

'Why ruin the event? Why make sure no one knew about it? Why go outside and tell anyone who looked like they might be coming in that it had been cancelled, any time I turned my back?'

Mary's mouth dropped.

'Yes, I know about that. Not everyone who works here is as disloyal as you.' After Violet had worked out what Mary had been doing, she had phoned one of the other girls. The girl was nervous of Mary, who had clearly been bullying her for months – years, even – but eventually told Violet what Mary had done the day before. 'Every time you went out back, she went and made sure no one came in. Not that there were many people. She had someone at the end of the street that she'd paid to tell women who looked like they were coming that it was cancelled.

There weren't many of them neither, though. I'm very sorry, Miss Cavalley.' Violet had reassured her. It wasn't the girl's fault. But she would have to keep a closer eye on things in the future. If there was a future. That very possibility looked in great jeopardy now.

'Disloyal? Why'd I be loyal to you, you tell me that, *Violet* Cavalley?' She spat the words out, and the way she spoke Violet's name jolted her.

'Or maybe I should call you May?'

Violet looked away. She felt as though she had been thumped in the chest.

'Yes, I know your pathetic little secret,' Mary continued. 'I overheard you telling that desiccated old fraud your story. Listened to the two of you, telling each other your tales of woe. "Oh, poor me, I got knocked up and then my pikey daddy killed my husband." Although he wasn't your husband, was he? Couldn't even get him to marry you when you were in the club. Shame.'

Before she could stop herself, before she knew what she was doing even, Violet's hand had reared up and slapped the woman on the face. Mary hardly moved. Her body was solid, her shoulders square. Her cheek began to turn pink, but she didn't touch it. She just looked at Violet with triumph in her eyes.

'What was your plan, Mary?' Violet asked, her voice as calm as she could make it. 'You were hoping I'd run out of money? Spend it all on smart invitations, on mail-order catalogues and new couture lines, and you'd sabotage me every step of the way? Watch me go bankrupt?'

Mary shrugged. 'I didn't really have a plan.' Any attempt at pretending she was innocent had been dropped now. 'I just wanted to see you fail.'

Violet nodded. 'Get out,' she said. 'I never want to see you again. I never want to hear from you again.'

And now, Mary smiled, her red lips cracking her face open.

'I'm sure. But the thing is, I said I didn't have a plan, and I didn't – then. I thought I'd just watch you ruin everything, little Miss Perfect – or not so perfect, watch you fall flat on your stupid smug face. It should have been mine, this shop. I've been here the longest. She should have left it to me.'

'So that's what it's about? You're jealous.'

'Of course I'm fucking jealous!' Mary cried. 'I've worked here for years. I gave that bitch everything!'

'The way she told it, *she* gave *you* everything,' Violet pointed out.

'She gave me nothing.'

'She gave you a job. She gave you a chance. She gave you her trust.'

'Nothing that means anything. Nothing real.' Mary snorted. 'I worked here for sixteen years, and just as I thought . . . Well. Then you came along and swept everything out from under my nose.'

Mary sighed. 'I never had a husband who left me, you know. I just told old Lizzie that because I knew she wanted a sob story. One of those tales of transformation she liked so much. I wondered for a while if you'd done the same – but then I saw you with your sprog, so that bit's true, at least. Anyway, I don't think you're clever enough to think of making something like that up.'

Violet walked to the door of the office. 'Leave. Leave now,' she said. She couldn't look at Mary. She closed her eyes, hoping that when she opened them it would be to an empty office. Her hands trembled by her sides, flooded with shock and rage. But as she stood, she heard Mary's footsteps coming towards her, and then not passing her by, but stopping in front of her. She opened her eyes, and found herself looking straight into Mary's. Don't look away, she told herself. Don't cry. Don't let her see how afraid you are, how hurt.

'I said that I didn't have a plan. But now I do. I think you're good, Violet Cavalley. And I think it would be a waste if you were to fail. I'd be out of a job then, wouldn't I?'

'You're out of a job now,' Violet said. The other woman tipped her head back and laughed. 'Ah, but I don't need a job any more. Do I?'

Violet stared at her. Mary leaned in, and whispered in Violet's ear. 'I've got you. And I've got your secret.'

She put on her jacket and walked out through the salon, towards the door. As she reached it, she turned and gave Violet a little wave.

'I'll be seeing you – Violet Cavalley.'

Violet waited for her to leave. Then she turned and went into her little office that had been Madame Fournier's and was now hers, sat down at the pale wood desk with Elizabeth's stationery set still on it, and wept. When the tears subsided, she wiped her eyes.

Mary might have ruined the first relaunch of the shop, but she would not be able to do it again. Violet would have to be alert, on her guard, watch her back. She might even, she acknowledged to herself, be forced to pay Mary off, though the idea of it was despicable to her. But there was one thing that she was certain of, and that was that Madame Fournier had left *her* the shop, had wanted *her* to have it and run it, and that she was going to honour Madame's wishes. She would not let Mary Wallop take what was hers.

Violet opened the accounts book. The previous day's figures were before her, neatly slotting into their columns. The book was nearly full. Slowly, Violet picked up Elizabeth's fountain pen and wrote a few words in both the columns. Under *Expenses and Outgoings* she wrote: *Madame Elizabeth Fournier. RIP. Mary Wallop.* And in the column for sales she wrote *Violet*

Cavalley. Then she drew a line under the three names and closed the book. She would buy a new one on her way home.

Violet had always intended to leave the small trust fund that Bryce had been using to pay for his studies, and which had passed to her on his death, to their son Flip. It would earn interest, so that when he was eighteen he could do what his father had done, and have the liberty to go anywhere, study or learn anything he wanted to. She would use it and replace it, Violet decided. After all, he would have much more, if she made the salon a success. There was no point it sitting in the bank while she struggled and lost the business. Then the money would have to be spent on surviving, and it really would all be wasted.

Still, the knowledge that she was doing the right thing – the only thing she could do – didn't make it any easier as she waited outside the bank manager's office, her palms sweating as she practised the little speech she had planned.

In the event, it was far easier than she had anticipated. The manager hadn't questioned what she intended to do with the money – after all, why should he? It was her money, to do with as she pleased. It still felt wrong, however. He had just pushed a form across the desk at her, the places where she had to sign marked with little pencil crosses, and then waited while she did so. Then he had slid it into his beige paper file and told her that the money would be available to be withdrawn in twenty-one days, according to the terms of her savings account. He had then left the room, without even glancing at her again or saying goodbye.

After this, Violet went back to the workshop, sat at Madame Fournier's old desk, opened a new sketchbook and began to draw.

*

Violet Cavalley's first solo collection, *Transformation*, was launched in 1968. On the same day, she re-opened the shop in Mount Street that she had spent the last five months taking to pieces and rebuilding. She had carefully packed away most of Madame Fournier's furniture and framed prints; keeping some of her favourite pieces to use in the revamped shop. She spent a day going around the shop, carefully deciding what would work in the new design, and what she would put into store. Everything that she wasn't using was boxed up and packed away. Everything she was keeping went to be cleaned and repaired if necessary, in the workshop if possible, or to a specialist if not.

She invited all of Madame Fournier's old clients. All of the women who had written to her after Elizabeth's death, and to whom she had spoken after the first, failed show. She also invited everyone in Madame Fournier's address book. She scoured the fashion magazines for names, sending invitations to singers and actresses and any young, hip names about London who might become customers, or wear one of her hats to an event and get it photographed. She knew that was the way to get people really talking about her, and something Elizabeth had always been too discreet to exploit.

But she shook it away, and carried on. Trusting her instinct. She designed the invitations herself; they were painted on the outside of little paper packets of Japanese water flowers, the delicate sticks of tightly rolled tissue that you dropped in water and which unfurled into beautiful underwater blooms. Sat up for hours after work addressing them, carefully stamping and taking them to the post office herself. She invited photographers to set up outside, and created a little walkway on the street with some pale lilac carpet surrounded by roses in pots, so the stars had a backdrop for pictures and the press could be kept at arm's length. She had a special cocktail mixed just for her, a potent blend of gin and violet syrup, served in flutes of smoky purple crystal. She had done everything she could think of to make the night and the show a success.

'If this doesn't work, then you really did choose the wrong girl,' she said in a whisper to Elizabeth in the salon, as she was closing up, the night before the launch. And then there was nothing left for her to do other than cross her fingers and hope.

On the night, the salon was crammed. Customers, fellow designers, even a pop star or two were all jammed into the small space. Violet had kept the idea of the different changing rooms for night and day, but had completely re-imagined them for a younger audience. The 'Night' room was painted dark purple, covered in metallic outlines of moons and stars. The furniture was black suede, the carpet a deep indigo. The 'Day' room was like walking into a chocolate box painting – the walls were painted pale blue with clouds, and everything was light and airy.

When everyone was there, Violet stood and cleared her throat. She thanked them all for coming, then said, 'I'd like to introduce you to my first real solo collection. *Transformation.*'

And then the show began.

The carpeted area outside the shop led guests in through the door, and as they entered, its colour got darker and darker until it became velvety black carpet running through the centre of the shop, where it served as the catwalk. The models would step on to it from the door to the office (which was acting as a tiny and makeshift dressing room, crammed full to bursting with girls in high heels crowding for the mirrors that were leaning up against the walls to do their make-up). They entered the room holding large paper fans in front of their faces, which they gradually closed as they stood in the centre of the room, revealing the hat or head-dress that each wore.

As they did so, the spotlight that had been set up in the corner of the shop would swing around, its beam growing in strength until the piece was displayed in its full glory.

The first model carried a fan with a woman's face painted on it, un-made-up and gazing straight ahead. When she folded it away, her own face was revealed, covered by a white veil suspended from the hat above it, painted with red lips, circles of light pink rouge and sweeps of black eyeliner.

Then came a girl with a fan painted to look like the fragile brown husk of a caterpillar's cocoon. She drew it back to reveal a pale-green silk cap covering one side of her head, from which swooshed an enormous silk butterfly made from feathers that had been stitched together into a panel and painted; they fluttered gently with each step she took, as though the creature was about to take flight from her head.

From behind an ash-grey fan emerged a plume of chiffon flames, which formed a high, flickering structure held together by gold wire; when you looked at it carefully, you could see the shape of a phoenix rising, its wings spreading out down the back of the wearer's head and its claws made from gold clasps which sat at the model's temples, wound into her hair.

On and on the models came, appearing out of the shop's small back room as if by magic, each hat a breathtaking example of transformation. The guests were entranced. Violet had worried that it might not work, that the combined effect of the hats and fans and lighting might all be too much, that they might not know how to take it. But as she stood in the shadows and watched them, as delight and wonder and surprise passed over their expressions like children seeing snow for the first time, she knew she need not have worried. They were in her thrall.

As the last model returned down the catwalk, providing the room with a final glimpse of her hat (a rose in full, lush bloom where the front had been a tightly furled bud), all the lights came up and there was a pause, and then a wave of applause filled the room. Violet's hands shot up to her mouth as a gasp of relieved laughter escaped in a yelp. She had done it.

The rest of the evening passed in a blur and rush of people shaking her hand and handing her their card, congratulating her and having their picture taken with her, patting on the head the sleepy, pyjama-ed Flip, who had been brought to see what was happening, as he sucked his fingers and stared, wide-eyed at all the glamorous men and women, interview requests and offers of lunch meetings and talk of magazine profiles and all sorts of other things that made Violet's head spin.

When, eventually, everyone had gone and Flip had been taken home to be put to bed by Ginny from down the road, Violet sat in the small silver velvet chair with a cup of tea and turned the lights down low. The buzz of the guests still lingered in the air and her ears were humming from the noise even in the silence. She sat for a while, looking out at the rain running down the shop window and the streetlights beyond. The window was filled with a model of a cherry tree, its branches extending into the four corners of the display space. Each quarter of the tree merged into a different season – icicle-encrusted bare branches; soft pillows of candyfloss-pink blossom, lush green tendrils, flaming orange and russet leaves. Hats hung from its extended arms and in among the leaves and twigs. Transformation. In the street, a little whirl of leaves whipped round and round, like kittens chasing their tails.

Her gaze fell on the lettering that covered the top section of the window. From her seat inside, the letters were reversed, and cast in shadow. The old, gold, cursive writing that had been there for so many years, saying *Madame Fournier, Milliner* was gone. In its place was a single word spelled out in bold silver capitals. *Cavalley's.* She let her gaze rest on the word for a moment. The name that she had teased Bryce about when they had first met, but which they had, as he had wanted, passed on to their son Flip when he was born. The name that she had taken, signing the deed poll forms when they arrived in the post, and had given to Flip, changing his name so that they were both Cavalley. Violet Cavalley. The name that marked the final stage of her transformation, a name that meant something, a name that she could be proud of. A name that people would remember.

Violet finished her tea and gathered her things together, intending to lock up the salon and make her way home through the night, walking off the remnants of the excitement and adrenaline rush before falling into her bed and grabbing a few hours' sleep. In the morning, she would start work early.

Before she departed though, she had one last task that she must undertake. One that she had left until the end of the night, not wanting to do it until she knew the launch had been a success. From her bag, she took the drawing that Bryce had made, and which she had had mounted in a simple silver frame. Carrying a chair to the door, she stood on it and hung the picture above it, checking it was straight. 'Thank you, my love,' she said quietly. 'Thank you for drawing my dreams.'

And then she got down, took a final look around the room, and locked the door behind her.

Cavalley's was open for business.

Part Two

Chapter Six

Fran stood in the living room of Tillie and Flip's flat, staring at the piece of paper in her hands. It didn't make any sense. It was addressed to her, care of Tillie. Fran hadn't wanted it sent to her home. Hadn't wanted to risk Violet opening it by mistake, or it being put into a pile of other paperwork and getting lost. A lot of paper came through the letterbox of the house in Slaidburn Street. This one was too important to lose track of.

At least, she had thought it would be. Had been so nervous and excited that morning when Tillie had popped up on her gmail chat telling her that a letter from the General Register Office had arrived for her. Had been distracted all through the day, not paying as much attention to her work as she should have been. She was loving it at Cavalley's, and today was the first day she had given anything less than 100 per cent. It had been exactly the right decision. She was learning more than she had thought possible, working a week in each department at first, just to get an overview of how everything fitted together. She had already done a week in the design studio, watching her brother Blue with awe as he designed a dress for one of the Swedish royal family, an apple-green confection made from hundreds of panels of lace stitched together with thread as fine as cobwebs. He fitted it on a tailor's dummy, creating the shape of the garment as he sewed, the form of the dress evolving out of nowhere, like a cloud, accompanied by his ever-present stream of words, a poem, almost, that emerged from his lips as the dress flowed from his fingertips. 'Nip, tuck, a bang for your buck, a buck for a bang, bang bang, shoot me down, prettiest girl in town, in this gown, green gown green fingers, fingers and toes and heads and shoulders knees and toes, knees and toes, so it goes, lovely lady, lady in red, lay me in bed . . .'

Fran had liked listening to him. It comforted her, reminded her of being a little girl and listening to him muttering at night as he paced the house. It had never been frightening to her. It was just Blue. Her brother.

Now she was in Human Resources, and though she would never have expected to find it interesting, she was discovering that she loved it here as well. Loved every part of the company her mother had built up, loved discovering how it all worked, how the cogs ran together every day. HR allowed her to get to know the names of all the key players, the ones she wasn't already familiar with, the ones who were important in a quiet, behind-the-scenes way. Like Sue Saunders, the woman who had been with Cavalley's for twenty years, working as a book-keeper, and who had passed up promotions and opportunities elsewhere in order to remain in her little, ordered corner of the place, keeping it running as smoothly as a Rolls-Royce. Or Martin Edwards, one of the Sales Directors who had ensured that Cavalley's had a stronghold in all of the Russian department stores long before any of their competitors, and who had grown the market in that country into one of the most lucrative parts of the company. And Pinnie Winston, the woman who supplied them with hand-dyed ostrich and coque feathers in colours that no one else could achieve. With each file that she pored over, Fran got to know the company better, to understand the people who had made it what it was and their role within it. She was determined that by the time her mother died, she would know Cavalley's inside out.

But today, the knowledge that the letter was waiting for her at the flat, its contents a mystery that could unlock so many other mysteries in her life, hung in the air around her, and she couldn't wait to leave at six o'clock. She rushed out of the office, walking smartly down the street to the flat, buzzing impatiently before realising that Tillie was probably still at work. She never usually finished before seven. 'Damn,' she said to herself, and turned, about to go and wait in the bar across the road with a glass of wine, when she saw Tillie waving at her as she hurried towards her, wearing a silky dress that was slipping off one shoulder, carrying a big battered leather bag, keys already out.

'I'm coming, I'm coming,' she called, grinning at Fran, who smiled back at her with relief. Tillie had on one of Violet's hats – a little turquoise circle that was pinned to the side of her head, with netting spinning out from it, covering one side of her face. She loved the hats, was a walking advertisement for Cavalley's, and wore them with the flair and style that Violet intended.

'Don't panic,' she said as she reached Fran and put her key in the door. 'I knew you wouldn't be able to wait a second past six.'

'Thank you,' said Fran, and she heard her voice tremble.

'Hey,' said Tillie, 'it's going to be fine. We'll have a glass of wine, you can open your letter and we'll take a look. All in your own time. Or if you've changed your mind, I'll chuck it down the waste disposal, and we can forget all about it.'

They were in the hall now and Fran followed Tillie into the mirrored lift.

'No. No, I haven't changed my mind. I'm just nervous.'

Tillie squeezed her arm then pressed the button for the penthouse.

It was just going to be a name, or two names, Fran told herself as they rose up through the building. It was silly to be so nervous. It wasn't as if either of her parents were actually going to *be* there. It was just going to be a name – of her mother, maybe of her father. A date, a place. But even that was so much more than she had ever had. They would be the building blocks of her story, of her past. A name hinted at a background – a mother called Maud would be very different from a Tracy; a father who was much older might imply a forbidden love affair, one who was left off the certificate, even more strongly. London was different from Leamington Spa or Liverpool. She might never have heard of the place she had been born in. Would she recognise their names, she wondered, as the lift pulled to a stop and the doors opened. Would there be some visceral, primal pull, some deep hidden memory from babyhood, from those first days or weeks before she had become Frangipani Cavalley, when she had been – who?

She was about to find out. She followed Tillie into the living room and took the envelope from her, remaining standing as Tillie slipped her shoes off and kicked them to one side, then brought a bottle of red wine and two glasses into the room and handed one to Fran. 'Thanks.' She took a gulp, then tore the envelope open, unhesitating, in a rush like a child ripping into its stocking at Christmas. She knew if she waited any longer it would be unbearable.

She thought she had prepared herself for every eventuality. But she had not prepared herself for the letter that she found herself reading.

Dear Ms Frangipani Cavalley,

Thank you for your application dated 15th September, requesting a copy of your adoption records. Unfortunately we are unable to fulfil your request, as there is no record of an adoption having taken place of any individual with your name. It may be that the adoption took place in Scotland or Northern Ireland, in which case you would need to contact the relevant Register Office for that region. I hope that this has been of assistance.

Yours sincerely . . .

Fran read it again. She didn't understand. There was no record of her adoption. Did that mean she hadn't been adopted? Of course it couldn't. She had always been told she was, and it would have been hard to pretend she was Violet's biological baby, since her mother's whole adult life was documented in newspaper and magazine archives. Fran had always valued the fact that no one had made a big deal of it, or tried to hide the fact of her adoption from her. It was just one of the realities of life. The only mystery had been who she had been adopted *from*. And now, having made the decision to try and find that out, she seemed to have come up against a dead end almost immediately. She could have cried with frustration. Instead, she wordlessly handed the letter to Tillie, who was standing in front of her, waiting. She read it, lighting a slim menthol cigarette with one hand as she did so, pushing her golden curls back and twisting them at the nape of her neck in one fluid movement. Fran always kept her hair loose, pulling it forward, the better to conceal her scar. She envied Tillie her unmarked face, her lack of need to hide behind a sheet of hair. But her almost sister-in-law was so beautiful and kind that she didn't resent it.

Fran was struck by the full force of Tillie's beauty now, as she looked up at her, and Tillie's bright blue eyes fixed on her dark ones, an intensity in them that Fran knew meant Tillie was thinking hard.

'Fran,' she said, 'have you ever seen your birth certificate?'

*

Fran hesitated outside Kalisto's front door. He lived in a flat in Soho, above a buzzy Italian restaurant. You had to go down a narrow alleyway past the side of the restaurant to access the small courtyard in which the entrances to the five flats above were located. The restaurant was as busy as ever, full of lunchtime customers drinking Campari and prosecco from little glass tumblers, and Fran wished for a moment that she could join them, abandon her plans and squeeze into one of the little wooden tables and while away the afternoon over plates of cuttlefish risotto and sticky almond cake.

Something about visiting Kalisto at home always made her nervous, always had done. She loved him as if he was part of the family – he *was* part of the family – and he had never made her feel anything other than welcome, but his flat was very much his private domain, a place into which he retreated, and one which she was wary of intruding upon.

She lifted the heavy brass knocker that was shaped like a skull, complete with eye-sockets encrusted with dark-red crystals, and was about to let it fall, when a voice called from inside the building.

'*Entre, entre, ouvres la porte, ma petite Frangipani.* It's open, come into my humble abode, stop lurking out there.'

Fran jumped, and then pushed the door open. 'Hello?' she said.

'I heard your footsteps on the stairs,' Kalisto explained as he came out to meet her in the hall. 'Such distinctive footsteps you've always had, you know, dear heart? Light, and yet decisive. Like a very determined angel hopping from cloud to cloud.'

Fran rolled her eyes at him, but couldn't help but grin at the same time. She handed him the square Patisserie Valerie box that contained the éclairs that were his favourite. Like Violet, Kalisto's sweet tooth was insatiable; Fran had grown up knowing that the place to find a toffee or a biscuit or even, occasionally, a perfect *petit four* wrapped in a napkin, was in one of Kalisto's capacious pockets. He took the box from her, and sniffed the air.

'Coffee *and* chocolate?'

She nodded. He looked at her appraisingly.

'My, my, you spoil me, and I thank you, but my dentist does not. This must be a more important meeting than I had realised, Frangelico.'

She didn't reply.

'Get a plate then, sugar plum. There's tea in the pot.'

Fran slid through the silver beaded curtain into the tiny kitchen, to find a tray already set with tea things. A daffodil-yellow porcelain teapot covered with crystal roses sat steaming. She put the cakes on to the tray and carried it through to the drawing room.

Kalisto sat on a chair that had been made from a wooden carousel horse, its seat scooped out of the animal's side, giving the impression that the person sitting in it was emerging from its belly, the horse's head sprouting from one shoulder and its tail at the other. Fran would have found it distinctly disturbing, had it been anywhere other than here, in this strange flat stuffed full of similarly bizarre objects. A taxidermy squirrel wearing full white tie and tails stood on the mantelpiece, baton in its hand as though mid-way through conducting an orchestra. The curtains were long and grand, pale pink toile that looked as though it depicted a bucolic idyll until you looked closely, when you realised that all the shepherdesses were bent over tree stumps, a wine bottle in one hand and their dresses hitched up around their waists, or giving blow jobs under a shady bower. In the corner of the room, an old-fashioned record player with a large brass trumpet played softly. Fran tried to drag her gaze away from the objects, but spotted something new – or rather, new to here – of a dusty bell-jar containing a huge, perfectly white butterfly that appeared to be fluttering against its sides.

'It's not real, petal,' Kalisto said, noticing what she was looking at, and lifting the bell-jar so she could see that the butterfly was a fabric one, on a slender wire. As she looked, she became aware that a tiny fan whirred away at the bottom of the jar, causing the insect's wings to vibrate, and giving the illusion that it was trying to escape.

'Made by a new protégé of mine – a student from St Martin's. I thought it was rather clever.' He put the jar back on its base.

'It's beautiful. And creepy,' Fran said.

'Isn't it? I think that's the point. But you can never quite tell. However, you're not here to talk about my latest discoveries, I fear.'

Fran took a folder from her handbag.

'No, you're right. I really wanted to talk to you about two things. But now I don't know which one to start with.'

Kalisto put sugar into his teacup.

'Start with the one that's tugging at your heart-strings, my sweet girl, because I can see by the frown on your pretty forehead that something certainly is. What is it? A boy? If some little bastard's broken your heart, I swear I'll break his legs, so help me Jesus, Mary and Joseph.'

Fran grinned. 'No. There's no boy . . .'

'Good. You stay away from them. Horrible, dirty creatures, they all are, and I should know. But if it's not a boy . . .'

Fran braced herself. Her perfume business could wait. She had thought she wanted Kalisto's advice on it, but now she was here, she saw that she didn't need it, not really. She could go straight to Violet with that – she had all her figures and research – and make her listen.

But she could not go to her with this question – yet. And Kalisto, this big, gay flamboyant Northern man who was, if anything, even more of a mass of contradictions than she was herself, felt like the closest thing she had to a father. Not a conventional one, certainly, but then nothing about the Cavalley family was, or ever had been, conventional. Ever since Fran could remember, Kalisto had been there, in some ways more of a constant than her mother. While Violet flitted around the world, missing school plays and the mornings before exams, because of her business, Kalisto rarely went outside London. He hated travel, was afraid of flying, could just about be persuaded to go to Capri, but avoided any trips abroad as far as possible. So he was often the one applauding Fran when she won a certificate for Most Improved at Maths, or brought home a wonkily coiled pen pot. The pot was by his desk in his studio still, almost twenty years later. He might not have lived at the house in Slaidburn Street, officially, but it was his home from home and he was there more than some of the rest of the family, floating through the kitchen or sitting in the garden in a straw boater and pink seersucker suit in the summer.

Kalisto had been there for every birthday party that she could remember, and most Christmases. When, one damp October day, she had fallen off her bike in Hyde Park, he had bandaged her bloody knee with a vintage silk Hermès scarf, letting the blood soak through its ornate pattern, never hesitating, never mentioning it again. When she had turned sixteen he had made her a party dress, the most beautiful dress she had ever seen, a Kalisto Kauffman couture original that had made her the envy of all of her friends. The dress was more adult than anything any of them were allowed and yet not immodest or inappropriate; a sequinned, beaded piece of peach chiffon that skimmed her body and fell into a gentle fishtail shape which shimmered in the light and cast its soft, flattering hues up on to her cheekbones.

And when she had come home after that trip, her face different for ever, her skin marked with the story of what had happened to her, a story that she would be retelling for the rest of her life, he had not flinched, nor had his eyes wandered down and on to the scar, but had stayed fixed on hers as he pulled her into his big, safe arms and told her she was the most beautiful flower in the world, and always would be. If that wasn't as good as the love of a father, then she wasn't sure she wanted to know what was.

And though Fran had never had a real father, she knew that you should be able to talk to them about anything, to go to them with all your worries and problems, no matter how big or small. So Fran swallowed her nerves, along with the fear that Kalisto would be furious with her for asking what she was about to ask; that he would tell her she was ungrateful, spoiled, or that he would simply refuse to answer and show her the door. She swallowed the horrible feeling that she was betraying her mother by coming to him and not her – and that by so doing she was somehow rejecting Violet, the person who loved her most in all the world. She swallowed all of those things, and she went ahead and asked the question.

'Kalisto – why have I never seen my birth certificate?'

Violet lay propped up on pillows on the iron-framed bed in her room in the house in Slaidburn Street, facing Patrick and Kalisto, who sat at the end of it. Travelling back from Capri had exhausted her, and her face was pale, with dark circles under her eyes.

Patrick was worried. Her colour was fading. It was as if the blood was seeping out of her, invisibly. He could see her moving further and further away from him.

Still, he kept on proposing to her. 'You can marry me now,' he said, when they had arrived back in the country. 'I'll take you straight to the Register Office. I'll sign a pre-nup like the Hollywood stars. You don't have to worry about anyone finding out who you are. It's all out in the open.'

'And you still want me? May Violet Gribbens, from Belton-by-Sea, whose father murdered her boyfriend?'

'Darlin' girl, I'd want you if you were the daughter of a dictator or a dandy. A fortune-teller or a freak.' He had touched her hand. 'We are not our parents.'

She had been grateful to him for that. For acknowledging the fear she felt and could not admit to. The joke that women turn into their mothers had never felt very funny to Violet. She looked at him now, needing him to tell her the truth once more.

'How can you even ask?' he said. 'Violet. You're the centre of this family. You're the one around whom it all revolves. And if . . .' He swallowed. 'If you're not going to be here to hold it all together, well . . .' He could not carry on. Kalisto handed him an ornately embroidered gold handkerchief.

'Did I do the right thing?' Violet then asked Kalisto, seeking out the truth in his eyes. He knew what she was referring to straight away. 'All those years . . . was it the right choice? For everyone?'

Kalisto hesitated, then said firmly, 'Yes, you did the right thing, Vi. You protected your family – all of them. Always have done. How can you even ask?'

'I need to know I'm not going to leave behind any – trouble. Any mess. When I'm gone, what if . . . I won't be here to protect her?'

Kalisto took her hand. 'But I will be. *We* will be.'

Violet looked over at Patrick.

Patrick nodded. ''Course we will be, darlin' girl. 'Course we will.'

Kalisto looked down at Violet, and could have wept. The feisty little girl who had first walked into his studio all those years ago, full of ideas, full of determination, was dying, and there was nothing he could do about it.

'Oh, little Violet. *Fleur de mon coeur.* We've come a long way, baby, you and me.'

'Yes,' said Violet. 'Yes, we have. You've done a lot for me, Kalisto. I know how much you've done for me.'

Their eyes met.

'I need you to do something else, now,' Violet told him. 'I need you to make me a wedding dress.'

Patrick laughed in surprise. 'I see. Is this you finally accepting my proposal then, Miss Violet?'

'Oh, I thought I should get you to stop badgering me once and for all.' She smiled at him. 'There won't be a big reception, nor a honeymoon, I'm afraid.'

'There'll be a honeymoon every day as long as I'm with you.' Patrick leaned forward and kissed her, and Violet closed her eyes and let him, and wondered how many days that would be.

And Kalisto looked at Violet, and could still see the girl she had been all those years ago in every single angle and plane of her face; could still feel the same energy and fire that had emanated from her skin, crackling through the air around her, that he had felt and which had taken them both so far, and wondered how he was going to break the news to her that another of the secrets she had bound to her soul and kept tightly inside for so long was about to be set free.

It had been playing with a wooden stacking toy of Flip's that gave Violet the idea for Stax. Her son came to work with her where she could leave him in his pram tucked in the shop's small back room, gurgling and chuntering to himself.

Violet was tired – not just in her body; she never bothered to even notice that – it was always the case and it was pointless paying attention to it, since it just made it worse. But today she felt tired in her soul. She had learned that the hardest thing about running her own business – and about being a mother – was that, in both cases, the buck stopped with her. In the end, whatever help she had, it was always up to her to make sure the shop was open for business, that her customers were satisfied, that they didn't turn up to an event wearing a hat that was too similar to a rival's. Up to her to ensure that her shop-girls were polite, that the windows were polished and the carpets free of fluff, that the couture salon where her ladies were fitted for their hats smelled of fresh flowers and resembled a beautiful dressing room rather than an anonymous shop, that they felt pampered and like the most important of all her customers from the second they walked in the gilt door. It was up to her to check that people were paid on time, that no one was skimming money from her and that the books were balanced; to keep working on her designs, and bringing in new business, trying to think of new ways of taking hats to people, showing the hip girls (and boys) who Violet saw queuing in the King's Road outside Lord Kitchener's Valet and Granny Takes a Trip that hats were as desirable as a suede mini-skirt or a Paisley maxi coat. Because Violet knew that the times were a-changing.

When she was a little girl, gazing up at Miss Hankins's hats on their stands in her hotel room as her mother pinned hems and adjusted seams, ladies wore hats. On a Sunday, or when going to the shops, or when travelling up to London – hats were part of women's lives in a way that was quickly dying out. Fashion was moving faster, it was becoming more throw-away – literally; girls were walking the streets in fragile paper dresses, Violet knew she would have to find a way to move with this new trend, a way to turn herself from the surprisingly young owner of an old-fashioned couture milliner's shop to the Mary Quant of the world of hats. That was the goal she had set herself, and she knew that to do it she had to go mass market.

Couture was indulgent, beautiful, magical – and seriously limited. The work she had done to the salon itself had started to bring in some younger customers – Right Honourables and daughters of peers, mainly – but it wasn't enough. The sheer amount of time that it took to design and make a couture hat meant that that side of the business was always going to stay small, expensive and exclusive. But that didn't have to be the only side of the business. Violet knew she could make Cavalley's bigger, make it into something special – she just had to find the right way to get things started.

Flip was sitting wearing his nappy on a blanket on the floor, while Violet half kept an eye on him and half-watched *Coronation Street* on the old television in the corner of the room. He was trying to hook one of the painted wooden rings of his stacking toy on to the central post, and getting it stuck. She leaned down to help him, taking the ring from his chubby grip and sliding it on to the post.

He grinned up at her. 'Ack.'

She smiled at him. 'There you go, poppet pie.'

He picked up another ring and waved it at her before raising his arms and putting it on the top of his head. 'Ack!'

Violet laughed. 'That's a clever boy. Does it look like a hat? One for Mama?' She picked him up and took him over to the small mirror on the wall, before taking the biggest ring and balancing it on top of her head. Flip giggled. She picked up another and balanced it on top of the first, and pointed at her reflection. 'Does Mummy look funny, with her funny hat on?'

He waved his arms around, trying to clap but his hands missing each other. Violet stared at herself in the mirror, at the red and green circles balanced on her head, creating a makeshift 'hat'. And suddenly, somehow she knew that she had stumbled upon something that could work – that could be huge. That might even just be the thing that could change her life.

Cavalley's launched Stax in November 1968, just five months after Violet had had the original idea. The range consisted of six basic hat shapes, broken down into their constituent parts and sold as such; they could be worn in hundreds of combinations, thousands, even. Customers started off by choosing the base – a moulded felt crown which formed the central part of the product, then adding a brim, in varying styles and widths, and trimmings. Whole new shapes could be created by stacking the crowns and attaching them to one another with specially designed clips, and before long it was not unusual to see girls catwalking down the King's Road with three of the crowns balanced in a teetering stack. The shapes were unisex and men loved them as much as women. A military coat could be accessorised with a hat reminiscent of a pith helmet but in yellow or royal-blue felt, or a black fez-shaped hat with a sequinned band.

Violet had the bases and brims made by a factory near Manchester, an old hat-makers on its last legs who were desperate for the business, any business, and who gave her a deal she could just about afford for the first order. She had read about the owners of Biba and their pink gingham dress selling out in days and the problems they had had fulfilling their orders for 17,000 of them when it was featured in the *Daily Mail*, and was determined not to make the same mistake. The items arrived on a Monday morning at her flat – she was selling them by mail order as well as in her Mount Street shop – in huge cardboard boxes. As she helped the delivery man unload the crates, watched by the local boys playing in the street, she had a moment of panic. What if no one wanted them? She had put all her savings, everything she had worked for into this idea which could turn out to be a horrible mistake. Fashion was fickle, and the trend-makers could easily turn their noses up at her hats, leaving her with a grimy flat full of boxes of useless felt parts and nowhere to turn.

But they didn't. She had advertised in the women's magazines, a rectangular slot which she had designed herself. *Stax – the new hat you design yourself*, it read. *Stack, swap, exchange! Be your own fashion designer with Stax*. At the bottom were three line drawings of a model wearing a round crown base with different brims – a wide floppy one, a sharp Trilby style, a small upturned boater – and surrounded by trimmings. Below were instructions on how to order the constituent parts, to which she had given indentifying letters. She posted the advert off, paid her fees, and then went back to work and waited.

The day after the advert first ran, Violet went to the post office to check the PO Box that she had opened and unlocked it with trembling hands. Her heart sank when she saw the single envelope inside. She tore it open. *I would like to order one crown style A and one brim style M in navy blue*. Violet could have wept. One order. But she told herself not to be ungrateful. These things took time. So she packed up her single order and sent it off. The next day she went back to the post office, steeling herself for another single order. You must stick it out, she told herself. What would Madame Fournier have done, had she given up at the first hurdle? Why should the world hand you success on a plate? What right do you have to it? You need to earn it.

Her fears were confirmed when the post office manager called out cheerfully as she walked up to her locker, key in hand, 'Nothing in there today, petal.'

Violet fixed a smile on her face, said, 'Oh. Thank you anyway,' and turned to go.

'Eh – not so fast!' Violet stopped. She didn't want to turn round and let him see the tears in her eyes, so she paused for a moment.

'It's all back here. You'd better take it with you, love, 'cos I don't have room for it.'

Violet spun around. The man was dragging a large mail bag from his spot behind the counter. She looked at it in astonishment. 'That's not . . .'

'Yup. All for you. Looks like you're going to be coming back here more often, eh?' and he beamed at her excitedly. Violet stared at the sack, and wondered how on earth she was going to get it home on the bus.

Orders continued to flood in. After the first day Violet enlisted the help of Ginny's brother-in-law Ray, who worked as a delivery boy for the flower market and was happy to pick up her sacks of mail and deliver them to her, then later, after his shift had finished, to take the orders to the depot. On the Monday morning after the ads had run, she got to Cavalley's to find a queue stretching halfway down Mount Street. The girls in the queue were not her usual type of customer, with their velvet minidresses and white patent boots, and sweeping Indian maxi dresses; there wasn't a pastel twin-set in sight – oh yes, there was. Standing between two young men in Afghan coats, who seemed to be passing a joint between them, was Miss Brigstock, one of her regular ladies, looking terrified, but waiting patiently in line.

Violet stood and watched for a second, her heart racing with excitement, and realised two things – firstly that she was going to have to get another shop, and secondly, that she had better go and rescue little Miss Brigstock.

In the first week of January 1969, Violet went to view a building a few hundred yards down the King's Road from Slaidburn Street. She was selling Stax and trimmings as fast as she could reorder the parts and come up with new accessories out of her flat, and had convinced Ray to leave his job at the flower market and come and work for her fulltime. She divested him of his canvas overalls and his van, took him shopping and gave him a new uniform of a red suit with velvet lapels and a dapper royal-blue shirt – complete, of course, with his own Stax – a red Trilby-style with a Union Jack print band. She put him on the back of a red Vespa Sprint with *Cavalley's* painted on it in shiny blue and white.

Ray quickly cast off his initial doubts about the clothes and took to frequently checking his reflection in his scooter's mirrors, adjusting his hat to his preferred rakish angle before getting out to make his deliveries. Violet had to chivvy him out of the door to stop him trying on different hat combinations. Quite a change for the boy who had, up until a few months ago, thought fashion was for 'girls and nancy boys' and had been trying to get his girlfriend to take a job in his dad's pie shop. The London-wide delivery service was already going down a storm with shoppers wanting a new hat to accessorise a night out or a hot date at short notice. They could phone their order in and have a Stax delivered to them within a few hours.

The lease was for the whole building – three storeys of red brick sandwiched between an antique furniture shop and a cosy bistro. Violet took Ray with her to look around it for moral support, and left Flip with Ginny. She was glad she had done so when, as they stepped over the threshold, a clump of plaster fell on to her shoulder and crumbled in dusty grey mulch over her clothes. The estate agent stepped forward smartly and brushed it off.

'Just needs a bit of TLC and it'll be a wonderful retail space,' he gushed. 'I can see it now – some new display cabinets, some nice white paint . . . lovely jubbly.'

'Needs a bit more than just love,' Ray commented, pulling another clump of plaster from the wall and rubbing it through his fingers.

The estate agent grinned widely. 'All you need is love, mate, isn't that what you lot say now, eh?' and he laughed at his own joke.

Violet's teeth clenched involuntarily. 'What about the damp?' she asked, looking up at the soggy patch in the ceiling.

'Surface only, nothing structural.' He turned towards Ray 'See there? It's just the plaster, be good as new in no time, mate.'

Violet cleared her throat pointedly. 'It smells of damp. That can't be just surface, surely?'

'Just needs a bit of an airing, love. Open a few windows, get some nice vases of flowers in . . . blow away the cobwebs in no time, clever girl like you.' He winked at her and then carried on addressing Ray.

'Talking straight, you're getting a bargain, damp or no damp. This area's become hot property, even if it feels a bit chilly today.' He guffawed again. Ray looked uncomfortable and shifted his weight from side to side – he could sense Violet's building rage. She spoke a little louder this time.

'Are the stairs safe? I'd like to look at the other floors.'

The staircase was uncarpeted and unpainted, and looked distinctly rickety.

'Why don't you stay down here, pet? Mr Cavalley can check

out the necessaries and you can wait outside – get a cuppa next door, maybe?'

'Oh dear,' said Ray.

'Why would I want to get a cuppa next door?' Violet's voice was sharp and cold. 'And Mr Cavalley is sadly deceased.'

'Ah. I do—'

'Don't apologise. Just stop talking to me as if I'm a brainless child because I happen to be a woman, and start telling me what exactly you are going to do to make this place available to me at a price that means I can make it habitable by next week, otherwise I will take the downpayment,' Violet reached into her handbag and pulled out a thick brown envelope, 'and take it to an agent who can show me a property that isn't about to fall down around my ears, and who might not be so rude and sexist as to assume that my assistant is the one in charge, when it is my business, my money, my name above the door, and my name on the papers that I won't be signing *unless you pull your fucking finger out*.'

There was a pause. The agent stared at Violet. Ray stared at the floor. And Violet stared back at the agent, hoping that he didn't call her bluff and force her to walk away from this building that was perfect, and which, even with the money she had made, she could only just afford if she managed to negotiate a ten per cent discount on the asking price.

The man's Adam's apple bobbed, and he put his hands in the pockets of his badly cut suit. 'Now you ask, I am authorised by the owner to accept a lower offer, should the property not be taken at its asking price. Maybe we should go back to the office to discuss it?'

Two days later, Violet had the keys in her hand, and the work really started. She went to the shop at 5 a.m., alone this time, and let herself in. She wanted to savour the moment. Madame

Fournier's might have her name above the window now, but it still had her benefactor's spirit in the very wallpaper of the place. But this . . . this was Violet's blank canvas, to do with what she would.

For a second she shivered, as her father's words rang in her ears. '*You'll never escape. You've done a deal with the devil, May Violet Gribbens – blood betraying blood begets blood. You're cursed. You remember that.*' She shook herself. She was May Gribbens no longer; she was Violet Cavalley, and her father's curse was superstition, gypsy guff. Nothing more.

Then she got down on her hands and knees and began to scrub.

For a week she worked from five in the morning until midnight, leaving the Mount Street shop in the capable hands of her staff and Flip with Ginny. She missed him, all day, worried that by the end of the week he would have seen so little of her that he would forget who she was, but in the mornings when she scooped him out of his bed, all warm and fast asleep still, and wrapped him in a blanket to drop him over the road on her way to the shop, he would half wake, and lock his eyes on to hers and smile, and she knew that he would never forget who she was, any more than she would forget him. 'We're a team, you and me, aren't we, Flip Cavalley? A team,' she would whisper to him.

She painted and sanded and varnished every day for a week. As it turned out, the estate agent hadn't been so far wrong about the state of the place. Once they had cleared all the rubbish and opened all the windows up they could see that the building was solid, if neglected and frayed around the edges. Ray's other brother Dave was brought in to replaster the walls, and he and Ray shored up the old wooden treads of the staircase, painted them silver and covered them with Perspex, so it looked as if you were walking up to heaven when you ascended them. The floorboards were solid, and Violet planned to cover them with rugs anyway.

She went next door to the antiques dealer who told her the best flea markets to go to, to buy rugs and side-tables and lamps, and she spent Saturday morning at the end of the week scouring the stalls, coming back with everything she needed to carry out her plan. They painted the front door black and silver, and repainted Ray's scooter to match. She bought sets of net curtains and dyed them black in her bathtub and sewed silver thread into them so they shimmered, and then hung them in the windows. There was no sign above the windows, just a nameplate on the front door, above the knocker that was shaped like a top hat.

Boxes of Stax came pouring in from the factory, and she had the girls in the Mount Street shop making extra trimmings and decorations in any spare moment they got. She knew that she would have to increase the range before long – Stax wouldn't sell for ever, the fad would pass on to something else and she wanted to make sure it was something of hers – but for now, she was going to strike while the iron was hot and sell as many Stax as she possibly could. Violet had plenty of other ideas up her sleeve for the future.

One of them, she needed to put into action before she could open; it was crucial to the success of her venture, she believed, but it was new and scary, and she was nervous. Still, it had to be done – she couldn't back out now – so Violet left Ray painting and his brother Dave hammering nails down into floorboards to make sure they were safe, and Ginny edging lengths of striped military ribbon, and took herself off down the King's Road. Near Sloane Square was an artists' colony – a large, imposing building called the Falconry, complete with wrought-iron gates with metal birds of prey glaring down at you as you entered. Violet looked up at them as she prepared herself to enter. She might dress in the latest fashions these days and sweep her fringe across her forehead like a proper dolly bird, but in her heart she still felt like a kid from the seaside playing with the grown-ups. The plumage of the birds who strutted around here was infinitely brighter and more exotic. The building was packed with studios containing every kind of artist. She could hear the music from outside – was it the Stones? It could be, there was a recording studio in the building, she had heard. Taking a deep breath, she walked through the arched doorway.

Inside, the air smelled of incense and pot and size, the glue made from rabbit bones that was used to make hats and which, once smelled, was never forgotten. Typewriters clattered. In the entrance hall, posters for gigs and exhibitions were stuck straight on the walls, and the light was gloomy. This was where Swinging London was all happening, and she could sense the miasma of creative energy in the walls of the place. And it scared her. She went upstairs, to a narrow corridor with a run of rooms leading off it, and began to make her way towards the end, where she had been told the man whom she had come to see would be found.

Kalisto Kauffman was a designer who had made his name a couple of years before when he had appeared in London, apparently from nowhere, and caused a sensation with his space-age-inspired designs that seemed to come from another planet. Silver jumpsuits and thigh-high boots made from Perspex flew off the shelves, even though they could only be worn by the slimmest-thighed customers and were impossible to walk in. A range of transparent shirts and trousers a couple of months later had all the old school reporters scoffing and muttering about 'Emperor's new clothes' and cemented his reputation as the *enfant terrible* of the fashion scene. He became the one whom everyone in the know wanted to work with. Violet had been reading about him in magazines and profiles for years, and had known since she moved to London that one of her main aims would be to meet him and somehow collaborate with him. And now, she thought she had found a way to entice the notoriously picky and temperamental man to consider working with her. She had managed to get him to agree to see her by phoning and telling him about her success so far with Stax, and that she had a proposition for him. Getting him on the other end of the phone had been enough of a job, but when she had eventually managed it he had been surprisingly charming and had told her to come to his studio the next day.

She could hear Kalisto's voice as she walked towards his room at the end of the corridor. It was unmistakable – a high-pitched Germanic lilt littered with random words in French and Italian and mixed metaphors, along with a few words that she suspected he might have made up, that seemed to carry for miles even when he was whispering, which he certainly was not doing now. It was not a bellow, which would have implied depth, rather a prolonged yelp, like a Yorkshire terrier singing.

'But this is *absolument* an *horreur*! A catastrophe of proportions *moltissimo*, veritable *moltissimo*. I am shocked – no, I am deeply saddened to the bottom of my core by this. Who would have thought, oh warrior of my heart, that when you agreed to stock my designs – no, no, *when I agreed to allow you to sell my children*, mes petits, *in your establishment*, that you would betray me like this with a spear in my spine?'

Violet paused outside the door, and listened. Kalisto was silent for a long time. Chatter about a recent magazine shoot came from one of the other studios, and Violet could hear someone sucking on a bong. She raised her hand to the door and was about to knock when a terrible wail came from inside the room.

'I will never surrender to you, you Brutus Maximus, you Mussolini of Chelsea! You . . .' there was a pause and then a stage whisper '. . . are DEAD TO ME.'

And then there was a crash, and a shriek from the street below. Oh goodness, thought Violet. Maybe she should come back another time. Yes, that was probably best. It didn't sound as if Kalisto was going to be as charming as she had hoped. He certainly didn't sound in the frame of mind to agree to what she planned to suggest. But then the door flew open and he stood towering before her, ushering her in with one hand, the other holding a cigarette in a long horn holder.

'Don't just stand on the doorstep, my *chérie*, looking like a tiny little terrified mouse. Sit down, tell me everything about yourself, tell me all,' and she was swept inside and deposited into a large leather armchair in the corner of his studio before she had time to turn tail and leave. Later, she would learn that Kalisto was as mercurial as Puck, and never held a grudge, partly because he could rarely remember what it was he had been angry about in the first place, such was his butterfly mind. He wore a floor-length tweed coat, lined with fur, that had a high collar and trailed on the floor, belted at the waist like a strange fusion of English country-wear and theatrical splendour. A sheer organza shirt peeked out from beneath it, and the look was topped and tailed with a matching tweed deerstalker hat and a pair of platform riding boots in polished leather. Violet took in the outfit, and knew that she had come to the right place.

In five minutes she had a cigarette pressed between her fingers in a pink plastic holder which he insisted she take away with her ('I make them in the long dark nights of the soul, *mein Liebe*, four o'clock in the morning is the time for creating frivolous fripperies while one dreams of Jeanie – or Jean') and a cup of herbal tea that tasted of straw. And ten minutes later, she had an agreement from Kalisto that they would work together.

On the Sunday before they opened she took Flip with her to the shop and let him play in the piles of empty boxes as she unpacked all the furniture and accessories and hats, and set everything up. Her assistant Betty helped, hanging clothes on rails and dressing the place according to Violet's instructions, and at the end of the day, as they stood surveying their handiwork, said, 'I don't know how you've done it, Miss Violet. It's as if it's popped up overnight.' But Violet had been dreaming of it for years . . . There was a knock at the door, three sharp raps. Violet went to open it. On the step stood Kalisto in purple patent platform shoes which added almost a foot to his already tall frame, a matching purple shirt with ruffles down the front and a long collar, and a white velvet suit. A purple silk scarf trailed over his shoulder almost to the ground, and a purple top hat was perched perilously on his bald head.

'*J'arrive, meine kleine Schokolade*. I come bearing my wares, a *pauvre* tradesman hawking his babies to the cruel world of fashion.' He stooped to kiss Violet on each cheek and stalked into the house. Behind him, an assistant began to wheel rails of silk and fur and velvet clothes towards the front door, while another girl was unloading crates from the back of a convertible sports car on to the pavement.

'I've rallied the troops, sugar plum. The fashion army is tooled up and bearing silver-topped canes, not terrible rifles. We come to fight the fight against mediocrity and the bland,' and his face twisted into a terrible expression of disgust. Violet stood back and allowed him and his entourage to sweep into the house.

They worked all day. Kalisto proved himself to be far more than a flamboyant clothes horse and over-the-top character;

he worked as hard as anyone else to get the place in order, the day punctuated by his cries of '*Quel dommage!* Someone light me a cigarette,' and 'No, no, no, not like that. Drape, dear-heart, DRAPE . . .'

Cavalley's House, King's Road opened on Monday morning, 12 January 1969. There was no sign above the shop; there had been no publicity. Violet hadn't had time, relying on word of mouth to get out, and it had. The door knocker was going every few minutes – it was already driving poor Betty mad opening it every time. She didn't understand why they couldn't just 'leave the blimming door open like every other normal shop. You do want to sell things, don't you, Miss Violet?'

But this wasn't like every other normal shop. The place was kitted out like a house. The door knocker was all part of it. You knocked, and waited to be let in. When you entered, you found yourself in a hallway (Dave had erected a makeshift wall and covered it in wallpaper left over from doing his mum's house up), complete with hallway rug, a small side-table, and an oversized hat-stand made from four normal ones nailed together and covered with Stax. On the wall, a cross-stitched sampler proclaimed that *Wherever I lay my hat, that's my home*'. Turning left, you found yourself in a large room decked out like a typical front room but on acid. An oversized settee made out of a double bed and the arms and back from an old settee found in a skip nailed on to the base, was covered in throws and embroidered shawls and silk scarves and tasselled pillows; it already had three girls lounging on it, one asleep beneath a crocheted shawl. Betty was pouring tea from a Portmeirion set and handing it round. In the corner, the television was playing *Coronation Street*, and on the wall, a large framed print of the Mad Hatter watched over proceedings.

Bookshelves held rows of paperbacks gathered from charity

shops, and in another corner a man flipped through a stack of records while a gramophone played the Beatles' *White Album*. Towards the back of the building, a small kitchen had been fitted and the cupboards filled with bars of chocolate, boxes of cereal, bags of crisps, tins of spaghetti hoops. A drinks cabinet held bottles of advocaat and gin and sherry, and someone was sitting at the small Formica table reading *Private Eye*.

The theme continued throughout the house. In the bedrooms, wardrobes lined the walls and became huge dressing-up boxes for grown-ups; hats in old-fashioned hatboxes were stacked in piles, on shelves; balanced in teetering towers on hat-stands and hung from ribbons in the window. Girls were stripping off and trying on Kalisto's clothes and shoes and Stax in front of full-length mirrors that were leaning against the walls, and on the landings.

A small box room that had once been used as a storeroom had been cleaned out and painted bright pink – the walls, the ceiling, the floor, and turned into a dressing room, with stools and dressing-tables and more mirrors, and bowls full of make-up. Jewellery boxes overflowed with long strands of beads, huge plastic coloured earrings, gobstopper rings. There were wigs on stands, hairpieces, false eyelashes, lipsticks, eyeliner pencils, scent, even a hairdresser's blowdryer – everything a girl needed to transform herself was there, to either buy and take away or pay to use there. You could easily walk into Cavalley's House dressed in your nightie and leave ready for a night on the town – and indeed, after a few weeks, someone did just that.

The bathroom was the same – a version of a typical bathroom but skewed, bigger, brighter. The tub was filled with bottles of bubble bath, packs of hair colour, body creams.

A second small room on the top floor had been transformed

into a psychedelic nursery. Mini Stax that Violet had ordered a small run of were flying out of the rainbow-painted door as hip young parents kitted their kids out in hats to match their own, and mini-velvet jackets and shift dresses in lollipop colours completed the look. The walls were painted with a bright, trippy mural – pink clouds and blue grass and swirling multi-coloured patterns created an entrancing scene. A huge toybox overflowed with toys and games – toy cars and pretend hairdressing-salon sets and rockets. In here the bookshelves held Flintstones and Jetsons annuals and a line of Daleks worked their unseeing way along the mantelpiece. 'Thunderbirds are . . . GO.' The theme tune blasted from a television set and the curtains were *Magic Roundabout* print.

At ten o'clock on Monday night, after everyone had gone home and the place had been tidied up after the onslaught of feet that had trampled through it that day, Violet and Kalisto sat at the little table in the kitchen, a bottle of cherry brandy between them. It was all that was left in the drinks cupboard. The day had been a roaring success.

'Fifty-nine . . . sixty . . . we've taken more than two hundred pounds,' Violet announced. 'Not bad for a day's work, eh?'

'Not bad? Sweetpea, it's fucking marvellous!' Kalisto threw back his head and laughed. 'You know, when you first came to me I didn't one hundred per cent believe it would work.'

'Why not?'

He raised an eyebrow. 'A shop that looks like a house? No till, people buying tins of baked beans and face powder and records with their hats and Kauffman originals? Where the pictures on the walls and the furniture is for sale?'

'OK, I know. It's unusual.'

'It's more than unusual, it's insane.'

'But it's worked.' Violet jangled the bag of money she was holding at him. Madame Fournier's words rang in her ears once more. '*Listen to your heart. Trust yourself.*' Well, she had, and it was working. The bag of money in her hand told the truth.

'It's more than fooking worked! You're a fooking genius!'

Violet turned and looked at him in astonishment. The smooth, European accent peppered with French and Italian had turned into a broad, Yorkshire brogue.

'Oh bollocks to it.' He took a sip of his drink and laughed. 'If we're going to work together, I'd better come clean. I can't keep it up all the bloody time. Kalisto Kauffman doesn't exist!' Now he slipped back. 'He's a fantastical phantasmagoria, a *délicieux mélange* of the *nouveau* and the *ancien*, *il maschio e la femina* . . . A transformation.'

From that day on, Kalisto and Violet became best friends. Their businesses grew side by side, feeding one another. Violet began doing all the hats for Kalisto's catwalk shows; he created ranges of clothing to be sold exclusively in Cavalley's King's Road, alongside her other goods. They worked, ate and played together.

'Ah, it's a shame I like the boys,' Kalisto would say, 'otherwise we could just marry each other and be done with it.'

Violet smiled. It was true. They never fought, they never got bored with one another's company.

'Actually, speaking of which . . . ' Kalisto said, as he was pinning a sheet of black chiffon to a tailor's dummy.

Violet glanced at him. 'Oh God. You're not going to pronounce your love for me, or something awful, are you?'

He snorted. 'Panic not, sweetpea, panic not. But I do have a favour to ask.'

'Go on.'

'The thing is, my parents are coming to visit. And they don't exactly know . . .'

'Oh God.' Violet knew what was coming. 'Kalisto, no.'

'Pleeeease? Sugar Plum? Light of my life? Just one dinner. Go on. It'll be fun.'

'Lying to your parents, Kal? It won't be fun.' Violet's eyes were disapproving, but she could not refuse him.

He grinned at her. 'Just one dinner. I promise.'

It wasn't just one dinner. It was never 'just one' anything, when it came to her best friend. But after the third evening of pretending to be Kalisto's girlfriend, of excruciating small talk and having to watch every word she said in case she mentioned one of his boyfriends or some wild night out, of sitting next to him and trying not to laugh at him in his sensible shirt and trousers, all affectations dropped (or most of them), not to giggle at his discomfort when he kissed her on the lips, she put her foot down.

'I'm not doing it again,' she told him, the night before his new shop was due to open, at the party for which his parents had made the trip.

Kalisto's face fell, but he didn't speak.

'And don't try and guilt me into it with that face,' she added. 'Come on, Kal. You have to drop the pretence some time. You can't exactly keep both sides of the coin going tomorrow night, can you?'

Kalisto sighed. 'Oh, all right,' he said. 'But if they disown me in front of everyone, I'm blaming you.'

Violet nodded. 'OK. I think we can take that risk,' she said.

The shop was full, as Kalisto's parties always were, with the oddest assortment of guests imaginable. Friends he had picked up from all sorts of places – fellow designers in thick eyeliner and dark bobs, flowers in their hair, and women in pinstriped suits, one with a monocle and hair slicked down in a side parting, who nodded pompously at Violet every time she passed by, and then tried to pinch her bottom, like a lecherous politician. The man who had once been in a band that had been famous for about three weeks in the summer of 1963 who now spent most of his time in parks, playing a set of pan pipes and chanting, when the mood took him. There was an actual politician, who arrived in a car with blacked-out windows and came in through the back entrance ('Not for the first time, you mark my words,' Kalisto boomed to Violet) and left as silently as he had arrived; there were models, their almost alien faces with features unnaturally prominent, pushed forward through their skin through years of starving themselves, bobbing above the rest of the guests like Chinese lanterns. The entire chorus of the latest musical were there, faces still thick with panstick make-up from the matinée, drinking more than they should and giving the room an impromptu rendition of one of their hit numbers. There were tailors and seamstresses, three lords and five ladies, Kalisto's chiropodist, charlady and at least four people whom he had found on the street and brought in, and, in the middle of it all, next to a woman in an orchid-patterned kimono holding a long cigarette-holder and wearing green platform shoes covered in sequins, and a man who was telling a small crowd that he was Kalisto's guru and spiritual guide, were Kalisto's parents.

Two dusty beige moths in a crowd of brightly coloured butterflies they stood, entirely still, polite but frightened smiles on their faces, neither knowing where to look or what to say.

'Well,' said Brian.

'Well, I say,' said Glenys.

'It's all very . . .'

'Very modern.'

'Yes. That it certainly is.' Brian looked around, unfolded his hands and refolded them, then changed his mind and put them in his pockets.

'All very lively,' he continued.

Glenys looked enviously at a woman passing by in front of her, wearing an eighteenth-century ballgown. 'What a wonderful dress,' she whispered, glancing down at her putty-coloured shift. 'So glamorous. I wonder if that's one of David's?'

'I imagine so. I don't know. Very impractical though, dear. Imagine the problems she's going to have getting through the door.'

When she passed them, the crowd parting like the sea for her enormous train, you could see that the back of her dress was quite transparent.

'Yes. Very impractical indeed,' said Glenys quietly.

'She's got a beauty spot on her . . . on her . . .'

'On her bottom.'

Brian remained silent, and bit his lower lip.

'Go and *talk* to them,' Violet whispered, putting her knee in Kalisto's back and trying to shove him out into the room. 'They're completely overwhelmed, poor things, they don't know where to look and, oh God, now the bloody Pied Piper's serenading your mother.'

Kalisto peered surreptitiously around the corner of the curtain into his shop, big beads of sweat on his forehead, which he mopped with a monogrammed silk hankie.

'Can't you?' he said, in his natural accent. 'Please? They still think you're my girlfriend. Go on, just to start with, then I'll come and join you. It'll be better that way.'

'Better for *whom*? Not for them. And not for you. This is your night. You need to be centre stage.'

Kalisto whipped the curtain shut as his father turned towards them.

'Please, Lady Vi. I can't do it. I'm terrified.' His voice was genuinely plaintive, and his face was white. He dropped his hankie on the floor and pulled another, even more flamboyant one, from a pocket in his frockcoat. Violet reached up to put her hands firmly on his shoulders; it was a stretch for her, since Kalisto was more than a foot taller than her in his socks, and tonight he was wearing stacked patent brogues.

'I know you are,' she said sympathetically. He looked relieved for a moment. 'And it's ridiculous,' she continued. Kalisto whimpered.

'They're your parents. They love you. They're good people. They'll accept it, they really will. And, more to the point, you're ruining your own party by hiding behind this sodding curtain like some overgrown Wizard of Oz. Now,' she said, firmly turning him around to face the curtains, 'get out there, and get *on* with it.' She stood on tiptoe to kiss his cheek and then gave him a shove, so he was propelled through the velvet. Then she crossed her fingers, and prayed.

There was a pause, and the room fell quiet. 'Come on, Kalisto,' she whispered to herself. She closed her eyes. That such an enormous presence could be so cowed both by speaking in public and his parents, that the prospect of combining the two was so frightful to him was something Violet would never understand, but there it was. She willed him, with every ounce of herself, to be all right, to say what he needed to say, feeling his rising panic, his sweaty palms and racing heart as though they were her own. Her mouth was as dry as she knew his would be, her heart fluttered in her chest. And then . . .

'Welcome, ladies and gentlemen.' His voice was slightly faltering, his German accent in place now. Don't you wimp out, Violet thought.

'Not that many of you are ladylike, or gentlemanly,' he continued, his voice gaining in confidence now, a familiar note of arch humour creeping back into it. 'There are more guttersnipes in this room than there were wigs in Versailles,' he carried on, adopting a French accent and, Violet knew, even though she could not see, giving a little florid bow. There was laughter and a smattering of applause.

See? she thought. You can do it. All you have to do is believe in yourself and follow your heart, and for a moment, Madame Fournier was with her again.

'But there is one lady and one true gent here this evening, without whom . . .' Violet could not resist peeking out from behind the curtain at this. There they were, Brian and Glenys Briggs, their wide eyes owl-like behind big, unfashionable glasses, their shoes sensible and comfortable.

'Without whom I would not be where I am today. I know, it sounds like an Oscar speech, doesn't it? Well, I may never win one of those, but I've got a shop in Bond Street, so screw you, I'm giving a speech.'

Laughter, applause.

'But without these people I really wouldn't be here – I wouldn't exist. Oh, Kalisto Kauffman exists, all right, but only until I take off my clothes and get into bed at night and turn out the light, and then I'm left with who I really am. Who I was born as and who, hopefully in a long time, I'll die as. David Briggs, from Hull, son of Brian and Glenys. Mum, Dad . . .'

Kalisto paused. 'I love you. And I have to tell you . . .' He reached his hands out and Glenys came forward and squeezed the arm of her son, then looked out at all of the people in front of her and blushed, and hurriedly gestured for Brian to get over by her other side. He took her hand, as Kalisto turned to them both.

'I'm sorry if you're disappointed, or find it difficult to accept, but it's time I was honest with you. Violet isn't my girlfriend. Violet, get out here.' He turned and gestured for her to come out. She stepped out from behind the curtain, and stood, waiting. 'I'm queer.'

The room was quiet. Kalisto waited. Violet also waited, her fists clenched tight.

'Oh David,' Glenys said eventually. 'We've known that since you were five years old. None of the other little boys at the village school wanted to play the part of the Virgin Mary in the nativity play, now did they?'

Chapter Seven

Kalisto watched as Patrick left the room. He had silently asked him for a moment alone with Violet, a question posed and responded to by a nod of the head and a meeting of the eyes in a way that was becoming more and more frequent around Violet since her family had learned about her illness. Somehow they felt less able to speak freely around her. She was turning into an invalid in front of their eyes, and she could feel it, and she hated it. *I am still here*, she wanted to rage at them, *still your mother, your partner, your best friend, still the person who has given you everything and who would drop everything to help you. I am not invisible and neither are you, I can still see the worried glances that pass between you, the things you want to keep from me. I am more than my illness, more than a dying woman, I am Violet Cavalley, and you must never forget it.* That is what she wanted to say to them.

But she did not. Instead, she lay in bed and watched as Patrick left the room, and then as Kalisto came and sat next to her and locked his fingers together, the big half-moons of his nails gleaming white, and then listened as he began to speak. He told her that Fran had come to him, asking about her birth certificate and why she had never seen it, and how he had tried to gloss over it, saying he was sure it was just coincidence, that there was no reason.

However, she had been sure, steadfast in her conviction that it had been kept from her, had cited as examples the time she had been going to apply for her driving licence and Violet had insisted on having all the paperwork done for her, presenting her with just a form to sign, when there was no reason Fran couldn't do it herself, and especially when Violet was usually keen that her children not end up as pampered brats who were used to having all their menial tasks and errands run for them. Had remembered when she was eighteen and had to get a new passport, and again, Violet had taken care of the forms and the administration of it, telling her that it was because there had been a confusion with the Passport Office and that it was easier if Violet dealt with them, that they would listen to her.

Fran had said she thought it sounded odd at the time, but since she had no real need to question it nor any desire to wrangle with dull bureaucracy, she had forgotten all about it. When Kalisto had asked her why she needed it, now in particular, she had told him about sending off for her adoption forms, and the reason why she had done so – why she had suddenly felt the need to know who she was and where she came from, now that Violet was slipping away from her.

Kalisto had seen the determination in her face and had known that she would, somehow, find out – whatever he did. As finding out by herself, by accident, would be the worst thing for her that he could imagine, he had told her that he would talk to Violet for her, and promised her that she would, soon, know the truth.

Violet let out a long, slow breath that hurt her lungs more with each second, and then she nodded. Fran was here, had come to the house with Kalisto, she was sure of it. Her old friend would have brought the girl with him, knowing that Fran was not going to rest until she got what she wanted, knowing that he might lose his nerve if he left it any longer. This time,

Violet was glad of the silent look that she was able to give him which told him all of that, and also that it was OK, that he had done the right thing.

'Tell her to come in,' she said quietly.

When Fran entered her mother's bedroom, she was struck by the unusual sight of Violet propped up in bed. It wasn't often that this happened. Violet had never slept much. Usually when Fran came in here she was sitting at her dressing-table, or was on the phone, pacing in the same way that Flip did, or sometimes sitting on top of the bed, on the covers not under them, magazines and drawings and sketchbooks spread out all around her – a beautiful spider at the centre of the web she was constantly weaving.

Now she was leaning against a pile of pillows, their silk covers the ones she had used as long as Fran could remember because they were meant to stop you waking up with wrinkles, wearing an oversized white shirt, the sleeves rolled up around her elbows. Stylish as ever.

She held her hand out to Fran. 'Darling girl.' Her other hand reached up and pushed the curl of Fran's hair back, tucking it behind her ear. Fran automatically reached up to set it free again, mother and daughter forming almost a mirror image of one another, in the same waltz that they had been dancing for years. Violet smiled, and dropped her hand to the cover.

'Sorry,' she said, and immediately Fran felt guilty, and wished she could take the gesture back.

Instead, she told her mother, 'Kalisto said you would tell me. He knows, doesn't he? He knows who my parents are.'

Violet gave a small nod. The time for hiding the truth in the shadows like a child hiding in its mother's skirts was gone.

'Yes, he knows. He has always known, Fran. I'll tell you everything, but please be a little patient. I need to tell you about what happened before, first. And please try to understand. You might feel angry – I'm sure you will. But please know that everything I've ever done, every decision I've ever made, has been what I thought was best for you. Everything.'

Her face was fierce and her voice was suddenly hoarse. Fran felt a lump grow in her throat and she tried to push it away, but she couldn't.

'Just tell me, Mama. Just tell me.'

1973

Violet would always remember the day that she first heard the name Sam Gilmour.

She was sitting at her desk in the office that adjoined her workshop, working on a new set of designs, when the phone rang and a voice that could have cut through diamonds said, 'This is Lady Ann Michelmore. Am I speaking with Violet Cavalley?'

Something about the woman's voice made Violet pause and look up from her work, instead of carrying on the conversation with the handset wedged between her ear and her shoulder while she drew and trimmed and sketched as she usually would. It was clear and light and very, very posh, not so much cut glass as polished crystal.

'Speaking,' Violet replied.

'I am to be married to Viscount Sam Gilmour in four months' time,' Lady Ann continued, 'and I am told you are the best couture milliner in town. I'd like to make an appointment to come and discuss my requirements. Should I speak to your secretary about that? I wish to visit as soon as possible; time is of the essence.'

Violet was taken aback. Ordinarily new customers had to

wait months for an appointment – she already had bridal couture bookings for the next two years in her diary. But something about this calmly confident woman was different. Violet agreed to see Lady Ann in a few days' time, and then put the phone down and paused. She had a feeling of – déjà vu? Not quite . . . But just something.

'Missus Vi'let? I'm not 'appy at all wiv 'ow this marabou looks on Miss Celia's pink 'at for the show. It's all mucky-looking, like.'

Violet pulled herself back to the workshop and Joan's concerns, but for the rest of the day she felt strangely unsettled.

The morning Lady Ann came to see Violet was a cold, bright day following a night of heavy rain that had made London feel scrubbed clean. Violet got into the workshop early, before anyone else, and put coffee and the heating on straightaway before taking her coat off. Then she went to the large windows in her office and raised the blinds. The view over the rooftops and towards the river never failed to make her gasp with delight, and she let her eyes gulp it in. The light was dawn-drenched watercolour grey still, and the river sparkled flashes of opal. An idea for a collection began forming behind her eyes. She grabbed a sketchbook and pencil and began scribbling, her handwriting and drawings filling the pages, almost bursting out beyond the edges of the paper. A collection inspired by the river, with all its teeming life and constantly moving rhythms. Houseboats, hidden treasures, glittering bridges at night. Police boats, pleasure cruisers, the old frost fairs with skaters and stalls, the South Bank and slabs of brutalist concrete architecture. Her pencil whizzed as she began to outline shapes and trimmings, to feel how she would translate the wonder of the river into a catwalk collection of couture hats that customers would pay thousands for, and the diffusion ranges which would be stocked in her high-end and mass-market boutiques.

'Ms Cavalley?'

She was jerked out of her trancelike state by Lady Ann's voice. The woman stood in the doorframe, a pale-blue silk square tied over her blond hair which was in a perfect chignon, dressed in a beige Burberry trenchcoat and glossily supple brown leather boots. She was the picture of English elegance, and Violet was suddenly aware of how haphazardly her dark curls were piled on top of her head, secured with a pencil, and how mismatched and chaotic her outfit felt by comparison. Lady Ann was young, younger than Violet even, but she looked like a grown-up and made Violet feel like a messy child. They shook hands. Lady Ann's was predictably cool and soft, her nails perfect unpolished ovals, and Violet wanted to hide hers behind her back, with their neon nail varnish that Flip had been applying the previous night, with great enthusiasm but less accuracy.

Oh, pull yourself together, Violet Cavalley, she told herself. You're the boss here. Why on earth are you letting this woman intimidate you, when she doesn't even seem to be trying to do so?

'Can I offer you some coffee?' Violet asked confidently, as she helped Lady Ann off with her coat.

'I confess I'm surprised to come here, rather than to the shop, and not to have been met by an assistant,' the woman replied. 'I assumed you would have girls here to meet clients, that you'd be too busy.' She smiled coolly.

'I always meet new clients here, not in the shop, to start with, and I prefer to see clients alone for the first time,' Violet said, walking towards the kitchen. 'I like to get a feel for people, get to know them. It's not as easy to do that when all the girls are here. In an hour or so the place will be heaving, radios going, chitter-chatter. You'll see one day, I'm sure, if we decide to work together.' She poured two cups of coffee and put them on a tray.

Lady Ann raised an eyebrow. 'Oh. I was under the impression that I had engaged your services already.'

Now it was Violet's turn to smile.

'Mm. I have my own way of working, Lady Ann. I choose my clients as much as they choose me, you see. Especially for brides. It's such a personal project, and I only take on a few. I can't work with just anyone.'

Lady Ann nodded. 'A true creative genius. That's what I read in the magazine. I suppose talent like that has to be cajoled rather than bullied into showing itself.'

The two women stared at each other. Violet wondered why she felt as if she was engaged in a tug-of-war with this woman, as if they were battling for something and she didn't even know what.

Later, she would look back and feel as though they had both had some kind of premonition, because the battle between herself and Ann might have been unspoken and unacknowledged, but it was the strongest of Violet's life; the whole time was one of uproar and upheaval that made her feel as though her soul had been torn into little pieces and scattered across the country. It would take years for that feeling to go – maybe it never entirely had.

She had first met Sam Gilmour that morning, two hours after Ann had arrived, and he had come to collect her. Despite her reservations, Violet could not resist agreeing to work on the wedding. It would be almost on the scale of a royal wedding, with scores of little bridesmaids and pageboys, it seemed, and the opportunity to create what would amount to nearly a whole couture collection for Lady Ann, both for her wedding itself and for her trousseau. She wanted an entire wardrobe of hats, from one to complete her going-away outfit, to ones for the country, ones for Town, a selection of cocktail hats – on and on, the list went. Lady Ann lived not just in another world, but was from another era, it seemed – one in which people still wore white tie and tails as a matter of course and took tea promptly at three and held house parties in the country, for which they had entirely separate wardrobes. It was a challenge, not least because of the time constraints, but one to which Violet knew she would rise and also relish.

'Here I am, darling girl, light of my life, come to whisk you away to your country idyll,' came a voice, booming up the narrow staircase.

Violet and Ann both turned towards it, instinctively. Ann half-stood up from the chair by the window where she had been sitting, while Violet rose from her seat at the large drawing-table.

And then he was inside Violet's studio and he was tall and blond, his hair thickly waved, and he seemed to take up all the space so that Violet felt pressed back against the wall. He suffused the room with his presence as he strode across it to take Violet's hand – and instead of shaking it, kissed it – and at the same time whipping his arm around Ann's waist and pulling her to him. The stiffly elegant woman who had walked into Violet's studio two hours ago seemed to melt away and she laughed as he kissed her neck, her body relaxing and her face becoming radiantly beautiful, as if his very presence ignited a light inside her.

And Violet could quite see why. Before she had even spoken to the man, she knew. It was Him. She had never believed in the idea of 'the one'. But suddenly there he was, right in front of her. Kissing Lady Ann.

'Violet, this is my fiancé, Sam Gilmour.'

'The famous Violet Cavalley. I'm honoured.'

'The honour is all mine. Your future wife is very ch-charming,' Violet stuttered. It was all wrong. He should not be embracing Lady Ann, he should be striding towards *her*. She even felt confused for a moment that he wasn't, so strong was her sense that the man she was meant to love had just walked into the room. Then she had to remind herself that he was not hers, and she felt a wrench inside that was physical, that took her breath away.

'Isn't she just? What on earth is she doing marrying a fool like me, I ask myself daily.'

Lady Ann giggled. She actually giggled. Only minutes before, Violet had been wondering if it was even possible – she had hardly cracked a smile since she arrived – and now she was like a simpering teenager. Violet excused herself to go and fetch water, her heart fluttering in her chest like a bird's, her palms sweaty. His eyes burned into her; it was as if he could see her naked and laid bare before him – not just her body but her soul too.

She had never felt desire like this. It wasn't just sexual, it was as though her whole body wanted to fuse to his. She wanted to hold her hand up against his, measuring the length of his fingers against her own. She already knew what it would feel like if she pressed herself up against him and kissed him, knew how her fingers would feel, running through his hair and down his back. Knew what the very edges of him felt like. There had been a look in his eyes that told her he felt it too, for he had smiled with the satisfaction of a bird of prey spotting a mouse in the field below, hunger soon to be abated, pleasure to come. The kiss on her hand had felt both instantly familiar and overtly erotic; it had been as if he were not chastely kissing the back of the hand of the woman who would help dress his bride, but a precursor to something deeply different. And wrong. Wrong, wrong, wrong, she reminded herself now, holding her wrists under the cold tap and trying to breathe.

And then there was a sound at the door of the kitchen, and she turned to see him there. He came in and shut the door silently behind him.

'Ann's just using your facilities before we go.'

'Oh, of course,' Violet managed to reply.

He took a step towards her, his eyes on hers. She was leaning back against the sink, her hands either side of her, propping herself up, because if she took them away, her legs might buckle. His height and breadth were even more obvious in the enclosed space. She could smell the limey scent of his cologne.

'I must say . . .' He paused.

Violet's mouth was dry; she swallowed. She couldn't speak.

'I am terribly glad you're going to be dressing my future wife. In the headgear sense, I mean.' The words sounded carefully chosen; he spoke slowly. Violet's head was immediately filled with images of her and Ann side by side, light and dark. Violet dressing her; while Sam undressed her. He smiled as if he knew what she was thinking. Then he took his hands out of his pockets and looked for a moment as if he was going to come closer. Violet held her breath. Then he gave a little laugh and turned towards the door.

'Bad idea.'

She still couldn't speak, she didn't trust herself, so she poured a glass of water and raised it to her lips. And then as she did so, he was suddenly upon her, taking the glass away from her mouth and covering it with his own, roughly, passionately kissing her, pushing her back against the sink with all his strength. And it was exactly as she had known it would be. His body was as familiar to her as her own; the second he touched her it was confirmed. *Oh yes*, her body said, *this is what it is meant to be like, this is what I am for.* As if it were dredging up a long-forgotten memory, but it was a memory that had not yet been created, that they were creating at that moment.

The glass clattered to the floor and shattered, pooling water around her feet, and he stepped back and opened the door, and Ann's voice carried down through the workshop towards them 'Sam? Where are you? I thought you wanted to leave and miss the traffic.'

He stared at Violet.

'I'll see you again, Violet Cavalley.' It was a promise. She knew that it was a promise.

And then he was gone.

And so, in another sense entirely, was Violet.

Working on what was essentially two new collections at the same time, as well as all her other one-off pieces, was demanding. But Violet's River Collection thrilled her, let her imagination skip forward in leaps and bounds and in directions it had never gone in before.

She had a Frost Fair hat which laid out a scene from the seventeenth century across a huge, wide-brimmed structure, the brim of the hat forming the frozen river, covered with skaters, carriages, bear-baiters and sleds, all in miniature scattered across an icily reflective surface.

A bridge was constructed over a frame which attached to the back of the wearer's head, making it appear as though it was floating above it, and a tiny battery pack, hidden under a section of the wearer's hair, contained the wherewithal to light up the string of tiny fairy-lights that lined the structure – a night-time scene familiar to all Londoners and recreated in millinery.

A soft, flowing stream of silk strands set on to a comb pinned on to the crown, trailed down the back in a rush, all olive greens and silvery browns, forming a puddle of a train at the wearer's feet, constantly moving and shifting with each step.

A houseboat hat in brightly embroidered felt sent its prow bravely out in front of the face. The finale of the collection would be the bridal head-dress or hat which Violet had designed. Inspired by the swan, it had a feathery veil swooping across the bride's face, partially concealing it.

The design for the head-dress that Lady Ann would wear on her wedding day was simple and regal: a gold circle that was almost more jewellery than hat or head-dress; a stiffened lace band rising up from the fine metal base and forming the shape of a coronet, which was encrusted with pearls and beading, giving the impression of a crown but a lighter, more translucent version. Then there was the rest. A fuchsia-pink pillbox hat with a piece of black veiling just over the eyes to match the fuchsia suit that she would go away in. Three cocktail hats, covered in feathers; velvet saucers with jaunty veils. A loose weave straw hat with a circle of silk flowers around the crown; a thick tweed for hunting. Lady Ann Gilmour's ice-blond head would be the best clad in London.

The wedding of Viscount Sam Gilmour and Lady Ann Michelmore is to take place in the Chapel of St Paul's Cathedral on 12th June. The guest list includes members of the British royal family, Irish nobility and a host of titled invitees in a ceremony which is expected to blend long-standing tradition with some controversial touches of modernity.

Lady Ann will wear a duchess silk gown and an antique lace heirloom veil, as worn by her ancestors. Contemporary florist James Montague has been engaged to arrange her bouquet.

But it is in her choice of headgear that Lady Ann has

really made a statement, by breaking with convention and engaging the services of milliner Violet Cavalley to create her head-dress and those of her retinue. In previous generations, Michelmore brides have all had their heads dressed by Green's of Bond Street, whereas Ms Cavalley is known primarily for the breathtaking flamboyancy of her designs. Still, the bold move has ensured that both the wedding and salon are the talk of the town, and this publication predicts that Cavalley's will be the destination of choice for every blushing bride next season.

Harper's Bazaar

And the publication was right. Lady Ann's decision and the coverage that followed brought a rush of new customers to Cavalley's doors, eager to see the designs that had been deemed special enough to break tradition for, and which were getting so much attention. They came in droves. They came clutching drawings that they had done for Violet to interpret and translate into a wearable version of the tiara or hat they had always dreamed of marrying in. They came with scraps of fabric from their dresses or trousseau, they came with friends and mothers, and maiden aunts, with their savings and their pay packets and their chequebooks at the ready. They came in such numbers that before long, Violet realised she was missing a trick, and took out a lease on a small shop in Pimlico, especially for her brides.

Cavalley's Bridal was small and on two floors; and an Aladdin's cave of sparkling, twinkly, flower-strewn confections. She covered every surface that she could upholster with ivory velvet, and what she couldn't cover with that, she covered with antique, burnished mirrors which reflected light upon light and made the little rooms look the size of a ballroom. She painted the front door a bright, pearlescent white, so it glowed to all the blacks and navys and forest greens in the rest of the street. And she filled the place with flights of fancy that made everyone gasp as they entered. A pair of love birds lived in an ornate cage by the gilt cash till, and cooed at the brides all day long. She stuffed the rooms from floor to ceiling with jewelled headbands and tiaras, veiled whirls of frothy tulle, feathered caps – everything a modern bride's heart could desire, and everything for her attendants as well.

Cavalley's Bridal was an instant success, and Violet wondered that she hadn't thought of it before. But things happened at the right time, she had always believed that, and maybe her heart wouldn't have been ready, until now, to cope with the mass influx of young girls in love and on the threshold of marriage who came to her door.

But the brides were not the only ones who came.

Mary Wallop came. The first time, Violet had just finished fitting a bride who worked in some incredibly high-powered job in the City and who was going to America to get married. She wanted a tiara modelled on the Manhattan skyline. When she first saw her out of the corner of her eye, through the window, Mary Wallop was just a flicker, a shadow so fleeting that Violet thought she had imagined her. Maybe it was nothing – a trick of the light. She returned her gaze to the bride's angular face and smiled at her, making sure her expression betrayed nothing of her worries.

'There you go, perfect.'

'I love it. Adorable!' the woman replied. 'Thank you so much. I'll bring a photo in when I'm back, if you'd like.'

'Please do.' Violet kept an album of all her brides now.

And then – there she was again. Unmistakable, this time. Tripping past the shop in a pale-yellow suit and matching shoes. She paused and watched as Violet's customer left. And then she walked in through the door as the woman passed, exchanging a bright smile with her.

'Enjoy yourself,' the woman said. 'She's the most talented milliner in London!'

Mary Wallop smiled. 'I know. I wouldn't come anywhere else. I'm just so pleased she's doing so well.' And when she looked at Violet, her eyes confirmed her pleasure. She really was pleased Violet was doing so well. Because there was all the more for her.

Violet begrudged every penny of the money she gave to Mary Wallop. Oh, she wasn't short of the stuff, not any more. But she hated giving it to this grasping, greedy woman who had done nothing to earn it.

How stupid she had been, Violet thought now, not to get rid of Mary Wallop as soon as she had hinted at blackmail, that day back in the salon in Mount Street. She should have called her bluff then. But she was too scared. The reason Mary's blackmail was successful was because she had found out Violet's secret, her deeply buried fear, and exploited it. Violet liked to think of herself as a strong person these days, someone who was not easily walked over, someone to be reckoned with. Every payment she made to Mary Wallop undermined that strength. But, as long as she wanted to keep her past hidden, there was nothing she could do about it. So she paid, and paid, and paid. And hoped that one day, she would find a way to stop paying.

At least she had the money to pay. Investors were throwing it at her, almost battering down the door of Cavalley's offering to invest in her business. It was boom time in London, and the attention she was attracting in the fashion world quickly spread to other realms, those of high finance and investment and venture capital – and other words that Violet, with her formidable but natural instinct for business, had never heard of nor considered relevant to what she still saw as her little shop business. But as the offers kept coming, from businessmen in London and Scotland and as far afield as America and China even, she realised that she should listen to what they had to say.

So she went to the meetings, an incongruous figure in amongst all of the power suits and padded shoulders and leather briefcases, dressed as she always was in her own unique way. They didn't know quite what to make of her, she could tell, this petite young woman of just thirty wearing little forties-style suits with nipped-in waists, and dresses that looked more like fancy-dress costumes than the designer gear they all wore, and a hat – of course, there was always a hat. They took her into glass elevators that went up the sides of buildings, and showed her presentations with graphs, and projected profit forecasts, and computer-generated images of shiny shops with her name above them in hundreds of towns and countries that she had never even heard of, and she listened carefully to everything they said, and then went home, put her son to bed and sat at her old wooden desk with a pen and paper, and drew up her own business plan.

Mary wasn't the only visitor she had around that time. Mattie came one night, after she had closed up and was sitting in the bridal shop, alone, drinking a glass of red wine and looking over her forecast for the year. She saw him through the window, looking up, after she began to get the feeling someone was watching her. He stood, motionless, staring in, his eyes wide and his cheeks hollow. She froze. His face reminded her of their father. Of his face at her door that day, before he killed Bryce. Of his eyes, as he sat on the floor, covered in Bryce's blood. She shook herself, and let him in. She didn't have a choice. As always, it seemed, with her family, she didn't have a choice. She opened the door, and stood back for him to enter.

Brother and sister faced one another. Violet's arms were folded across her draped jacket. Mattie's hands were shoved into his pockets as usual. As their father had always done. Violet shuddered, reminded once more of Jimmy.

'What do you want?' she asked, unable to look at him.

'Dad's dead,' Mattie said.

Violet swallowed. Her mother had died not long after Maggie. She'd rung up the church, to check that there would be a proper headstone for Maggie, ready to pay for one if needs be, and the funeral director had asked her which M. Gribbens she was referring to. 'The little girl, or the mother?' he had asked. Violet had said she would pay for both. But she hadn't shed a tear for her mother. Not after Maggie. However, the force of knowing she was an orphan, was free from the clutches of her family, hit her square in the chest, and she looked at Mattie with more affection than she would have thought possible. He was the only one left, after all.

'What happened?' she asked, but thought she already knew.

'What do you think happened?' Mattie's face was full of hate.

Violet looked into his eyes. Was her younger brother still there, somewhere inside this angry, rough-edged man? Could she see the remains of the boy she had played with for so many hours in the fields, holding his hand when he got scared inside the dark centre of the woods, slept with under piles of quilts that smelled of woodsmoke and apples, snuggled up with, to keep warm? Her eyes pricked with tears as she remembered, and realised that no, she could not see him there. This was a stranger.

'I don't know, Mattie,' she whispered.

'Don't call me Mattie,' he spat. Ah, there he was, just for a second; the defiant, defensive boy was back. But then, just as quickly, he was gone again. He stood and turned away.

'What do you want me to call you?'

He shrugged, wouldn't look at her. 'Nothing. Just don't . . .'

Her heart went out to him, despite herself. She could see the deep hurt that lay under the thick layer of bravado and aggression he was wearing like a cloak.

'Tell me. What happened to . . . to Dad.'

It was hard to say the word. Mattie spun around. 'He killed himself, didn't he? In prison, like I knew he would. He couldn't live locked up. Couldn't do it. He was a free man, but he died like a caged animal. It's wrong. It was wrong, what you did to him.'

Violet lowered her head.

'When?' she said, wondering why she was asking. She didn't want to know. Didn't want to hear any more episodes in the long line of tales of despair and misery that was her family. Her old family, she reminded herself.

'Fortnight ago, mebbe,' he said gruffly. He looked vulnerable. Despite herself, Violet instinctively wanted to go to him, to comfort him, but then he turned and shouted at her, his face red and full of rage, 'He bled out on the floor, alone, and it's your fault, it's your fuckin' fault,' and the feeling was gone, to be replaced by pure fear as Mattie rushed towards her and slammed his fists on the little table between them, sending the glass jug and water glasses flying.

'Mattie, don't!' she cried out. 'Don't!' her hands shielding her face. When she looked up again, he was sitting down, white-faced.

'I'm not going to touch you,' he said. 'I'm not—'

He stopped. *Not Dad*, she completed in her head, knowing he wouldn't finish the sentence himself. Too loyal, despite everything. His father's son in many ways. Not that one, though.

Slowly, quietly, she sat back down. She could hear his breath coming hard, as he regained control of his temper.

'Well,' she said eventually. 'Thanks for coming to tell me. I appreciate it. I assume the funeral . . .'

'Been. No one wanted you there.' The snarl was back as he

bottles of champagne and one stolen kiss across the table later, Violet was almost crying with sweet, confused emotion. She had never been this happy, not with anyone. Sam was her other half, her mirror, her soulmate. A *coup de foudre*, she had heard it called, and never really understood why. The phrase had seemed melodramatic, but now it made absolute sense. If anything, it felt like an understatement. The thunderclap that spread across the sky, rolling the clouds out of the way, rending it in two, had nothing on the power of the attraction she felt for Sam. Her thighs shivered as she sat opposite him, her wrists turned themselves upwards as she reached her hands over the table, exposing their pale undersides and blue veins to him, as though she was giving him her very lifeblood. She would give it willingly, she would give him anything.

For the first time since Flip had been born, she did not think of her son, or of Cavalley's, for a full three hours. She was drunk with Sam, drinking him in, inhaling him. The fact that they were breathing the same air struck her as miraculous, at one point, and then she laughed at herself. She had gone quite mad; there was no other explanation. And yet she had never felt such clarity, such sanity, in her life.

They talked, almost non-stop. He understood her. It was extraordinary, but she felt as though, after a lifetime of not quite fitting in, of struggling to make people understand why she was doing what she was doing, she had finally found the other side of her oyster shell, the person to whom she had to explain nothing at all.

'I've always wanted to go to Paris,' she began, 'to visit the L'Etoile boutique,' he finished, and she gazed at him.

'You've made your own family,' he said, when she told him about Flip and how proud she was of him. 'You've built it out of nothing,' and that was it, that was exactly what she had done, and he could see it. He could see her. Every inch of her.

When they weren't talking, they just stared at each other. It wasn't just her who felt it. She could tell by the intensity with which he gazed at her, as if he could see into her soul, and the matching intensity with which his long leg pressed against hers under the table. The way his fingertips grasped her wrist and stroked it as he reached for the bottle of champagne.

When they left the restaurant, Sam pulled her down a side street and kissed her, hard. His hands grasped her waist, pulling her to him, and she let herself into him. When he finally let her go, he rested his forehead against hers, and stared deep into her eyes.

'Oh Violet,' he whispered. 'Violet eyes.'

Her legs were shaking under her and she held on to him for support, and for the strong warmth of his body inside his wool Crombie coat.

'Yes? What?' she whispered back, her voice challenging, flirtatious.

'Don't . . .' he said, and his voice was low.

'Don't what?' but she knew what he was going to say. Their faces were so close together that all she had to do to kiss him was push her lips forward a little, and she did so now, letting them brush against his. He bit her bottom lip suddenly and sucked on it and she gave a little yelp, and let her body sink down a fraction, enjoying the sensation as she moved against him.

As his lips released hers, they moved again, forming themselves into words, still around her lips. She inhaled his words as they came out of his mouth. 'Don't make me fall in love with you,' they said.

She breathed them in, the delicious power that they gave her, that she knew was already hers. Then she kissed him lightly.

'I'm afraid it might be too late,' she whispered back.

*

She had been right. It was too late for both of them. They were lost in each other, lost in love; they had been from the moment they had met, and they both knew it.

'My family's all mad, you know,' Sam murmured in her ear. It was the weekend after that first lunch and they were in bed in a suite in Claridge's. Violet laughed.

'I mean it.' He flopped back on the bed and reached for his pack of cigarettes. Violet stretched over him and reached for one too. He held them away from her.

'Give me one.'

'You said you were giving up.'

'I can't. Especially not when I'm with you. You make me want to smoke.'

'Oh, it's my fault, is it?'

She shrugged. 'You just have that effect on me.'

'A deeply, darkly addictive one?'

'If you like.'

'I do like.'

'I don't know if I do.'

'Really?'

She leaned her head over his chest and pulled the cigarette out of the packet with her teeth. It crackled as he lit it for her and she inhaled. She looked him in the eye.

'No, actually.'

Violet sat and crossed her legs, pulling the rumpled sheet around her waist. She stared at him appraisingly. The bed was in the centre of the hotel room, which was dark red and dramatically decorated. A high ceiling bore a black chandelier that dripped dark cut crystals like drops of blood towards the floor. The walls were all shades of dark red, red on red, and the curtains were heavy.

'You aren't any good for me,' she continued. Sam had retrieved a lump of hash from the bottom of the cigarette packet and was slowly burning it with his lighter, and crumbling the soft brown fragments into a cigarette paper containing tobacco. His chest was golden and smooth and his blond hair flopped over his forehead. He shrugged a shoulder.

'Darling girl, I never promised to be good for you. And you wouldn't be here now if I had. Why on earth would you want to fuck someone who's good for you? Wholegrains are good for you. Aerobics are good for you.'

Sam pulled a curl of her hair around his finger, then ran it over her bottom lip.

'Sam Gilmour is bad for you. I told you so from the start. Absolutely, definitively . . .' He tugged the sheet down from around her waist so she was naked on the bed, and stared at her appreciatively, then he stuck the joint in between her lips so both his hands were free. She inhaled, and he pulled her towards him and on to his lap so she was straddling him.

'Incontrovertibly . . .'

He leaned forward and she blew smoke into his open mouth. He held his breath before exhaling, and then lowered his lips to her nipples.

'One hundred per cent.'

He lifted her hips up slightly and then lowered her back down on to him. She closed her eyes and sighed as she began to move.

'Bad for you.'

Later, as they lay in the bath, drinking champagne, Violet rested her head back against the roll-top enamel and sank into the bubbles.

'What did you mean when you said your family were all mad?'

'What I said. Completely fucking bonkers, the whole Gilmour dynasty, such as it is. Mad, bad and dangerous to know. I told you.'

'About you. You haven't told me about the rest. Go on, tell me about the Gilmours.'

'Ah, it's like a bride's father sniffing out the goods, checking the family lineage. Checking what you've got yourself into? Too late, Lady Vi. Just like my dear father-in-law, you're too late. You're in too deep now.'

'Don't call me that.'

'Why not? You're my lady.'

'I'll never be your lady.'

Sam smiled. 'You always will. Not in name, maybe, but in my heart. Although what you were doing earlier was hardly ladylike behaviour, now was it?'

Violet sighed. 'Fucking hell, Sam.'

'What?'

'Stop it. It's hopeless.'

'*Au contraire*, it's full of hope. All perfect and waiting to be dashed. Tragic. Delicious.'

'Dashed hope isn't delicious, you fool.'

'Think of the romance.'

'It's not romantic either.'

'You know, if I thought you believed that I'd ditch you right now.'

'You wouldn't dare.'

'No. I couldn't. I'm addicted. In far too deep.'

'It'll end eventually. It has to.'

'You wanted to know about my family.'

'Don't change the subject.'

'Why not? I don't like the one you chose.' He poured champagne into her glass.

'All right. Tell me.'

'It goes back generations. Hundreds of years of Gilmour men and women, all utterly off their rockers. Alcoholics, gamblers, degenerates. If we weren't so rich we'd all be in the gutter.

Although some of us have ended up there, even so. There are a couple of murders in the family tree. My Great-great-aunt Elizabeth was, I think, suspected of poisoning one of her husband's mistresses.'

'I hope that doesn't run in Ann's family as well.'

'No, you're safe there. Straight as a die, all of them.'

'Good. How about your parents?'

'Mad as two boxes of frogs.'

Violet laughed. 'Really?'

'Really. What about yours?'

Violet shivered. 'They're both dead.'

'I'm sorry. I didn't know.' Sam stroked her upper arm.

'It's all right. I wasn't close to them. Tell me about yours. Go on.'

'Are you sure?'

'Positive.'

'Very well. My mother . . .' Sam sucked on the joint. 'What can I say? She's very beautiful. That's the first thing you notice about her. The beautiful and damned, my father calls her.'

'They're still married, aren't they?'

'Yes. Well, in name. In spirit? I'm not sure two people who both had affairs on their honeymoon can ever really be said to have been married.'

'Really?'

'Scout's honour.'

'You were never a Scout. They wouldn't have had you.'

'Hah. You caught me out. It's still true.'

Violet rested her head on his chest. 'I believe you. Thousands wouldn't. Go on.'

She was somehow keen to know, now, about the darkness that lay in his past. With every word, she felt closer to him – not the sexual closeness that she had felt the first time they met, but a deeper closeness, a sense that they were the same, that she had finally found someone who understood her. Who came from the same darkness.

'My mother. Everyone who meets her thinks she's wonderful. Everyone who knows her thinks she's a bitch. She's staged suicide attempts three times, each time coincidentally when my father was on the verge of getting rid of her once and for all. Carefully managed – no lasting damage or real danger. She single-handedly drove one of her lovers to jump off the edge of a cliff, though. She's run through three family fortunes, and she doesn't give a fuck about anyone else. Not my father, not her children.'

Violet stroked his arm, but there was no sadness in his voice. Just a brisk, matter-of-fact tone.

'She's the only person I've ever met who I can honestly say is one hundred per cent selfish,' he said, grinding the joint out in the plant that sat next to the roll-top bath. 'Well, apart from my good self, maybe.'

Violet wriggled a little against his body. 'Ah, but you're not selfish, are you?'

He took hold of her hips and slid her up him roughly. 'Oh yes, I am.'

She gasped as he pulled her on to him.

'Anything I give you is purely for my own pleasure.'

As he moved her body, the water splashed out of the side of the bath on to the black and white tiles. Violet let him push and pull her limbs through the water, giving herself up to his pressure, his desires, feeling his hands bruising her thighs, and not caring. He could do anything with her, as long as he was with her. She was utterly, hopelessly addicted to him.

Mary Wallop's visits continued. She would arrive, always at the shop, always making sure there were people around, to increase the weight of her threats. 'I'll tell,' she would remind Violet. 'I'll tell everything. I'll take out an ad in the paper, I'll shout it from the fucking rooftops, and you'll be finished. Everything you've worked for – everything Elizabeth worked for – it'll all be gone.'

She wanted cash, and plenty of it. Violet found herself having to lie to Gerald about her spending habits to cover up the holes in her accounts.

'I'm terrible at keeping track of money,' she told him. 'I've frittered it all away.' And he just nodded. They both knew Violet Cavalley was no fritterer. But it was not his place to comment, so he said nothing.

It was after one of Mary's visits that Violet told Sam. She and Mary had fought. 'I'm not going to do this for ever,' Violet had told her, her words sounding hollow even to herself.

Mary had laughed. 'You'll do it for as long as I say you'll do it.'

'Who would pay you off if you told?' Violet had bluffed.

'I'd find another way to survive, sweetheart,' Mary had said. 'I always do. The question is – *would you*?'

Violet had arrived at the hotel where she and Sam had arranged to meet still upset. She had redone her make-up, holding a cold flannel over her face to try to get her eyes to stop looking so puffy, but as soon as she sat down he knew. Took her hand across the table.

'What is it? What's happened?'

'I'm fine. How was your day?'

'Violet, you can't fool me. Tell.'

And she had burst into raw, ugly tears and told him. Told him everything. From Bryce, to her father, from Madame Fournier's kindness to her, to her death, right up to Mary's blackmailing. Sam had sat, smoking and listening, his face growing harder and harder as she talked. When she finished, he stood up.

'You stay here,' he said.

'Sam, no.'

'I won't have this little trollop holding anything over you. I'm going to sort her out.'

'I mean it. I don't want you to.' Violet held his wrist. And she did mean it. She didn't want to be beholden to anyone. Didn't want Sam cleaning up her mess for her. 'Promise me, Sam. Promise me you'll leave well alone. I'll deal it with. I've got a plan.'

He took her in his arms. 'A plan?'

'Yes.' She nestled her head in his chest.

'I don't believe you.' He sighed. 'Promise me you have a plan – an actual plan – and I'll promise you I won't get involved.'

Violet wrapped her hands around the back of his neck, lacing her fingers together and pulling him to kiss her. And both their promises were forgotten.

Violet had enough on her mind. Sam's wedding was to take place in a month, and she was still working on his bride's collection. She avoided seeing Lady Ann as much as possible – the sight of her filled Violet with guilty jealousy that she was sure showed in her face – but a certain number of appointments were unavoidable.

It was at her final dress fitting that Lady Ann made her position clear. Violet had gone to the boutique of the designer who was making Lady Ann's dress – a small, smart shop just off the Fulham Road – in order to fit her veil and the tiara. Lady Ann was standing in front of the full-length mirror, in the slim column of silk embroidered with the intertwined initials of her own and Sam's families. A little jacket with a high neck and stiffly puffed sleeves that ended at the elbow and curved out like tulips gave her a regal look, and her hair was set in soft, perfectly circular rolls that added to the impression of royalty. Violet was standing on a little stool, pinning the veil carefully into Lady Ann's hair, attaching it to the tiara. She could smell her perfume – Penhaligon's Lily of the Valley, Violet knew. She had smelled it on Sam. Seen receipts for it in his wallet, once, when she had been getting cash out. Violet tried not to think about Sam.

She took a pin out from between her teeth, where she had been holding it, and fixed the last section of veil to the jewelled head-dress. It was one of the finest pieces Violet had made for a bride. 'I want it to become an heirloom for our children,' Lady Ann had said, when they were discussing it. 'I want it to last beyond us, to be a symbol of the joining together of our families.'

'There,' Violet said softly now, as she adjusted the final diamond-ended pin, and prepared to get down from her stool. 'Perfect.'

Before she could get down, Lady Ann reached up and put her hand on Violet's arm. The woman's touch was cool on Violet's skin, but her voice when she spoke was cooler still.

'He won't give you what you want, you know.'

Violet froze. 'I'm sorry?'

'Don't be.' Lady Ann's voice was slightly amused now. Violet looked up, and the two women's eyes met in the mirror. Lady Ann wore a very faint smile.

'Don't be sorry. I'm not a possessive woman. I was not brought up to believe that fidelity is the most important thing in a marriage.'

Violet wanted to look away, but found that she could not. She felt ashamed, but not regretful. She could never regret Sam or what they had.

'But I am going to marry him. And I won't divorce him. And he won't divorce me. Marriage, for us . . .'

She paused. She did not say, 'for people like us', but Violet became very aware that she was standing on a stool, dressing this woman, whose fiancé she was sleeping with. Violet was subservient here; she had not been brought up like Lady Ann, or Sam, had been. She would never be one of them.

'Marriage for our families may not involve sexual fidelity, but it is about something far bigger. History, family and permanence. Sam will not leave me for you once our families have been joined together.'

She gestured to the embroidery on her dress.

'That's what it's about. You see, Violet, you may be able to give him all sorts of things – I'm sure you can. I'm sure, in lots of ways, you are better suited to him than I am. But you can't give him what he really needs, which is a family to join to his, and an heir. And you don't know him. You don't know what he really needs, who he really is. Trust me, there is a side to Sam Gilmour which you do not yet know and which you do not want to discover.'

Lady Ann paused, then continued, 'And, if I might say so, you don't strike me as the sort of woman to be satisfied living in the shadows. Long-term.'

Violet got down from the stool now and turned away, packing her things into her bag. She felt utterly humiliated. The other woman's apparent lack of anger or jealousy only made it worse.

'You may not want me to be sorry,' she said now, her hands working fast to pack away her materials, 'but I am. I'm sorry you found out and I'm sorry if it hurt you. I'm not the kind of woman who does this. I never thought I'd do it. But I'm not sorry I met Sam. And I'm not sorry for loving him.'

She raised her head again now and looked at Lady Ann, her eyes blazing with passion and love and sadness. Lady Ann smiled at her sadly.

'No, I don't expect you are. I understand, Violet. I do understand. But, neither am I.'

*

When Sam opened the hotel-room door to Violet that evening, he looked dishevelled, his blond hair messy and his shirt undone at the neck and untucked. A cut-glass tumbler of whisky in his hand and a cigar in his other filled the room with their peaty, heavy fragrance. The sheets of the bed were untidy, crumpled. Violet looked around the room. 'When did you get here?'

He didn't answer, just stood in his shirtsleeves pouring another whisky from the decanter while the cigar smouldered in the heavy glass ashtray. Violet's throat burned with its smell. She shrugged off her coat and went to him. Stood behind him, rubbing his shoulders. His body was tense, his muscles stiff under the cotton of his shirt. She let her hands slide down and around his waist. He grabbed her wrists roughly and pulled her around in front of him.

She drew her breath in sharply as he then used one arm to hoist her up on to the side of the large upholstered wing chair, so she was perched on its wide arm. He didn't look at her. He ran his hand up along the side of her body, let it reach her shoulder and brush against her hair. Then he wound a hunk of it around his fist, muttering softly, 'Violet, Violet . . .'

Her eyes searched his face. Where was he? Not in the room with her, that was certain. His large hands were pulling at her clothes, his breathing heavy and his mind distracted, tumultuous. She put her own hands on his shoulders, trying to get him to look at her.

'Sam, you're drunk. I'm going, OK?'

She couldn't be here with him like this. The smell of the room, the whisky and sweat and smoke was too much. It was suffocating her.

He looked up at her. 'You can't go.'

She pulled her coat on. 'Oh yes, I can. I'll call you tomorrow. We need to talk.'

'So talk.'

She shook her head. 'Not now. There's no point. You won't remember.'

She was angry. How dare he be drunk, how dare he be so selfish? He knew she hated it – and why. But more than that, she needed him; she had come to him today shaken by her confrontation with Lady Ann, needing him to tell her it would be all right, or even that it wouldn't be all right – *something*. Something, to make her feel less alone.

Violet went over to kiss him goodbye, but instead he lifted her up, scooping her up under her bottom and half-carrying, half-throwing her on to the bed. She lay passively for a moment, gazing up at him. She couldn't believe he'd done it. She pushed herself up on her elbows, trying to shrug off her upset.

'Now I really am going.'

'No.' He held on to her arm, his eyes somewhere else, his grip firm.

'Sam, let me go. What is it with you today?'

'Why did you talk to Ann about us?'

She took a breath. 'I didn't. She talked to me about us.'

'I don't want you talking to her.'

'Believe me, I'd rather avoid it as well, but I'm making the hats for her wedding – for *your* wedding.'

'What did she say about me? That I was mad, bad, dangerous to know?'

'No. She said she loved you; she said she understood that I loved you.' Violet sighed. She didn't want to relive the conversation with her lover's fiancée.

'She's a wicked woman. You're both wicked women. *My* wicked women.' He laughed, and drank another gulp of whisky.

'Not for ever, Sam,' she said under her breath. 'We can't both be your women for ever.'

As she said it, she knew it was true. Lady Ann had been right. She could not love him part-time, from the shadows, for much longer. She could not be the lady-in-waiting, knowing that she would never be the lady, for much longer.

And she knew something else. Something she had realised that afternoon, when she had left Lady Ann's dress fitting and had to run into a nearby alleyway to be sick. At first she thought it was nerves, the adrenaline let-down of the encounter catching up with her. But as she stood there, hand against the wall to steady herself, trembling all over, she recognised the feeling in her stomach as something different. She was pregnant.

She had not wanted to do it like this, but it seemed that she had no choice. She would ask him just once. Give him the chance. So that she never had to look back and wish that she had said something, so that she could not accuse herself of having simply walked away.

'Will you leave her? Will you leave Ann for me? Will you marry me, instead?'

This was the one chance. She would marry him in a heartbeat, if he would have her. Build a life with him, and Flip, and the child growing inside her. Whatever they faced from other people, whatever scandal and disapproval it meant enduring, she would have endured it for him. But she could not be his mistress, pregnant with his child, while he built that life with Ann.

Sam's hand faltered as he struggled to relight his cigar. He did not look at her. She waited. She was not going to ask twice.

Violet looked at him, tears falling from his eyes, as he stood there, his shirt undone and damp now, the still unlit cigar in one hand, the other pushing his hair back over his head. He did not speak. She took a deep, tremulous breath.

'Goodbye, Sam,' she said, as she walked out of the door. And as she pulled it shut behind her, she thought she heard him whisper, 'I'm sorry.'

He was drunk, he was dishevelled, she was almost afraid of

him, and he had rejected her and broken her heart, and yet as she stood sobbing in the hotel corridor, she still desired him. Still loved him. Would still walk a thousand miles for one stolen moment with him. And that scared her more than anything. She turned, and forced herself to walk away.

By the time she gave birth to Sam's son, Violet had forgotten the promise he had made her, his promise not to interfere with her arrangement with Mary Wallop. She was wrapped up in work, in the cocoon that she drew around herself when pregnant, in the baby kicking and growing inside her, in Flip and in the bustle of the life she had built. So when she got a letter from Mary, saying that she would not be contacting her again, she felt nothing other than relief. It was like a gift, she felt, a gift to her unborn child. Now he – for she knew it was a boy – could be born into the world without his mother fretting and worrying about her past. She could be free. *I have been lucky enough to find a man who loves me and will take care of me, and so I have no need for your kindness any longer*, the letter said. Kindness, thought Violet. That's one way of putting it. *Thank you for your generosity until now. I will not forget it.*

Violet shook her head, and then threw the letter away. Mary might not, but all Violet wanted was to forget it.

Sebastian Cavalley, who had been conceived in complete secrecy, emerged into the world in public – or nearly. Violet went into labour just as she had walked off the catwalk at Kalisto's show, having taken her bows with him to another round of rapturous applause from the world's fashion press. The show had been a hit – their biggest yet. The ultra-modern, angular clothes with exaggerated lines and tightly wrapped structures were offset by Violet's headgear – strange floating bubbles that bobbed over the models' heads like jellyfish and gave them an alien, otherworldly look. All the way through the show, Violet had been shifting uncomfortably from foot to foot. She felt as if a nerve was trapped in her back. She actually felt as if she was going to go into labour – but she was three weeks early. Still, it did feel awfully like . . . *no*. She got a dresser to bring her a stool to perch on and ignored it, so she could watch the end of the show, and take her turn. It turned out to be a mistake.

As she stood at the end of the catwalk, the flashbulbs popping in her face, she felt a contraction spread through her body like a great juddering wave, and she clutched Kalisto's hand.

His grin remained fixed. 'What is it, *ma chère*? You're crushing the bones of my hand.'

'I'm having a fucking baby.'

'Oh bollocks.' His accent dropped and he spoke in his broad natural twang, but still his teeth flashed in the glare of the bulbs.

'Smile and walk, darling, smile and walk. You can still walk?'

'Not for much fucking longer.' Violet breathed out through gritted teeth. 'Get me off here or *Vogue* and *Bazaar* are going to get more exclusive photos than they bargained for.'

Kalisto's hand had become sweaty and clammy. 'All right, darlin'. Don't panic. Panic ye not.'

'I'm not panicking.'

'I am.' He steered her around and back down the catwalk. As soon as they reached the wings, Violet sank to the floor and let out a cry. Kalisto looked on in horror.

'Get a doctor. Get an ambulance! Help!' he called.

Violet grimaced. 'No time,' she gasped.

'What do you mean, no time?' His voice was high and panicked.

It would be fine, Violet told herself. Something about Kalisto's panic and the shocked, heavily made-up faces of the models staring down at her made her feel calmer, more in control.

'I'm having the baby. Here. Now. It'll be . . .' She clenched her teeth and paused as another contraction hit. Waited. Waited. Gradually, it subsided, and she could speak again, so she did so quickly before the next one began to swell and rise up again.

'It'll be fine. I've done it before. It'll be fine.'

Oh God, there was another one coming already. This was quicker than her previous experience of labour. She made her hands into fists and braced herself. It was clear that this baby wasn't waiting for anyone.

As he had started his life, headfirst and shooting forth from his mother like a cannon ball, so he continued it. Sebastian Cavalley, as Violet named him, went at life running. From the off he was wild, brave, charming and utterly appallingly behaved.

Just like his father.

'And by the time he was two . . .' Violet continued, as Fran sat on her bed, knees drawn up to her chin, listening intently to the story of the brother she had never known.

'Go on,' she said, nodding in encouragement as Violet paused. She shouldn't push her, she told herself, the memories were clearly difficult for her. So she waited, as Violet breathed deeply, her face pained.

But then she watched in horror as her mother let out a sudden, awful sound that was somewhere between a gasp and a yelp, and Fran knew that the pain in Violet's face had not been caused by the dredging up of old memories, but by the cancer inside her. Something was very wrong. Violet slumped a little, as if to try and protect herself from the waves of agony that Fran could see crashing through her body, and Fran cried out.

'Mama! Mama, hold on, I'm here.' She wanted to take her hand, comfort her, but Violet's arms were tight and twisted round, cramped, her hands up near her face as though to ward off the blows of some unseen assailant, and Fran was afraid to touch her. Instead, she fumbled with her iPhone, cursing the sliding touch screen that her fingers slipped over, missing their mark as she tried to unlock it, finally managing to bring up the keypad and swearing, as she did, that she would get a proper bloody phone with actual keys, waiting as it rang and hearing herself speak in a voice that did not sound like her own, to the operator, requesting that an ambulance come, 'soon, as soon as possible. My mother's very ill, I'm scared that she's dying,' and then hearing the words come from her mouth, dropping the phone, overwhelmed with fear that they were true. And as Violet's limbs softened finally and the pain seemed to subside a little, Fran crawled up the bed and curled up next to her and sobbed, her body wrapped up in a little ball next to her mother's, willing her not to die, not yet, not yet, not now.

Chapter Eight

Two days later

Flip stood in the large drawing room of his mother's house in Slaidburn Street, pacing around the room as he planned who should sit where for the family conference he had called, now that Violet was out of immediate danger and safely back home upstairs with a nurse on standby twenty-four hours a day.

Patrick would sit here, in the leather club chair by the fireplace. Blue could go nearest the door, on the smaller sofa or standing. He liked to be able to see his exit, tended to become agitated if he felt trapped. Fran and Tillie could take the larger sofa. Kalisto would perch on the arm of a chair, or on one of the stools. He always did. Flip himself would stand, the better to take charge of proceedings, better able to move around if necessary. Not that he wanted to dominate things, but . . . someone needed to be in control.

Mattie could go in the corner furthest from the door. Surrounded, Violet's brother had agreed to attend the meeting after Flip had been to visit him at the serviced apartment in London where he had been transferred when the rest of the family returned from Capri. Violet had insisted that he be where someone could keep an eye on him.

'I've got a strange feeling,' she had said to Kalisto. 'He's a bad penny. He always has been. He's only ever brought a cloud with him. And now – it's like my father said. "Blood betraying blood . . ."'

Kalisto had soothed her and shushed her, and watched over her while she fell into a disturbed sleep. He had wished she could rest, now more than ever. She deserved to rest. But it was as though the darkness of her past was rising up to meet her as she took each step closer to death.

Kalisto was here already, leaning against the marble fireplace, his lilac top hat under his arm. Flip was glad of his company. Kalisto was a force to be reckoned with in more ways than one.

Tillie put the bottles of water down on the coffee table and rubbed Flip's back.

'It'll be fine,' she whispered. She worked her thumb in between his shoulderblades, trying to unknot the lumps of tension sitting there. He pushed his shoulders back and breathed out deeply.

'Will it?'

'Of course. You're family. You love each other, despite everything. And you all want the same thing. We *all* want the same thing.' She moved her hand up the back of his neck, and he tilted it from side to side. It clicked.

'I suppose.'

'You know it. We all want Cavalley's to stay strong, stay united. We all want it to succeed now, and in the future.' *When Violet is gone.* She did not say the words, but they were in both their minds. 'It's part of your family, as much as you and all the others are.'

Flip nodded, and kissed her. 'And you,' he said.

Tillie smiled. 'Yes. And me, now,' she replied. 'Are we going to tell them today?'

'Not now. I can't . . .' Flip rubbed his hand over his face. 'I just can't.'

Tillie and Flip had married the day before. Unable to wait any longer, shaken by everything that was emerging and falling apart around them, they had decided on the way back from Capri that they would marry as soon as possible, and they had. Just the two of them, and two witnesses, at Westminster Register Office, and lunch afterwards. Flip had apologised for the lack of grandeur. 'Not very romantic, I'm afraid,' he had said. But Tillie couldn't have thought of a more romantic wedding. It was everything she wanted.

'She loves you,' Tillie said quietly.

'She should have told me how ill she was before now. I would have – I would have –'

'You would have cosseted her. Insisted she slow down, stop working. Fretted. Let it distract you. Wouldn't you?' Flip shrugged. They both knew she was right. Tillie smiled. 'You would. And that's why I love you. You're determined. You protect the people you love in the way you think best. But I can see why she kept it from you. Sometimes people just need to keep on going for as long as they can. She's not a quitter. You'd be the same.'

'Whose side are you on?' Flip asked, but his voice wasn't angry.

'Yours, you idiot.' The doorbell rang, and Tillie moved towards the door. 'Always yours. You know that. But I owe her a lot, as well.'

Flip nodded. 'Yeah,' he said. 'Don't we all.'

He waited outside, watching again, as he had in Capri, this time from the driving seat of his hired car as the family arrived, one by one, at the house in Slaidburn Street. Flip and Tillie were already inside; they would be getting ready for the conference they had summoned the rest of them to.

First to arrive was Kalisto, his clothes flamboyant but with a steadiness to his gait and manner that spoke of a serious core that only those who knew him the best were ever really allowed to glimpse. Then Blue, jittery and full of tics and nerves, his stride uneven, making his way along the pavement and up the steps of the building as though weaving his way through a forest of invisible trees. No Adam by his side today.

And then there was Fran. Beautiful despite her scar, more beautiful than she would ever see, she walked quickly with her head down. She paused for a moment outside the block, looking around her. Then, as if shaking herself, she carried on inside.

The Cavalleys. Rich, powerful, privileged. And cursed.

He stared at the building once more. It was time for him to make his entrance.

The siblings were gathered, all seated in the places Flip had steered them towards. Kalisto had gravitated towards the windowseat, where he sat now, his long legs stretched out along it, his body framed by the wooden rectangle as though he were in a photo-shoot. Kalisto lived his whole life as though he was in a constant photo-shoot, always on show. Which, in a way, he was. Fran was next to Tillie, sitting close to her, looking worried. Always looking worried. Blue hovered by the door, smart as ever in a lilac linen shirt and white trousers of the sort that only he could wear for more than five minutes without getting them grubby and creased. His fingers fluttered by his side. Adam was not with him, and Blue was feeling his absence, as he always did when he was without his touchstone. Flip stood. Time to take charge.

'OK. So here we are. All of us together. Before our . . .' Flip paused. He didn't know how to refer to Mattie. 'Uncle' sounded wrong to him; too familiar. Too much of a reminder that Violet had not always been who she was now. Had come from a past that none of them were familiar with, and never would be. 'Matt' sounded like a friend, a mate he might meet down the pub. And the man who had turned up at the villa in Capri certainly wasn't that. He could hardly call him 'Mr Gribbens', though.

'Before Violet's brother arrives, I just want to talk about why we're here.' He felt awkward suddenly; his hands felt heavy, his arms as though they were in the wrong place. It wasn't a sensation he was used to. He was in control, normally, composed, determined. He knew what he wanted and he knew how to get it. Suddenly he was all stumbling and angles. He pulled himself together.

'All right. Next. I'm sorry to sound as though I'm chairing a board meeting. But – well, I guess that's what it is, sort of.'

He looked around the room at the faces of his family, and realised the truth of the words he spoke. They were the ones who would be in charge soon. They were the ones who would take Cavalley's forward. And he would lead them.

'Firstly, we all know that Mama took a turn for the worse, as they say, the day before yesterday. Fran was there with her and dealt with what must have been a very frightening time with great maturity and strength.' Stop sounding so stiff, so formal, he berated himself. This is your family. But he knew that he couldn't help it. It was just how he was.

He looked at Fran, acknowledging his praise, looking pleased even as she tried to pretend it was no big deal. 'Well done, darling,' he said, and she gave him a little smile.

'Of course she has the best possible care. Mama is doing all right. She's a tough lady, as we all know. But it has brought it home to all of us, I think, how little time we might have left with her. Which brings me to the main reason for gathering you all here: our imminent guest.' He cleared his throat. 'Understandably, Mama was very upset by his appearance in Capri. We don't know why he's here – well, we do to an extent; he obviously wants money. But we don't know why he hasn't come out of the woodwork before now. Where he's been, what exactly his plan is. Obviously, there's no question of him having any involvement with the family business, so don't panic about that. But Mama hasn't yet told me how she wants to deal with the situation. Patrick, do you have anything to add? Has she spoken about him today?'

Patrick nodded. 'She's keen for you to handle it all, Flip. She's not paying him off.'

Flip replied, 'Good.'

'Says he can tell who he likes, what he likes. But she's willing to pay any debts he might have, get him out of trouble – as a gesture of familial goodwill. Doesn't want anyone saying she won't take care of her own. But it's not a pay-off. She was very clear about that. She won't be blackmailed again, she said.'

Flip turned back to the rest of the room. The strategy seemed sensible to him. The gossip mill would be whirling into action already. It followed Violet everywhere she went, commenting on everything she did. By offering Mattie help with his bills, she was heading off blackmail demands before he could come out with them. By making it clear that she would not be bullied, she claimed the upper hand. But Flip had an additional idea.

'I'm going to suggest to her that she gives an interview. Tells the touching tale of being reunited with her brother; tells the story of her background herself.'

Kalisto pointed a manicured finger at him. 'Clever boy. There's nothing for him to tell if she tells it first.'

'Exactly. And I think it will be good for her. She should feel as though she has nothing to hide now.'

Patrick agreed. 'As long as she's strong enough. It's a good idea – bring him into the fold. Keep your enemies close . . . I'll suggest the interview to her, if you like.'

'Thanks.' They both knew Violet might resist if it came from

Flip, but that she would go along with almost anything Patrick suggested.

'Secondly, the position with Cavalley's in the coming months.'

He didn't say 'after Mama dies', but they all knew that was what he was talking about, and a sense of sadness was palpable in the room. Each one of their lives would change for ever when she was gone.

'We don't know the details of Mama's Will, but it's fair to assume I will remain in my current position, and be in possession of a controlling stake in the business.'

'I don't think we should assume anything,' Fran said quietly.

The heads of her siblings turned towards her and she blushed. She hated being the centre of attention, but she had to speak out. 'She doesn't seem sure about what she's going to do with Cavalley's. I wouldn't be surprised if she hasn't made up her mind yet.'

Flip gave a little noise of irritation. 'Fran, darling, I don't want to shout you down, but I don't think you know what—'

'You can't ignore me just because I'm the youngest,' she interrupted. 'I'm not a child any more, Flip. I'm going to be working at Cavalley's – I am already. And I know Mama as well as any of you.'

Tillie spoke next. 'Look, the only way this is going to work is if we're all in it together. We know Violet's ill. We know she's conflicted – confused about the future of Cavalley's, and it means so much to her that her vision can get clouded by emotion. The best thing for the company is for it to remain in the family, not get floated on the Stock Exchange or something, where we wouldn't retain the control we do now. And I really believe that Flip's the best person to remain at the helm, at least at first.'

'It's not your decision though, is it?' came a voice from the doorway. The Cavalleys all turned towards it. Standing there, looking for once calm and in control, in a well-cut long dark skirt and raspberry-sorbet-coloured cashmere cardigan, was Boodle.

Tillie glowered. 'No, it isn't our decision, as such, but—'

'But nothing. It's not your decision, full stop. It's Violet's. And I think it stinks that you're having meetings about the future of her company – *her company* – behind her back. She's not dead yet, you know.'

Boodle's bottom lip jutted forward and her eyes were dark. She entered the room and stood next to Blue, whose fingers were dancing a sonata. 'Not dead,' he muttered, 'not dead again, dead again, no, no, alive alive oh, oh, oh, oh, what shall we do with the drunken sailor . . .' His eyes darted around the room, not knowing where to alight. Fran went over to him, laying her hand on his arm.

'It's all right, Blue,' she said. 'No one's dead. It's all right.' She shook her head at Boodle.

'Sorry,' Boodle mouthed. Fran shrugged. It was done now. But Boodle should have known better than to start talking about people dying so baldly with Blue in the room; she knew he couldn't handle it. But it wasn't all down to Boodle. The tension had been getting to him before then, Fran could see it. His head turning from side to side, his lips moving in a silent recitation. He couldn't be left out of the discussions, but they were almost too much for him. Fran fretted about her older brother almost constantly, her instincts to protect him battling with her desire for him not to be treated like a child.

'Why are you here, Boodle?' Flip said angrily.

'I'm here to make sure my son – *our son* – isn't left out of things. To make sure he isn't forgotten. He's the only grandchild.'

A flicker passed across Flip's face.

'And he has as much right to an inheritance as any of you.

You should want the same thing, Flip. You should have included him from the start.'

Boodle's chin was pushed forward in an expression Flip remembered well. She would not be beaten down, when she looked like that.

'I'm sorry,' he said stiffly. 'You're right. Mungo should be involved. Is he in the car? Why don't you go and ask him in.'

Boodle faltered. 'He's not in the car.'

'But you wanted him to be involved.' Flip frowned. 'You said, quite rightly, that he should be part of the conversation. I apologise for not thinking to include him from the start – but why did you not think to bring him?'

'I'm his mother. I represent him,' she blustered.

Flip shrugged. 'He's old enough to speak for himself now, don't you think? Why don't you go and ring him, get him to come over.'

Boodle looked furious. 'Fine. I'll call him a car.' She opened the door to the hallway, her hand reaching into her bag for her mobile. As she did so, the buzzer to the apartment sounded, and the assembled family seemed to freeze. Flip looked around at them.

'Right. Here he is. Let's put Mr Gribbens in his place, and then we can all get on with running Cavalley's, and making sure the family is as solid as it can be.'

No one had heard Boodle go outside to get her Filofax that contained her life, including the details for her car account, leaving it on the latch as she stood in the street calling an Addison Lee car to pick up Mungo and bring him to Slaidburn Street, and then sending Mungo a text telling him to be ready to leave in five minutes. It took her ages, she was a complete Luddite when it came to mobiles, and her podgy fingers didn't help. So she was sitting in the front seat of her car, busy trying to send the message when the man slipped in through the front door of the family house without her noticing. She would not let her bloody ex-husband get one over on her, make her look stupid. Mungo would be here, and he would be part of the Cavalley family conference.

No one heard him walk down the thick, soft carpets of the hallway, to the room where he could hear his family talking. No one knew he was there, until he spoke. His voice was quiet and a bit rough around the edges, as if he hadn't used it for a long time. It felt like that to him, even. As though he had recently woken, and was speaking for the first time after a long, long sleep.

'Hello, Flip. Still playing "I'm the King of the Castle", I see.'

Flip didn't move, at first. He didn't spin around, or even turn. He just stared in front of him, at the faces of his family who were positioned so they could see the man who had just walked in through the door. And they confirmed what the voice had told him and what he could not believe – *could not believe because it could not be true*.

Sebastian.

Flip took in their expressions, one by one. Patrick, shocked and yet calm, as he always was. Not much ruffled Patrick's feathers. Kalisto, on the other hand, looked appalled, his jaw hanging open in a cartoon-like parody of shock and dismay. With Kalisto there were never any small gestures. Tillie slid her hand into Flip's, and he could feel the blood pulsing through it as he gripped on to it for support, her bones fragile under the skin. Blue's eyes widened, and then shot away from the door, seeking something else, as though by fixing themselves on a new image they might be able to supplant the one they had just taken in, erase it. After skitting around the room for a few seconds, they settled on the floor, and then he began to speak, as Flip had known he would, a low, whispered stream of fear. 'Back again, back again, never coming back again, but no, now he is, back from the dead, back in my head, give us this day our daily bread, forgive us our trespasses, forgive us, forgive . . .'

Flip's heart felt as if it would burst with sadness as he listened to his brother, but his sorrow quickly turned to rage. Finally, he began to turn around. As he did so, his eyes alighted on the final face in the room. Fran's forehead was set in a ripple, recognition slow to come to her as she searched her memory for an image of the face she saw in front of her, and eventually matched it with old photos of the brother she had never known. Sebastian.

Sebastian who, as far as they all knew, was dead, had been dead for years, since the terrible accident that had almost broken Violet, which she had seen as yet more proof of her belief that she was cursed, that her family would never be happy or find peace, that she was doomed to lose everyone she loved, sooner or later. It had taken her a long time to recover. Had taken all of them a long time to recover – and they had never been the same since.

And now, there he was in front of him. Sebastian.

The room was silent, at first. Not a breath could be heard; even Blue's ever-present recitation was missing as the Cavalleys stared at the man who had just walked into their midst, who was both stranger and member of their family.

Flip felt disjointed. Half of his brain was telling him that this could not be happening, that Sebastian was dead, long dead and long buried; the other half felt as though it was waking up to a realisation that had been there, somehow, all along. Sebastian was not dead. And that meant that he had never been dead.

The man who stood before him now was very much alive. The same features, but softened a little by age. His hair was still thickly waved, blond and shot through with a little grey now, sweeping back from his forehead. He wore a plain white shirt and tan trousers, relaxed, casual clothes that one might wear for a walk in the park or a picnic. Something about their studied nonchalance filled Flip with a rage that soared up through him, overtaking the confusion, the part of his brain that was trying to fit the pieces of the puzzle together. His heart thumped in his chest and his palms were sweaty all of a sudden, as though he were afraid. He was *not* afraid – what was there to be afraid of? But still his heart raced.

The silence was broken, after a few seconds that felt like an hour, by Sebastian himself, and that increased Flip's anger. What right had he to speak first? What right did he have to just walk in here, call him brother and smile at him, as though no time had passed since they last saw one another, as though no promises had been made and kept by Flip, as though no tears had been shed for him.

'It's something of a shock to see me, I know,' he said, 'but I was hoping someone could tell me what's happening with Mother. I'm very worried about her. It's why – well, obviously, it's the reason I've come back. From the dead, so to speak. Sorry.'

But he didn't look sorry. Not to Flip. In the corner of the room, Blue whispered, 'Back from the dead, playing dead? Roll over, roll over, I'm the king of the castle, all fall down.'

Sebastian looked over at him and smiled. 'Hello, Blue. I've missed your rhymes.'

He glanced at Kalisto, whose face was expressionless, but whose presence was impossible to ignore. Sebastian walked over to him. 'Kalisto. It's been a long time.' Kalisto did not move. Just shook his head, almost imperceptibly. Sebastian held his hands up, and took a step back. All right.

He turned to Fran, who was sitting motionless on the sofa, staring at him. She didn't know what to say to the brother she had never known, who her mother had just started telling her about, whose photo she had seen but who she did not remember. She didn't understand what was going on. She could not connect what she was seeing and hearing with what she had always been told.

'I'm Sebastian,' he said, and his voice was quiet now. 'You must be Fran. Frangipani.'

'Fran,' she said, and he nodded.

'It's nice to meet you.' He didn't hold his hand out to her. Instinctively, without really thinking about what she was doing, Fran stood up and kissed him on the cheek, her hands touching his shoulders. Then she stood back, surprised at herself, but not sorry. She might not understand what this meant, what any of it meant, but this man was her brother, just as Flip and Blue were. Someone should show him that he was welcome.

Sebastian lowered his head. 'Thank you,' he whispered.

Finally, he turned to Flip. The two men faced one another. Tillie stood just behind Flip, wanting to reach for him and hold him, but knowing that she must let him be.

They stood in silence. Flip could think of nothing but all the pain that his family had gone through after Sebastian's death. The funeral, that took place on a grey, wet day, Violet crying her heart out next to him as she buried her son. The days after, when she would see no one, talk to no one apart from Kalisto, just stayed in her bed, crying and listening to the radio, strange stations from foreign countries playing their lilting, crackling music through the long nights. Fran, little more than a newborn, propped up in her bouncing chair, where everyone would give her a nudge as they walked past and make her giggle as she bobbed up and down, but who would then suddenly look around herself as though searching for someone, and burst into ragged sobs. Years of a hole in their family, a second hole, because there had already been Scarlet's death to contend with, so Sebastian knew, he would have known the damage it wrought, and he had – had what? Faked his own death? Causing such devastation as he did so, that Flip could not bear to think about it. The thoughts and questions flew through Flip's mind, rendering him mute.

And then, from the doorway, came Boodle's voice. 'Oh fucking hell,' she said, and Flip looked over Sebastian's shoulder and saw her standing there, Mungo by her side, her plump, jowly face wobbling as she looked from her ex-husband to her late (as she had thought) brother-in-law, and, with typical lack of ability to self-censor, blurted out, 'Violet. How on earth are we going to tell Violet?'

But even as Boodle said it, and even as Sebastian opened his mouth to speak Flip knew what his reply was going to be. Of course.

'You don't need to worry about that,' Sebastian said. 'She already knows.'

The punch landed square on Sebastian's jaw, and his head rocked with the force of it. He didn't react, at first. Kept his head tucked into his neck, and lifted his hand to touch the already swollen side of it.

Flip was breathing hard, rubbing his knuckles. He hadn't been in a fight since he was at school. But seeing Sebastian walk into the house, relaxed, tanned, his blond hair swept back in easy waves, his shirt open, looking for all the world as if he had just popped round after a short holiday, ready to slot back into family life as though nothing had happened, made such a rush of rage rise up in Flip that he could not help himself, and let fly at his younger brother. Rage at Sebastian, rage at Violet, that he would not be able to express to her. She had known? How? Since when? Flip hated being left out of things, hated unanswered questions, and the sheer number of them flying around his head now was more than he could handle without lashing out; so lash out he did.

'You fucker,' Flip gasped. 'Where have you been? Why couldn't you just stay away? Stay fucking dead, if you were such a fucking coward that you had to run away. Stay . . . away.' He spat the words out.

Sebastian raised his head. 'Well. What a welcome home, brother.'

Flip shook his head. 'You're not my brother. Not any more. You're dead.'

'That would be more convenient for you, wouldn't it?' Sebastian said slowly. 'I can see why you're angry. Flip, the Crown Prince, heir to Cavalley's, never did like competition, did he? Never did like sharing the limelight. You must have been furious when I was born. And then the twins. All those new additions to the family, taking attention away from the little Prince.'

Flip charged at him once more, and his body slammed into Sebastian's with a thud. The two men grappled, their bodies intertwined, a tangle of strong arms and elbows and shoulders struggling for dominance over one another.

'Hit a nerve, didn't I?' Sebastian grunted.

'Why don't you disappear again?' Flip growled. 'We were all happier when we thought you were dead. Everyone was better off when you were dead.'

Flip's face was flushed. Sebastian, in contrast, looked calm, the only sign of distress the mark where Flip had hit him that was becoming more visible on his jaw.

From the doorway, Violet watched, unable to move or speak. Patrick had slipped out of the room and gone to get her, knowing that her presence would break up the warring brothers faster than any intervention by anyone else, knowing as well that she would want to see Sebastian with her own eyes. He had carried her down the stairs – had insisted, though she said she could perfectly well walk. 'Save your energy,' he had told her. 'I think you're going to need it, my love.'

He put her down outside the drawing room, so she could walk in herself. As soon as she did, Flip and Sebastian moved apart, and in these two grown men she saw her sons, as young children, caught fighting as they had so often been by her before, heads hanging, shamefaced.

She took a step towards Sebastian, and held her breath. It was him. Patrick had told her upstairs. 'He's back,' he had said, and she had known, straight away, who he was talking about. There was only one person he could have meant: Sebastian, her beloved boy, her bad boy, her Prodigal Son.

'He was dead and is alive again,' she whispered now, and the room fell quiet around her. 'He was lost and is found.'

Her eyes swam with tears and she wiped them on her sleeve, and then held her hand out to him. He did not take it. Instead, he pulled her towards him, wrapping his arms around her fragile body, wanting to hold her tightly, but restraining himself. She inhaled the lemony scent of him, mingled with sweat and airports and cigarettes, and, despite everything that his reappearance meant, despite all the upheaval she knew it would bring, was glad. How could she not be? Though his arms hurt her ribs as they held on to her, she embraced him tighter; though her breath felt short in her chest, she stood for longer than she had in days as she hugged him.

From over Sebastian's shoulder, Violet saw Flip standing, his fists still clenched, his face a mask of rage and hurt. The pain she had caused him – was causing him still – cut through her. She stepped away and reached a hand out to him, willing him to take it. He did not.

'My boy. My boys. I can't see you fight.'

'Don't worry,' Flip said, pulling on his jacket. 'You don't need to. I'm leaving. Fuck this. Fuck this fucking family.' He walked quickly out of the door, his head down, his jacket crumpled around his shoulders. His mother wanted to reach out and smooth it. Smooth the lines from his forehead. But he was full of anger and she could not reach him.

Tillie ran after him. 'Flip! Flip, wait, darling . . .'

But he was gone.

Flip and Tillie sat side by side on the bench outside the World's End pub. He had grown up in this part of London, in these streets, his mother pushing him in his pram up and down the King's Road, had learned to walk through Battersea Park and past the boutiques and bars of Chelsea, his sturdy legs waddling along step by step, until he wobbled and fell down. His teenage years had been spent here, hanging around outside bars, sitting at pavement tables drinking more coffees than he could handle and smoking French cigarettes until he saw Violet or one of Cavalley's employees heading his way, when he would shove the cigarette into a friend's hand or throw it into the gutter. It was home, still, in the way that the place where you had grown up always was. Tillie's hand was in his, and this gave him comfort.

'When do you think she found out?' Tillie asked him. Flip let go of her hand as he reached into his pocket to light two cigarettes and pass one to her.

'I don't know,' he said.

'I mean, do you think she's known . . .'

'All the time?' The question had been knocking at the edges of his consciousness since Sebastian had spoken those words. '*She already knows*.' What had he meant? He had sounded so unworried, so sure of her knowledge. And the look on her face when she had come into the drawing room – it had not been one of surprise, but of acceptance, of relief, almost.

Flip could not accept that. 'No. She wouldn't have lied to me. Not like that. Not for all these years. We – we're closer than that. I would have known. I would have seen she was hiding something.'

Tillie took his hand again. 'Yes,' she said. 'I'm sure you're right.'

They sat in silence for a minute and then, together, they watched as a cab pulled up and Mattie got out of it. Not long ago, his presence in London had seemed like a big threat. How to handle him had felt like the most urgent problem, one that the family must all pull together to deal with, protect Violet from, close ranks against. Now it didn't seem important at all.

'Patrick will deal with him,' Flip said, and Tillie nodded.

'I know it might seem like the worst timing ever,' Flip added suddenly, 'but I think we should go on honeymoon.'

She turned to him in surprise. 'On honeymoon?'

'Yes. Nowhere far. Just to Capri, for a few days. No bothering with booking hotels, we can just go. Get away from all of this.' He gestured at the cab, which was pulling away from the kerb, and the house, where Patrick was letting Mattie in through the front door. Flip rubbed his head with his hand. 'It's too much, Till, you know? Mama. Mattie. Sebastian. I need . . .'

'You need to clear your head. You're going to need to be able to think.'

'Yes.' He looked at her. 'You understand me, Tillie Cavalley. You know me like no one else.' It was true. She knew exactly what he needed, she knew how he ticked, when he needed to be held and when to stand well back, knew that when he was sulking, the best way to make him laugh was to mimic his grumpy, folded face, and that when he was frustrated with work, sex was one of the only things that could calm him down and release that knot in his left shoulderblade.

She smiled. 'I know. I know.' And her smile was suddenly a little sad.

'Hey – what?'

She shook it off. 'Nothing. Just – oh, you know. You're not the only one feeling the pressure here.'

He pulled her towards him and kissed her curls. It was true. She supported him so much that he sometimes forgot how much weight she must be carrying as well, how closely she worked with Violet – what good friends they were. And Fran. She and Fran were thick as thieves, had been plotting something recently. He had meant to ask Tillie about it, but had got distracted. Still. There would be plenty of time on honeymoon, however brief. He stood, and gently tugged her arm to pull her up.

'Come along, Mrs C. Let's go. We'll take the jet. I'll talk to Mama when I get back.'

'Flip – are you certain? She . . .'

Flip nodded once, firmly. 'She isn't going anywhere, not for a while. The doctor said. I have to get out of here, Till. I'm going to be no good to anyone, least of all Mama, if I don't. And watching me fight Sebastian sure as hell isn't going to help her. I need to sort my head out. I'll speak to Kalisto from the car.'

Tillie took his hand again as they crossed the road and walked back to the house. She would do everything she could to support him. She was his wife now, after all.

Violet sat on the windowseat of her drawing room, the cushion beneath her still warm from Kalisto's body. She was exhausted. The pain she had felt two days ago was returning, she could feel it. It was masked by the morphia pills the doctor had given her, but they wouldn't keep it at bay for long. He had told her so, sadness in his eyes.

'You must rest,' he had said.

'I don't have time to rest, Doctor.'

'You have to. If you don't . . .'

'I'll have less time?'

He had nodded. And she had shrugged. As long as she had time to put everything in order, that was enough for her, she had thought then. She would have time to see her children, to tell them how much she loved them, to make her peace with the world.

But that had been then. Now, Sebastian was back, and suddenly things weren't so simple any longer. She had more to attend to, more to do, and already she could feel herself fading, feel the pain returning. Seeing him again had taken more out of her than she had expected, and she was no longer at peace with her fate, but was raging against it, even as she knew that by battling she was using up precious energy. She wondered how much longer she had left. Was it like an egg-timer, the grains of sand sliding through a narrow opening? How many hours? How many minutes?

There was a knock at the door, and Violet paused before speaking. Part of her just wanted to shut them all away, lock the door and sleep. But she had responsibilities. She had promises to keep.

'Come in.'

It was Sebastian.

'Patrick wanted me to tell you Flip and Tillie have gone to Capri. Couldn't bear to be in the same city as me, I guess.'

His voice was light but she could see the hurt in his eyes.

'He'll be back. He's always been like that. Remember when you were little and you fought over that rocking horse? The one he shaved the mane off, pulled its eyelashes out, even, because you told him it had mange?'

Violet gave Sebastian a look, and he nodded. She smiled despite herself, as she watched the memories on his face.

'He had to go and sit in the summerhouse in the garden and think about things for three hours before he could come back inside. He needs time to process things, Flip. Always has done.'

Sebastian went to the seat near her, sat on its arm. 'And me?' he asked.

'You?'

'What was I always like?'

She looked at him. 'Headstrong. Wild, wayward – charming. Clever, but with no sticking power. You never bloody well finished anything. Funny, but you could be cruel when you wanted to be. A talker, a communicator, an entertainer, a practical joker, but afraid of being trapped, afraid of being forced to confront what you had done.'

'Can dish it out, but can't take it?'

Violet's eyebrows lifted. 'If you like.' She could hardly deny the truth of it. The essence of Sebastian's character, of who he was and his place in the family that she had built, was what had led them to this place, and they both knew it.

'And now?' she asked. 'Is that what you are like now?'

'A leopard doesn't change its spots – that's what they say, isn't it?'

She shrugged. 'Sayings are worthless. Tell me. Tell me who you are, Sebastian. Tell me why you are here.'

'I found out how ill you were. I wanted to – I had to see you.'

She shook her head. 'I don't believe you.'

He laughed, his voice shocked. 'My mother's dying, and that's not enough?'

'To risk it all. To risk everything I have protected you from, all these years? Your security, your freedom. Your family. No. You're not that sentimental, my darling boy.'

He lowered his head. 'OK. All right, it's not the only reason. I came back because I found out you were dying, because you *are* dying, yes. And because I knew that it would be my last chance to find out who my father is. I couldn't let you die without telling me, Mama.'

Violet stared at her son. That was closer to the truth. Her eyes searched his face, trying to see in it the story of the years that she had missed. What had time done to him? What person was he now? The same? Different? How? What sort of man had the boy she had known become? Time could change many things, but never the essence of someone. He was unmistakably her son. And he was unmistakably Sam's son. The man she had loved so passionately was visible in every fibre of him. None of her other children were so strongly like one of their parents. '*Sam*,' she had to stop herself whispering. It was almost as though he was there in front of her again. His hair, his hands, the way he stood and held himself. It was Sam made flesh in Sebastian. She missed him still.

Chapter Nine

Violet lay awake at night sometimes and wondered how she had ended up in a position where she had two children, by two different men, neither of whom were part of their children's lives. If it had been someone else in her shoes she would have thought them reckless, feckless, irresponsible. And yet, looking back at her life, she found it difficult to imagine it happening any other way. The choices she had made had seemed the right ones at the time – so how was it that she had ended up here? In the heavy darkness of the middle of the night, she thought she knew. It was the curse that she was running from. The words her father had whispered in her ear, that day in court; they slipped in through the cracks in the windows, they whipped through the gap under the door.

It was as though her success in business was inextricably linked to failure at home, as though she must pay for each shop that opened and each new line that succeeded, with a personal tragedy, a failure, a loss. She missed Sam so much. Sebastian was growing, and every day he looked more like his father. The reality of parenting an eight year old and a six year old by herself and running a growing business, trying to feed all three, nurture all three, was wearing her down. When she looked in the mirror, she saw someone far older than her years. 'The weight of the world on your shoulders,' Ray said sometimes, when he saw her at work, head hunched over her accounts or sketchbook.

So when Kalisto turned up one day, bearing in one hand a new dress that he had made for her, and in the other the name of a man who he said was going to call that evening, she took both. 'He's a rag-trade boy, like us,' Kalisto boomed. 'Well, sort of like us. *Un peu* rougher around the edges, to be phenomenally frank, but to be one hundred per cent honest once more, we can't all be born as refined as you and me, my darling.' He winked at her as she rolled her eyes.

'I don't have time for a date,' she complained. 'I've got to finish the Art Gallery Collection and I need to do a set of drawings for an American bride.'

Kalisto winced dramatically. 'American? *Quelle horreur!*'

Violet smacked his arm. 'And I have to check the building plans for Paris. Honestly, Kal, I just can't.'

'He's already expecting you,' said Kalisto, bustling her towards the stairs. 'Sweetie pie, light of my life, I'll tell you something. You can't *not* go on a date. When was the last time you had sex?'

'Kal!' Violet blushed. 'I'm not telling you . . .'

'Oh God, *that* long? It's worse than I thought. Now get upstairs and do something about that nest of hair before he gets here. I'm babysitting. And if you're not ready by the time he's here, I'm going to set you up on a date with that man with a glass eye who sells flowers by the station and looks at you funny when you walk past.'

Violet shrieked, and ran upstairs.

Half an hour later, Violet walked down the stairs of her house a transformed woman. The dress Kalisto had made for her was of dark-red pleated fabric with bell sleeves that swished as she walked, and had a deep V neck. She sashayed into the room, and Flip's mouth dropped open, making her laugh.

'Well, well, *meine kleine Schokolade.*' Kalisto whistled between his teeth. 'We do scrub up well nicely.'

Flip ran to her. 'Mummy,' he said, 'you look like a princess.'

Violet laughed. 'Let's hope I'm going to meet a prince then, eh?'

The doorbell rang, and Kalisto went to answer it. From the living room she could hear him greeting her date.

'Darling Dorian. You, my delicious boy, are in for a treat indeed.'

And, after a final check in the mirror, Violet left the room and walked down the hallway of her house, towards the waiting, welcoming arms of Dorian Eve.

They had married quickly. Eight weeks to the day after they first met, he had proposed, bringing her breakfast in bed on a tray, with an oval opal ring balanced on top of a croissant.

'Violet Cavalley,' he had said, his face serious, 'I love you. I love you more than I realised was possible, more than I had dared to hope might be possible. I loved you the moment I saw you. I loved you before we met, I think. I will love you until the stars fall from the sky, and the moon turns dark. I love you, I love your children, and I think I will die if I have to go another day without being married to you.'

Violet had laughed. 'You're going to have to wait a while,' she said. 'Unless you want to elope.'

'I will,' he said, leaping on to the bed. 'I'll take you to Gretna Green, right now, like runaway teenagers.'

'No! I can't. I'm a respectable woman – a mother of two. I can't elope.'

'When, then?'

'Hang on. I don't think I've actually said yes, yet, have I?'

Dorian threw himself face down on the pillows, dramatically.

'Oh God. Don't say you're going to refuse me. I can't take the humiliation. I'll have to jump off the roof.' He grabbed her wrists and pulled her on top of him. Her foot caught the breakfast tray and knocked it on to the floor and she squealed.

'Leave it,' he commanded. 'Leave it! You're not going anywhere until you say yes. Go on – say yes. Such a tiny word – hardly even a word at all. Yes.'

Violet looked down at Dorian, her toy boy, she called him. He was five years younger than her. Owned a boutique selling cheap, fashionable clothes with a quick turnover, but had his eye on better things. He had big plans, and he wanted her to be part of them. And she was intoxicated by him. By his youth and energy and enthusiasm. By the way he looked at her as if she was the only person who counted in the world. By the fact that they seemed to be two sides of the same coin. Both in the same industry, both from unhappy families (Dorian had grown up in care, in a succession of homes so dreadful-sounding Violet was almost grateful for her childhood), both lovers of travel, of creating, of living. He bowled her over, and she allowed herself to be caught up in the utter romance of the force of his affections. Every day, he would meet her from work, a bouquet of flowers in his arms, until she told him to stop. 'My studio looks like I've just had a baby,' she said, when he turned up with yet another three-foot-tall arrangement in his arms.

'Now, there's an idea,' he whispered in her ear, as he leaned to kiss her. 'We'd make exceptionally good-looking babies, I think. It seems selfish not to start straight away.'

Giggling, she pushed him off. He wrote her long letters, sending them to her through the post, proclaiming his passion for her; he wrote her short notes, leaving them tucked into her knicker drawer, proclaiming his desire for her; he wrote her poems and bombarded her with words of love from the first night they spent together, making her quite dizzy with the passion and excitement of it all, until even Kalisto, last of the Great Romantics, wondered aloud whether things were moving a little too fast.

'You introduced us,' she said. 'You can hardly complain now. It's what you wanted, isn't it? For me to be happy. In love?'

'Yes,' he said. 'Of course it is, my little *pain au chocolat*.' His voice was quieter than normal, but Violet hardly noticed. She was rushing out of the front door to meet Dorian.

And, 'Yes,' she said, staring into his eyes. 'Yes, I'll marry you.'

After the wedding, Violet and Dorian started trying for a baby immediately. Violet wanted Flip and Sebastian to have another brother or sister, another playmate. She wanted to create the big family she had dreamed of, and that she and Bryce had talked of when they were first living in London – a family full of noise and laughter, a unit, a team. She wanted her children to have allies, to feel the security of familial support that she had never felt and that she had longed for so much.

This need to build up the family for both of her sons was felt keenly by Violet, but she knew that the impulse for it, the reason that lay behind the need was slightly different for each of them. For Flip, it was because of the ever-present guilt that she felt about Bryce. Every day she saw something new of her first love in her son's face, sometimes mingled with something of herself, sometimes simply a flash of him. A flicker, of the first man she had ever loved and who had ever loved her back, would flit across her firstborn's brow, a shadow of him would pass behind his eyes, and she would be pierced by sadness, have to fight the waves of panic that washed through her body whenever she thought of that dreadful day in her old kitchen. She hoped Flip remembered nothing of it, but she could never be sure. What thumbprint might the incident have left on his memory; what mark of violence had her father passed on to her son, despite her attempts to protect him? She knew that she would probably never be entirely confident that it had had no ill-effect – that, try as she might, the shadow of uncertainty would follow her for ever. But she would bear that burden, as long as it did not touch Flip. For Flip, she wanted only good things. She wanted him to feel surrounded by love and family. Bryce's family wanted nothing to do with their son's partner and child, giving the lie, in Violet's view, to the intimacy in the family portrait that Bryce had painted in her mind while he had been alive. There was nothing she could do about that. She had to focus on the parts of their son's life that she could affect.

And then there was her other son, Sebastian, who had never known his father, who Violet felt in some primal, visceral way should be kept away from the man who had been her second love – a love that had almost overtaken her with its passion. She might not have been able to protect Flip from the violent end that his father had met, but she could stop Sebastian from being touched by the violence that she knew was latent in his father. She had seen it in Sam Gilmour's eyes as they sought out hers in bed, had felt the strength of it as he grabbed her wrist, pulsing through his veins. And when she had felt the pulse of her son's life forming, deep inside her belly, had known that she must shield him from it.

She never told anyone who Sebastian's father was. From the moment she had found out that she was pregnant, and had forced herself to turn so resolutely away from him, she had kept the knowledge tied up tight inside her, a secret that she could only keep by sheer force of will, and by reminding herself of the sound of Flip crying into her shoulder as his father bled out on the floor before her.

When Sebastian himself eventually asked, as she had always known he would, who his father was, he had been almost six. She had pulled him on to her lap in the big squashy velvet armchair in the kitchen, and for a brief moment, had thought she wouldn't be able to answer. But of course she had to. She was Sebastian's mother, and she owed it to him to answer his question – even if she was going to do so by lying.

'You know that Flip's daddy died,' she said.

'Yes. But he's not my daddy.'

'No. No, he's not.'

'So where's my daddy?'

Violet took a deep breath. 'Your daddy has to stay a secret.'

He didn't reply.

'He has a very important job, you see. And no one can know where he is, or he might be in great danger. When we made you . . .'

Sebastian sniggered at this point, despite the seriousness of his expression.

'Yes, all right. When we made you, he was in the middle of a very special assignment. No one must know that he was here, in London. Do you understand?'

Sebastian looked down at the Knight Rider toy car that he had been playing with, and made a 'Brrrm' noise, running it along her thigh and up her arm. Violet gently took it from him. Suddenly she had an idea.

'Look, it's a bit like in *Knight Rider*. Michael and KITT have to fight the baddies, don't they?'

Sebastian nodded. 'So my daddy is like Michael. Or KITT?' he said.

Violet paused. She hadn't really thought the finer points of this analogy through, she realised, and was reaching the end of her *Knight Rider* knowledge.

'Well, sort of like both.'

'How?'

'More like Michael. Because he's a man, not a car.'

Sebastian giggled.

'But a bit like KITT,' she went on, 'because he always gets people out of trouble, when they need it.'

'Like James Bond,' the little boy said.

'A bit like James Bond as well, yes.'

Sebastian nodded, satisfied. Then: 'Can we have Alphabetti Spaghetti for supper?'

Violet nodded and kissed his head, and wished that all the questions in her life could be resolved as easily as that last one.

Scarlet Eve was born at midnight on 21 May 1977, exactly on the cusp of the two days. Blue came into the world four minutes later, predicting his name by emerging into the world not breathing properly, tinged with icy-blue like something from under the sea. Violet had lain on her back in the theatre, her lower half hidden from her by a green curtain of surgical fabric, feeling woozy and disconnected as she waited for word that he was all right and for her babies to be brought to her. Her perfect twins, a girl and a boy. In her dreamy, shell-shocked post-birth haze, she felt as if she had created two halves of the very world, her own miniature Adam and Eve, Yin and Yang.

Later, when the three of them were all back on the ward, and she sat, propped upright in her bed, feeding them, she remembered that image and laughed. How silly. And yet, it had given her an idea for the babies' names . . .

When Dorian arrived at the hospital the next morning, holding Sebastian and Flip's small hands and bearing a huge bunch of flowers under his arm and the remains of a hangover from wetting the babies' heads last night, she was sitting in bed, Blue grizzling in her arms and Scarlet asleep next to her. She raised her face for his kiss and said, 'I've thought of the names. Scarlet and Blue. Oh Dorian, aren't they beautiful? Like two parts.

Primary colours. They'll always be linked to each other, you see? Two sides of the same coin.'

Dorian leaned down and picked up Scarlet. As he shifted his arms, trying to make sure he held her securely, her head supported like he had always known babies' heads had to be, she woke up and opened her eyes. They were the shape of teardrops, and they fixed on his.

He stared into her eyes, and felt nothing but terror at the need that he saw there, the unending, undying need. It choked him. She was his for ever and ever, and there was no turning back now.

'Isn't she beautiful?' Violet whispered, but he could not speak. She smiled, thinking he was overwhelmed with emotion. 'Here,' she said, 'take Blue as well. Look, you can hold them both at once. One in that arm,' she turned Scarlet around so she fitted into the crook of his elbow, 'and one in this.' He stared down at them. His eyes filled with tears, and Violet lay back on the pillows and sighed happily.

'Darling,' she said. 'Look what we made.'

Dorian gulped. And nodded. She looked up at him. He was young, Dorian, unprepared for the responsibility that he was going to be faced with now. He had gone from being a single man to a married father of two and stepfather to two more in the space of just over a year; enough to rock anyone's foundations. But she was sure of him. He would step up to the plate, and prove all the nay-sayers wrong, she knew it. Because there *were* whispers – that it was too quick, that she was trusting him with too much, that he would buckle under the pressure. People always talked, she told herself. Couldn't help themselves. And while they talked enough when things went wrong, they talked all the more when things were going well, when you were finally finding happiness. It was as though they couldn't bear for everything to be going well, had to try and find a chink somewhere. 'He's very young,' Gerald said nervously, one day when Violet was about six months' pregnant. 'I don't wish to pry, Violet, and your personal life is your own concern, but I would be remiss in my duties if I didn't ask whether you were one hundred per cent sure of his track record as a businessman before you merged certain of your assets with his.'

Violet's response had been swift and steely. 'I am as sure of him as I am of you, Gerald,' she had said, and her voice had brooked no argument. Kalisto had also spoken to her, voicing a worry that she was plunging her family headfirst into this new life too quickly, without knowing enough about him. 'Have you met his parents? Where do they live? Are you sure of who he is – how can you be?' he had asked.

'I'm not some nineteenth-century princess,' Violet had shot back, 'and you're not my guardian. Who do you think you are, asking whether I've met his parents? You introduced us, why don't you tell me?'

'I don't know,' he had answered quietly. 'I don't know him well. I just thought he'd be a fun person for you to go on a date with. I didn't realise you were going to install him at the head of the table after one fuck. Just how good was he, exactly?' His voice had been bitter and he had regretted the words as soon as they were out of his mouth, recognising them for what they were – fragments of jealous spite, bullets of hurt at feeling pushed out of the new clique Violet was forming with this boy.

But it was too late. It was the first, and worst, row they had ever had; she refused to speak to him for a week afterwards. Kalisto had only been able to pacify her when he came round with a pair of red patent leather shoes that he had had specially made for Dorian, but which they both knew were really a peace offering for her.

They had made up, but the scar of their row remained. Violet felt his slight wariness when he came to visit them all in the hospital, not wanting to intrude, hovering around the edges of the room in a way that she found at once irritating and endearing, and, as she felt those two emotions side by side, she laughed. Kalisto looked at her, unsure.

'What?' he asked.

She shook her head. She couldn't explain what she had realised – that she had experienced, for the first time, what she had heard people talk about when they referred to their siblings or parents – a combination of affection and frustration that signalled their closeness in a way that she had always wondered about. He was her family. She held Scarlet out to him.

'Nothing. Get over here and take this baby, will you? And you'd better have brought me something to eat, I'm bloody starving.'

Violet took her baby twins home a week later. Kalisto picked her up from the hospital.

'I'll meet you at the house,' Dorian had said. 'I'll be there later. There's something I have to do.'

He would be picking up a gift for her, Violet was sure. An eternity ring, maybe, or a diamond bracelet. She looked down at her rings. The large diamond in her engagement ring twinkled and sparkled. Maybe it would match that. Maybe it would be something quite different. She turned to look at the twins in their matching cribs in the back of the car, rearranging the blankets beneath their chins. She didn't mind what it was. She had everything she needed. Her family.

Dorian wasn't at home when they arrived back. There was no sign of him. Violet walked through the whole house, looking in every room, realising as she went, that all of his things were gone. His shoes were not by the front door, lined up alongside Flip and Sebastian's. His cufflinks were no longer on the top of her dressing-table in their little tray. His post was not lying, half-opened, on the kitchen table. The only sign that he had ever been in the house at all, was the lingering smell of the musky aftershave he wore. And of course the twins, gurgling softly in their baskets.

Violet rang for Ginny to come and watch them, and Kalisto drove her to Dorian's shop. Even as they drew up outside, she knew there would be no one there. The building had that feeling about it. Deserted.

When they went inside, using the key that Violet had on her key-ring, they both stood quite still, staring.

The room was empty. Violet was unable to move, unable to breathe, unable even to blink. She felt as though she had been plunged into a great vat of water and was suspended in it, floating motionless, paralysed. Her limbs did not feel as though they belonged to her, her arms hung uselessly at her side. She tried to raise them, to point at something, to make some kind of gesture that might express her horror, her shock, but they were like dead weights, puppets' arms with the strings cut. Her blood rushed in her ears, loud and pulsing, the only reminder that she was in fact alive.

The room was not entirely empty, as she had first thought. There was a set of shelves in the corner nearest them and, leaning up against one of the shelves was an envelope.

She made Kalisto wait in the car.

'I want to stay,' he said, his face worried. 'Vi, let me stay. You shouldn't be alone.'

'I have to be alone,' she said. 'I just have to be. Please.' Her voice was almost a whimper. She felt like a wounded animal that must crawl into its hole to die in private. Could not bear the idea of Kalisto watching her as she fell apart, as she knew she was about to.

Dear Violet, the note said. *I'm sorry*.

And she let out a wail. 'Oh no,' she yelped, through hot, thick breaths. 'Oh no, oh no.'

I never meant for the twins to happen. It wasn't about them, it was always about the job. I got carried away. You – you were more than I had bargained for. And I let events overtake me. I'm sorry for that, and I'm sorry for the burden I'm leaving you with. I thought for a moment that I might stay. Be normal. Live a normal life. But then . . . well, they were born, and I saw the future in their eyes, and I knew I could never do it. It's kinder this way. And this was always how it was going to be. Don't take it personally, Violet. Try not to hate me. Don't waste your energy. Like I say, it was always about the job. It's just what I am.

Dorian

Later, Violet found out that it was not just Dorian's shop that had been left empty. His current account had been closed, the balance removed in full, in cash. Her account, which he had access to, was also empty. The shop tills had been cleaned out. She didn't have to take her rings to the jewellers to know they would be fakes.

And Violet was alone once more.

Although this time, it was worse. Because this time, in reality she was far from alone. She had four young children to support, who relied on her, and her alone, to provide them with food, clothes, a roof over their heads. She had a business with an ever-growing number of employees who were also relying on their salaries from her to do the same.

And she had not a penny to do it with.

'I'm afraid I can't imagine a way that it could be worse, my dear,' Gerald Petherbridge told Violet bluntly when she asked him how bad a situation she was in.

She nodded, her light-grey dress emphasising the pallor of her face. He was worried about her, Gerald thought, as she sat before him, her baby twins in their carriers on the floor beside her. It was too much for anyone to be expected to shoulder.

But she sat and listened calmly as he outlined the severity of her position to her.

'There's simply no money,' he said. 'He's pretty much taken the lot. You have your savings account – but I'm afraid that is somewhat depleted due to your recent withdrawal.'

Violet had bought Dorian an antique Rolex watch as a wedding present.

'And, in contrast to when you last found yourself in a comparable scenario . . .' Gerald was thinking back to when Violet first sat before him, in this very office, after Madame Fournier's death. 'On this occasion, your overheads are far higher. The expansion of the business that you have undertaken in recent years has been immense – as you know. And I hope you also know, and don't mind me saying, how much I admire you for it.'

Violet smiled sadly. 'Thank you,' she said. 'You're a good friend to me, Gerald.'

'Oh!' He looked surprised. 'Well, of course it is my pleasure.' He looked a little embarrassed.

'You warned me,' she continued, 'and I didn't listen to you. Worse – I was very rude to you. Unforgivably so. But I hope that you will forgive me, nevertheless.'

Gerald Petherbridge was not a man accustomed to showing emotion. 'Of course, my dear. There is nothing to forgive.'

He patted her hand twice across the table, and then cleared his throat and continued, 'But I'm afraid all of this does mean you have an urgent cash-flow problem. There are many people relying on you.'

'Yes, I know,' Violet said. 'I . . .' She picked up Blue, who had started to grizzle, and lifted him on to her shoulder, patting and shh-ing him.

'I'm going to have to go away and think about what to do,' she said.

'Of course. But . . .' Gerald wasn't sure how to continue.

'Don't take too long, right?' She finished for him.

He nodded. 'Indeed. That would be my advice.'

A frown passed across Violet's face.

'The oldest trick in the book,' she said, looking into Blue's big eyes as she held him before her. 'Isn't it? Oh Gerald, what a fool I have been.' And, to the lawyer's horror, she burst into tears.

As they stood in his office, Violet sobbing and, one by one, Blue and Scarlet both also beginning to cry, Gerald took out a clean linen handkerchief, handed it to her, and patted her on the shoulder, wishing beyond wish that he could take the poor young woman in his arms, and make all of her problems go away.

No one could make this go away. Violet knew this as she stood on the street outside Gerald's office, both twins squalling in their pram. Dorian Eve had taken from her everything she had worked so hard for, sacrificed so much for. All of those nights sitting at her desk in the corner of her bedroom while Flip slept alongside her, all the time she had spent producing new collections and going round London, sticking flyers and posters up to make sure people knew Cavalley's was there, all of the time she had spent on her hands and knees, scrubbing the floors of old properties she had bought and renovated for her Cavalley's House shops . . . all of those hours with Bryce, drawing her dreams . . . It was all going to disappear, be swept away like dust, and there was nothing she could do about it.

'There's simply no money.' Gerald's voice rang in her ears as she pushed the twins home. Without cash in the bank, she could not pay her workers, the mortgages on the properties, the overheads, for materials. A business tax bill was due, as was a large payment to the building firm she used to carry out all the renovation work on the properties she bought. And there was nothing to pay them with.

As it all began to sink in, Violet did what she had always done, and walked. She pushed the twins along the river, the motion of the pram soothing them as she weaved her way down the Embankment, over Waterloo Bridge, down towards Battersea and the park, and back over the river towards Chelsea and home. As she walked, she pondered as she had done so many times before, the wheels of her mind turning over and over like the wheels of the pram. But this time, she came up with no solution. Cavalley's, the company she had built with her bare hands from nothing, was dead. And it was all for love.

But just as love had threatened to destroy her work, it would be love of a different kind that saved it. A week after she had been to see Gerald, Violet was sitting at her kitchen table, a pot of tea in front of her, feeding the twins and sifting through the household bills at the same time, trying to work out which ones were the most urgent and which she could put off. The shops were still going, for another week. She had transferred her remaining savings into the business account so the staff salaries could be paid. She would not see those who worked for her out of pocket because of the wickedness of one man, and the stupidity of one woman.

She opened yet another envelope with a feeling of numb dread. How much would this one be? But, instead of a bill, to

Violet's surprise, a cheque fell out. She opened the letter folded around it. It read:

> *Dear Violet,*
>
> *I have heard that you are in a difficult situation, and would like to help. As I believe I told you once before, your previous employer and mentor, Elizabeth Fournier, showed me great kindness, and I was never able to repay her in her lifetime. I am glad, therefore, of the opportunity to do so, albeit indirectly, now. Please accept the enclosed as an interest-free loan, repayable as and when you are able. No strings attached.*
>
> *Yours, with affection*
>
> *Clare Montgomery*

Violet's hand went to her mouth. The cheque was a large one: it would pay half of the builder's bill. But, of course, it was nowhere near enough. The chasm of the debt she had been left with yawned before her. Sighing, she carried on opening her pile of letters. And, one by one, alongside letters of support, of solidarity, of encouragement, cheque after cheque fell out on to her kitchen table.

As she sat there, weeping with relief and gratitude, Kalisto appeared in the doorway.

'Oh Kal,' she said. 'It's saved. Look . . . I can make it work. I can carry on.' She picked up a handful of the letters and held them up to him, and as she did so, Violet looked at the smile on his face and saw that it was one of pleasure, but not surprise, and she fell quiet.

'I just dropped by to tell you that the girls in the studio came to see me today. They won't take their salaries for a month, they said. I tried to talk them out of it . . .' he shrugged, trying to look as though he were telling the truth, '. . . but they said someone else had paid them already. So, you've got a bit of breathing space, at least. And it looks like you've got some other benefactors, and all.'

Violet put the letters and cheques down, walked over to him and wrapped her arms around him. They didn't quite reach together at the back, even now.

'Thank you,' she said. 'Thank you so much.'

'Oh, I didn't do anything,' he replied.

'Stop it.'

Kalisto sighed. 'All right – I might have spoken to a few people. But Vi, it was all my fault in the first place. If I hadn't set you up with him . . .'

She patted his back. 'Ssh,' she said. 'It doesn't matter. It just doesn't matter. I'm sorry,' she whispered, as they held one another. 'I'm so sorry I didn't listen.' And as they stood there, she knew that she had been wrong. Dorian was not her family. Kalisto was, and her children, and Gerald and all the men and women who worked for her and who demonstrated their loyalty to her every day. She did not need to bring a man into this to make it complete – it was complete already. She had everything she needed, right here.

Scarlet was a showgirl from the very beginning. Inside the womb, even, she was doing backflips and shoving Blue out of the way. He lay quietly, never really changing position, down one side of Violet's belly, when she was pregnant with them, but Scarlet seemed to be all over the place, flicking like a fish, in a way that Violet could not understand, given that there were two of them in there. How did she find the space? But Scarlet found the space.

From when she was tiny, she was always dressing up, always at the centre of things. Performing came as naturally to her as sleeping, which was the other thing she did a lot of. When she was a toddler Violet would often turn around and see Blue at her ankles, as usual, wanting to be close to her, and wonder where Scarlet was, and then find her fast asleep in any corner that she could find – a laundry basket, a pile of towels waiting to be put away, curled up on the bottom stair. 'That girl could turn any surface she came across into a stage or a bed,' Kalisto would say, as she pushed a carefully printed and decorated note under his office door announcing the performance of yet another Scarlet Cavalley Production.

It was as though she burned out her energy so quickly that she had to recharge it constantly, Violet thought. She was like a little firefly who buzzed around the room, lighting up every corner of it and not leaving herself with anything, so she flopped, suddenly, into sleep to regenerate herself. She had the gift of charming persuasion, as well; could talk her brothers, in particular, but everyone else she came across, in general, into doing what she wanted them to, which was usually to take part in a musical or a parade or a talent show that she was racing around organising. Many was the time that Violet would enter a room and find her three sons lying on the ground, in order of height; Flip at the bottom of the human pyramid with Sebastian on top of him, as Scarlet clambered up a chair to balance on top of them all, shouting for Violet to 'Come and take a photo of the Magnificent Christmas Tree of Cavalley Boys, topped with their human fairy!' Or seated behind a table, holding up score cards as she tapdanced before them, urging them to 'give us the scores on the doors'. They went along with it, all three of them unable to refuse their ebullient, ever-grinning sister. Even Blue, to whom performing was as unnatural as sitting and reading the comic books he loved to his twin, forced himself to play her games. Anything to see her smile.

Blue was different. He had always been different. Life to him was not the stage and playground it was for Scarlet; it was eminently serious, a labyrinthine maze filled with hazards and opportunities for disaster. His imagination was florid and uncontrollable. He would spend hours sitting on the floor, a roll of paper in front of him, creating detailed pictures full of imaginary creatures and distant isles and letters and numbers, a whole world flowing out from his pen. That part of him was familiar, at least, the part of him that drew his dreams. But the dreams themselves were unrecognisable to Violet. His mind was tilted slightly, it seemed. He saw things differently to other people. The imagination that created these pictures terrified him – he would wake at night screaming, sweating and his eyes searching the corners of the room for visions seen only by him. He could not rein it in, could not stop the galloping creatures that marauded through his brain, creating terror around every corner. In Blue's mind, through his eyes, the world was a dangerous place.

When Violet told him bedtime stories, he would stop her constantly, interrupting with everything that came into his mind.

'There once was a princess in a castle—'

Was she trapped? Had she been locked in? Was there a monster, a dragon, an alien? Were there vampires near the castle that sucked her blood out? Was her blood really blue?

He read all the time, and though Violet tried to regulate it in order to control the flow of information into his brain, keep it to things that would not jar too much and be turned into ever more frightening prospects once inside, she couldn't stop him absorbing almost everything he came into contact with, like a sponge, and then retaining it, twisting it, his synapses fizzing and short-circuiting, or so she imagined. And then it would all pour out, to whoever he was talking to at the time, wherever they were, mad, rambling tales that Violet could piece together because she got used to the chaotic thought processes which turned a glimpse of a man in a fancy-dress costume, dressed like Robin Hood, into a book that came to life and sucked children into its pages where they would live for ever. He had no sense of what was real and what was imagined, no invisible line between what other people thought was normal and what he saw as being real.

Eventually, when he was ten, she could no longer pretend it was an overactive imagination, normal childish nightmares and games, nor could she stand the way people looked away when he began to talk, their eyes silently hoping he would not trap them in one of his long, nonsensical rants from which they could not escape without seeming rude. Not that he noticed; all you had to do was say, 'I don't want to listen any more, Blue,' and he would stop in his tracks, relieved, almost, to be stopped. If something didn't pause him he could carry on indefinitely. Blue had no sense of social niceties.

The first doctor she took him to had no idea what to do with him, and suggested boarding school. That was a short appointment. The second prescribed 'play therapy', the third sedatives, the fourth, fifth and sixth hospitalisation, electro-convulsive treatment and a course of vitamins respectively. None of them knew what was wrong with him, what was different about him. There was no name for his condition, they said, and when Violet suggested that maybe he didn't have a condition, maybe he was just himself, they looked sceptical, and made another note.

In the end, it was Scarlet who found the key that unlocked something inside Blue. They were fifteen, and Scarlet was playing the lead role in the school production of *Romeo and Juliet*, hoping that if she was good enough, Violet would finally give in and let her go to the stage school that she had been agitating about for the last two years. Violet was standing her ground for now, insisting that she get an education, but her arguments against it were starting to sound weak even to her. The rest of the cast had been provided with costumes from the school store, but Scarlet wanted to stand out. She wanted something special. Kalisto was in the middle of a collection, or she would have asked him, but Violet had firmly warned her not to do so. So, one day, when they were at home, and Blue was sitting reading, his lips moving quickly as he took in the words and pictures, instead of doing what she usually did, flopping on the floor next to him and replacing his book with her lines so that he could test her, she gently took it from his hands and put a sketchpad in them instead.

'Design me a dress,' she said, on a whim. Blue looked up in surprise. His eyes flicked between hers.

'Go on,' she continued, 'a beautiful dress. A party dress. For me to wear in the play. What you think I would look best in. Something romantic and lovely. Please?'

He stared at her for a while. She wondered whether he was going to shut down, as he sometimes did. But then he nodded once, briefly, lowered his head to the page and started to draw, quickly filling the space. Scarlet sat and watched as shapes and scrolls grew, spilling out to the edge of the piece of paper.

'Here,' he said eventually. She held out her hand and smiled at him, expecting – what had she been expecting? A childish vision of a princess dress, probably. What she got was something entirely different.

He had drawn almost an entire collection in one page. It wasn't just a costume, it was a full-scale theatrical concept for a production, ornate and detailed. A dress with an asymmetrical sheath shot up from one left shoulder into a high, structured collar, and was cut high on the leg on the same side, with a kind of side train facing it. Light flicks of Blue's pencil indicated that the dress was metallic, a shimmering, silver fabric. The woman in the drawing had hair that was twisted up on top of her head in a coil that shone like a snake; a silver rope was twisted through it. Another dress was a black micromini, strapless and covered in large circular gold plates, like a suit of armour. There was a suit with similar metal plates on the shoulders, jutting out like the exoskeleton of an insect; trousers cropped to just below the knee and trimmed with a thick band of sequins.

'Mama?' Scarlet called, her eyes still fixed on the paper. 'Come and look at this.'

Violet looked up at her son in surprise.

'Blue. Why didn't you show me? You must have been doing this before. Do you have more?'

He shook his head.

'But this can't be the first time you've drawn dresses like this, darling,' she protested, and then stopped and said, 'OK, it is. It is, don't worry, I know you're telling the truth,' because she could see the look of rising panic on his face that he got if someone thought he was lying. She looked back at the designs in wonder.

'No one never asked me to draw a dress before,' he said. And she realised that it was as simple, in his mind, as that.

Violet put him to work. She knew instinctively that this was what he needed. She arranged a table in the corner of the workshop for him, and told him that if he could come up with a complete collection, she would help him launch it. He didn't need telling twice. All his energy from that moment on was channelled into his designs. It was like watching someone come to life.

It was what he had needed, what he had been waiting for, it seemed. Suddenly Blue had a purpose, a place where he could be himself and where that self was valued, not just by his family, but by the outside world. He continued to go to school – Violet told him he must get his GCSE's – but every spare minute outside of school was spent working on his designs, poring over books and fabrics and trimmings, standing in front of a mannequin, pinning his toiles into place. The job gave him a clarity that he had never had before, had never known was possible. When he was concentrating on his drawings, on his dresses, everything went calm inside his head. The buzzing that set his teeth on edge quietened, the sense that someone was always just over his shoulder, whispering in his ear and about to step out in front of him faded away. The shapes in the pavement and clouds became less threatening.

As the fifteen-year-old Blue thrived, Sebastian, at twenty, worried Violet more and more. He had been a handful for years – wayward, rebellious, stubborn, with all of Flip's will and none of his self-control. He drank, he smoked, he broke almost everything he came into contact with, whether things or people's hearts. And yet he was charming and charismatic in a way that unsettled Violet every time she saw him use it, because it was so strongly reminiscent of his father. His father's genes ran as clearly and as strongly in him as a mountain stream, and Violet knew that it boded ill.

He was a very different young man from Blue. By the time *he* was fifteen, Sebastian Cavalley had been expelled from three minor public schools, and Violet was at a complete loss as to what to do with him. He was clever, but refused to work at anything he didn't find interesting; nothing diverted him for more than short periods of time. He could talk his way out of trouble when he wanted to – but he didn't even bother to do that.

'I don't understand,' Violet said to him, after receiving the third phone call in as many years asking her to please come and collect her son 'as a matter of some urgency'. 'I shouldn't say it, but you don't have to get caught, at any of these things. Obviously I'd rather you weren't doing them at all, but it would seem we've gone past that point.'

Sebastian shrugged and lit a cigarette. She sighed and passed him the ashtray, pinching one of his cigarettes for herself. She didn't have the energy for that argument, as well.

'If you're going to do all of this stuff, why do you have to make it so blatant? It's not as though you're just stupid. I don't think I'd mind as much, if that were the case. It's as if you want to get caught.'

The first expulsion had been when he was thirteen, for hacking into the school's computer system, downloading copies of forthcoming exam papers and selling them to the older boys. 'It's not cheating,' he had said when caught, in the interview with his mother and the Headmaster. 'I didn't use the answers myself, so how can it be? And it's really not my fault if your security measures aren't up to scratch.'

The Headmaster had knitted his bushy brows together, and Violet had taken her son home. Though she had grounded him all over the summer holidays, she had secretly been quite impressed with his abilities. It wasn't as if he'd been bullying anyone, she told herself, or doing anything really awful. It was entrepreneurial, almost. 'Entrepreneurial, my backside,' Kalisto had said when she'd told him about it that night. 'I know he's your son, Vi, and you love him – we all do. But the boy's heading for trouble.' She shrugged it off. He would be fine; he'd just been bored at the school, not stretched enough. All she had to do was find him the right school, and everything would be fine.

Next, he went to a school that was known for being tough on wayward children, and academically rigorous. They took a dim view of Sebastian's lack of enthusiasm for attending classes, and he was thrown out when it became apparent that he was responsible for a poker night which meant that at least five of his schoolmates were forced to sell belongings or swipe money from their fathers' wallets in order to pay their gambling debts.

The third and most recent establishment to expel him was

one that prided itself on taking boys and girls who had got into trouble at other schools, and 'bringing their talents to the fore'. They had an excellent art and drama facility, a full recording studio and a relaxed uniform policy. That one put up with Sebastian's persistent truancy, with his disregard for all of the rules and his habit of disappearing off to London for the weekend without telling anyone, because they saw a 'unique intelligence' in him. However, they gave up on him when he was caught with the Headmaster's underage daughter in his bed.

'I don't care if I get caught,' he said now, holding the cigarette in his cupped hand, his thumb sticking through the hole that he had worked into the sleeve of his grey cashmere V-neck.

'You've made that abundantly clear. But you seem to seek it out.'

He shrugged again.

'Oh, stop shrugging at me, Sebastian. I can't keep sending you somewhere new every time you fancy breaking the rules.'

'So don't.'

'You're fifteen. You have to get an education.'

He smiled at her and stretched. 'Not today, I don't. Take me out to lunch, Mama? I'm starving. I haven't had a proper meal for weeks.'

'I am not bloody well taking you out to lunch. Not until you tell me why you keep doing this.'

He looked at her with big eyes. 'I just get bored.'

She stood her ground. 'Not good enough.'

Sebastian sighed. 'OK. You want to know why? I'll tell you. It's because . . .' He took a deep breath; his bottom lip trembled.

Violet leaned forward and took his hand between hers. 'Sebastian, my little boy. You can tell me anything – you know that.'

He nodded, his head lowered. When he spoke, his voice was a whisper.

'It's because I don't fit in anywhere. I feel like an outsider everywhere I go . . .'

'Oh Seb.'

He raised his head and looked her straight in the eye. 'You know, Mama. I think . . . I think it's because I should have been born – a girl.'

Violet froze. She could feel her face set into an expression of horror as she tried desperately to work out what to say. Then, as she scrambled for words, Sebastian burst out into great peals of laughter, flopping back on to the sofa, his arms over his stomach as he guffawed. She threw a cushion at his head.

'Oh Sebastian. You little shit.'

When he had stopped laughing, Violet took him out for lunch.

She gave in to him too much, she knew she did. But he was beguiling, her second-born boy; he had a force of personality that bowled her over. Maybe she should have stopped Sebastian in his tracks earlier. But how? Disciplining him didn't work, he just came up with loopholes, or ways to get around her rules that she found impossible to argue with. Bribery didn't work either; he would, again, find a way of getting what he wanted, and conveniently dropping the part of the deal that didn't suit him. When she called him on his behaviour he would look up at her with those big eyes, an awareness within them of what was going on that astonished her. It was as if he was saying to her, 'I know what I'm doing, and I know you know – and we both know that you can't stop me.'

After expulsion number three, she stopped trying to find boarding schools that would take him. She had thought sending him away was the right thing – he'd wanted to go. But maybe it hadn't been. Clearly, she had done something wrong, in a big way. Maybe treating him like an adult was the way forward, involving him more in the decisions she took. He was going to be sixteen, before long, after all.

So, she sat him down at the kitchen table with coffees and cigarettes, and told him they weren't getting up until they had a plan that they could both live with. She ran her life from that table, it seemed, it was the house's heart. 'Mission Control', she called it. That day it was full of mood boards for a wedding Violet was working on, for the daughter of a Russian oligarch, all gold embroidery and jewels worked into ropes that would be plaited through the hair of the seventeen attendants; the plans for a new salon Cavalley's was opening in San Francisco were spread out on one side of the table. Two huge glass hurricane lamps sat in the centre of the table, big white pillar candles half-melted inside them. Trilby the tabby cat had wound himself around one of them, and was asleep in a patch of sunlight. On the other side of the kitchen, Kalisto and Violet's housekeepers were planning the menu for a dinner party they were hosting together.

'Right. Where do you want to go to school, Seb? And "nowhere" isn't an option.'

'In a few months it will be. You could home school me until I'm sixteen.'

'No chance.'

'It's the law, Mother. You can't argue with the law.'

'Fine. You can leave school at sixteen if you plan to support yourself from that point on.'

He stuck his tongue out at her.

'No, I didn't think so.'

Sebastian sighed languidly. 'You're so . . . bourgeois, Mother.'

Violet raised an eyebrow at him. 'Well, that's as may be. But, while you're under my roof. Et cetera.'

He poured some more coffee and picked up the drawing closest to him. 'Terribly ostentatious in their tastes, these Russians, aren't they?'

'Don't change the subject!'

'Oh, stop fretting, Mama dearest. It's sorted.'

'It's not . . .'

He stood up, his jeans low on his hips, his rugby shirt frayed at the edges. Anyone would think he was homeless, the way he dressed these days, Violet thought, and then inwardly rolled her eyes at how old she sounded to herself.

'It is. I'm going to stay at Miles's house tonight, by the way.'

'You're grounded. I told you.'

He grinned at her. 'It is sorted. I've already been accepted into Westminster. Here . . .' Sebastian pulled a crumpled piece of paper out of his back pocket. 'You just need to sign the fee stuff.'

Then he leaned down and kissed the top of her head. 'See you tomorrow.'

He blew his little sister a kiss, and Violet despaired. He was always one step ahead of her. Just like his father.

Part Three

Chapter Ten

Capri was ahead of them. Flip rolled his head from side to side, trying to unkink the muscle that had locked in his neck, as it did whenever he got tense. The skies were dark around the helicopter and a flicker of rain spattered against the window suddenly, tugging Tillie out of her reverie. She straightened up. As she did so, there was a low, heavy rumble which seemed to come from underneath the helicopter, and a slight juddering.

Tillie looked up at Flip, who gestured to the pilot.

'All OK?'

The pilot nodded briefly but didn't speak. Flip leaned forward, speaking to him through the headset he was wearing.

'We're nearly there, aren't we?'

'Yes.' The pilot bit his lip. The weather was getting worse. Visibility had been low but he was sure it would be fine. The bigger companies were anal about not flying, downed tools at the first sign of a cloud. He thought it was bollocks. And he needed the money the client was offering. But the light had almost gone now and it was getting windier. And if he was completely, 100 per cent honest with himself, he had a tiny niggling doubt at the back of his mind that the heli was not running quite as it should. He'd been fiddling with it before they left but the guy had been so keen to get there, and then he'd come up to him and offered him a bonus if they left now, straight away – as long as the aircraft was safe, of course. 'We're on our honeymoon,' he'd said, 'we've only got a couple of days. Please?'

And he had said he was sure it was. Had winked at the man's beautiful young bride, who had looked at him with pleading eyes, and couldn't have refused her anything. Now, though, as he felt himself struggle to keep the chopper straight, he wasn't quite as sure as he had been. He began to bring it round, taking it lower to try and move out of the wind, heading for the north of the island. He wanted to get them landed as soon as possible, before the weather got any worse.

Flip stroked his wife's thumb with his own. 'It's fine, darling,' he told her. 'I've done this trip a thousand times. It's a bumpy bit around here, for some reason. I promise you, it's fine.'

He smiled at her, reassuringly, but her expression was still worried. Tillie was afraid of the water. She always had been. Something to do with her parents.

'I can't,' she had said, her face closed and tight, and he had started to come up with reasons why she must, fearing that her refusal was to do with her feelings for him and wanting to talk her round.

'But I want to take you away from everyone and have you all to myself. It's so beautiful,' he had started, 'and the boat I rent is amazing, four staff to every passenger and everything you can dream of, and—'

'Flip, I can't. Please don't push me.' She had turned away and continued to clean her make-up brushes, long elegant slivers of black wood, carefully dipping them in cleaning solution and gently wiping layers of foundation and powder and eye-shadow from them. Now she began to dry them with a soft piece of cloth. Her hands worked slowly, calmly, though her expression was anything but.

She chewed her bottom lip. Flip flopped back on the sofa and poked her with his foot.

'Have you gone off me?' he pouted. He expected her to smile and turn her golden curls to him, but she didn't, just carried on wiping the brushes. He was concerned now, and sat up.

'Hey. You can say, you know. Just tell me. I'm too old to play games.'

Now she did turn to look at him, and he was appalled to see tears flowing down her face.

'It's nothing to do with you,' she said as she wept.

'Oh Tillie, what on earth is it? I'm sorry, I'm a fucking idiot. Please don't be about to say "it's not you, it's me," or something. You're not, are you? Tell me you're not.'

She tried to smile but couldn't. 'No, I'm not.'

'Then anything else is fixable. Whatever it is.' He shuffled along the sofa to her and held out his arms for her to move into, but she stayed at her end, perched on the edge of the seat.

'Now I am worried.' She always wanted to curl up in his lap, like a cat; she would wrap herself around him and draw her legs up high, resting her tiny feet on his chest. It made him feel extraordinarily protective of her. Now, however, her thin body was tense and stiff.

'Tillie, whatever it is, I'll support you, I'll help you. I love you.' Something in him told him he should shut up now and so he did, and waited for her to speak.

Eventually, she did.

'You have to promise not to quiz me about it. I can't . . . I can't answer lots of questions.'

'All right.' She had stopped fiddling with her brushes now and her hands lay still in her lap.

'It's the boat.'

She took a gulp of air in a big breath, as though just saying the word had caused her some trauma. Later, he would come to know that that was exactly what it had done. He waited.

'I can't go on . . . on them. I know it sounds stupid and pathetic, but I just can't.'

She wiped tears away from her face with the back of her hand, and Flip watched for a moment while she tried to get her ragged breath to slow once more. While she did he stood and went to the kitchen and poured her a glass of cold white wine, then padded round to the sofa and handed it to her.

'Thanks.' She sighed.

Flip wanted nothing more than to bundle her up and make everything better for her, but he knew that he couldn't – and more, he knew he shouldn't. There was a battle raging inside her but it was one she had to fight alone.

'When I was a teenager, my father took me out to sea. He . . .' She shut her eyes briefly and then continued, 'he hadn't been in a good place. To say the least. But afterwards, after all that was over, he was broken. A shell of the man he had been before . . . It was awful to see. And I wanted to do anything I could to help him. To salvage something.'

She must have heard or sensed that Flip was about to speak because she cut him off.

'He died in a boat, in a fishing accident. I was there. I really can't talk about it any more.'

He never asked her about it again. It explained why she had reacted as she did when he first quizzed her about her family. Flip remembered it now as he shifted in his seat, feeling the helicopter juddering beneath him. They had been eating dinner at a sushi bar in Soho, choosing little plates of sashimi and nigiri off the conveyor belt and popping salty edamame beans into their mouths from the pods, drinking cold, sweet sake in little frosted glasses. It was their third date, and they were dancing through that grey area between comfort and awkwardness in each other's company, where every touch is full of sex and possibility and every sentence might mean one thing or might mean something else, and your mind and body are awake and alive, and everything is something of a surprise and yet almost inevitable.

He had asked her about her parents, as you do. He was falling hopelessly, hopefully in love and wanted to know everything about her, every detail, every memory. Every bad joke she had ever told so that he could reassure her as to its hilarity, every friend who had slighted her so he could rage on the injustice of it, every childhood scraped knee and cut finger so he could check for lasting damage and kiss it all better.

But instead of telling him all of that, she fell unexpectedly quiet. 'They're both dead,' she said calmly and quietly, and then, 'Don't apologise,' as he opened his mouth. 'It was a long time ago.'

'Still.'

'Yes. Not ideal. But there we have it. Sorry to make you feel awkward. There's no easy way of saying it.'

Flip refilled her glass. 'Tell me about them? Not, you know, how . . . I mean, what were they like?'

Tillie half-laughed. 'Indefinable. Beautiful, both of them.'

'Unsurprisingly.'

She smiled. 'They were . . . they were . . . they weren't a "they".' She paused. 'She was one thing, he another. My mother was restrained, my father notorious. My mother was cool, my father hot-headed.' Her face clouded over. 'Sorry. I don't find them easy to talk about.'

'I understand,' he tried to reassure her. She didn't reply. 'Well, half. My mother's alive, obviously.'

'Obviously.'

'But my father died when I was a baby.'

Tillie turned to him. 'Let's go. I want to see whether we've got something else in common right now as well.' She ran her hands up his legs and stopped. 'Oh. I think we do.'

He raised an eyebrow at her, and she grinned, and all thoughts of parents, dead or otherwise, disappeared from his mind.

The helicopter pulled sharply to the right and tilted down. Tillie shrieked as the horizon lurched sideways and she felt the air give way beneath them.

'Jesus!' Flip shouted. 'What the fucking hell do you think you're doing? You're terrifying my wife.'

But by the look on his face in the pilot's mirror it wasn't just Flip's wife who was terrified. The man's own face had suddenly gone grey and his hand was gripping the armrest tightly.

The pilot tried to make sure his voice was calm and even when he spoke. The last thing he needed if there was a problem was two passengers panicking and shouting and screaming in his ear.

'It's fine, please, Mr and Mrs Cavalley, don't panic. My apologies. We'll be on the ground in no time.'

The helicopter juddered violently and Tillie turned to Flip. Outside, a sheet of rain battered against the window, sending a sudden cracking sound through the aircraft. The view from the window was blurred by cloud, but Flip could just see that they were nearing the island: trees and rocks were visible in between patches of mist. The sound of the rotor blades' rhythmic chops added to the noise. The wind roared.

'I'm scared,' she said, and her voice was quiet and small. He took her hand in his. Never had he wanted so much to tell someone that everything was going to be all right. Never had he felt less confident that it would be.

Flip hated himself. He had promised to protect his wife from everything. Promised he would never take her on a boat, or make her go in the sea. And now he was in a rustbucket of a helicopter above the ocean with her trembling with fear beside him.

Out of nowhere, a high-pitched whine filled the cabin, and Tillie's grip on Flip's hand tightened. He stared ahead. The back of the pilot's neck was covered with beads of sweat. Flip knew that could not bode well. He put his arm around Tillie.

'I love you,' he said. 'We'll be all right—'

And just then, the pilot cried out, and Flip jerked his head up to see a jumble of green and mist and slate grey surrounding the windows of the helicopter, and they lurched to one side, and the air that just a little while before had felt so safe, so solid even, beneath them, holding them up as if by magic, suddenly melted away and a chasm opened up in the sky, or so it seemed, and they began to fall, down, down, down . . .

For a few seconds as they fell, Flip understood how time could become pliable, how it was not the fixed entity that people and logic deemed it. It stretched, in the moments after they went down, as if the craft itself were suspended from a piece of elastic, dropping, pulling itself out and becoming longer, longer, almost as in a dream. He felt light-headed and as if he were floating. He tried to turn his head towards Tillie, to see her beautiful face, but found that he could not move. So he just let his head rest against the side of the seat where it had become stuck, and waited.

Then, as if someone or something had let go of the piece of elastic and had pinged it back, time rushed forward in a jumble of screaming and tearing metal. His body was jerked up and down and from side to side – and he wondered if he would be ripped apart like a rag doll in the jaws of a pet dog. And then the image was gone because it had been replaced by a very big, very loud impact, and then . . .

Flip's eyes flickered open. There was blood in them. It was like a red film, sticky, warm. He blinked but it didn't clear. He tried to open his mouth but his jaw wouldn't work. It was as if the muscles weren't connected. He couldn't move. A cloud of darkness rushed in front of his vision again and he began to spin, but fought against it. Dragged his consciousness to the forefront, with an effort of will. He felt sick and swimmy, with a swooshing noise in his ears. Where was he?

And where was Tillie? She had been with him. Were they in a car? He didn't know. He had a bad feeling, somehow, but he couldn't place it. He wasn't in any pain though. That had to be a good sign. Didn't it?

He forced his eyes back open. They had shut again, for a moment, by themselves. And as he did so he somehow managed to raise his head, very slightly, just an incline of a few millimetres. He gazed up. It looked as though he was in a forest, or a wood of some kind. Dark leaves and branches were around him, hazy, and a bit blurred because of the blood in his eyes. He tried to raise his hand to wipe it away but he couldn't. Arm wasn't working. Why was he in a wood? He opened his eyes again. *Come on. Wake up*.

His eyes alighted on something beyond the trees. Higher up. He could only half see it. It was beautiful. Gold and blue, set into what looked like a slab of rock. Then he realised. It was the Virgin Mary. Even a heathen like Flip recognised the familiar pose of the Madonna, her arms folded around a Baby Jesus, her smile beatific. A ray of sunlight shone on her from somewhere, and the gold glowed behind her. She looked so kind. So peaceful. She looked like someone . . . a memory from long ago. Flip's eyelids fluttered. As he gazed at her he heard voices. A woman, an Englishwoman, was crying out. It sounded as if she was in pain. Terrible pain – like an injured animal. He should try to help her. He needed to be able to move.

He licked his lips. For the first time in his life, inspired maybe by the Virgin Mary before him, Flip prayed. *Please, let me move. Let me get out of wherever I am, and help that woman crying. Is it Tillie? I don't think so. But please God, I'll do anything. Anything. Just let me get out of here.*

Still staring up at the face of the Madonna and repeating his silent prayer like a mantra, Flip pushed, with every ounce of strength that he possessed. From below, there came a terrible creaking noise, and then, for the second time in the last few minutes, the ground gave way under him. As he felt himself fall through the air once more, he saw the Madonna's face fade away, and as she faded, he knew who she looked like. His wife, his first wife, his first love, holding Jasper in her arms. Flip tried to stretch an arm towards her, to his son. But he could not move. And when he opened his mouth, his lips formed her name. The name of the woman who, apart from Tillie and outside his family, was the only woman that he had ever truly loved.

'Cressida,' he whispered. 'Cressida.'

It had been October when Flip got in a taxi and headed for Heathrow, no luggage in the boot of his car and no ticket in his pocket, carrying only his passport and wallet and an overwhelming desire to get away from England, from the final days of summer that lingered heavily and refused to go away, reminding everyone in the family when they woke and saw yet another glorious blue sky, of the day of Scarlet's death. There was no joy for any of the Cavalleys in the Indian summer that everyone else was basking in, just endless agonising regret, and memories of a beautiful girl, hair as golden as the sun that shone on them all, lying broken on the ground.

Violet had gone to Thailand. Cavalley's was on hiatus – she had announced that she would not be producing a collection this autumn, and had taken herself off, alone, to a retreat where she could draw, and read, and try to heal. Flip had wanted to go with her, but she had insisted on going by herself. 'I need to go somewhere where I don't have to think about anyone other than myself for a while. And Scarlet. Where I can go into a cocoon for a bit and hope that I've rebuilt myself by the time I emerge. Darling boy, I'll miss you, but if you're there with me I'll be your mother, even though you're pretty much all grown up, and I just need to be Violet for a month or two.'

He understood. She needed to try and begin to get over her daughter's death, and she couldn't do that surrounded by her other children. Some would have pulled their remaining offspring closer; Violet herself might have done so at different times of her life, indeed. But something about Scarlet's death, the violence and horror of it, had shaken her to the core, and the whispers that had come afterwards had made it worse. It had all happened so quickly – and he could see that the only thing she knew how to do was to retreat.

So he decided to do the same. Flip had never had a gap year, not like other boys his age. And when he arrived at Heathrow and stood in the departures hall staring up at the wall of screens, his eyes running down the list of destinations, he felt for the first time in his life that he was truly free to go and do whatever he wanted for a few weeks. He had never felt like that before, not really. Flip carried a weight of responsibility around with him in the way that only firstborn children do. The closeness he had with his mother had been at the expense of a childhood entirely free from cares. He had always, since he could remember, felt he had to look after her as much as she did him, and with the births of his younger siblings had come more people in his family that he felt must come under his wing.

Turin . . . Paris . . . Brussels . . . Bologna . . . Frankfurt . . . Nowhere grabbed him. He wanted to go somewhere beautiful, somewhere he could focus on things outside of himself, somewhere he could eat good food and walk and swim. He wanted to go to Tuscany, he decided, as his eyes alighted on Pisa and looked along to the right to see what time the flight was departing. 11.40 – he could still make it if he got a move on.

Just a few hours later he was looking out of the plane's window as it slowly taxied around to the airport hangar, already unbuckling his seatbelt, eager to get going. He had a curious sense of weightlessness. No one with him, no luggage, no younger brother or sister to take care of. 'You're the eldest,' Violet had always said to him. 'You have to look after your brothers and sister, you have to help them. It's your job.' He knew she had done it to make him feel important, in part, to make sure that after Sebastian, and then the twins had arrived he never felt excluded or pushed out of this new family she had created, and it did that – but it weighed him down as well.

Today, however, he was free. He almost laughed as he stepped off the plane and on to the tarmac. He was really free. And this was how he would honour his sister. She would have known exactly how he felt, he realised now – she would have understood the incredible lightness that filled his heart and his head in a big rush, the exhilaration that pulsed through his veins and the thrill of knowing he was here, just him – not Flip Cavalley, Violet Cavalley's eldest son, not an older brother, not an Economics student. He was just Flip.

Since Scarlet died he had felt guilty every time he had smiled, or eaten a meal that he had enjoyed, as if taking pleasure in anything at all was wrong, a betrayal of the girl who would never experience a meal or a smile or a song again – but now he saw how wrong he was. She had taken such joy in life, she was always telling him to 'lighten up, big bro' – she would press her small hands to either side of his face and force his cheeks up into a smile when she saw him frowning over his books or the newspaper. She, of all people, would know that he needed this.

He should probably buy some supplies, he thought as he walked quickly through the airport, hire-car key in his hand. It would be sensible to pick up a toothbrush and toothpaste, a map, some water, a sandwich or something. But he wasn't going to do what was sensible, to be the one to remember the tickets and make a note of the passwords somewhere no one could find them, and make sure there was milk in the fridge.

As he drove the little Fiat convertible down the long road leading out of the airport, Flip fiddled with the radio until he found a station playing something he recognised, turned the music up as loud as it would go, and put his foot down.

It was like a sign. Flip didn't believe in signs, in love at first sight, in things happening for a reason. Almost twenty years of life under the shadow of Violet's belief in destiny and a curse and Fate had turned him against the idea of any sort of higher power, any kind of guiding force behind events in his or anyone else's life. Things happened because you made them happen, or someone else made them happen, or just because. Cause and effect, or chaos theory – these were the sorts of ideas that made sense to Flip, not God, or curses, or any kind of unalterable predestination. But that first time he caught sight of Cressida, just after he had thrown caution to the wind along with his jacket, and opened his heart and mind to whatever the universe might bring him, made him think again. It was as if he had been given exactly what he needed, exactly when he needed it. And more than that – as soon as he saw her, he felt an unmistakable twinge of recognition, along with awe at her heart-stopping, breath-stealing beauty. It was as if he already knew her, but he had never seen her before in his life. He would never have forgotten that face.

He had parked his little red car in a side street of the small village on the outskirts of Florence where he had ended up after a few hours' driving between fields full of sunflowers and vines. Despite his newfound sense of spontaneity, it was late afternoon now, and he thought he had better find somewhere to stay for the night. As he worked his way up winding stone streets lined with lemon trees he began to see signs for Fiesole and a hotel, and started to follow them.

Spotting a cashpoint, he decided to pull over and get some lire out before driving up the last steep section of hill towards the building that he assumed was the Villa San Marco – the hotel he had been heading for. That was when he saw her. She was sitting on the edge of a circular stone fountain, one leg stretched out in front of her underneath the stream of water, the other tucked underneath her so she looked like a bird perching on a pylon. An old man sat on the other side of the fountain, smoking a cigar and watching her. Her hair fell in loose ringlets down her back and her limbs were long and elegant and she was laughing at something the girl next to her was saying.

And Flip then did something he had never done before. He followed his impulse – at the risk of looking stupid, of her laughing at him in front of her friend and all of the locals starting their *passeggiata* and the old man smoking his cigar – but he didn't care. Didn't think twice. Just got out of his car, went over to her and said, 'Hello. My name is Flip Cavalley. You're the most beautiful girl I've ever seen in my life, and if you don't agree to come out to dinner with me right now, then I'm going to jump in that fountain.' And then he waited, eyes searching her face for a clue as to what her response would be, focused only on her, uncaring, not seeing anyone else. If his eyes hadn't been fixed so ardently on her oval face and pale grey eyes, he would have seen that they too were waiting to see what she would say. It didn't matter that half of the onlookers couldn't speak English – it was quite clear what the good-looking young boy had been asking.

A sudden laugh escaped her mouth as she turned her head and looked at him. She must speak some English, he hoped, to have laughed like that, surely? It was the slightly embarrassed but flattered laugh of someone who knew exactly what he had just said.

The girl gazed at him, looking him up and down. Flip felt very aware of his shortcomings – his unruly hair, the shirt he had been wearing all day that was now less than fresh, his average height. And he waited.

She tilted her head to one side, and as she did so he noticed how long and elegant her neck was. Pale, as though she were not sitting in the Italian sun but had been shaded from the elements all of her life, like an orchid under a glass bell. She had a row of little pearl studs climbing up the side of her ear, and he wanted to reach out his hand and run a finger up them. But still he waited.

'Go on, then,' she said, and he was so surprised that this girl who looked like a medieval princess, albeit one dressed in a Guns N' Roses T-shirt and leggings, had actually spoken to him, that at first he just blinked and said, 'Sorry?'

She smiled gently, just a slight inclination of the corners of her mouth, and said, 'Go on then. I can't possibly agree to go out for dinner with someone I've only just met, who drives up to me in a red sports car and interrupts my conversation without so much as a by your leave. What on earth would my mother say? So it looks like you're going to have to do as you said, and jump into the fountain.'

Her friend sniggered, and Flip noticed her properly for the first time; she was a solid girl who looked as though she played lacrosse somewhere, with hair dyed an uneven shade of hennaed red hanging in a greasy bob next to her slightly sweaty cheeks. She clearly didn't think he was going to follow through on his threat. She was probably used to being the sidekick while boys chatted up her far more beautiful friend, and who dealt with the constant reminders that she was not the pretty one by putting the boys down, making sure they did not pierce the bubble that she had created, making sure they did not take her friend away from her.

Well, I'll show her, he thought. I'll show them both. And, without taking off his shirt, trousers, or shoes, without taking his wallet out of his pocket or his watch off his wrist, Flip put one foot up on the fountain's stone wall, pushed himself up on to it, and then dropped straight in with a big splash.

Flip heard a shriek of surprise from the girl and a gasp leap forth from his lungs as the freezing cold water rose up to his chest and the water splashed her, and then a round of applause and whoops from some of the men and women standing in the square, and he grinned, ignoring the cold and dipping his head in the water before bringing it up again, shaking the water from his head like a spaniel emerging triumphant from a lake with a pheasant between its jaws.

'Ha!' he cried out, full of pleasure at the surprise he had caused everyone watching, but most of all the surprise he had given himself. This was not the sort of thing Flip Cavalley usually did, but it felt good, and it felt even better when he looked up, wiping the water from his face, and could see that the girl's slightly mocking smile had changed to one of admiration.

He waded slowly through the freezing water, and then stood before her, his arms spread, basking in the warmth of her smile.

She gazed at him, held out her hand and touched his wrist.

'Your watch is going to be ruined,' she said. 'It looks awfully expensive.'

Flip looked down at the Rolex that his mother had given him for his eighteenth birthday, and realised that she was almost certainly right. It had stopped at 5.41, the minute he had jumped into the water. In any other circumstance he would have been furious, but he didn't care. He took it off and handed it to her.

'Not ruined,' he said. 'Now it's always going to show the time when I met you. Why would anyone want it to do anything different?' She blushed, and her friend made retching noises from beside her, but the girl hushed her, took the watch, and then held out her hand for him to shake.

'My name is Cressida Vale,' she said, 'and I think you've earned that dinner.'

On the morning of their wedding, exactly a year to the day they had met, Cressida placed the newly mended watch in a box, wrapped it up and gave it back to him. When he turned it over and looked at the back of it, he smiled: engraved on the metal disk was the time and date they met.

As he was getting ready later, he lifted the watch out of its box and put it on. There was only one time he needed to worry about today.

They were married in a castello just above the little town on the edge of Florence where they had met a year before. The same day and month, the same place, the same two young lovers staring into each other's eyes and smiling, except now, they were doing so not as boy and girl meeting for the first time, but as man and woman on the cusp of being married and then, a moment later, as man and wife.

Flip turned to the group of family and friends and held his new wife's hand up into the air in triumph, the watch proudly visible on his wrist. He caught his mother's eye, and smiled at her. They weren't just man and wife, they were parents-to-be – Cressida was two months' pregnant. But they had told no one, not even Violet. They didn't want the day to be overshadowed by whispers of shotgun weddings. It was a day for them, and the baby was their secret, which they held between them like a glass bauble on a Christmas tree, something magical and fragile. Flip couldn't wait to tell his mother though. There would be no admonitions from her about them being too young, needing to wait and grow up first, he knew; she hadn't done so when he had told her he had met his wife, because that was how he thought of her after just a few days – his partner, his soulmate, his mirrored self.

Violet had thrown herself into the wedding preparations for her firstborn and his beautiful girl with the enthusiasm of one with plenty of ideas and plenty of money to make them happen. She had always thought that she would be mother-of-the-bride herself one day: Scarlet would have married before too long, she felt sure. But with her death that role had been taken away from her, so Violet had used the money and spent it on Flip's wedding. If she had learned anything in her life so far, it was how important it was to live for the present. Life was too short not to, she knew all too well.

'We look like something out of *The Godfather*,' Flip had joked, as the fleet of cars had set off, sleek and black, with young men in shirtsleeves and shades, and girls in floating dresses in the back. As they passed the fountain where he and Cressida had met, he wound down the window and waved to the old man who sat there again, on the edge, smoking his cigar and watching them pass. Violet took Flip's hand.

'Nervous?' she asked, but she already knew the answer. She could feel the energy emanating from his body; he was leaning forward in the leather seat of the car as if urging it forward.

'No,' he replied, 'I just can't wait to get there and marry her.' He turned his head to his mother. 'Thank you,' he said.

'What on earth for?'

'I don't mean for the wedding,' he replied. 'I mean – that too, of course, it's—'

'It's what you deserve, and it's my pleasure,' she interrupted firmly.

He nodded. 'I mean for everything with Cressida. For accepting her, and us. For not saying we're too young, or we'll regret it, or don't know what we're doing.'

She squeezed his hand. 'I could hardly talk on that front, could I?'

'Not everyone would understand.'

'Darling boy, I know what it's like to be young and in love and desperate to start your own life. I just hope you aren't trying to escape from our family in the same way I was.'

'Never. I want to bring Cressida into it, not run away from it.'

'Good. She's a lovely girl.'

'And that's the other thing. Thank you for never making me feel as if I only had one parent.'

She looked at his serious face. The car had pulled to a stop outside the high stone arch that billowed with white muslin drapes, but they remained inside the car.

'Oh Flip. I'm just sorry you did only have one.'

He blinked and she saw the familiar will in his eyes that had been there since he was little. A stubborn determination that enabled him to do anything he set his mind to, whether it was to climb up the side of his cot when he was hardly walking, or get a place at the oversubscribed degree course he had set his sights on, or marry the girl he had seen sitting on the side of a fountain in Italy. And Violet was proud of it, despite the fact that she knew that such pride was a kind of vanity, because it was pride in a trait he had inherited from her.

Flip looked towards the archway, and then at his watch. 'We should go in. She'll be here in a second.'

The new Mrs Cavalley, Violet thought to herself, with a twinge of sadness and a realisation that she was no longer the most important woman in her son's life. And then she looked at him again, seeing the excitement and joy on his face as he got out of the car and strode to take his place under the flowered bower. How could she begrudge him this happiness, for the sake of her own place in his heart? It was pure joy. She followed him into the garden and sat down to wait for his bride.

When their son, Jasper, was born six months later, Cressida was immediately devoted to him, with a fervour that surprised even her. She had known she would love their child, had waited excitedly for him to be born, had imagined the whole thing over and over again as her due date grew closer, but none of her daydreams and imaginings prepared her for the solid thump of love that hit her like a punch in the chest when Jasper was handed to her.

He was a perfect mixture of her and Flip. While she knew lots of babies looked more like one parent than the other, and was ready for her son to look more like his father, or neither of them, he came out embodying both of his parents equally, as if he had been formed by someone picking the best bits of each, adding them together, and then smoothing over the joins. He was born with a full head of Flip's thick hair, his long eyelashes and Cressida's pale grey eyes, her slim, languid limbs and Flip's snub nose, her full lips and long neck.

Flip was equally smitten. The three of them made a striking picture on their frequent walks through Pimlico and along the river, over the bridges and through Battersea Park, these two young lovers with their baby, hands intertwined on the handle of his pram.

Flip had found a piece that he had never known he was missing until now. His whole life had been lacking a crucial part, and he wondered at how he hadn't noticed it. Maybe it was like people who were born deaf or blind, they simply never knew what it was like to hear or see. He found himself in possession of a new level of empathy for those sorry individuals who were single or childless. He became particularly nice to his siblings, buying them gifts and inviting them round for Sunday lunches where they could gaze upon the wonder that was Jasper and Cressida, because he felt that he must share his unbelievable good fortune with his family, who were less lucky than he was.

Naturally, they found this new Flip baffling and nauseating in equal measures (apart from Blue, who just went along with it, as usual, and drew strange and wonderful murals on Jasper's nursery walls). 'Just humour him,' Violet told her other children. 'He'll calm down soon enough. He's in love.'

And as much as she was happy for him, she envied him a little as well. He had found with Cressida what Violet had almost had, once, with Sam: that magical crystallisation of love and sex that so rarely seems to collide in one pairing. It was wrong to be jealous of your own child, but she couldn't help it. It seeped in around the edges of her pride and love, it crept up the sides of her heart as she sat on the little sofa in their flat, cuddling her grandson under the guise of giving Cressida a break; a break that they both knew she didn't need or want.

'Too ra loo ra loo ra lay,' she sang to him, cradling his head in her hands and letting him lie in the crook of her arm, as she had done to Flip when he was tiny, examining his face. Flip was in there, and Cressida, and there was a faint flicker of her own image, sometimes, but it disappeared as quickly as it came, like seeing something in the corner of your eye that disappeared when you turned your head towards it. Was Bryce anywhere to be seen? Not yet. Maybe he would emerge later, in a sprinkling of freckles across the boy's nose, or in something more subtle. Maybe Jasper would shrug like his grandfather, or walk like him. Her grandson made Violet think of Bryce in a way that she hadn't done for years and years. It seemed so long ago now, her time with him. 'He would love you though,' she whispered to Jasper now. 'He'd be so proud. He'd have photographs in his wallet that he'd get out at every opportunity, and Flip would be embarrassed but pleased as well. I know he would.'

And she kissed her grandson on the nose, and said a silent thank you to her freckle-nosed American boy, who had been the start of it all.

It happened on Cressida and Flip's first wedding anniversary. They had taken Jasper back to Tuscany, to the hotel they had stayed in when they first met and had fallen in love.

'We'll show him the view from the restaurant,' Cressida had said. 'He'll like that, won't you, little man?'

Flip had touched her hair and kissed the top of her head. 'I'm sure he'll be thrilled. Five-month-old babies are known for their appreciation of Florentine vistas, I hear.'

She kicked him. 'He will. He's unusually advanced for his age, you know.'

Flip smiled. 'I know he is.'

Jasper gurgled.

'See? A genius.'

They smiled at each other. They might be teasing, but they also knew that secretly, in their hearts of hearts, they both believed their son was specially gifted, set apart from other babies by his intelligent eyes and unique nature.

He did seem to like it, Flip admitted, when they got to the hotel, the day before the anniversary, and set his little carrycot up on the table, facing the city, so he could see out. The restaurant was located in a long stone cloister with high arches overlooking the hillside below and, further down, Florence. It was hazy, the air full of the blue-green of the hills, and the sun caught the roof of the Duomo and made them screw up their eyes as they looked towards it. Cressida shifted Jasper's seat so he wasn't facing into the sun as it set, and they sat there, the three of them, their perfect little circle, Cressida and Flip with plates of hand-rolled ravioli and big glasses of the wine they had drunk two years ago, and they all grew sleepy and slow until Cressida took Jasper on to her lap and he fell asleep there, his hands up in front of his face, 'like a boxer', as Flip always said. 'If anyone tries to make him into a boxer, they'll have me to deal with,' Cressida always said in return.

After a while, she carried him back to their room and put him down, turning the monitor on and walking back over the square of lawn to the bar to join Flip. Before she left their bedroom she undid her hair, letting it fall over her shoulders in the way he liked so much. Maybe they would conceive another baby tonight. Maybe . . .

They had fallen back in through the door of their room and into bed, too focused on each other's bodies to care about shutters or windows, tumbling on to the four-poster bed, Cressida pulling her crepe dress over her head and letting her hair fan out as she straddled Flip, him gazing up at her in wonder as she began to move on top of him, her hands behind her so she looked like Venus de Milo, her spine arched and her shoulders back. Afterwards she flopped down next to him, resting her head on his chest and falling asleep there. Flip lay awake for an hour or more, stroking her back and feeling her heart beat next to his. He was the luckiest man in the world, and tomorrow – tomorrow he would show her that.

He had made big plans. The box containing the eternity ring that he had picked out and brought with him was safely tucked away in his washbag, the babysitter was booked, and he had been arranging the evening of their anniversary for months. He had booked the castello where they had married for the night. The courtyard where they had had their wedding breakfast would be set up for dinner again, but this time, it would be him and Cressida only.

He couldn't wait to see her face when she saw it, all decorated. He had ordered the same red roses to be placed in huge vases around the space, and dark-red candles everywhere – on the stone floor, in the little alcoves, making a path leading into the courtyard. There would be music, a solo violinist playing as they arrived, who would then melt away as they began dinner. After dinner there would be fireworks, reaching high into the sky above them, creating a magical ceiling just for them. And then, he intended to get on one knee, and present her with the diamond-encrusted eternity ring, and make love to his wife underneath the blanket of darkness.

He was getting excited just thinking about it, and forced himself to think of something off-putting so he didn't wake her up. Flip's desire for Cressida appeared to be limitless. It hadn't waned when she was pregnant, or just after the birth; if anything, it had increased in strength. He had always become bored by previous girlfriends quite quickly, finding them a turn-on only until he got to the stage of familiarity, and then discovering that fondness dampened his ardour for them. But with Cressida, the more he fell in love with her, the more he wanted her; the more he got to know her, the more he chased after her. He could not get enough of her, and he could not believe that he was able to keep on going to bed with her for the rest of his life.

Later that day, Flip looked back to that moment, lying in bed, the moonlight glowing pearl-soft on his wife's pale back, and could not believe that he was never going to go to bed with her again. How his life had not just changed that afternoon, but crumbled away into nothing, into a pile of dust.

'I'm going to take Jasper down to the fountain,' she had said. 'I want him to see where we met.' And he had smiled at her indulgently and kissed her and kissed his son and stayed behind so he could make the final phone calls so that everything that evening would be just so. Vanity, that was all it had been – typical stupid vanity. He had wanted everything to be perfect, so perfect that she would walk into the castle and be overwhelmed with joy and gratitude. He had wanted to impress her, and so he had let her walk out of the door and go down the hill alone; he had let her and their son walk to their death.

The coach had been going too fast, Cressida walking too close to the wall that curved around the road, so she wasn't easily visible as the vehicle rounded the corner; the driver had been laughing at a joke told to him by the tour guide, whose bottom he was eyeing up in the rearview mirror as she read out her spiel to the group of tourists facing her. The tyres were a bit balder than they should have been and the brakes a bit less responsive, since the coach's owner had lost a lot of money gambling and so hadn't been as up to date with the repairs as he should have been . . . There were a hundred reasons and there were none at all.

'Oh my darling boy,' Violet said to him as she cradled his head in her lap, as he sobbed on her like a child, after she had flown out later that day, after she had taken the phone call that had rendered her motionless in the hall of her house, as she stood statue-still listening to Flip's terrible, keening wails as he told her to 'Come, please come, you have to come,' and her heart breaking all over again.

'You didn't know, you couldn't have known. How could you have?'

And yet she knew how he felt. She knew that ragged, desperate regret, that urgent need to turn back the clock, to walk backwards along the line of time that had riven his world into two distinct eras of before and after – that he should have known, that if he had loved her more, he would have sensed something, done something differently. It was how she had felt after Scarlet, that if she had been a better mother, a better person, she would have saved her daughter.

She stopped herself. She could not save Scarlet now. And Flip could not save Cressida or Jasper. She could try to save Flip though. And, as he raged and wept, she knew that he would need it.

How his life could have changed so dramatically, for better and for worse again, like the waxing and waning of the moon that had lit Cressida's back so softly that last night, Flip had no idea. He could make no sense of it. The only conclusion that he could reach, during the long months that followed her death, was that it was a punishment of some sort. That the curse he had always shrugged off as being the product of his mother's overactive imagination – a fantasy, almost, that made sense of the drama of her life – was real. Now, as he stumbled through the nights and suffered through the days, he understood. It was the only explanation for this horror which must have a reason, could not just be a random and unlucky roll of life's dice.

The night after he had returned from the hospital, while he waited for Violet to arrive, he ordered a car to take him up to the castello. The hotel staff looked at him with furrowed brows and concerned eyes, urged him to stay at the hotel, to rest. He just closed his eyes and repeated his request, and in the end, they did as he asked. He told the driver to take him the back way through the village, so he did not have to pass the place where it had happened. He had seen it once already, when he had raced down there after he heard it.

He had heard it – that was one of the cruellest things. The hotel was close enough so that he had heard the squeal of brakes, the screech of tyres and the thud of the coach as it slammed into the thick stone wall and – he knew now – into Cressida and Jasper. 'She probably wouldn't have felt anything,' the doctors said to him. 'And your son was almost certainly asleep. It all happened very fast.'

Probably. Almost certainly. Words that left that chink of room for 'maybe not'. For the chance that they were wrong, or lying, or just didn't know, and that she had felt every ounce of the tons of metal slamming into her body with their unstoppable force, that she cried out for Flip to help her even as she was being crushed and he was running down the hill towards the scene – worse, that Jasper had been awake and gazing at his mother's face as she tickled his feet and looked into his eyes, not seeing the threat coming towards her, and that he had stared at the coach as it pummelled into them, not understanding what was happening as the wall of yellow metal came closer and closer . . .

He couldn't bear it, he couldn't carry this, he couldn't . . . He stood in the courtyard, dressed for their anniversary dinner, the flagstones strewn with red roses, and then he walked round to the side of the building and he began to climb.

'I wish you had just let me jump,' he said to Violet later, back in the hotel. She had arrived and been told where he had gone, and had known, straight away, that further disaster lurked. He had been sitting on the edge of the ruined section of wall when she got there, grief showing in every line of his body, as though his very soul had been broken, not just his heart. Her heart broke again, for him, when she looked through into the courtyard and saw the empty table, perfectly laid as though for a prince and his princess, the table set with the silver and glassware that had been there a year before, the flowers and candles everywhere, and her son, her beautiful, bereft son, sobbing his heart out above it all, inches away from hurling himself on to the scene and letting his blood mingle with the red roses.

'I know you do, my darling,' she whispered, as she rocked him, 'but you won't always, I promise. One day, maybe not for a long, long time, but one day, I promise you, you will be glad I didn't.'

And that day had come, finally, when he had met Tillie. It had taken years, but Violet had been right. Until that moment it had been a matter of counting the hours, then the days, then the weeks, willing time to pass and simultaneously wanting it to go slower, because every hour that passed took him further away from Cressida and Jasper. He had worked, he had drunk, he had done little else. He had stumbled through the first few months in a haze of Bourbon and blues bars, late-night drinking clubs in Soho where even the hookers, coming in for a last warmer before going home to their own beds, left before him.

He had felt hollowed out, through those years. No one could reach him. He shut himself away from his family, even from Violet, although he had never turned away from his mother before. She was busy, anyhow, he told himself, with Blue and his madness, and Fran, who was tiny still, and who, despite adoring her, Flip could not bear to be around much. He stayed away from babies, from everyone and anyone who might remind him of what was lost, and that was almost everyone. He fell blindly into his unintended marriage to Boodle, then eventually left her; he rolled around London with a crowd of artists and musicians who asked no questions, nor anything else of him; he sleepwalked through his life, the only constant an unending, unyielding pain, that, in time, he learned how to cover up, learned how to live with it, in a way that was not really living but existing. He accepted that he would never be happy again.

And then, he met Tillie. And the world turned on its head once more.

From the road below, the helicopter could just be seen. It might have been completely hidden, because of the angle of the hill and the thickness of the trees, if it were not for the fact that one of the trees had snapped when it landed, and the chopper had tipped on to its side so the blades stuck up in the air.

It was a taxi driver who saw it first, stopping on the bend to investigate, and quickly realising that the accident was a bad one. Within moments the area was full of men trying to scramble down the slope to get to the body of the heli, afraid of what they were going to find there, all too aware of the dangers of getting too close. The cliffs were perilous; it could slide further down, taking them all with it, at any moment.

'*Vieni qui!*'

'*Rapidamente! Fai in fretta!*'

Soon, the sirens could be heard from the base of the hill.

Violet had returned to her bed. The conversation with Sebastian had taken a lot out of her. But she had insisted that Patrick ask Fran to come and see her.

'You're too tired,' he had protested. 'You have to sleep.'

'I'm too tired not to, Patrick,' she had said. 'I'm scared I'm going to run out of time. I can feel it. I have to finish what I started. You have to help me.'

He had nodded then, and done as she had asked.

'Hi,' Fran said, and Violet turned to face her.

'Darling girl,' she said. 'We need to finish our conversation, don't we? We got rather interrupted.'

Fran nodded. She moved to her mother's side.

'Why has he come back now? Where has he been?'

Violet paused before answering. 'He's come back, my love, for the same reason as you are here now. He wants answers – to questions that have been hanging in the air for too long. And I don't blame him, not really. Not for this, anyhow.'

'What did he do?' Fran asked.

'I think he'll want to tell you that himself. You see, darling, he wants some answers, but he also wants to tell the truth. And that's good. He wants the same things you do,' she said again, and the look in her eyes was distant.

'I'm sorry I applied for a copy of my adoption certificate,' Fran said quickly. And she was. She wished she could turn the clock back, wished she had never started any of this. Wanted it to be like it used to, when her family was unconventional but solid. Flip, Tillie, Blue, Violet, Kalisto. They had been fine. And now everything was shifting and changing, the ground was unsteady beneath her feet, and she didn't like it. She rubbed a tear from her cheek, angrily.

Violet took her hand in both of hers. 'You mustn't be sorry. I'm the one who should be sorry. Again. I've made a lot of mistakes, Fran. A lot of things I covered up that I shouldn't have.' She smiled at her daughter. 'Tillie told me about your perfume business, earlier. Before they left.'

Fran looked surprised. 'Really?'

Violet nodded. 'She slipped up to see me. Said she thought

you might feel I shouldn't be bothered with it, but that she believed it could be a wonderful success, and that I should know about it. She was right, wasn't she?'

Fran blushed. Tillie was right about the first thing, at least. She hadn't been going to tell Violet. Had thought it all seemed very silly, all of a sudden.

'Darling. You must do it. It's brilliant, quite brilliant. I'm just annoyed I never did it myself.'

Fran laughed, and her laughter was full of tears. Her mother wasn't just saying it, she really did look cross that she hadn't been the one to have the idea. But more proud than cross.

'I know you'll make it work,' Violet said. 'I know you'll grow up to be a wonderful asset to Cavalley's. The best of all of you, maybe.' Violet lifted the girl's chin with her finger. 'My Boy Scout Butterfly, that's what I always called you, isn't it? That's just what this company needs.'

Violet leaned her head back on her pillows. 'Right,' she continued, feeling afraid. This was it. She had to tell Fran the truth about where she came from. She knew she was risking everything by telling her now. Knew that it would be easier to leave it until after she was gone, and to leave the job to someone else. But that would be the cruellest thing she could do. Fran deserved an explanation from her mother, because that was how Violet saw herself, whatever her birth certificate might say.

'You're a beautiful girl, Frangipani Cavalley,' Violet whispered.

'But who am I?' the girl asked, tears falling down her cheek and on to Violet's fingertips. 'There are no records of my adoption. I sent off for them, but there aren't any. *Who am I?*'

Violet looked at her. 'You're Frangipani Cavalley,' she said. 'Just like you always have been.'

'I want to know my real name,' Fran insisted. 'My birth

name. It's important, Mama. Surely you can understand that? I need to know, before you die. I need to know where I came from.'

She was crying now, her face distorted. Violet's chest was tight with the awareness of the pain she had caused her daughter, and with the effort the conversation was costing her.

'You're Frangipani Cavalley,' Violet said again. 'And Sebastian is your father.'

Fran's hands lifted to her face. Sebastian. Her brother – not her brother. The man she had met for the first time today, who had walked back into their lives as if rising from the dead. Her father? Her head swam and buzzed with confusion.

But she had no time to take it in, no time to ask Violet how, why, when – because suddenly the door was opening, and Patrick was standing there, and Fran knew that something awful had happened, something worse than any revelations about who had been her father or who her mother might be, because his face was all twisted and wet, as he looked down at Violet and began to speak.

'I need you to be brave, my love, my darling,' he was saying, 'I need you to be very brave.'

And Violet was looking up at him and Fran thought how young she looked, not like a mother, or a grandmother at all, but like a young girl, lost, confused, reaching up for Patrick's hand as he knelt by the side of her bed as if in prayer.

'There's been an accident,' he began, and Violet made a noise like an animal in pain, as though she knew already how much the words he was about to speak would wound her, had felt it even before they found their mark.

'It's Flip and Tillie. Their helicopter went down. There was a storm. We don't know, yet, whether . . . we don't know what's happened to them, Vi. I'm sorry. I'm so sorry.'

And his head dropped and he wept, great sobs, and held

tightly on to Violet's hand as she screamed out in pain, a pain that no amount of morphine could soothe nor any doctor treat, until she had no voice left to scream with any longer, and could only lie, helpless, as the ambulance was called to her side once more.

Chapter Eleven

The next day

Fran sat in the family room at the hospital, staring at the man who, until yesterday, she had believed to be her brother. Who, until a few days ago, she had not known at all, since she had believed him to be dead. And now he had walked back into their lives – not dead at all, but more alive, it seemed, than any of them – this man who, she knew now, was her father. It didn't make sense. She had grown up knowing that she had been adopted by Violet, but not from whom. She had never felt the need to know, until recently. She had always felt different, yes, but that was because she was adopted, wasn't it? Not blood.

But she *was* blood. Just not in the way she had imagined. Violet *was* her mother – in every sense that counted. She was the one who had rocked Fran to sleep, who had sat at the kitchen table with her, valiantly trying to help her with her maths homework despite being worse at numbers than any of her children. Who had taken Fran travelling with her, trying to make up for her being so much younger than her siblings, and for the past that they shared and that she did not. Who had protected her – from more than she had ever imagined, she realised now. Yes, Violet was her mother. She was her mother, *and she was her grandmother*. And this near stranger in front of her was her father.

Her head swam with it all. With questions.

'Why?' was the first. Then: why had they hidden this from her? What had he done? Why had he gone away for so long, and never come back for her?

Fragments of her past were suddenly falling into place. Violet's expression when people told her that she and Fran looked alike: half-proud, half-worried. The look that ran across Blue's brow on the rare occasions that his dead brother was mentioned. Of sadness, she thought now, and of not wanting to say the wrong thing. Poor Blue. How hard it must have been for him, in particular, to know what to say and what to keep within. Blue, who had always been her ally, particularly since Russia.

She stared at Sebastian, and wanted to know him. But more, almost, she wanted him to know her. He was her father, and where had he been? He had not seen her first steps, nor did he know what her first words had been. Probably didn't even know where she had gone to school, what subjects she had taken exams in; the names of her friends – any of those apparently insignificant details that weave together to make a life. And she found she wanted to hurt him, make him aware of how much he had missed, of how much she had gone through without him.

'Do you know how I got this?' she asked him, pointing to her face. She pulled her hair back, tucking it behind her ear, so that he could see the whole length of her scar, running from under her eye to the edge of her jaw. He tried not to wince, but failed. He did not look away though. He nodded.

'I read about it,' he said. 'I have kept an eye on you, you know. Then – and more recently. I watched you.'

She looked at him, quizzical.

'In Capri. I was going to come and find you all there – at the party. But then someone else kind of stole my thunder.'

Mattie had arrived in Capri, instead. Of course. She remembered now, the strange feeling she had had in the gardens, and at other times in the last few days there, that eyes were on her back.

'Sorry,' he said. 'That's creepy, isn't it?'

'Yes, it is a bit. But it's OK. How did you find out about the accident?'

'The Cavalley family are pretty well covered in the press. And the internet made things easier. I didn't read everything, but I saw stories, now and then. It happened in Russia, didn't it?'

Fran nodded. She was filled with the urge to tell him everything that had happened to her. So she began.

Fran looked out of the tall window of the hotel room on the Nevsky Prospekt in the centre of St Petersburg. She thought the city was the most romantic place she had ever dreamed of, let alone visited, in her whole thirteen and a half years. It was winter now, and colder than she could have imagined, but she didn't care; she was transfixed by the beauty of the place. The hotel took up the whole corner of a block, and was a big, ornate hulk of a building that looked like a palace. It was breathtaking inside.

A huge marble entrance hall greeted you when you entered – full, most of the time, with women with bright blond hair in fur coats and thick-necked men in fur-trimmed overcoats. Violet ushered Fran past the men and women when she caught her staring at them, at their red lipstick and the big cigars and scowls. They were prostitutes, Fran knew, or mistresses, both of which seemed to her to be unbelievably glamorous. Fran had been harbouring fantasies of life as a Russian Tsarina since they got here, aided by life in the hotel, which attended to her every whim in consummate style, with the staff treating her as though she was far older than her years. Used to being the baby of the family, coddled and patronised in turn by her two much older brothers, this was one of the best things about being there. Flip was in London and America, flying between the two, so it was just her, Blue and Violet.

And, much of the time, it was just her. Violet and Blue were working all hours on the costumes and head-dresses for the opera that they had come over to design. It was a production of *La Traviata*, modernised and set during the Cold War, and it was already attracting a lot of attention, not all of it positive. The director was a notorious political agitator, as well as an artist, and had been arrested by the KGB more than once. That was another thing Fran was fascinated by, but Violet had banned her from asking him about it. Fran knew Violet was having an affair with the bearded older man, she could tell by the way they smiled at each other during the rehearsals that Violet sometimes sat in on. Fran had long known how to tell who her mother was sleeping with.

Fran would wake up in the mornings and stretch her feet out to the end of her big bed. Her room was all white and gold, and she would open the shutters and look out of her window to the street below. She never tired of watching the glamorous women and macho men making their way to work, queueing for the bank to open, the men standing on street corners selling silk stockings and tiny black kittens from within the vast lapels of their thick coats. She was desperate for a kitten, but her mother said the hotel wouldn't allow it. She bet they would, especially if she asked Sergei the concierge, who had taken a shine to Fran with her unusual, exotic looks and her eagerness to learn everything about the city and its history. From the day they arrived he had given her itineraries of places to go and visit – the obvious tourist places at first, like the Hermitage, and the Summer Garden, but then after a while, when it became obvious that her desire to learn would not be quenched by the obvious, he had drawn up a complete immersion in Russian culture for her to work her way through. Had arranged for a cousin to escort her around the city, had even taken her to places himself on his days off on occasion, so enchanted had he been by this girl who for once was interested in the city around her, not just in the money to be made or the deals to be done and then the flight home, like most of the guests who passed through the glass doors of the hotel he loved so.

She would say hello to him every morning on her way to breakfast, picking up information about where she was to go that day, or telling him about what she had seen the day before. She would eat – alone, often, but pampered by the staff – in the Art Nouveau ballroom with its immense stained-glass window at one end and its spotlit arches, filling up with omelettes made in front of her by the chef in his tall white hat, and caviar on blinis and smoked salmon, all the delicacies that she had learned to love. A lady harpist played for the guests as they ate, and when Fran entered she would smile, and begin playing. And so her days began.

Her walks and tours around the city had taken her along the miles of iced-over canals, overlooked by faded houses with ornate iron balconies. They took her to Palace Square, to the Winter Palace and the statue of the majestic *Bronze horseman*, rearing up, frozen in time. But her favourites were the churches. Piped and whirled and curlicued from the outside, all painted like a child's birthday cake, they were a world away from the dull, austerely grey churches she had been to in England. They seemed to have a sense of joy to them, of celebration and glory and pomp. Inside they were even better, dark and dense and packed tight with history and mystery. They were scented with incense and full of icons, little jewel-like images of gold-leafed Virgin Marys in front of which old women knelt on creaking knees to click their prayer beads. Some days, when there was nothing else planned for her, Fran would go to her favourite church, the tiny one on a corner near the hotel, that she was allowed to walk to by herself, and slip into a wooden pew at the back and just sit for hours, watching in dusky silence as the women came and went, lighting their candles and repeating their prayers in front of the images. It gave her a feeling of peace that she had never experienced before and didn't entirely understand. She didn't need to try, either; it was something that she did not need to pick apart and intellectualise, as she did with everything else.

Today, though, she was not going to the church, or to the opera house. Today they were all going to the circus.

From the outside it looked like an old-fashioned cinema, painted yellow and bedecked with white blobs, topped with a big sign in the now familiar cyrillic lettering. When she had first arrived in Russia, Fran had found the letters impossible to get used to; she had been keen to learn the alphabet as quickly as she could, so that she could at least pronounce the words she saw in front of her, and repeat them. Violet laughed at her, but Fran knew it was the way to anchor herself in the chaotic world that her family seemed to occupy. There weren't many things Fran couldn't make herself feel better about by learning about them. 'Always looking things up in encyclopaedias,' Violet would tell her friends affectionately. 'The brains of the outfit', she would call her, which made Flip compress his mouth into a hard line. He didn't like to feel overshadowed by his baby sister, not when he was the eldest and the one who was working so hard for the family business.

So she could take charge a little now, as she and her mother and Blue went into the building, feeling pleased with herself as she read out loud the signs for the toilets and cans of soft drinks, and the stand selling brightly coloured toys and mechanical animals made out of tin that rode round in circles when you turned a key, playing jangly music as they went.

'Where do we sit?' asked Violet, as they entered the auditorium. Fran craned to read the tickets in the dark.

'There isn't any reserved seating, I don't think.' She looked around her. 'Why don't we go here?'

'No, let's go at the front,' said Violet. 'Come on! It's not every day you go to the circus. I want to be right up by the action.'

Fran hung back, reticent. She didn't want to go at the front, at all. She knew there would be clowns – what if they picked her out, and made her do something? Her cheeks flushed just thinking about it. It was her worst nightmare. Once at school they had been to a Christmas gang show and the master of ceremonies had called all the girls up on stage, to take part in a song. Fran had tried to hide in her chair but had been jostled along and had hated every second of it, standing as far back as she could, terrified all the time that he would pick her to sing a line by herself, or worse. She didn't know what could be worse, but the fear of unspecific humiliation stuck in her throat.

Slowly, she followed Violet to the front row where her mother had already settled herself down. Blue followed silently behind, as usual. He talked more these days, but he still wasn't exactly chatty. Fran liked that, however. He didn't say anything unless he had something to say – even if there were quite a few occasions when what he had to say wasn't all that easy to understand.

They sat companionably while the auditorium filled up, Blue folding the programme into tinier and tinier squares in his hands until Violet gently took it away from him, Fran drinking her can of sweet, sticky Fanta and nervously wondering how it would begin.

Then the lights went down, the chatter quietened, and the show began.

It took her breath away. There were acrobats hanging from thick ropes with their faces painted black and white, twirling their bodies upside down from what looked like a fingertip and leaping over each other, landing on the floor in tight balls and rolling along like pinwheels. There were glossy black horses, decorated with silver buckles and rhinestone bits, ridden by women in jewelled leotards standing on one hand, legs straight up in the air, and pink and white feathered plumes on the horses' foreheads like fountains. Cossack dancers, moustachioed and dark, kicked their way around the arena, their eyes flashing, their backs straight and their bodies proud and stiff. An elephant balanced on a ball in an impossible-seeming feat that had Fran working out the force that the elephant would be propelling downwards in an attempt to stop herself worrying about it tipping over and falling on its back like a beetle. Fran had the family imagination in some ways, but it worried her; she didn't like her mind running away with her. So she tamed it with exercises, calculations. She stared as a woman dressed in a shimmering turquoise and indigo costume with a shiny black mask that made her look like a dragonfly leaped on to the elephant's broad back and did a handstand on it. Her mother, she noticed, was transfixed, gazing at the spectacle, her hand flying over one of her ever-present notebooks without even the need to look down at the page. A circus collection was coming up, then.

As the elephant was led away, there was a drum roll, starting softly and low, and growing in volume as it slowed down, the thrum becoming a rhythmic thump . . . thump . . . thump. There was a ripple of whispers around the audience and Fran could feel everyone tensing and holding their breath. What was going to happen?

Just then, a man came out from the curtains at the back of

the stage area and undid a fastening in the fabric; at the same time, from the roof, an expanse of netting began to unroll. More men appeared and fastened it to points around the circle, so it formed a tent over it. Fran chewed the inside of her lip. Out of the corner of her eye, on the other side of the aisle, she saw someone leaning down, unrolling something. She turned, and saw that it was a stagehand unrolling a long hose, the flat sort that firemen used, and positioning it so it was pointing at the sawdust floor in the centre of the stage. Why was he . . . ? Then it became clear.

The drumming got louder, joined by bells and cymbals, and the curtains at the back opened to let a Noah's Ark of a parade through, led by a tiny, wide-eyed monkey wearing a red fez. He scampered around the ring, his little arms and legs dancing as he led his fellow performers. He was pulling an ant-eater on a leather strap, followed by a goat, a miniature pony, a small cow – and then, to the crowd's excitement, the big cats: a pair of tigers on jewelled leads, followed by a lion, his mane combed out to look even bigger than it was, prowling behind the other animals led by their trainers. Fran couldn't help it, she reached for Blue's hand to hold. He patted it gently, kindly, and they sat back to watch the show together. Violet watched them, and smiled to herself.

After the show, as they were gathering their belongings, the man who had been standing with the hose at the side came over to Violet and touched her on the shoulder.

'Excuse me,' he said in a dense Russian accent, 'you are invited to . . .' He ran out of words, and made a brushing motion with his arms.

'I'm sorry?' Violet said.

'You are invited . . . come to see. The director.'

'Oh,' Violet said. 'All right. Thank you.'

They followed him across the stage, picking their way through the sawdust floor and then through the dark-red curtains at the back. Violet was suddenly reminded of walking through the wooden doors into the caravan back in the apple fields, for some reason, all those years ago. Something about a smell, probably. It was usually a smell that took you back like that.

Backstage, the light was shadowy and Fran had to be careful to avoid tripping over any of the various bits of equipment and furniture that seemed to be everywhere. Huge coils of thick rope, harnesses, cages for the smaller animals . . . the place was crammed. A tall woman, made a foot taller by her plumed head-dress, stalked past them, not meeting Fran's eye as she gazed up at her admiringly. Her face was coated in a thick mask of make-up, with big arches of exaggerated eyebrow and orange and yellow face paint blended into one another so that she looked almost like one of the animals.

'Here,' the man who had fetched them said, as they reached an outside door. The three of them were all still a bit bemused as to where they were going and what they were doing, but they followed as he gestured for them to go through it.

They found themselves outside in the biting wind, in a square behind the circus building. Standing by a large cage, with its door open, containing one of the tigers that they had just been watching, was a thin, wiry man dressed in a big overcoat that almost swamped him. He turned as he heard them approaching.

'Ah, Ms Violet Cavalley, and Blue, and Frangipani . . .'

Violet held out her hand for him to shake, and he kissed it with a bow.

'Mr Sidorov told me you were coming to my humble circus. I thought you would like to see my family close up.'

Violet smiled her brightest smile. She was charmed by this elfin little man, Fran could see, and she rolled her eyes inwardly.

'Come, come . . .' He took Fran's elbow and steered her towards the side of the cage.

'Oh no, I don't—'

'Oh, I am sorry, I apologise.' He took his hand off her. 'Are you frightened? I understand. But they are trained, my children. You think it's strange that I call them that? Maybe it is. But, there we have it.'

He rattled on, his words coming out like a train going over tracks, and Fran couldn't help but be somewhat charmed by him as well. He moved lightly, quickly, hopping from foot to foot in his enthusiasm.

'Come – right, not Mr Tiger, no. Let's see, someone else . . .'

He moved over to another cage where a small bear, no taller than his shoulder, stood gazing out at the group. His eyes were huge, and Fran melted a little inside. There was something pathetic about the big animal, in his chains.

'You like him more, yes?'

She nodded.

The man opened the cage door. 'Let's visit him. He's one of my favourites as well.'

Fran hesitated, watching as the man stepped inside and went up to the animal, who lumbered towards him and placed a paw affectionately on his shoulder.

'Come? Come!' The man held his arm out and Violet and Blue both entered the space. Fran held back.

'Come on, Fran. Don't be rude.' Her mother gave her a look. And Fran stepped into the cage.

The director of the circus was demonstrating the dance that he had taught the bear to do with him, a sort of slow, lumbering waltz, the animal's big paws on his shoulders. He had taken the bear's chains off, to better show them the dance. They lurched around the cage, the man singing a folk song as they went.

'Here, see? Miss Franny, Miss Franny, we dance for you.'

Fran laughed. The bizarreness of life with her mother suddenly struck her. She was standing in Russia, a bear and a circus director giving her a private dance show.

Or they were. And then, all of a sudden, they were not. She didn't even know how it happened – didn't remember anything about it later. There was just a whirl and a shout as the bear spun away from the director and towards Fran and, before she had a chance to run away or even turn her head, still standing on his hind legs, far taller than her, he swiped.

The blow caught the side of her head and tore down her face, a great rend of skin that left her cheek torn in two like a piece of silk, the edges jagged and frayed, and her jawbone exposed. She didn't fall down, Violet would always recall later, her beautiful girl. She just stood there, swaying slightly, like the flower she was named for blowing gently in a soft African breeze. Her expression was unsurprised, as if she had known that something like this would happen, her eyes sad, and her face – her face half-gone.

Violet had run to her, her hand clutched to Fran's face and blood pouring out from between her fingers until someone brought cloths and bandages to try and stem the flow. Cradling her like a baby as Fran gazed up at her, not making a sound, not moving.

There had been a cacophony of noise and activity, of circus hands shutting the other animals in and getting the Cavalleys out and calling for help, and then an ambulance and a hospital where Violet had to try desperately to make herself understood, where she saw what it was like, for the first time, to be in a strange country and unable to understand anything. And she got separated from Fran, who was wheeled into the operating theatre, and then couldn't find out where she had been taken afterwards or get anyone to tell her anything, for hours and hours, until she had managed to get hold of the director of the circus on the phone, and he had come and shouted at the nurses in great splurts of fist-waving Russian, and she had been taken along to Fran's room and seen her baby, her little surprise grandchild who had been so perfect, such a perfect, flawless thing, her skin pallid but still in stark contrast to the starched white sheets, her face mostly covered by bandages, and all connected to wires and an IV of fluid being pumped into her arm, and it had been Scarlet all over again, her daughter, her little girl, hurt – and nothing Violet could do to help her.

Blue had been standing behind her, following Violet like a shadow since it happened. He stared at Fran now.

'My sister,' he said.

'It's all right,' Violet told him.

'I'm scared again,' he whispered.

'Don't be scared, Baby Blue.' She took his hand.

'Will she die again?'

Violet blinked. From the depths of her memory, she recognised the phrase. He had said it before.

'I'm scared again, will she die again?'

It was what he had said after Scarlet. She remembered now. For months, he had been silent, and then when he spoke, that was what he said. 'I'm scared again, will she die again?'

She hugged him close, but his body was stiff in her arms. 'No, Blue, she won't die. She won't die again. I promise.'

'Mama told me the rest of it,' Fran said. 'What happened after, I mean. I don't remember much.'

She wanted to tell him she had felt alone, had needed her father, but the truth was, she had not. Violet had been everything she needed.

'I didn't need you,' she said fiercely. 'I didn't then, and I don't now.'

Sebastian nodded slowly, and she saw that she had hurt him more with those words than she might have anticipated. So he did care, then. A little, at least.

'I should tell you,' he said, 'what happened to your mother. Then when you know, you can decide whether you want anything more to do with me.'

Fran bit her lip. This wasn't a story she wanted to be told, she sensed. But, 'All right,' she whispered. 'Go on.'

And he began.

Catalina was a nineteen-year-old singer in a jazz band at a Cambridge nightclub. Sebastian had been after her for months, but she was holding out on him. He paced around his little attic room at St John's College, night after night, waiting for her to call, hoping for a knock on the door and a warm, silky body to slide in next to him in bed. She never did. Other girls did, of course – that had never been a problem for him. Although, often, they only came once.

But Catalina didn't come at all. She resisted. She teased him, standing in the little bar that she performed in singing smoky, sultry songs of women with soft lips and men with hard hearts, as he sat at the table drinking Caipirinhas. He was trying to show her that he could understand her culture. He knew that she was laughing at him every time she looked his way. But still he came back. Again, and again.

One night, he left before the set had finished, so enraged had he become by sitting there, night after night, never getting closer to her, never getting what he wanted. He slammed up the narrow wooden stairs of the tiny underground bar, the stairwell papered with old film and concert posters, his feet thundering on the steps. It felt as if even the women in the posters were laughing at him, with their perfectly arched eyebrows and upholstered, uplifted chests. He pushed the door open with his fist and breathed in a big gulp of the cold air. Fucking damn her! A group of earnest-looking undergraduates walked past him down Trinity Street, one pushing a bicycle, another hefting a satchel of books on his hip that was so heavy it was twisting his spine out of shape, and their breath made clouds in the air as their laughter escaped. He launched at them with a growl as they passed and they scattered with yelps like a box of kittens, and he shouted after them.

'Go on! Get back to your books, like good little boys and girls! Off you go. Fuck off!'

One of them looked over their shoulder at him as they went, her expression bemused, a shrug in her eyes. Fuck it. He must be drunker than he thought. He leaned against a cold wall, his head tipped back, looking up at the stars. He thought for a moment that he might be about to cry with anger and thwarted desire. Then berated himself for being such a wanker. For God's sake. Of course he wasn't going to cry.

The next day, he was sitting at a table in the café where he liked to breakfast, nursing a macchiato and a sore head, when she slipped into the seat opposite him. He looked up in surprise. If it had been a few hours earlier he would have assumed he was still half-asleep, or half-drunk, or both. But no. She was really there, sitting at his table, smiling at him and calling over the waitress to order a fry-up and a double espresso.

'And I want the bacon really crispy, and the eggs poached, and a double order of toast. And brown sauce. Thank you.'

Sebastian burst out laughing. 'Brown sauce?' He mimicked her lisping South American accent asking for one of the most British of condiments. 'Really? Well, I never.'

'Of course! What else with fry-up? I love it. My father was from Hull. He gave me love of brown sauce and Yorkshire pudding. And science.'

Sebastian raised his eyebrows. 'Fair enough.' Suddenly he had an appetite again. He called the waitress back, ignoring her put-upon expression, and ordered exactly the same. Catalina gazed at him with amused eyes.

They stared at each other across the table. Catalina's full lips formed a gentle curve of a smile, and her hair tumbled in thick black waves over her shoulders. She was perfectly delicious.

'So,' they both said at the same time, eventually. She giggled. 'Go on,' she said.

'Oh, it's not important. I was just going to ask how your father ended up in Columbia.'

'He fell in love with my mother. She was a singer as well. They met in a music hall and he followed her back to South America when she went home to look after her mother, who was sick.'

'Sensible man.'

'No. Not sensible. A romantic fool. But a good man, nonetheless.'

'And they met in a music hall, you say?'

She nodded, sipping her coffee and looking at him over the brim of the cup.

'Fate, then,' Sebastian commented.

'Ha. No, not Fate. A coincidence.'

Sebastian shook his head. 'Fate. It's obvious. Look at us.'

'Us?' She threw her head back laughing and her teeth shone white. 'There is no us, silly boy.'

'There should be.'

'Should there? You left early last night.'

'You noticed.'

'Of course I noticed. Every night you are there, sitting at the front, with your drink, with your big eyes . . . then last night suddenly you go halfway through. What, you think I'm blind? Or stupid? Or are you just playing the tortured lover?'

'Don't tease me,' he said. 'I don't play. Not at love.'

She was trying not to smile again, he could tell, but he ignored it.

'Ah, I see. Well then – tell me why you left.'

The waitress put their food down in front of them and Catalina began to tuck in straight away, shaking brown sauce into a huge puddle at the side of her plate and shovelling sausage and egg and bacon on to her fork before dipping it in. She didn't seem to be as interested in what Sebastian had to say as she was in her food, and suddenly he felt very much on the back foot. And he wasn't sure he liked it. Well, she could whistle for it. He wasn't going to just pour his heart out to this girl, all because she had shown up here and asked him to, after all this time. No, he deserved more than that. More consideration. He ignored his food and lit a cigarette.

She tutted. 'Did your mother not tell you it's rude to smoke while someone is eating?'

'Yes. I ignored her. Like you've been ignoring me.'

Catalina shrugged. 'I have not been ignoring you. You haven't said anything to me. Just mooned.'

'I have not . . .'

'Oh Sebastian, I am teasing you again. I'm sorry. You don't like it, I know. Come on. I have come all the way here to find you, so you have achieved your goal of getting my attention. Stop sulking.'

'I'm not sulking.'

'You are! Don't spoil your lovely face with a frown.' And she put her fork down, reached across the table and rubbed the corner of his mouth with her thumb, pressing his flesh upwards as if to force a smile. He ducked his head to one side like a child avoiding his mother's handkerchief with a dash of spit to wipe away ice cream – but he did smile.

They spent the morning together after breakfast, walking along the River Cam, telling each other about their lives, their families. Catalina was from a strict Catholic background, the eldest of six daughters and the only one to leave Columbia so far.

'Three of them already have babies,' she told him, 'one is still at school, one . . .' She trailed off.

'One what?'

'Has gone down a bad road,' she said quietly. 'I don't want to talk about it.'

'OK. What about your parents – what do they do?'

A shadow passed across her face. 'No. Another time. Tell me about your family now.'

So he did.

Later, he took her back to his room and made her tea and toasted crumpets on the little grill in the corner. He got out the copy of *Vogue* with Violet on the cover while the kettle boiled. It always worked.

'Here she is,' he said, handing it to her. 'That's my mother.'

Catalina looked it over with an appraising eye. 'She is very beautiful,' she said. He smiled, and waited. Ordinarily, this was where the girls stood up and took the magazine out of his hand, and kissed him, dropping the glossy to the floor as they did so. They loved the thought of going to bed with the son of someone who had been on the cover of *Vogue*; they loved the thought of free hats and sitting in the front row of the shows next to him; they loved *him*. But Catalina just smiled and continued to sit there.

'Tell me what you are going to do after you leave Cambridge,' she said. 'Are you going to work for her?'

Sebastian was a bit thrown, but he handed over her tea and crumpets, and answered her question. 'Oh no. My brother's gone into the family business. I'm not following in their footsteps.'

'So what, then?'

'I've got lots of ideas. Lots of possibilities and offers, you know? Just need to decide which ones I'm going to follow up, really,' Sebastian blustered. The truth was, he had no idea what he was going to do when he graduated next year – *if* he graduated at all, that was. His grades were less than stellar; since scraping into Cambridge to read History by some miracle and a lot of very expensive hours spent at a London crammer, he had let his studies drift and had only just managed to get through his first-year exams. Now, well into his second year, things were not looking any better. He was coasting – bright enough to get by on the minimum of work, and he and his tutors both knew it.

So did Catalina, by the look on her face.

He sat down next to her, took the magazine from her hands. It fell open at the article about Violet and the family. It was a lifestyle piece, laid out so that it looked a bit like a family photo album. In the centre of the double-page spread was a big photo of Violet on holiday, somewhere in the Caribbean, in a large hammock, with all of her children piled in on top of her. She wore a white floppy straw hat and a striped bikini, and a wide smile. Flip was tanned like a native and grinning as he held a massive slice of watermelon up to the camera; Blue had his face hidden in Violet's shoulder and Scarlet lay next to him, her small hand just visible holding his at the bottom of the frame. On Violet's other side was a young Sebastian, his hair bleached bone-white by the sun. Other photographs, scattered across the spread, showed the twins modelling, Violet as a young girl walking along the King's Road with Flip trundling along on his tricycle beside her. Violet and Dorian in hospital with the twins as babies. Sebastian on his first day at 'big school', standing in the garden in his smart new, too big uniform. That had to get her, surely?

'Happy families,' Catalina said. 'Lucky boy.' She flicked the pages, her eyes skimming the text with no apparent real interest. Was the girl made of stone?

'No, poor *un*lucky boy.' Sebastian's voice was smooth. 'A beautiful girl in my room, and she's more interested in reading about my mother than letting me kiss her.'

He pouted and leaned in, his hand moving to push the magazine out of the way. *Come on, come on*. He shut his eyes as he got closer. He could taste her already.

Then he felt a firm hand on his chest, and opened his eyes again to see Catalina shaking her head.

'No. Sorry, Sebastian.'

'What do you mean, no?'

'I should not have come to your room. I made a mistake – I'm sorry.'

And before he knew it, she had hopped up, and was on her way out of the door, leaving Sebastian alone with an erection and an old copy of *Vogue*, wondering quite what had just happened.

'She wasn't – you know, easy,' Sebastian said to Fran now. 'I don't want you to think badly of her. That's why I'm telling you this.'

Fran frowned. 'I don't think badly of her.'

'Good. Because she wasn't a bad girl, your mother. She just – we shouldn't have been together.'

'Were you happy?' Fran asked. For some reason, it felt important that she know.

'I was bad for her.' Sebastian sighed. 'Bad for everyone, bad for myself. I'd been sent down from Cambridge . . .'

'What for?

He looked embarrassed. 'Dealing in cannabis. Violet managed to persuade the college not to tell the police. She had to get me out of trouble a lot of times. Like I said, I was bad for everyone, then.'

'You were young,' Fran said softly. Sebastian's heart

contracted at the understanding in her face, at the empathy she was showing him and which he did not deserve. He hadn't come back with the intention of playing Daddy, not really. He had come back because his mother was dying, and because he was sick of hiding away. He would face the consequences, and he knew that the might of the Cavalleys, their wealth, their success, would protect him, at least to an extent. He was no longer prepared to lurk in the shadows and watch Flip in the spotlight. He was no longer happy to bum around Australia and South America with a fake passport, living on money wired by his mother to a motel, a bar, picking up women and dropping them every time he moved on. He was getting older, he wanted comfort, he wanted to enjoy the perks of being a member of this family, to be acknowledged as part of it. He wanted his life back. And if he was really honest, he had loved the idea of the drama of it all. Rising from the dead. It was the ultimate way to get attention. This had not passed him by, had been the thing that had tempted him back the most, maybe, all those weeks ago when he had first found out about Violet's illness, when the seed of the idea that he could come back had been planted.

But there was something about looking into the eyes of his daughter, as she waited patiently for him to tell her the truth, that made him feel like a complete shit. And, more than that, made him want to be less of one. It was the first time in a very long time – maybe ever – that Sebastian had felt inspired to try and be a better person. And it was taking him somewhat by surprise.

'She got pregnant,' he continued. 'I moved to London, brought her with me. We fought a lot. Drank together, a lot, before she was pregnant. And after you were born. We weren't good parents, Fran. I wish things had been different. But you know, for you, it's probably better that they weren't. Violet's a better parent than either of us were, or were ever going to be. That's the truth of it.'

But you were my *parents,* Fran wanted to say, yet found herself unable to do so. *I was your child, and you gave me away. Why did you give me away?*

The car was the most expensive one in the showroom, and the flashiest. Long and yellow, it clung to the ground like an animal making itself as low as possible, harnessing every ounce of its muscle and energy in order to leap forward. The salesman started the engine and it growled with a roar that made Sebastian's heart jump in his chest.

'Is it the fastest? Is it the fastest one you've got?' he asked.

The salesman smiled. 'Oh yes, sir,' he replied. 'It's the fastest we make. And,' he leaned in and lowered his voice, 'for our most,' he paused, and put emphasis on the next word, '*valued* customers such as yourself, there are tweaks that can be made to increase the engine capacity still further. For when one is driving abroad, of course.'

Sebastian smiled. 'Of course.'

When he pulled up outside the house, Catalina was sitting on the porch, smoking. Her eyes lit up when she saw the car. She was bored. She was often bored. The nanny looked after the baby, so she didn't have much to do there, apart from take her for a walk in the afternoon to show her off a bit. She liked it when people stopped to look at the huge pram, with her baby inside it all dolled up in a dress and bonnet and surrounded by toys. She didn't like the rest of it so much. The feeding and crying and grizzling. Babies were a drag, she had realised, very quickly. So it was a good job Sebastian had hired a Norland nanny to be there the day they brought Frangipani home from hospital. Anyhow, they were young, they couldn't be expected to spend all their time being puked on and jiggling a crying baby. That was for old people, like the nanny. She was at least thirty, an age that Catalina was still young enough to find unimaginable.

Catalina wasn't very interested in her child. Catalina was interested in clothes and shopping, in parties, in dancing till her calves ached and her hair stuck to her back with sweat, in staying up to see the sun rise and sleeping in the silk sheets of her Emperor-sized bed until afternoon, and, having found a man who had enough money to make sure she could do all of these things, she saw no point whatsoever in continuing her studies. Her days were lazy ones. She would get up when she woke, normally around 1 p.m., and call for the nanny to bring Frangipani to her. After kissing her, and making sure the baby was wearing an outfit to her liking, the child would be taken away again, to do whatever the nanny did with her, while Catalina bathed and dressed. Then she would have coffee and a cigarette in the garden, or on the porch so she could watch people go by. She would walk to Selfridges, wheeling the pram proudly in front of her, to meet friends for coffee or just to shop. Most days she would arrive back home with one of the store's distinctive yellow bags, whether handbag- or shoebox-sized, or just containing Sebastian's favourite treats from the Food Hall.

Today, she had bought a very expensive new watch, putting it on her Gold Card, and was a bit worried about how Sebastian was going to react. He was generous – could afford to be, and it wasn't as though he had earned the money, so why would he care? But sometimes he lost his temper over the silliest of things. Sulky, he was, sometimes. He was cheating on her. She knew it. Had been since Fran was born – before, maybe. She was not stupid, she saw the signs, smelled the wine that he never drank on his breath, read the receipts in his wallet for dinners for two when he said he was going out with his friends, and gifts that never found their way to her.

So Catalina was pleased when he came home driving the expensive yellow car, lowering the window as he pulled up to the door and calling out to her, 'Fancy a ride, darlin'?' She shrieked, and leaped up from the porch, running down the steps and into the passenger seat, where she kissed him. They both ignored the hoots of the vehicles behind them. 'Sebastian, it's beautiful.'

'Isn't she? I thought we'd go for lunch.'

And he revved the engine, and they took off.

They were sitting at a table eating oysters and drinking champagne near the sea by five. Lunch was a moveable feast in Sebastian and Catalina's world. Everything was. Money made their lives revolve around their whims and wishes. If a shop was closed, it could be opened; if the baby cried, the nanny would quiet her; if a restaurant was full, a table would somehow become available.

Lunch lasted till midnight. They left the restaurant arm-in-arm, Catalina still in bare feet and the vest and short skirt she had been wearing outside the house when Sebastian picked her up, laughing, drunk, kissing.

Money had made their lives easy until now. But money could not stop the car from spinning out of control as Sebastian took the sharp bend on the cliff-top road too fast, and his reflexes, slowed and dulled by wine, could not catch up in time. Money could not stop his hand from slipping, sweatily and clumsily on the wheel as he tried to right it and only succeeded in pushing them further towards the fence. Money could not stop the vehicle from hanging perilously over the rocks as Sebastian scrambled to undo his seatbelt and get himself free of the car, nor could it mean that he was able to get around to Catalina's side, to her slumped, unconscious body, in time to pull her free. Money could not save her as the car, its bright yellow bodywork scratched and dented, crashed on to the rocks below.

Sebastian stood, in the cold night air, the wreckage of his trophy down below him containing its awful cargo, breathing hard. Oh God, what had he done? He felt sick with fear and regret. And panic.

He pulled his phone out of his pocket, and stared at it. His thumb hovered over the base of the keypad. He should have dialled 999 – he knew he should. But he was afraid. He knew he was drunk, and he knew it was his fault. So instead, he called his mother.

'I can't do it, Mama. I can't go to prison. I know what happens there, to men like me. You know what happens there. You can't send me to jail, Mama. Please.'

And she could not. She knew how it felt to stand and condemn your own blood to the certainty of pain, horror, to a future changed for ever with the words you spoke, however true. She knew what prison could do. She would not, could not, let prison kill her son. Could not send him to that fate.

'Don't cry, my darling boy,' she said, cooing down the phone to him as she had when he was a child, away at boarding school, insistent that he wasn't homesick and yet sobbing secretly to her in the dead of night. 'I'll help you. It'll be all right. Mama will make everything all right.'

'And she did,' he finished. 'In the best way she knew how.'

Fran scratched her head. It was too much to take in. 'You killed Catalina,' she said slowly, 'and Violet hid you. She protected you.'

Sebastian nodded. 'I was her son. A bad one, yes. But – it's Violet. Family is everything to her.'

That was true. How many times had Fran heard that, as she was growing up. 'Don't tease your little sister, Flip. She's your family – you might need her when you're older.' 'No, you can't go to the cinema by yourself, we're all going together. Family outing.' 'I don't care whether you have a date with Princess Diana, you're going to Fran's piano recital, and that's the end of it. Family comes first.'

Family. But only Violet's unique definition of family – the family she had created.

'How . . . ?'

'The car was in the sea. Catalina's body . . .' he paused. 'They didn't find her for a while. They assumed mine had drifted away. In a sense, it had. Sebastian Cavalley had drifted away.'

He looked sad, and for a moment she felt sorry for him, and then caught herself.

'Why did she have to lie to me though? Why not just say she was my grandmother, that you were both dead? I don't understand why she lied about that.'

'I didn't either,' Sebastian replied. 'Not at first. Not for a long time. It's only now I realise that she was trying to break the chain.'

'I don't know what you mean.'

'Have you never heard her saying it? "Blood betraying blood begets blood". It's what she believes. What she thinks has ruined us all. It's crazy, but . . .'

Fran had heard it, she recalled now. *Blood betraying blood begets blood*. Just an old wives' saying, she had thought. But it was obviously more than that.

'It's all about family,' she said quietly, and he nodded.

'The way Violet saw it, handing me over to the police would have been betraying me. She couldn't see me go to prison, so she protected me. And lied to you. The Cavalley curse – she believes in it. And I think she thought she could keep you safe from it, keep you in a bubble, as long as you didn't know you came from that violence. That blood.

'She made everyone promise – Flip, Blue, Kalisto – they all promised not to tell you who your real parents were. The press never got hold of it,' he continued, answering her next question before it was out of her mouth. 'I wasn't a good partner to Catalina, like I said. I kept her pretty quiet. The pregnancy and everything . . . No one knew you had been born, outside the family.'

'The family.' Fran ran the words around her mouth. *The family*. Different from the one she had thought it was. But, in so many ways, still the same.

Fran had gone in to sit with Violet. Sebastian was in the waiting room alone. He stood and went to the window. In the small courtyard garden of the private hospital, Blue paced up and down, covering the same ten squares of paving stone back and forth, back and forth, a cigarette in his hand, smoke rising slowly into the air as he walked. His mouth worked. Sebastian watched for a moment, then went outside.

'Still saying your nonsense rhymes, Little Boy Blue?' Sebastian asked. 'It's reassuring to see that some things never change,' he continued. 'Still turning things over and over in there, aren't you?'

He walked over to Blue, tapping him gently on the head. 'Knock knock, anyone home?'

Blue gazed at him and Sebastian laughed. 'Don't panic, Blue. I'm not going to tell anyone your secret. You remember your secret, don't you?'

Blue's eyes widened and the speed of his pacing increased as he pulled away from Sebastian.

'Of course you remember,' Sebastian said. 'How could you forget something so terrible? Such a tragedy? I know I couldn't.'

His face was sad now. 'It's all right, Blue. We're brothers.' He took Blue's arm and pulled him close. 'Brothers. That means we trust each other, yes?'

Blue nodded, a quick jerk of his head. 'Brothers in arms, brotherly love, band of brothers, blood brothers,' he whispered, and at the last stopped, his brow furrowed, his voice a whisper.

Sebastian took his elbow, and began to walk him down the street. 'Blood brothers, that's right. Good boy, Blue. I'll put you on the bus and you can go home now. Home to Adam. Yes?'

'Home,' echoed Blue. 'Home on the range, home is where the heart is, my heart, my heart, cross my heart and hope to die, to die, to die.' A tear ran down Blue's cheek as they walked, but he did not wipe it away.

They had all been at the house in the country that Violet had rented for the summer when it happened. Violet, Kalisto, Flip. Sebastian, Scarlet, Blue. The Cavalley Family. 'We need to get out of London,' Violet had declared one sweltering July morning, after having spent all night sweating and tossing and turning, throwing the windows open in a vain search for fresh air. She had breezed downstairs dressed in a white cotton fifties style sundress with her hair tied up in a big pink bow, one of the costumes that made her children cringe, and started rifling through the phone book as she lit her first cigarette of the day.

'I'm going to rent a house – we'll summer there. It'll be like a big house party, so invite all your friends. We'll have a birthday party for the twins! A big, summery, sixteenth birthday party.'

Blue gazed at her with wide eyes. 'Don't look so scared, sweetie. It'll be fun.' She touched his cheek. Such a delicate boy.

Violet flicked through the pages of the phone book for a while before saying, 'What am I looking for? Estate agents? How do people do this?'

Flip reached behind the sofa and chucked one of the Sunday supplements over to her. 'Small ads. Look, there are hundreds of them.'

'Aha! That Law degree going to good use at last.'

She ruffled his hair absentmindedly as she smoked and sat down at the kitchen table. 'Here we go. "Near Whitstable. Large family house one mile from beach, mature garden with swimming pool, grass tennis court, croquet lawn." Croquet! We can have Pimm's. It'll be like something out of *The Great Gatsby*.'

'Mum, not everything is something out of a book or a movie, you know,' Flip chided. '*Great Gatsby*, indeed.'

Violet stuck her tongue out at him, then reached for the phone and began to dial.

'Aren't you going to look at others?' he said. 'Research the area?'

'No, I don't need to,' she told him. 'I can tell. I have a good feeling about it.'

She was right, even the naysayer Flip and the worried Blue admitted when they went there to see it. She had already paid the deposit and booked the house for two months, so it was a good job she had chosen well. But even she was surprised at how perfect the place was. As they drove through the gates at the end of the drive, the six of them all crammed into the secondhand Land Rover she had bought for the occasion, they all gasped, and the kids craned their necks out of the windows to get a better view. The sea seemed closer than a mile away, because the house was high up and the garden rolled down the hill, followed by fields and then sand dunes, so you could see it from most of the rooms in the house. The drive was long and curved and the house was a big, pale stone Georgian block with dove-grey framed windows and a wisteria climbing up the side. There was an apple orchard and a proper walled vegetable garden, a summerhouse and barbecue by the swimming pool, hammocks in the trees and bicycles in the outhouse.

'Oh,' they all said, as Violet parked the car, in a brief moment of quiet as they all imagined the coming weeks in this beautiful place, and then the air was filled with screeches and bickering as the children fought to get out of the car and grab the keys from Violet's hand and get inside and choose bedrooms and explore.

'I never want to go back to London, ever again,' Violet said as she got out and stretched. Kalisto unfolded his long legs from the passenger seat and got out as well, stalking around the side of the car and breathing in deeply and dramatically.

'FEEL the sea air, Violetta,' he pronounced, spreading his arms wide and exhaling noisily. 'Feel it! I can sense it cleaning my very BONES!'

'Come along, then, Prospero,' she said. 'We'd better bag the good rooms before my brood claim them, otherwise there'll be no uprooting them.'

Kalisto waved his cane. He was dressed for the occasion in his version of a country squire's dress – a cropped tweed riding jacket with scarlet breeches, and one of his collection of canes. This one was red with a devil's head carved out of marble as a handle.

'Aren't you boiling?' asked Violet, slipping off her silk cardigan. She wore a pink and blue striped prom dress underneath, with a pink net underskirt and bare feet, her toenails painted blue. Her straw hat was dyed blue to match. They had already attracted quite a few strange looks as they drove through the village. They were used to it.

Kalisto sniffed. 'Hot, cold, who cares? Fashion does not conform to such low details; it is not dictated to by the whims of the weather.' But he ran a finger around his collar nonetheless.

'I want to have a party here,' Violet said, as they went round to the side of the house and saw the wide, flat lawn stretching out ahead of them. 'Don't you think? For the twins' birthday. Pitchers of lemonade, bunting, games. A bonfire at night and a hog roast, and people can camp on the lawn. A proper celebration.'

'Aye,' Kalisto nodded, slipping into his true accent briefly as he did when he was feeling a bit emotional. 'Yes. A celebration. You deserve one of those, Lady Vi, you do, kid.' He squeezed her shoulder with his big hand.

'Oh, Kal, don't . . .' She reached up and wiped a tear away from the big man's cheek. 'You silly thing.'

He took a deep breath. 'I'm very proud of you, you know. Look how far you've come.'

'Look how far *we've* come,' she said gently. 'We're a good team, aren't we? If a funny-looking one.'

She pointed at their reflection in the French doors of the house, and they both laughed. It was a bit like one of those mirrors in The House of Fun at the fair or on the pier: tiny Violet with her wild curls and bare feet; huge Kalisto with his shining bald head and broad girth. He put his arm around her, and they went inside.

They spent the next week planning the party, dreaming up a Willy Wonka-esque vision that would put a film set to shame. The twins mostly left them to it, occasionally dropping into the kitchen and vetoing some particularly '*embarrassing*' or '*completely gross*' idea one of them had had, like when Kalisto suggested creating a live carousel with Shetland ponies tethered to a large roundabout.

It was Scarlet who came up with the idea for their entrance. She was obsessed with roller skating and spent hours practising her twirls on the patio outside the kitchen, spinning around with one leg bent up by her knee, dressed in legwarmers and a ra-ra skirt. Blue didn't need convincing. He would have done anything his twin asked him to, since he was utterly in her thrall. So was everyone. Scarlet was beautiful and vivacious, sunny and funny and talented. She was the sort of girl that people wanted to hate but couldn't, because she was genuinely nice and warm and generous. She was destined for big things, everyone said so. You could see it just from looking at her.

So when she told her brother that arriving at their party being pulled along on roller skates on garlands of flowers, from behind a bedecked Land Rover, would be 'the most cool thing, EVER, totally brill', he just looked up at her for a moment, and then nodded, and went back to working on the design he was drawing for her costume for the party, making sure it was roller-skate friendly.

Everyone was arriving, or had arrived – scores of cars and minibuses rolling up the drive, tents filling the bottom end of the garden. A marquee dressed up to look like a Big Top had been erected in the centre of the lawn; coconut shies and stalls with candyfloss and fresh lemonade were everywhere. A huge spit-roast pig was turning away, dripping its fat on to the ground.

Sebastian chewed on a piece of grass and watched the Land Rover that he knew contained Blue and Scarlet chugging gently at the end of the drive, waiting for the signal. Across his lap lay the girl who worked behind the bar in the village pub. She was drunk on the bottles of cider they had taken from the house and brought up to the top of the hill with them, and her fingers were working away at Sebastian's fly. He was slightly drunker than her, having also downed a stiff vodka and orange that he had sneaked from the party supplies earlier. Violet didn't like him drinking, even though he was almost eighteen. He didn't know why she was so funny about it. All of his mates were allowed to drink at home. But not him. He sighed, and let the barmaid's slim fingers slide inside his boxer shorts. Fucking Scarlet and Blue, he thought, looking down at them from his position. Typical that 'the twins' should have the biggest party of any of them. Why was it that simply being twins made people think they were more special, more than the sum of their parts? Neither he nor Flip had had a sixteenth birthday party on this scale. It would be his eighteenth in a couple of months, and nothing had been mentioned about any big bash for him.

He fantasised. Maybe he would get Violet to hire the 231 Club for him. He could invite everyone from school, all the guys from cricket, all the girls that he seemed to pick up hanging out on the King's Road at weekends. It would be cool. Violet would do it, he was sure. She never said no to him. He would outdo the twins with their stupid country party that looked like something for children.

He pulled a cigarette from the pack in his back pocket and flicked his Zippo lighter. It sparked, but didn't light. Damn. He shook it. Empty.

'Got a lighter?' he asked the girl, who was enthusiastically but inexpertly rubbing at him.

'Don't smoke,' she said. 'I've got something else you might like though.' And raised her striped vest top.

'Yeah. In a bit. I really want a smoke.' He felt through his pockets.

'Come on,' she pouted. 'I want to play, Seb.'

She stuck a finger in her mouth and sucked it, leaning forward to kiss him. She smelled of sweat and cheap cider, and he pushed her away. He didn't even know why he'd got her up here – it wasn't as though he fancied her much. Must have been bored, he supposed.

She lost her balance and flopped backwards, her legs sticking up into the air, and he laughed. 'Ow!' she said. 'Fine. I'm going.'

Sebastian shrugged.

He watched as she stumbled down the hill. Scarlet and Blue had got out of the four-wheel drive and were affixing themselves to the long strands of flowery rope that were attached to the back of it, hooking them around their waists. Blue looked nervous. Sebastian could tell he was nervous, as he was doing that thing with his shoulder. Sebastian suddenly noticed that the girl had dropped a make-up compact in the grass. He opened it: a mirror. Something from his days in the Scouts, before he had been expelled, came back to him. They had been taught how to start a fire. You got a mirror, angled it towards the sun, and . . . He began to experiment. He really was dying for a smoke.

The car was starting to move now. It had been sprayed in rainbow stripes, like a helter skelter, for the occasion, and plastic flowers in all the colours of the rainbow were stuck all over it. A sound system had been installed with speakers on the top, which had started up, playing 'I'm Forever Blowing Bubbles'. As it moved off, bubbles began to float out of it, and for a minute, Sebastian wished he hadn't been so stubborn and had stayed down at the party. Oh well. He would go down in a minute, when his siblings had done their big show-off thing, slip back and pretend nothing had happened. He really fancied a hot dog.

The car was chugging slowly along the drive. Sebastian stared. Blue was fussing about something, his hand starting to flap. He was shaking his head from side to side. That was another of the things he did when he got upset. A lot of things upset Blue. Scarlet turned her head towards him, then back to the front. Blue's head-shaking got worse. Both shoulders were going up and down now. Scarlet took one hand off the ropes and patted his shoulder. She wobbled for a second, then righted herself.

Sebastian was bored now. He picked up the mirror and tilted

it towards the sun. As he did so, he realised that a spot of bright light appeared near the big stone pillars that were positioned in front of the lawn. The drive was long and windy before then, more of a track than a drive, though people kept on calling it the latter. 'To sound posher,' Flip said scornfully. Flip was going through what his mother said was a 'socialist phase'.

It was quite a big puddle of light, like the spotlights that they had in the theatre. He tilted the glass again, slowly. The pool got a bit bigger. Sebastian positioned it so that it was hovering at around what he thought would be the right height, and waited.

He only meant to reflect the flash into Scarlet or Blue's eyes for a second. Just enough to startle them, spoil their entrance. Something in him tugged as he saw them waiting there, perfect, bathed in sunlight. His sunlight. He thought that if he directed the glare towards them they might stumble, wobble. That it would break the perfect glow that surrounded them, just for a moment. He didn't realise what else it would break.

Scarlet didn't die until two days later, in the end. Internal injuries. It sounded relatively innocuous, as a phrase. What it actually meant was that her organs had been crushed, twisted out of their natural placement and ripped apart inside her, bleeding into her body, pumping blood into places it was not meant to be, until her system slowly began to shut down.

The full weight of the Land Rover had gone over the right-hand side of her thin body, crushing her beneath its bubble-blowing, rainbow-coloured bulk. After it happened, there were a few moments before anyone quite understood what had gone wrong, and the vehicle sat there, tilted up slightly by her body under the wheels on one side, still pumping out translucent circles of filmy oil, still playing its ice-cream-van-like tune. Blue was crying, a low, guttural sound that was like no noise he had ever made before, or would make again. The shock juddered out of his lungs, as people began to realise that the car had stopped, too soon, and that they couldn't see Scarlet's golden curls bouncing behind it any longer, and that something had gone terribly, awfully wrong.

The driver, a local man from the village who had driven the ice-cream van until his retirement and from whom they had bought the musical equipment, taking it out of his old van, never got over what had happened. He maintained that there had been a light that had blinded him momentarily, that he had squinted his eyes shut and covered his face with his arm but that it hadn't helped; his eyes were filled with a white light that pierced into the back of his skull. Just before, he had seen Blue wavering, Scarlet reaching out to steady her brother, he said, and he was worried that the boy was going to fall and take his sister down with him, and so he had reached down to change into second gear, but somehow it had been reverse, and he had still been unable to see, and confused by his blindness and the fact that he could feel the car going backwards, he hit the accelerator.

Blue had twisted out of the way, already leaning to that side, shying away. It was Scarlet, who was leaning towards him, who took the full impact of the blow. The car wasn't going fast, but it was heavy, and that was all it took once her body had got caught under its big wheels.

The driver had all sorts of tests – brain scans, MRI scans – to see if he had a tumour, or had suffered a sudden migraine or some kind of seizure that might explain the sudden light he described. No one else had seen it. There was nothing in the grounds to explain it. After a while people began to assume that he had made it up, that he had become confused, or – or they didn't know what. But his explanation just didn't sound that plausible, and a young girl was dead, and he shouldered the responsibility.

As did Blue. He didn't utter a word for months after Scarlet died. No one could get him to speak. He just sat and stared ahead of him, dully. Eventually he began to draw. Violet breathed a sigh of relief when she saw him reach for his pencil and sketchpad as he sat in the corner of the kitchen on the floor, a position he had begun to favour. He's starting to come out of it, she thought. He's going to be OK. But when she saw his drawings, later that night after he had gone to bed, she wept. She had been expecting to see dresses again, wondered what he would have come up with, but this was no cruise collection or assortment of designer knits, this was a return to his old drawings – all madness and fire and twists of metal, jagged edges and hard scratches with his pen that had dragged on the paper.

When he eventually did open his mouth, it was to repeat one sentence, over and over again, like a mantra that was meant for comfort, although there was nothing comforting about his words. 'I'm scared again, will she die again?'

Over and over.

There was a link in his mind between his fear and her death. It was as if he was reliving it all the time, a doctor eventually explained to Violet. He had joined the moments together, one following the other, and though Scarlet was dead he was still in fear of her dying – a fear which led to a memory of her death. And underneath it all was the fear that he himself had caused the accident to happen.

The worst thing was that Violet could not tell him that it wasn't his fault because, whatever had made the driver shield his eyes and hit the wrong pedal, it did seem that if Scarlet had not been leaning across to comfort Blue, then she might not have gone under the wheels. Would have been rolling along behind him, facing ahead, so that even if the driver had braked and reversed still, she would have been knocked to one side, or would have seen it coming and been able to get out of the way. A broken leg, maybe, some bruises and wounded pride would have been the worst of her injuries. Instead – instead, this.

So while Blue repeated his mantra, Violet repeated her own. 'Blood betraying blood begets blood.' Somewhere inside herself, despite knowing that it was illogical, old traveller nonsense, she believed. She believed it was the curse of her father that had killed Scarlet. And that therefore it was *her* fault.

Sebastian kept quiet, as well. He didn't tell anyone at all what he had been doing. By the time he got back down to the party, with the girl's compact in his pocket, everyone was wailing and calling for ambulances and trying to lift the Land Rover up off Scarlet's body, and he had just waited, a slow, dull shock spreading through his body as the irreversible, terrible magnitude of what he had done hit him.

And then he had looked up, and his eyes had met Blue's . . . and he knew.

Sebastian and Blue stood alone in the kitchen. Blue did not speak, just stared. But Sebastian knew by the way his younger brother looked at him, his eyes judging, mistrustful, that he had seen. That had been why Scarlet was twisting to comfort him. The glare that Sebastian had been directing had worked; it had hit Blue in the eyes and made him wince. But it hadn't entirely blinded him. He had squinted up, trying to see what it was that was hitting his eyes like a migraine, and he had seen his brother. Sitting up on top of the hill, mirror in his hand. For a second, their eyes had met. Just a second – not even that. And that was when he had cried out, and Scarlet had turned to comfort him.

Sebastian leaned in towards him. 'It's all right, Blue,' he said quietly. There was no one around. 'I won't tell.'

Blue looked at him, confused.

'You know it was your fault, don't you? We both know. You couldn't be a grown-up. You thought you saw something, and you got frightened. Scarlet tried to help you, and she got hurt. I won't tell.'

Sebastian put a hand on his shoulder. 'You didn't see anything, Blue. Your head's making things up. There was no one on the hill. I wouldn't tell anyone you thought there was, or they'll put you in hospital again. Bad hospital. You don't want to go to the bad hospital again, do you?'

Blue shook his head. 'No. No no no,' he said, 'no thank you, thank you kindly, thank you and you and you . . .'

Sebastian squeezed his shoulder. 'It's all right, Blue, mate. It's all right. We're brothers.'

Chapter Twelve

Violet lay in her hospital room. It was off the main corridor, and outside, she could hear trolleys being trundled past, and orderlies speaking to one another. There were a few chairs, a small table, some papers. A jug of water and a plastic rose in a little jar. The depressing contents that filled similar rooms all over the world, rooms where people waited, staring ahead with glazed eyes, just as she did now, waiting for news, hoping that the worst would never come, hoping that each sound of footsteps would not be the ones that brought their lives to a crossroads or a cul-de-sac. Half-desperate for news, half-wanting to put off for ever the moment that they feared most of all.

She stared down at her hands, resting on her lap, and thought how old they looked. When had they got like that? She didn't remember. It had crept up on her sneakily, in the way aging did. One day you were sixteen and everything was ahead of you, and the next, you were . . . old. The sort of woman they called a doyenne rather than a protegée. A grandmother, a widow. Not that she had had to be old to be a widow. She raised her head. Her mouth was dry. Patrick sat by her side.

'They'll be here, soon enough,' he said. 'Everyone will be here.'

'Flip?' she asked, and her voice was unrecognisable. 'I need to see Flip.'

Patrick's eyes crinkled, and he said, 'No. I'm sorry, my darling. Not Flip. Shh, don't cry. Don't cry, lovely girl.'

And then later, as her children stood around her, the door opened and in walked Tillie. Her head was bruised, her face marred by a cut down one side, but she was otherwise unharmed.

'Tillie?' Violet swallowed. 'Have you brought him? Have you brought Flip?'

Her children looked at one another, uncomfortably. Tillie turned to them. 'Can we have a moment?' she asked, then turned back to Violet and gently took her hand, as Sebastian, Fran, Blue and Patrick left the room.

'Soon,' she said softly. 'Flip's coming soon.' Her voice was soothing. 'Violet, I need to tell you some things.'

She pulled up a chair, and sat close to her mother-in-law, still holding her hand.

'You're not the only one who's been keeping secrets,' she said.

Violet's eyes widened.

Tillie picked up her bag from the floor and put it on her lap.

'I understand why you did lots of the things you've done, Violet. You wanted to protect your children, didn't you? Fran, for example. You didn't want her to be the child whose father killed her mother.'

Violet didn't understand. It was true – but what did it have to do with Tillie? She dragged her mind into the room. It kept threatening to drift. Back into the past . . .

'Not all of us had someone to protect us like that, Violet. Some of us did have to grow up as the girl whose father killed her mother. I can see why you'd want to protect Fran from that. I can understand. It's not a good thing to live through.'

Something was swimming into focus, as Violet stared at Tillie. Something was falling into place, in the back of her drug- and pain-addled mind. She looked at Tillie, at her blond hair, her cool eyes and, from the murky depths, it emerged.

'Can you see it now?' Tillie asked. 'Can you see them?'

Violet nodded. Yes, she saw them. In the past, in her memories, and here in front of her.

And then Tillie reached into her bag, pulled out an old-looking envelope, worn at the edges, and handed it to Violet, who took it and turned it over. As she did so, she saw her own handwriting on the front – and gasped. Then, as Violet closed her eyes for a moment and tried to still her heart which had started banging in her chest as if it was a caged animal desperate to escape, and stop the black fuzzy darkness from closing in around the edges of her vision, Tillie spoke again.

'You know. Somewhere inside yourself, you've always known. You know that I'm Sam Gilmour's daughter.'

Violet didn't need to read the letter Tillie was holding to know what it said. She remembered it, word for word.

Dearest, my darling, my most beloved Sam,

I write from my bed, in a hotel in Rome where I am doing the hats for a new show and wishing beyond all reason that you were here with me. In my bed, inside me. You are in my mind and my heart though, so that will have to do for now.

I have been surviving on the memory of the night you came back to me like a poor blackbird in winter, picking for scraps in the snowy, frozen ground. I could not believe it, when I opened the door, to see you standing there, all dishevelled and as devastatingly handsome as ever – have I told you how handsome you are? Only a thousand times. And I will tell you a thousand times more.

Somehow I had always known that our story was not

entirely over, I think. I must have done, mustn't I, or else how would I have been able to carry on? God, I sound like a breathless teenager, not a respectable milliner and mother of five. A mother of five including yours, of course. He is the other thing that has kept me close to you, in heart if not body, of course. Your boy. Our boy.

Maybe now, one day soon, he can know you. Know you are his father and be so proud to call you that. I know he will be. He has been yearning for you for so long, to have what the other boys have, and it has broken my heart that the one thing he wants most is the thing I could not give him – you.

Will we tell him together, do you think? Or maybe you'll want to tell him by yourself. Boys together . . .

We can discuss. I must rush and prepare hundreds of beaded capelets for the chorus.

Love, love, love,
Violet

'Where did you find it?' Violet whispered.

Tillie shrugged. 'In his things, after he died. It broke my mother's heart, you know. You were the only one . . . oh, not the only other woman. There were strings of them. You knew that, didn't you?'

Her voice was cruel. Violet didn't reply. She had to save her breath now.

'But you were the only one that mattered. He would never have left her, but he always loved you. And when he went back to you – it broke her. That was what – that was what drove her mad. That was what started it all. She knew she'd lost him, and it made her lose her mind.'

The rest was unspoken. Their memories like two halves of

a Fabergé egg, joined together, neither complete without the other, closed. Holding the truth at the heart of it.

It was a month after he had come back into her life that it had happened. Sebastian was ill, he had been running a temperature all day, and Violet had been up and down stairs checking on him all evening. Kalisto was there and they were sitting at the kitchen table working on their new show after dinner. It was quiet. Outside, snow fell.

The phone rang and it was Sam. Violet carried the cordless handset into the hall. Kalisto didn't know she was seeing him again – he would not have approved. She couldn't blame him; she didn't approve of it herself. It was Kalisto who had had to pick up the pieces after their affair ended before. Violet couldn't blame him for not wanting to do it again.

But Sam had worked his way back into her affections. Ah, who was she kidding, there was no work involved. Her heart had been wide open to him, the aching gap in it entirely evident, and when she had seen him, quite by chance, at a party, she had fallen in love with him all over again. Had never been out of love with him, she had realised. So she went against her better judgement, and agreed to see him again. There was no judgement, when it came to Sam.

'Hello,' she said quietly, standing by the fireplace in the front room and looking at her reflection in the overmantel mirror.

'I have to see you,' he said. Straight away she could hear the wine in his voice; it was thick with it, and with lust.

'Ah, darling Sam. I miss you too. But not now.'

'I'm coming over. She's driving me insane, Violet. Questions, questions, always questions. She won't let me leave the house unless I tell her where I'm going. She waits for me, in rooms, in the dark. I don't know what to do.'

'It's not a good night.'

'Please.'

'Honestly, Sam. I can't.'

'I don't know what to do, Violet. I can't cope with it any more.'

She bit her lip and watched it turn cherry red in the mirror, suddenly angry.

'You have to,' she said sharply. 'She's your wife. Your responsibility. You made your choice, Sam. You can't have it both ways now. When you chose your marriage over me and your son, I stopped belonging to you.'

The noise he made then was a savage one, a cry that came from somewhere deep inside.

'You will always belong to me. I'll show you. I'll fucking show you.'

And he hung up.

Violet stared in the mirror and rubbed the smudges of eyeliner away from under her eyes, twisted her hair back. Pulled her outward self together.

'Do you mind if we call it a night?' she said, when she went back into the kitchen. 'I'm exhausted. And I think I'm going to be up with Sebastian in the night again.'

Kalisto looked up at her. 'Everything all right?' He glanced at the phone in her hand.

'Yes. Just . . . just Flip.'

He nodded. He didn't believe her, but he didn't push it. Just gathered his drawings and slid them into his leather satchel.

'All right, chuck. Ring me in the morning.'

'I will.'

He paused by the door as if about to say something, then thought better of it, kissed her cheek and walked off into the night, tweed flat cap on his big bald head, vintage mink coat flowing behind him. For a moment as she watched him go she wanted to call after him and get him back, spend the night sitting curled up on the sofa drinking red wine and gossiping. But she didn't.

The next day she awoke to her doorbell ringing, over and over again, and the knocker going. She lay in bed for a second, startled, and then quickly got out, pulled a jumper and jeans on and went out on to the landing. She left the bedroom so quickly that she didn't notice the lights coming from outside in the street. She had been up in the night with Sebastian, as she had predicted, and was a bit dazed from interrupted sleep and strange dreams. There had been nothing more from Sam, although she had thought there might be more drunken phone calls – a visit, even, despite her telling him not to. She wouldn't have been surprised if he had just turned up. It was partly why she had sent Kalisto away. He must have passed out.

That would probably be him now, she thought as she ran down the stairs two at a time. 'All right, all right, I'm coming!' she called out. Jesus. She was going to go mad if it was him now. It was part of the deal. He didn't come to her house, any more than she would go to his. The last thing she wanted was Sam turning up here all the time. At all, in fact. Sebastian was only small but he was eagle-eyed.

'Sam, I'm coming! What the bloody hell do you think . . .' she called, trailing off as she pulled the door open and stood back.

'Oh.'

'Ms Cavalley? Violet Cavalley?'

A policeman stood in front of her, the collar of his waterproof jacket up against the snow which was coming down in little clumps behind him. Next to him, a short, dumpy female officer stood, her frizzy hair sticking out from the sides of her helmet. She had obviously been brought along to provide tea and comfort, Violet thought, then wondered why they hadn't told her who it was – Flip, or Sebastian – and then realised she had bare feet, and all of her thoughts came in a jumbled rush, while she invited them in, then stood and waited for them to announce their specific doom-laden mission.

When they did, it was not what she had expected at all. Not at all.

'Ms Cavalley, we understand that Viscount Gilmour rang you last night.'

'That's right.'

'Can you tell us what you discussed?'

'It was personal.'

The officer nodded. 'I understand. But I'm afraid it's very important indeed that you tell us.' The man spoke slowly, with a thick Birmingham accent, the combination of which irritated Violet, over her worry.

'Why?' she snapped.

'Because we need to establish exactly what Viscount Gilmour did last night and where he was between nine p.m., when he rang you, and midnight.'

Violet folded her hands in front of her chest. The policeman seemed to take up so much space in her drawing room. He was enormous. She could hear the woman clattering about in her kitchen, making tea. Rifling through things, probably. She would have to go and stop her. Blue and Sebastian were asleep upstairs.

'All right. But first, I need you to tell me exactly why that information is so important. If he's in some sort of trouble, if he's hurt . . . I want to know.'

Violet tried to keep her voice under control. She didn't want the man to see how worried or upset she was. He glanced towards the door into the hallway. He was obviously waiting for the WPC to finish faffing about with the tea and join him.

'Oh for goodness' sake!' Violet got up and walked smartly

into the kitchen. 'Hello, could you join us? Don't worry about the tea. Your colleague would like a word.'

The woman looked confused, but followed Violet into the drawing room.

'There you go. Here she is. She can hold my hand. Now will you please just tell me what on earth is going on?'

The man leaned forward and rested his elbows on his knees, uncomfortable in the low, feminine sofa she had shown him to.

'I'm afraid Viscount Gilmour is in a great deal of trouble, Ms Cavalley. You see, it would appear that Viscount Gilmour murdered his wife last night.'

Violet stared. The WPC looked at her warily, but she didn't notice. She was just watching the policeman's thick, bumbling lips as they moved in what appeared to be slow motion. He continued. It seemed that, now he had got going, he had warmed to his part.

'Viscount Gilmour . . .'

'You pronounce it Vy-count.'

He paused. 'I beg your pardon?'

'You keep pronouncing it Vis-count. It's Vy-count.'

'Right you are. Vy-count Gilmour has been taken into custody and is likely to be charged with the murder of his wife, Lady Ann Gilmour, later on today. So you can see, Ms Cavalley, this is a very serious matter indeed.'

'I wrote to him,' Violet said to Tillie, her voice almost inaudible. 'During the trial. I told him I could never see him again. That he could never see Sebastian. He'd been asking to see him. Wanting me to tell our son who he was. I told him no.'

She wept.

'He is my brother then,' Tillie said. 'I thought so. They look alike, don't they? He—' She broke off. When she spoke again it was in a soft voice, almost a whisper. 'He went mad, I think.

Her death,' she couldn't bring herself to say murder, even now. 'The trial, you . . .' She looked down. 'It was too much for him. I think he was trying to kill us both, that day he died.'

The signs had been there since the end of the trial. Probably before then, but Tillie had been staying with her uncle in Ireland while it was going on, kept out of it. Kept away. But afterwards, after he 'got off', as the tabloids all put it, or was found 'not guilty of the murder of his wife, Lady Ann, after the trial collapsed due to a lack of evidence and a series of blunders on the behalf of the Metropolitan Police', as others described it, he collected his only daughter and took her back to their family home in County Clare. He had hired a brilliant lawyer, Mr Camino, who was frequently referred to as 'Mr Casino' because of his propensity to take on cases where it looked certain that the house would win, and get his clients off. And then he would move on to the next case, and the guilty rich returned to their gilt-cages, and rotted in them, rather than in prison.

Or that was what happened to Sam, anyhow. Tillie could tell from the moment she walked into the big stone hall of their castle, back from boarding school, to see her father rearranging all the paintings on the walls in an obsessive, manic way, to ensure that the portrait of her mother was in the exact centre of the wall, that he was not, and would never again be, the same.

He was older, sunken inside, somehow. His hair had greyed at the edges and his skin was papery. It had only been a few months, nine at the most, since she had seen him, but he looked like an old man now. However, that was not the biggest change.

The biggest change was what she saw when she called out to him, thinking he hadn't heard her come in, and he turned to look at her – and she saw his eyes. They stared at her, completely blank, for almost a full minute, while she stood waiting, full of teenage awkwardness. He just – gazed. No recognition, no love, no familiarity. There was, during that period, nothing there at all.

And then, just as she was about to turn and run out into the garden, into the wild garden down to the lake, he spoke.

'Tillie . . .'

'Daddy.'

She wanted to go to him and hug him, and took a step forward to do so. He smiled, very slightly, and then turned away from her, head tilted up towards the big stone wall, half-empty, half-hung with their ancestral portraits. The rest were on the floor, propped up against the wall. Half-empty mugs and wine glasses were scattered around. He had clearly been working on this project for a while.

'Can't Johnnie help you with that?'

'Hmm?' He didn't turn. Johnnie was the village boy who helped the gardener, did odd jobs – or who had done. It didn't look as though the gardener had been for a while.

'Johnnie, Daddy – you know. Some of those frames look awfully heavy.'

'No, no. Johnnie's not coming any longer. Too many people around, cluttering up the place . . .' He trailed off, and paced slowly up and down, his hands in his pockets. 'I think this one,' he pointed to an old portrait of one of his great-uncles, 'could go, don't you? He has a disapproving look. I've never liked him.'

Tillie faltered. 'If you like, we could take it to Christie's?'

'No, no, let's get rid of him now.'

'What do you mean, Daddy?'

Suddenly, with a burst of energy, he picked up the picture by its frame and strode out of the big front door, carrying it in one hand. Oh God. What was he doing? Tillie followed him out into the garden and down the sloping grass to the old gardener's shed at the bottom. He threw the painting on to the remains of what had been an old bonfire, and plunged into the shed.

'Daddy, what are you doing? You can't—'

'I don't want him around any longer,' Sam called out from inside the shed, 'glooming and glowering at me all the livelong day.'

A crash came from inside the shed.

'Looking down his big old Gilmour nose . . .'

Tillie smiled, despite her growing anxiety. Her father had always hated his nose. She didn't know why. It was straight, the right sort of size. 'It's just a nose, for goodness' sake,' her mother had used to say. The girl's throat caught at the thought of her mother. 'He just doesn't like the notion of inheriting his good looks from anyone,' Ann had used to say. 'Likes to think they're all his own invention.'

Her father had always been vain. Tillie had inherited that from him; she was self-aware enough to know. Neither of them could pass a mirror or a pane of glass without glancing at their reflection in it.

'It's not vanity, it's common courtesy,' he had told her once. 'You and I are simply polite enough to check that we are putting our best face forward, for the benefit of those looking upon us, at all times.' And her mother would raise an elegantly arched eyebrow and stroll off to her garden. Lady Ann was a beauty, but one who had no time for adornments or frivolity.

Tillie was jerked out of her thoughts by the sight of her father emerging from the woodshed bearing a pile of kindling, splinters of wood in his hair. He chucked them on top of the painting with a crash and rummaged in his trouser pocket.

'Oh Daddy, you can't, you mustn't.' She took a step closer, one hand out in front of her, almost about to touch his arm. But something held her back. It was as though touching him would ignite him as well as the pile of wood and sticks and priceless art in front of her.

He put a firelighter in the bottom of the pile and held a cigarette lighter to it. It glowed and smoked softly, and then caught the stick of balsa wood above it. Within a couple of minutes, the blaze was going strong.

Tillie stood and watched her father's face as he watched the family portrait, which was worth many thousands of pounds, burn, and knew that things were very wrong.

They didn't get any better over the summer. Sam never slept, he hardly ate. He spent most of his time wandering around the huge house, up and down the corridors, going through old trunks in the warren of attics, starting projects like cataloguing all of the wine in the cellars in a database and working on it feverishly for days on end, and then losing interest and abandoning it. He wouldn't have anyone to help in the house, saying that they were 'fine by themselves, the two of them', that he didn't want people coming in and interfering. 'But it's Johnnie and Caitlin,' Tillie had said. 'They've been coming for years, Daddy, it's not like strangers.' But he would have none of it. 'They're not family,' he said, 'not blood. I don't trust them.'

And so the house got dirtier and more chaotic, although Tillie tried to keep things going, to make them decent meals and to clean the place. But she was only fifteen, and Sam's projects created piles of junk and mess, and he was constantly taking glasses and plates into little-used rooms and forgetting about them, so they began to run out in the kitchen, and Tillie couldn't keep up.

That wasn't all. Sam's behaviour got more and more erratic. Tillie would wake up in the night to hear him playing the same old Gershwin song, over and over again, and when she crept downstairs she would find him in the breakfast room, or the library, the music bellowing and her father, drunk, passed out, the music on loop, playing 'Someone To Watch Over Me'.

The sad, crackly voice filled the room like the moonlight, and regret washed through the air. Tillie reached into the old turntable and lifted the arm off the record. When she was a child, her father had played her Dolly Parton on the same record player, and they had pushed the furniture back and danced around the room. The house was filled with memories. But they were being replaced by different ones now.

He would wake, every time. Dazed, eyes blinking. 'Turn it back on,' he would whisper, half-asleep in the half-light. It was as though the only way he could find sleep was with the background of that song playing. And she would put it back on, then go and sit next to him, pulling up a chair, or just sitting on the arm of the chair where he slept, and watch over him.

'I assumed it reminded him of her – of Mummy,' Tillie said now to Violet. 'I thought it must have been their song. It didn't really seem like it – but I didn't have any reason to think otherwise. Teenage romantics. But I thought . . .'

Tears were streaming down her face now, and Violet's.

'I thought he was dreaming of her watching over him, still with him, even though she was dead.' She gulped. 'Even though I knew, though I never admitted it, that he had probably killed her. That he had beaten her to death. He was mad, wasn't he? He was mad.'

Tillie was sobbing like a child.

'And I would sit there with him, watching him sleep, and think, At least he's missing her. At least he is dreaming of her, remembering her as they used to be, when they were happy. And . . .'

She couldn't finish. So Violet completed the sentence for her.

'And it wasn't her he was playing the song for. It was me.'

Tillie put her hand over her eyes and wept as she had never wept before. Violet felt her hand being squeezed tight, as the girl cried. And Violet closed her eyes, and remembered.

The first time, that first time, he had played the song to her on the piano, in the foyer of a big, faded hotel in the South of France. They had managed to plan an escape there for the weekend, stealing away for a few hours of carved-out time, time they weren't entitled to, time they created by pushing their real lives back and holding them at arm's length for as long as they could.

The hotel was old, out of the way, unfashionable. It was the sort of place where families returned year after year, and were given the same table each time. The rooms were full of mismatching furniture and the waiters were all almost dead. They didn't care. They weren't here for the ambience.

It was late, two or three o'clock in the morning. They had long stopped counting the hours – it only reminded them how few they had left. They were facing each other in the windowseat, overlooking the sea, a bottle of champagne between them, when suddenly Sam leaped up and bounded over to the piano.

'What are you doing?' Violet asked.

'Serenading you. That's what lovers do, isn't it?'

'In fairy tales.'

'And why can't this be our fairy tale? You're princess enough.'

She smiled. He pushed his hair back from his face and began to play, his long fingers splayed out over the keys.

'I'm rusty,' he said, the notes coming slowly, faltering.

'Go on.' She stood and went over to the piano, resting against the curve of it. He looked up at her.

'That's better. Inspiration.'

He continued to play, growing in confidence as he found the notes again and sang the beautiful words of the love song.

She joined in, and they sang in harmony, their voices flowing together.

Tillie let go of Violet's hand as she stopped crying. Wiped her hands on her skirt.

'Do you want to know what happened the day he died?' she asked coldly. 'Do you want to know what you drove him to?'

Violet didn't respond. She knew she didn't have any choice but to listen.

That day, Tillie woke to the sound of her father banging the big brass gong that had once been used to summon guests for dinner. She got up and dressed, and went downstairs to find him standing in the hall, still banging away with the stick, his hair wild. He was dressed in a bizarre outfit of tweed trousers and various jumpers, topped with an old shooting cape and a thick scarf. He obviously hadn't slept again.

'Awake, awake, awake! Are you awake?'

'Dad. What does it look like?'

'Like you're half-asleep still, Sleepy-head. Come on, get dressed in something warmer. Wrap up warm. Plenty of layers.'

'Why? It's not that cold.'

'Oh yes, it is. We're going out on the boat.'

She should have known something was not right – more not right than it had been, even. He was too high, too buoyant, he was suddenly full of a vigour that was on the edge of mania. Later, she would come to understand why. It was because he had seen the way out, and was taking it. It was a new project – like cataloguing the wine or rearranging the paintings or digging over the vegetable garden; the inception of the plan had given him a burst of energy that would carry him through the initial stages of it. Only with this plan, by the time that first burst died out, it would not matter any longer.

Tillie pulled on her old pair of Hunter's that stood by the door and which were too tight now, and a Barbour, and followed him outside. The early-morning air was cool and the grass was dewy as she tramped down the slope, following in his footsteps.

By the time she reached the edge he was already standing in the water, in his fishing waders. The rods were in the boat, ready.

'Dad . . .'

'Come on, hop in. It's the early fisher who catches the worm.'

'We haven't been fishing for years, and the boat hasn't been used for years – it's all dirty. Is it even safe?'

'I know we haven't been fishing for years. That's why we're going now. Come on, it'll be fun. You'll be going back to school before long.'

She sighed, and got into the little blue boat. They had fished together a lot when she was little. He would come and wake her up when it was still dark and take her out, making sandwiches for their lunch in the kitchen out of anything they could find in the larder, creating a mess of crumbs that they knew they would be in trouble for when they got back later, but that was all part of the fun. He had taught her how to cast, how to tug the line gently, teasing the fish, tricking them into thinking it was food.

'You have to think like they think. Gently. Slowly. Fish aren't in a hurry. You can't be in a hurry,' he had said.

So she couldn't say no to him now.

It happened quickly, and yet it seemed to happen slowly. One minute they were in the middle of the big lake, Tillie idly holding her rod over the water, slowly tugging the line in as her father had taught her. It was a movement that came as naturally to her now as walking. It was peaceful out here. Tillie felt the boat bobbing gently beneath her. It calmed her.

And then, without any warning, the bobbing suddenly stopped and became a great lurch, and the boat pitched to one side, pulling her over. Tillie was flung backwards, and shouted out as she tipped over with the boat, feeling the wood hold for a moment and then capsize, and she was drawn down into the freezing water.

'On purpose,' Violet said, and it was not a question.

'That's why,' Tillie took a deep breath, 'that's why he was wearing so many layers. Why he told me to wrap up warm. So that we would sink more quickly.

'And I think it worked. I mean, obviously not with me. It was the fishing rod that saved me. It got caught on the side of the boat, and I held on to it, and sort of floated while I kicked my boots off. And I was younger, and stronger, and . . . But it worked with him. He died quite quickly, I think,' she told Violet. 'I mean, I don't know, of course. But I think he would . . . he would have been trying to. He would have been waiting for it.'

Violet nodded. 'Yes. I'm sure he did.'

Whatever the truth of it, they both needed to believe that.

'It's important to have everything out in the open, don't you think?' Tillie went on. 'I do. That's why I told Mattie and Sebastian about your illness. I've been doing a bit of spring-cleaning for you.'

Violet could feel her strength fading. She felt very light, as though she weighed nothing at all. It would be so easy to just float away, to drift . . . but she had to wait. She had to wait for Flip. She pulled herself back.

'But how did you know about Mattie?' she asked. 'How did you find out who I really was?'

Tillie smiled. 'I found someone who was very keen to tell me all about you,' she said. 'It was luck, really. I found Mary Wallop.'

Violet's eyes flickered.

'He was a generous man, my father. And he loved you very

much. You shouldn't have sent him away that night, you know? You should have taken responsibility. He couldn't bear it alone, and you turned him away. You turned him away.'

Violet didn't answer. She couldn't. There was nothing to say. It was all true.

'I found letters between him and Mary Wallop. He kept everything. There were trunks and trunks of letters and papers when he died. I spent months going through them all. And I found some from her. Thanking him for the money, telling him she'd received it. Confirming that she'd written to you "as agreed". So, I went to see her.'

Violet felt sick. The thought of Sam, beautiful, golden Sam with Mary, made her shudder.

'He had promised you he wouldn't do anything about her, hadn't he? You should have known him better than that. My father was a good man. He would never see someone he loved struggle like that, without helping.'

'He promised,' Violet said.

'He broke his promise. To help you.' Tillie's voice was hard. The tears were gone and only hate remained.

'He paid her off. A lump sum, more than he should have, never to contact you again. Made her promise to tell you she'd married, emigrated. Didn't want you to find out what he'd done, feel beholden to him. Even after you'd left him.'

'He married *her*,' Violet said, the injustice of the accusation stinging. 'He married Ann. He chose *her*.'

'He didn't have a choice,' Tillie said. 'You know that.' She carried on. 'But she found out. My mother. That was the start of it, really. It was her money, you see. It was all her money. The Gilmours had the title, the pedigree, and the stately home that cost a million pounds a year to keep going. The Michelmores had all that – but they also had the cash.'

'I would have—'

'What, paid for him? Would you? Would you really?'

Violet couldn't answer.

'Mary helped me a lot, you know,' Tillie continued. 'Telling me all about where you came from. Your filthy gyppo family. Your murdering father. Everything. So it wasn't hard to find Mattie, feed his fire. Tell him you were dying. Tell him he should come and claim what's his. Set the cat among the pigeons. And Sebastian – I found him as well.'

'How?' They had hidden the trail so well. She had been sure of it.

'Oh, Violet. Through Gerald, I'm afraid. He's a sweet man, but he's a sucker for a pretty face and a nice pair of legs, isn't he?'

Violet was shocked into silence.

'Don't worry,' Tillie carried on. 'I didn't sleep with him, if that's what you're thinking. God, I can't think of anything more disgusting. Didn't need to, anyhow. Just distracted him. Watched, waited. That's all it takes, normally. Patience. Observation. Once I had the password to his computer, it was easy to look through the records. And once I found the wire payments, I knew I was on to something. Like I said, a pretty face – and some ready cash – get you far in life. But then you know that, don't you?'

'I'm glad,' Violet said quietly. It was hard to speak now. 'I'm glad he came. I'm glad you did what you did. I'm glad you brought them back, both of them. It made me tell the truth.'

Tillie tilted her head to one side. Her eyes flashed. That wasn't what she wanted, but it didn't matter now. Not really. Making Violet's last weeks difficult had been a bonus, a game. The real prize, she had already won.

'Mary helped me in other ways as well, right from the start. She told me how to get my job with you. Told me everything about Madame Fournier – about your sense of duty,' her voice was sarcastic, 'about passing on what had been given to you.

So I did as she advised me. I transformed myself. That's what you did, isn't it? Transformation? I became the talented ingénue. I didn't need to make much up, thanks to you. Thanks to what you did, I was an orphan already, wasn't I? And I was good at my job. I just – I just played it up. Made sure you heard me saying how much I needed a mentor. Someone to guide me, take me under their wing. Once you had done that, it was only a matter of time before Flip noticed me.'

Flip. Hold on, Violet told herself. All she wanted now was to see Flip.

'And now I'm the third Mrs Cavalley. A widow, so young,' Tillie carried on. 'It's tragic.'

Violet felt a rush of pain to her chest, and a croak escaped from her throat that sounded inhuman.

'No!' she cried. 'No, not Flip. Please no.'

Tillie nodded sombrely.

'I'm afraid so, Violet. He died, your precious son. Flip died.'

Tillie watched as Violet's eyes shut, and tears slid down her cheeks. And she sat and waited, as the sick woman's breaths became slower, and noisier, and rattled in her chest. And she took her hand and held it, and whispered in her ear as she died.

'It's all right, Violet. It's all right. You see, we were married before he died, so his share will all go to me. I'll take care of everything. After all, it's going to be my name above the door, isn't it? I'm Mrs Cavalley now.'

Tillie shut the door of Violet's room gently behind her, and walked down the corridor to the room where the rest of the family were waiting. As she went, she let the tears fall from her eyes.

'I'm sorry,' she said, as she reached her in-laws. 'I'm so sorry. There wasn't time to come and get you. She's gone. Oh God, she's gone.'

And she sat on the edge of Flip's bed, where he lay, his body bruised and battered, his left arm badly injured, almost completely crushed, and covered in a dressing, and held him as he wept. It was a miracle that he was not more badly injured, and that Tillie had escaped with barely a scratch. A few cuts and bruises, that was all. The pilot had not been so lucky – he had died in the crash.

'I'm sorry,' she whispered again. 'I'm so, so sorry.'

Chapter Thirteen

The day of Violet's funeral was bright and clear, and afterwards, the family gathered at the salon in Mount Street to pay their respects to her. Friends and associates who had, just a few months before, raised their glasses at her sixtieth birthday in Capri, now came together once more to drink a final toast to the woman who had built up this empire of hats from nothing, from a speck of an idea and a drawing that still hung above the door.

The window of the salon was filled with Violet's best designs. Hats from her River Collection, an original Stax, some of her first wedding tiaras, head-dresses from the catwalk shows she had designed for Kalisto, all vied for attention. Over forty years of work and life were here.

Guests spilled out on to the street. Her long career in the worlds of fashion and design, working with Oscar winners and rock stars and royalty, meant that the crowd that turned out to bid Violet farewell was as varied as it was immense. Paparazzi formed a catwalk, almost, lining either side of the small street leading to the church, their flashbulbs lighting the way of the mourners in a starlit procession as they walked in to pay their final respects. They were not just mourning Violet, they were honouring her, and the legacy of Cavalley's.

Cavalley's.

When the guests had finally gone, the children, along with Kalisto, Patrick and Gerald Petherbridge, stood in a line outside the front door of the salon where it had all begun. Flip held a bottle of champagne in his hand. He popped the cork, then poured all of them a glass, his right hand holding the bottle, Boodle holding the tray. His left was still bandaged. He glanced at Boodle as he poured, and smiled at her. 'I don't want there to be bad feeling. We're all family, after all. I'm going to try to do better. With Mungo. With everything. I can be a good father, Boodle, but you might have to help me.'

Boodle nodded. 'I know you can, Flip. And of course I'll help you.' To both their surprise, she flung her arms around his neck and hugged him.

'Sorry,' she sniffed, as she pulled away.

He shook his head. Boodle had nothing to be sorry for.

Mattie was not there. Violet had given the interview that Flip had suggested, had done so a few days before her death, and had told the world the story of where she had come from. As he had anticipated, far from shaming her, it had covered her in even more glory; the press had gone crazy for the tale of the little gypsy girl who had built the most successful millinery company in the world, and when she died, the fashion trade had been plunged into mourning. Mattie, bitter, ignored and now relatively wealthy, had melted away once more.

Flip finished pouring the champagne. Kalisto, wearing a hat from Violet's first Transformation Collection, a pale-grey top hat with a feather trim and a smart, thick grosgrain bow, wiped away a tear, and held his glass aloft.

'We've come a long way, kiddo,' he said to the silver-painted name above the door.

'To Cavalley's,' Flip called, and they all raised their glasses, and repeated it after him.

'To Cavalley's.'

Fran raised her glass along with the rest of them. 'To Cavalley's,' she said. 'To you, Mama,' she whispered under her breath. For Fran, the toast was more significant than any of them knew. For in her pocket, she held a letter, written the day before Violet died, and addressed to her.

Afterwards, the siblings lowered their glasses. They began to fade away, slowly, none of them wanting to be the first to leave. Fran filtered off first, slipping away quietly with Patrick.

'I want to go to her grave,' she told him, 'now that everyone's gone. Will you come with me?'

He nodded. The two of them said their goodbyes, then made their way, arm-in-arm, down the street.

In the end, it was just Flip, Tillie and Sebastian in the shop.

'We'd better lock up,' Flip said and Sebastian nodded. The brothers had begun to mend the rift between them. Slowly. Flip picked up his bunch of keys.

'I'll just check the offices,' he said.

'Do you want me to go?' Tillie asked.

'Actually,' Sebastian said, 'can you give me a hand with something, Tillie? I just need to move a table that I got stuck with earlier. Forgot about it till now. I'd ask Flip, but . . .' He gestured to his brother's injured arm.

'Course,' Tillie said. And as Flip went up the back stairs to the offices above, she turned to Sebastian. 'What table?' she asked.

'There's no table, Tillie,' he tutted. 'Don't be stupid.'

She looked at him appraisingly.

'I heard you,' he said quickly. They could hear Flip moving around upstairs; he would be down in a moment. 'In the hospital. I heard you – I was outside.'

Tillie stared.

'What are you going to do?' she asked.

'Nothing,' he said, grinning. 'Sis. Nothing – yet. We're going to run Cavalley's, just like Mama wanted. You, and me, and Flip, and Blue, and Fran. All one big, happy family. I just want you to remember – for the future, you know? I don't intend to let Flip have all the fun for ever. At some point, I'm going to want to . . . step up, let's say. Have a bit more input into how things are run. Not yet. I've got plenty on my plate for now. I want to get to know my daughter, and I need to deal with the court case. But, sometime, I'd like to take a more active role in the family business. And when I do . . . well, it would be good to know I've got some support.'

Brother and sister, siblings in blood and in law, stared at one another. And Tillie acquiesced. 'Of course,' she said. 'You'll always have my support.'

Just then, Flip came back downstairs and into the salon.

'All right?' he said.

'Yes. Just telling Sebastian he's got our support with the court case,' Tillie told him, taking his hand.

Flip looked at his brother. They had had a rough journey, but they were getting there now. Flip stretched his good hand out, and Sebastian shook it. 'Of course, mate, of course. We've got you back. After all, we're family, right? Got to stick together.'

Sebastian smiled. 'Absolutely.'

The three of them went out into the street, and as Flip locked the door, they took one final look at the building.

Cavalley's was still open for business.

Epilogue

Dear Fran,

If you are reading this, I have passed away. Once, I read those words, and they changed my life for ever. Now, I am writing them. And though it brings me great sadness to do so, I know that it is the right thing, and that I, too, am writing the letter to the right person.

It has been a rocky road for all of us recently, hasn't it? And yet it feels now as though it could not have happened any other way. My family – our family – has never gone quietly.

Darling girl, I underestimated you, I fear, and I am sorry. I should have seen the talent that lay behind the eyes of my little Boy Scout Butterfly earlier than I did. I wish so much that I had, and that I had had longer with you, to teach you more of what I have learned. But maybe it is meant to be like this. Maybe, like me, you are meant to learn by yourself. It stood me in pretty good stead, after all.

It is not too late. Because, as of this morning, Cavalley's is yours. Flip, Blue and Tillie must all retain their jobs. It is one of the conditions under which I am leaving you my company. Yes, I'm afraid there are a few strings attached, darling girl. Gerald has all the details in my Will. Flip will be angry at first, but he will get over it. He is to remain as Managing Director, for at least the next three years, in any case – you are not yet ready for that responsibility. I want you to learn; I want you to launch your perfume and make it a great success. Then you can take the lead role, day to day. Until then, you will have the majority stake. I have realised in the last few days that there must be a guiding hand, a single deciding vote. Cavalley's cannot be run by committee, it will falter and die; but it cannot be run by anyone other than my family. Cavalley's is *my family, as are you all.*

Look after it for me, my beautiful daughter, my love.

Mama

Patrick and Fran entered the small churchyard together, both pausing as they got to the gate, reluctant to go in. It was hard to think of Violet here.

'You never got to marry her,' Fran said, when they were by the side of the grave. It was not yet marked, and a small vase of violets and the freshly mounded soil were the only signs that her mother was buried here.

Patrick sighed. The wind blew his hair around his face and he pushed it back.

'No, I didn't,' he said. 'But she finally said "yes". That's enough for me.'

From her pocket, she pulled out the letter and handed it to Patrick – but he shook his head.

'She told me, sweet girl,' he said. 'She told me what she was going to do, and I told her she was right.'

Fran slid it back in her pocket. 'I'm nervous,' she said. 'I'm scared that they're all going to hate me.'

Patrick smiled, and took her hand. 'No one's going to hate you, Fran. They're going to see that she's done the right thing. She knew what she was doing, my Violet did. All along.'

He knelt by the grave, and touched the soil gently.

'Anyhow, you're family. And family comes first – remember?'

Fran nodded. Family comes first. She then produced a beautiful, deep-purple glass perfume bottle from her pocket, and laid it next to the vase, its thick, cut glass and flowerlike stopper catching the last of the sunlight. The gold lettering on its side spelled out her name, as Fran and Patrick slowly walked away.

Violet.

Have you read Jessica Ruston's

dazzling debut novel

LUXURY?

Read on for a taster . . .

Prologue

1981

From somewhere behind the hazy, green-blue blur of the horizon, a solidity began to form itself into the shape of a shore, a gently curving bay, a steeply peaked hill. As the boat drew closer, tacking round to approach from the west, it was as if an unseen hand was sketching in the details of the island – the deeper blue patches in the water indicating a reef off one side; then a spike of pale sand snaking its way into the sea; then a fuzz of flickering green – palm trees sprinkled down the slopes of the hill.

Logan exhaled. 'Oh, man. It's just like she said. Look – the jetty's still there. Take it round to that side.'

He pointed to the narrow structure of greying wood, its spindly legs rising up from the water, and motioned to his friends at the helm to head for it. The three young men were all tanned and relaxed from their summer in the sun – their 'last summer of freedom', as they had named it. They wore nothing but shorts and had let their hair grow long, in the knowledge that come the fall they would be in suits and short haircuts as they went off to begin their lives as adults, as Harvard graduates. This summer was a stolen slip of time between their student years and things 'getting serious', as they put it.

As Johnny leaned forward to bring the boat round, the muscles in his shoulders undulated under his skin. 'Looks pretty rickety,' he commented.

'How long is it since anyone was here?' Nicolo called from the far side of the deck.

'Not a clue,' Logan replied. 'Twenty years? More?'

They edged closer to the jetty.

'Let's stop alongside,' he told them. 'I want to see if it's sound.'

They slowly manoeuvred the boat so that it bobbed alongside the jetty. Logan hooked a leg over the handrail that ran round the boat's deck, and hanging on to it with one hand, he stretched forward and stamped on the jetty, testing its strength.

'Seems OK. I guess the worst that can happen is I get to go for a swim sooner rather than later.'

He swung his other leg over the side and hopped down on to the landing stage. There was a rustle of a breeze through the trees that lined the beach, and the faint swishing of the sea all around them. Otherwise, all was silent.

Johnny and Nicolo watched from the boat. The wood creaked as it absorbed Logan's weight, but it stood firm, and he spun round to face his friends, arms aloft and a wide grin on his face.

'Come ashore, my friends, my brothers. Welcome to L'île des Violettes!'

Putting his thumb and forefinger between his lips, Nicolo let out a long, high-pitched whistle. Johnny whooped with excitement and quickly secured the boat, then the two young men leaped off it to join him. The noise they made as they ran down the jetty and on to the hot sand startled the birds in the palm trees, who rose into the sky like a cloud of smoke, clacking and squawking.

They raced into the undergrowth, not caring that their legs were getting scratched. The air was cool and dry, and felt refreshing after hours spent on the boat.

'It's like a secret world,' shouted Nicolo.

'*Treasure Island*,' Johnny called back.

'*Lord of the Flies*?' responded Nicolo.

'Ha. Turning on each other?' Johnny chased after Logan. 'Not us, my friend, never us.'

Logan had stopped running and bent over to catch his breath. Johnny and Nicolo caught up with him.

'I feel like Robinson Crusoe – with two Man Fridays!' He was panting, his face a big grin, challenging his friends. Nicolo and Johnny looked at each other and shook their heads.

'Asking for it, don't you think?'

'Begging, I'd say, man.'

Logan chuckled, and before they could catch him he took off again, weaving through the trees. Whooping like savages, Johnny and Nicolo gave chase, until all three of them burst out of the glade of trees on to a rocky promontory. The view stopped them in their tracks.

'Wow.'

Without realising it, they had made their way to the highest point of the island, and from here they could see the shape of the whole mass. It was picture perfect. Blue skies, turquoise sea, leafy trees and sandy beaches. And as the three young men stood staring down at it, all of them felt a secret, powerful tug in their chests. All of them wanted it to be theirs.

'What's over there?' Johnny said suddenly, breaking the silence, pointing to a building. Even from a distance they could see that it was tumbledown, decrepit.

'Don't know,' said Logan. 'Why don't we find out?'

Later, the three of them lay on the sandy floor of the ruined building, a bonfire burning nearby, and the empty bottles of beer that they'd fetched from the boat discarded on the ground next to their sleeping bags. They gazed up at the sky. Tomorrow they would return to the mainland, give the boat back to its owner and catch their flight home. Back to real life, where Johnny would go to law school, Logan would begin his MBA as one of the youngest students ever to get a place on the prestigious Harvard course, and Nicolo would start work at a construction company in New York, learning the real nuts and bolts of the business. They'd got First, their fledgling hotel company, up and running, and it was doing well. They were raring to go. Their lives as men were beginning.

'So what do you think, Father Flores? Does she live up to your expectations?'

Nicolo leaned over and flicked the side of Logan's head with his thumb and forefinger. 'Don't call me that. And yes, she certainly does.'

'Why "she"?' asked Johnny.

'Fuck's sake, J. This place is a woman. A beautiful, uncharted, wild woman, just waiting to be tamed.'

'Ha. By you?'

'Yes, by me. No – by us.' Logan's voice was confident. He didn't doubt his words, and neither did his friends.

'We'll come back here, yes?' Johnny's words were stretched out, long with tiredness and alcohol.

'Yes. This is our future, guys. One day, we'll be back here – not as kids, but as men. As the men who own this place. And everyone will see that we made it.'

Logan raised his fist into the air. '*One man with a dream, at pleasure, Shall go forth and conquer a crown . . .*'

Johnny followed suit. '*And three with a new song's measure . . .*'

And finally Nicolo: '*Can trample an empire down.*'